WOMEN on WOMEN 2

"One More Time, Marie" by Madelyn Arnold
Forty years of building a life together are shattered by a
single act of homophobic violence, leading two women
into a cold labyrinth of bureaucracy that denies the
intimacy and fullness of their lives.

"What Has Been Done to Me" by Jacqueline Woodson
A mother and daughter share a birthday, but they have
different ways of remembering a shared past . . . the past
the daughter must escape to go on with her life.

"When 98.6 Is Less Than Zero" by Nisa Donnelly
In an imagined meeting with an old lover, a woman
struggles to integrate memories of old pain and past desire
into her present life with a new lover.

"Dry Fire" by Cathy Lewis
A woman cop, "out" to her fellow officers, confronts
subtle and not-so-subtle hostility from them as she
attempts to cope with the violence and devastation she
experiences daily in her job.

And 24 More Outstanding Stories

NAOMI HOLOCH lives in New York and has been
teaching French literature at SUNY-Purchase for the past
seventeen years. She is the author of several short stories
and a novel, *Offseason*. Together, they are the editors of
Plume's *Women on Women* series.

JOAN NESTLE is co-founder of the Lesbian Herstorv
Archives in New York City
Country, as well as editor o
Femme-Butch Reader.

WOMEN on WOMEN 2

An Anthology of American Lesbian Short Fiction

Edited by Naomi Holoch and Joan Nestle

A PLUME BOOK

PLUME
Published by the Penguin Group
Penguin Books USA Inc., 375 Hudson Street,
New York, New York 10014, U.S.A.
Penguin Books Ltd, 27 Wrights Lane,
London W8 5TZ, England
Penguin Books Australia Ltd, Ringwood,
Victoria, Australia
Penguin Books Canada Ltd, 10 Alcorn Avenue,
Toronto, Ontario, Canada M4V 3B2
Penguin Books (N.Z.) Ltd, 182–190 Wairau Road,
Auckland 10, New Zealand

Penguin Books Ltd, Registered Offices:
Harmondsworth, Middlesex, England

First published by Plume,
an imprint of New American Library,
a division of Penguin Books USA Inc.

First Printing, June, 1993
10 9 8 7 6 5 4

REGISTERED TRADEMARK—MARCA REGISTRADA

LIBRARY OF CONGRESS CATALOGING-IN-PUBLICATION DATA
Women on women 2 / edited by Naomi Holoch and Joan Nestle.
p. cm.
ISBN 0-452-26999-7
1. Lesbians—United States—Fiction. 2. Short stories, American—Women authors. 3. Women—United States—Fiction. 4. Lesbians' writings, American. I. Holoch, Naomi. II. Nestle, Joan III. Title: Women on women two.
PS648.L47W65 1993
813'.01089206643—dc20   92-35983
                                                                        CIP

Printed in the United States of America
Set in Kabel and Times Roman

Dedicated to the memory of George Stambolian,
editor of the *Men on Men* series

Contents

Introduction   11
Alley Ways (1918)   *Helen Hull*   17
The Cat and the King (1919)   *Jennette Lee*   35
Miss Russell   *Cherry Muhanji*   53
Eating Wisdom   *Jesse Mavro*   65
Tracking Down Vivienne   *Carolyn Weathers*   73
One More Time, Marie   *Madelyn Arnold*   79
Monster   *Michelle Cliff*   92
Night Life   *Naomi Holoch*   100
Be Still and Know   *Brigitte M. Roberts*   112
Past Sorrows and Coming Attractions
      Edith Konecky   116
Snake in the House   *Gail Shepherd*   142
La Ofrenda   *Cherríe Moraga*   156
The Waking State   *Gerry Pearlberg*   164
How the Butch Does It: 1959   *Merril Mushroom*   169
Mighty Muff   *Mary Wings*   175

Dry Fire   *Cathy Lewis*   181

A Bicycle Story   *E. J. Graff*   189

What Has Been Done to Me

     Jacqueline Woodson   203

Invented Sisters   *Annie Dawid*   211

When 98.6 Is Less Than Zero   *Nisa Donnelly*   223

State of Grace   *Lucy Jane Bledsoe*   232

Commercial Breaks   *Cass Nevada*   255

Alfalfa   *Nona Caspers*   265

Chelsea Girls   *Eileen Myles*   275

AmaizeN   *Lexa Roséan*   290

A Good Man   *Rebecca Brown*   294

An Amazon Beginning   *Ellen Frye*   335

Married Ladies Have Sex in the Bathroom

     Sally Bellerose   344

Author Biographies   346

Introduction

" 'If you tell a story for good, it's true,' " says the protagonist of a novel excerpted in this collection. In Volume 2 of *Women on Women*, lesbian writers continue the task, sometimes joyful, sometimes disturbing, sometimes painful, always demanding and exhilarating, of telling stories "for good." However the individual writer directs her imagination to integrate fantasy and experience, each work of short fiction included here embodies a "true"—that is to say, a lived—facet of lesbian existence and an affirmation of that existence.

Volume 1 of this series represented a ground-breaking collection: it was the first time that a large mainstream press published a collection of American lesbian short fiction. Yet Volume 2, by virtue of the moment in time in which it is appearing, may be more urgently controversial. The national elections in November 1992 capped a year that saw various community and state-wide attempts, some successful, to remove antidiscrimination laws protecting gays and lesbians, and to prohibit lesbians and gays from working as public employees, invoking explicitly or implicitly the notion of homosexuality as "unnatural" and "perverse." The National Endowment for the Arts is retreating every day from supporting any work that is sexually explicit or homoerotic. Several of the selections included would in fact undoubtedly fall to some censor's ax. The political realities of this period underscore what has always been true: the act of creating art that gives voice and form to a "minority" experience is a radical act threatening, as it does, the superficial self-portrait of a society whose "coherence" depends on the continued invisibility of many of its members.

As in the first volume, we have chosen to open the volume with works from the early years of the twentieth century. Such a perspective allows us some insights into the interrelation of literature, the social and political constraints of a period, and the history of the lesbian community. Both "Alley Ways" by Helen Hull, published in 1918, and "The Cat and the King" by Jennette Lee (1919)[1] offer, among other things, muted yet intense depictions of young homoerotic friendships that never transgress the socially acceptable. Each remains consonant with the values of the times and translates erotic potential and attraction into longing and sentimental fantasy rather than manifest passion. Such "innocent" portrayals of friendships among girls were shortly thereafter no longer possible as Freudian tenets filtered through, in one form or another, to large sections of the general public, and "inversion" became a recognized "danger" for young women as well as men. Yet these stories are a touching if painful reminder of the extraordinarily persistent and complex desire that is female sexuality.

A number of the contemporary stories are closer in theme to these early ones than may at first appear. Profoundly effective forces are still at work that fragment the lesbian experience and drive it back into invisibility, even once it has seen the light of day. In "Miss Russell," the intensity of her love for another woman, which dates back to her college days, is buried for years along with her identity as an artist. She has no way to name and conceptualize its importance,

[1] We thank Lyndall MacCowan for bringing this story to our attention.

so it remains for too long invisible even to herself. "What to call it? How to call it? No good-byes. No ending." Family ties may bind in such a way that the possibility of a confrontation or choice between the "conventional" and "unconventional" does not even arise, as in "Alfalfa" or in "State of Grace." Race and class differences intensify such a conflict in "Invented Sisters," leaving the protagonist on a collision course, incapable of visualizing an integration of her attachment to her African-American woman lover with her connection to her family, yet unable to entertain the possibility of loss of either. In the story "Be Still and Know," the narrator must somehow find a way to bend the forces of her family's religion to her lesbianism. And if being visible as a lesbian to oneself and the world is in certain contexts now "acceptable," there are always boundaries beyond which this visibility threatens to become inadmissible, as in "Waking State" when sexuality becomes too transgressive even for the lesbian protagonist. Edith Konecky's "Past Sorrows and Coming Attractions" gives us a young protagonist who has acquired all the institutional trappings to prepare her for adult life, yet who is so distanced from a vision of self, that she retreats into the bedroom of her childhood, convinced she is dead.

The interface of lesbian identity with society is never a neutral event, even when it is apparently uneventful, for underneath the surface is the fault line created by difference and discontinuity. "Dry Fire" captures the uneasy yet functional integration of an "out" lesbian into the police force, an integration threatened periodically by tremors of hostility that are a constant reminder of the underlying antagonistic forces at work. The "straight" world unknowingly steps into the lesbian world in "Night Life," to create, in this instance, an unexpected moment of intimacy.

There are, of course, many moments when lesbians go about the business of being and becoming without a heightened awareness of waiting for the "Big One." "Mighty Muff" and "How the Butch Does It" raise with irony and humor

issues of self-definition and power within our own community, while "Chelsea Girls" brings on stage a variety of characters that interact unself-consciously given their common
marginality. The universal tragedy of sexual abuse of the
child with its battering consequences is evoked in two other
stories—"Bicycle Story" and "What Has Been Done to
Me"—as the victims, two lesbians, attempt and perhaps fail
to get on with their lives. Friendships form across genera-
tional, class, and gender differences; people help each other
to live, to return to life, as in "Eating Wisdom," and to leave
it. Whether death is "timely" as in "Tracking Down Vivienne," or brutally tragic as in "A Good Man," the authors
evoke an extraordinary tapestry of attachment and loss in
which the dying and the living help sustain each other.

And of course there is Love, there is Sex. Relationships
go along exuberantly, playfully ("AmaizeN"), then they
don't ("When 98.6 Is Less Than Zero," "Bicycle Story"),
but they did, and others will ("Commercial Breaks"). They
may defy by their very enthusiasm the structures around
them and survive victorious, if a bit tired, as in "Married
Ladies Have Sex in the Bathroom." Inevitably, there is also
Death, a loss compounded by the losses that arise out of the
infinite variety of fears and internalized prohibitions that
dog every relationship ("La Ofrenda," "One More Time,
Marie").

"Monster," "Snake in the House," and "Amazon Beginning" present, each in a different way, a vision of family that
nourishes and strengthens the child/author who will identify
herself as a lesbian, for these stories offer portraits, whether
mythical or "real," of a father, a mother, a grandmother
who do battle more or less willfully, more or less explicitly,
more or less successfully as individuals in exile, as outsiders
who love, resist, create, survive in problematic relation to
the culture around them.

Many pressures come to bear on lesbian fiction, pressures
that are, not surprisingly, similar to those that come to bear

on our lives. In an effort to correct the dramatically tragic stereotypes of desperate women leading a desperate existence, which have in the past been used to characterize lesbian experience, lesbian writers have sometimes relentlessly pursued the happy ending in their fiction, just as we have attempted at times to romanticize our lives. Neither our writing nor our lives can be held to such simplistic formulas. "We must," as the German poet Rainer Maria Rilke wrote, "trust in what is difficult."[2] Our lives are full of contradictory experiences. So should our literature be, accepting the difficult and transforming it into a vision of community, continuity, and hope. It is in this spirit that we offer this collection.

—The Editors

[2] *Letters to a Young Poet*. Trans. Stephen Mitchell. New York: Vintage Books, 1986, p. 67.

Alley Ways
Helen Hull (1918)

Cynthia hurried between the sheeted counters toward the door. She had lingered so long that the other clerks had gone, and Mr. Bell himself stood, just shaking off his managerial airs, in final directions to the basement man. He unlatched the door for Cynthia, who slipped past him with a grave good night. Within her gravity, though, hung streamers of delight; she was proud of Mr. Bell's black-haired suaveness, proud of it as something belonging to her, since he managed the store where she clerked; she delighted in her own importance in being thus let out of the secretive, closed shop. She glanced down the street to see whether anyone had noticed her emergence. At the sight of a girl loitering before the windows a few stores ahead she shivered, a forbidden streamer fluttering out. Queenie wouldn't take a hint, then. Cynthia walked slowly toward her, framing bits of self-defense. She had waited as long as she could; Queenie should have been blocks ahead of her. Instead, there she was, dropping into step beside her, a sick furtiveness glinting in wide, blue eyes.

"If you're tryin' to shake me, say so."

"Don't be silly!" exclaimed Cynthia, and the relief that chased off the furtiveness in Queenie's face banished her

own faint resolve. She couldn't strike at her brutally, as her
mother had demanded.

"Was it Bell kept you? You're awful' late."

"No. I—I couldn't come earlier."

They swung off the main street, Queenie struggling to keep
step.

"If you tried to shake me now, after all I told you"—her
plaintive voice came over Cynthia's shoulder—"I don' know
what I'd do."

"Has anything happened?"

"Say, you don't need to run home, do you?" She plucked
at Cynthia's arm, and with a little laugh Cynthia slackened
her stride.

"Nothing's happened, Queenie?" she repeated.

"I saw him."

"Queenie! Again! Where?"

"This noon. He was waiting—down near the river."

"What did you do?"

"I acted like I didn't see him; and then—I tried to run;
and then I got home somehow."

"You didn't talk to him?"

Queenie shook her head, her eyes staring into Cynthia's
in dogged appeal.

"Good for you! Oh, Queenie, good for you!" Cynthia's
cheeks flushed.

"Well, you said you'd help me if I didn't talk to him."

"And you said you couldn't help it; and now you've proved
you could." Cynthia's voice rang out in young triumph.

"I was afraid he'd wait for me tonight." Queenie glanced
at the warehouses they were passing. "He turns me all to
water. You don't know."

"I knew, if you wanted to do it, you could." Cynthia
nodded wisely at Queenie. She glowed with her triumph;
she had projected her own strength into this girl. "I'll walk
down your street with you, and then if he comes—" She
ended with a note of scorn.

"I keep thinking it's him I see."

"Don't think about him. He isn't worth it."

"He ain't worse'n most men."

"But if you think about other things—"

"What things?" Queenie's full lips twitched. "You can pretend you ain't thinking about it, but it's right there." She seized Cynthia's arm, a curious gurgle in her throat. "See! Is that him?" She pulled Cynthia to a stop in front of a little drugstore, peering in between the red and blue bottles.

"Don't stop and stare!" Cynthia jerked her along.

"I wasn't." Queenie turned her face slowly back to Cynthia. Little blotches of color showed under the soft, pale cheeks. She clung to Cynthia's arm, pressing it against her body. "Oh, I don' know how to bear it!"

A strange tremor moved through Cynthia. She dragged her arm free.

"Don't act so here on the street," she said gently. "Someone will notice you."

They were almost to the river. A wagon passed them, the pitch of its rumble changing hollowly as it came to the wooden bridge.

"You see"—Cynthia went on as the girls reached the bridge—"it is wicked to feel like that, now you know he has a wife." Queenie's emotion was strange wine on her lips, dizzying her.

"I didn't know that when I got to loving him." Queenie stared down at the muddy, sluggish current.

Cynthia grew stern.

"You do know now," she said, "so you must stop."

A group of workmen straggled past them, one of them grinning, teeth white in the grime and tan of his face.

"From the yards," said Queenie, pointing to the tracks across the river.

"You aren't listening."

"Oh, I hear you. But what am I going to do?" Queenie clung to the rail. "Sometimes"—she flung up her hand—"I think I'll jump in. Living so handy to the river, I think of it."

"Nonsense!" Cynthia drew her again into a slow walk. "Don't you talk that way. You've got a job, and there are lots of things for you to do."

"Job! It's all right for you to talk, coming in for two weeks of the sale. How'd you like selling notions all the time? 'Yesm'm, these are five cents. No; them are ten.' Fine way to live, ain't it!"

"I think it's fun."

"You got something else ahead. Would you stay doing it?"

"Well"—Cynthia hesitated—"the family wouldn't let me. It was all I could do to make them let me do it these two weeks. But I think I'd like it. You could get to be head of a department."

"Get laid off for the dull season!"

They had reached the end of the bridge, and Cynthia stopped impatiently. Queenie's apathy roiled the clear water of her wisdom—a lip wisdom that she echoed unquestioningly.

"If you won't make any effort yourself!" she cried. Queenie sucked in the corners of her mouth; an incongruous dimple flickered in one cheek. Her huge sailor hat had slipped back, and her fair hair lay in moist curls around her forehead and ears. She looked almost like a baby, thought Cynthia, pityingly, so that she hurried on. "But of course you want to. Now let's think. If you don't like the store, why not try something else?"

Queenie shook her head.

"I set out to be a private secret'ry, but I didn't have the mem'ry. I saved up, and took a course, but I couldn't learn it."

"Well"—Cynthia walked on—"there must be something. I'll think about it."

They came to an alley squeezing between old sheds.

"Would you"—Queenie hesitated—"would you have time to come down a piece with me?"

The two stepped into the dingy passage, Queenie shrinking close to Cynthia.

"I always feel he might step out the other side of this."

There was nothing beyond the sheds, though, but a mud path close along the river, with a cluster of shacks.

"Third one's where I live," said Queenie, defiantly. "'Tain't much and it's full of kids. You better go back now." She clutched at Cynthia's arm. "You won't shake me, will you? Just feelin' there's somebody knows, gives me more spunk."

"Of course not. I'll help you, Queenie." Cynthia flung up her head, her voice vibrating in her throat. The squalor of the houses by the river, the strange, dirty alley, this soft, trembling Queenie—all became an entrancing mystery lying in her hands for her to shape. "Good night," she whispered. "I'll see you tomorrow."

She ran back through the alley, half expecting to be halted by a stranger, by him, perhaps.

As, breathless, she reached the street she heard a loud "Cynthia!" and there was her father pulling up his horse. She climbed in beside him, her "Hello, Father!" as nonchalant as her quick breath permitted. Confusion whirled within her for a moment, and then quieted enough to be recognized as despair. What were all her defenses, now that she had been seen coming out of the alley itself?

"Little late, aren't you?" her father asked.

"Why, not much."

"Your mother asked me to pick you up."

In the pause that followed, Cynthia set her chin, her eyes on the smooth rapid motion of Daffy's flanks. She wouldn't say a thing. He could go ahead, if he had to. After a moment he did, casually.

"What's so attractive about that girl, Cynthy?"

"I tried to get rid of her tonight"—at her father's glance a flush prickled in her eyelids, and she went on—"I did. I waited until the store was locked up. She was still hanging around. She begged me to go down the alley."

"Well"—he touched up the horse—"you've had enough of the store. Your mother needs you around the house."

A lurch of the road cart threw Cynthia against her father,

and she saw, incredulously, the lines down his lean cheeks deepen. He wasn't joking. He had swung over to the other side, then. She had lost her amused ally.

"But, Father, the sale lasts all this week. I can't stop."

"Bell's won't go out of business. If you won't play fair, you can't do what you want to."

"It isn't playing fair to go back on somebody that needs you."

Her father looked around at her.

"You can't do that girl any good. She's a poor lot. Your mother told you to drop her. That's all there is to it."

He turned the horse under the elm trees of the drive, and walked her in silence to the steps of the house. There he waited for Cynthia to get out. She stood for an instant by the wheel, her eyes entreating him. But with a flick of the lines he said:

"I'll just tell your mother you aren't going to work anymore," and Cynthia, lagging up the steps, knew bitterly he meant that as a concession, the only one he could make her.

Supper was ready; she could hear her mother moving about the kitchen.

"I'll be right down," she called halfway up the stairs.

As she splashed her eyes with cold water she pressed her fingers against them, so that the blood in the tips pounded on the eyeballs.

"Oh, I hate them!" she thought. "I won't go down!"

Then Robert called shrilly:

"Cynthy! Supper!" and she went slowly down to the dining room.

Through the desultory supper talk she was aware of her mother's gaze drifting about her, retreating if she looked up restively. Robert, eyeing her over his bread and butter, announced between bites:

"Huh, Cyn looks sick of her job."

"I am not!" Cynthia flashed at him, and winced as her mother replied:

"Hush, Robert! Cynthia is tired."

Later, in a dark corner of the porch, Cynthia looked into

her black mood. It was all distorted images of herself: the self Mr. Bell would think her for "quitting her job," when she had said she could work two weeks; the self he would think her if he learned that she was being dragged away like a baby; the self—this all a shattered image—that Queenie would think her when she failed to appear in the morning, failed to keep that promise to stand by her. Gone were the bright images she loved of herself as a person of independence, as a superior saleswoman, and, brightest of all, sharpest, as a wise benefactor. Within the house voices droned, her father and mother talking. A little impotent rage blew through her, blurring the distorted images into a microcosm of humiliation. The screen door opened, and Cynthia, at the sight of her mother's figure, large in the dusk, drew back into her corner, a hard shell closing to about her heart.

"Cynthia?"

"Yes."

"Oh, there you are." She settled into a chair near Cynthia, rocking leisurely. "Your father says you aren't going to the store anymore."

Cynthia's shell strained altogether.

"You haven't been yourself since you were there. It's too hard work."

"Other girls do it," cried Cynthia.

"They have to. You don't."

There was a silence, in which Cynthia felt tiny flames of antagonism lick out from her contracted heart. Then her mother spoke again in the tone of one offering diversion to a sulky child.

"Rachel Meredith came in this afternoon. She said her dresses had come home. Why don't you go over now to see them, if you aren't too tired? You won't have much more chance to see Rachel."

Cynthia stirred in her chair. She did want to see Rachel. She wanted to refuse her mother's suggestion, but after a moment of perversity she knew she wished more to see Rachel.

"I might go over," she admitted.

"Don't stay too late, although you won't need to get up early tomorrow."

Until she was out of sight of the house Cynthia walked slowly; then she quickened her steps until she was almost running. The huge elms gathered the night in pools under their branches; waves of light ran out from the windows she passed, breaking into curious white foam on rose bushes or dropping on smooth, pale lawns. The self of humiliation drifted away from her. Rachel would help her, would know what to do for Queenie. The thought of Rachel sang through her—tall, sweet Rachel, with white, light-touching hands.

She crept noiselessly across the grass to the side of the Meredith house. The French windows stood open to the screened porch, and just within one of them Rachel sat reading. Cynthia caught her breath in a second of hushed adoration; mystery lay about Rachel, like the soft light on her dark hair and graceful neck. Tonight and tomorrow she could sit there reading; then she would be gone, changed. The thought of the strange man who was to come Friday to marry Rachel stirred in Cynthia jealous wonder. She wanted Rachel to look up, to see her standing there. Suddenly, with the breath of some warm night scent, Queenie seemed to press against her, quivering, imploring—Queenie in love, too. Her image dimmed the mystery about Rachel, and Cynthia moved impatiently away from such disloyalty. At the sound Rachel glanced up, and, with a soft "Cynthia!" came out to the edge of the veranda.

"Don't stand there staring, little moth!" she said with a laugh. "Come in!"

Her voice was a warm rain of confusion falling deliciously upon Cynthia. She stumbled on the step, and then Rachel drew her inside the screens, laying an arm about her shoulders, and led her up the broad stairway to her own room. There was mystery here, too, in the disorder of the quiet, spacious chamber, in half-filled trunks, and piles of soft colors and textures on low chairs. Two nights more, and the beautiful disorder would be gone.

"Sit here, child." Rachel pushed to the floor a mass of

tissue paper, and Cynthia crouched on a corner of the couch.

"They must all be packed tomorrow, and I knew you'd wish to see them."

Cynthia watched mutely, her eyes on the slender hands that caressed the fabrics, shaking out folds of silk, touching bits of embroidery. Rachel slipped her arms into a bright mandarin coat, and wheeled in front of Cynthia. Incongruously, Queenie seemed to fling up her hands there, clumsy, short-fingered. Rachel, turning back to Cynthia, paused.

"What is it?" she asked.

The coat dropped from her shoulders, and she stepped near the couch. Cynthia shook her head; Queenie had no place here.

"I believe you'd like me not to be married, little dumb thing!" Rachel touched Cynthia's cheek with cool fingers. "Is that it?"

"Oh, no; no!"

"Want to be rid of me, eh?"

"Rachel!" At Rachel's laugh Cynthia flushed. Perhaps Rachel guessed how she reveled in the exotic pain of losing her.

"There, I won't torment you. Come, we'll go out on the porch. This is all, except loads of silver. Mother can show you that, if you like, afterward."

On the veranda again, Rachel sank into her hammock, and bade Cynthia pull her chair close.

"Now," she said lazily, "tell me what you've done today."

"I can't go back to the store." Cynthia plucked at the fringe of the hammock. "Father saw me—coming out the alley where Queenie lives. She's that girl, you know."

"I thought you decided last night to avoid her."

Cynthia drew her hand hastily away.

"She—needs somebody," she protested.

"Oh, Cynthia," Rachel's voice rallied her, "your heart's too great for the world. That little alley girl doesn't need my Cynthia."

"But I can help her."

"Cynthia dear, Lottie used to live down there near the river. I asked her if she knew these McQuades."

"Well." Cynthia was hostile. Whatever that hired girl knew did not matter.

"This Queenie has a bad name. Her mother can do nothing with her."

"It's a stepmother. And, Rachel, she wants to—to do what's right. I know."

Rachel reached for Cynthia's hand, held it in her cool, firm grasp.

"It's you that's good, dear. You can't understand yet. You can't alter mud. You just get smirched yourself."

Cynthia held herself rigid against the sweet thrill of Rachel's touch.

"But suppose—you fell in love"—she sought for tangible form to give her confused thoughts—"and then—he was married. Wouldn't it be hard?"

"Cynthia," said Rachel, releasing her hand, "you are an absurd child. If the girl were decent, she wouldn't be in love with a married man."

For a shivering moment Cynthia sat silent. Bending over a deep, lovely pool to touch it, she had found it polished glass. Then Rachel, with a sudden movement, drew her out of her chair to her knees by the hammock. The bewildering sweetness of Rachel's arms around her, of Rachel's throat against her hot cheek, sent that moment scuttling away, an ugly spider, to some remote corner of her being. She needn't know it was there. With a little sob she relaxed into the fragrant darkness.

"Don't think about it." Rachel's lips brushed her ear. "We have so few hours left. You are worn out—that horrid store!"

Think? She could think of nothing with Rachel lavishing light hands about her. Cynthia, sitting by the swaying hammock, felt the mystery creep about her, too. Rachel was so rich in love she could pour it out until the swimming joy became pain within you.

When Cynthia came slowly up the walk to her own house,

voices on the porch ceased, and the red star of her father's cigar glowed out.

"Yes, the things were very nice," she said in a vague way, moving on toward the door.

"Going to bed?"

"Yes. Good night."

Later, lying in bed, she heard that interrupted talk picked up again. She was too drowsy to care. With her mind full of the drifting images at the border of sleep, she was sinking, sinking, when, unguarded, out scuttled the horrid spider of doubt, rousing her to full wakefulness. Her mother and Rachel had talked that very day. Rachel had connived with her mother. There was surely something wrong in such easeful dispensing with Queenie. But Rachel's good-night kiss was there on her lips, seducing her to languor, and she slept.

The next morning she bent to household tasks with eager humility. She was unconsciously trying to force herself back to an old order of things, as though only thus could she be sure of loyalty to Rachel, of matter-of-fact tranquility at home. Her father was to stop at Bell's to say she wouldn't be down. Who would be given her counter? And Queenie —she saw her fumble with the cord of a parcel, count change into some customer's outstretched hand, always with her eyes toward the door, watching for her. At her mother's approach her thoughts would scatter, a swarm of flies driven from a bit of refuse, to gather black as soon as she was left alone.

Toward noon she put on her hat and sought out her mother.

"I'm going after my money," she said stubbornly. "Mr. Bell might not be in this afternoon."

Her mother lifted her eyes from the white stuff she was sewing. For a second her needle continued its little pricking sound along a seam.

"I wanted you to try on this skirt," she suggested. "You want it for Rachel's wedding, don't you?"

"I'll be right back." Cynthia fled.

The street was hot and still. The shadows huddled close
about the trees, and the sweetish odor of tar swam in the
glare. Cynthia's hurrying body sucked in the heat, grew
heavy with it; but the discomfort gave her a dim relief. When
she came at last to the bridge she stopped, peering off at the
gray huddle of shacks. A breath from the river touched her
moist forehead, and she looked down at the water, above
which hung a wavering glow like molten air. Then she went
on more slowly until she stopped again inside the doors of
Bell's store.

It seemed dark and cool after the street, the aisles stretching back empty, interminable. She made her way between
the counters, a dull sense of severance moving in her. The
woman behind the silks nodded to her; she could see Mr.
Bell's sleek head over the office partition.

Someone seized her arm. Queenie, with reproachful, swollen eyelids, made a grimace of caution toward the office, and
drew Cynthia into the shelter of the tall thread cases.

"I thought you wasn't ever coming."

"I can't work anymore."

Queenie's lips twitched in her pallid face.

"Has a bad name." Cynthia seemed to hear Rachel's low
voice. Poor Queenie! She looked as if she had melted a little
and sagged down.

"Why not?" Queenie thrust her face close. "Is it—me?
They won't have you seeing me?"

"They think the work's too hard." Cynthia's quick words
fell back from Queenie's grin of contempt.

"Oh, I know; I ain't such a fool. You're too good." She
leaned heavily on the counter, her eyelids growing redder.
"Well, Bell's kicked me out, too. 'Won't need your services,
Miss McQuade, after tonight.' They's just two things left."
She broke off at the approach of a customer, who looked
curiously at the two girls, fingered some ribbons, and trailed
on. Cynthia waited tensely. "One's the river, th' other's him.
Anyhow, he wants me."

"I'll ask Mr. Bell." Cynthia's fingers clenched into Queenie's arm. "When he knows I'm going to leave—"

Queenie's pale eyes hung on Cynthia's an instant.

"Oh, you needn't bother." She edged away.

Had she felt that echoing speech—"You can't alter mud." Cynthia drooped. Her power had run out of her; she had somehow lost her grip on Queenie. With a shrug Queenie tucked her blouse into her tight belt, and presented herself to the customer who had drifted back.

After an irresolute moment Cynthia made a rush toward the office. Awkward, aware of the dust on her shoes, she seated herself by Mr. Bell's desk. He looked up from his papers.

"Yes, Miss Bates?"

"I just came for my salary, Mr. Bell."

"Oh, yes. Your father stopped in this morning. So you've had enough of salesmanship?" He smiled, and Cynthia saw him changed to the Mr. Bell of church socials, his authority dropping away.

"They think so," she confided.

"Next time you want a job"—he pulled open a drawer—"I'll give you a recommendation." He counted out three half-dollars. "Up to last night, wasn't it?"

Cynthia drew her finger along the edge of the desk. Into her manner came an alloy of flattery. Instinctively, to gain her request, she sought to please his suave maleness.

"Mr. Bell, there's something I wanted to ask you." Her breath fluttered. "As long as I have to—resign"—she offered that phrase as a small jest, and at his smile hastened on—"couldn't you keep Queenie McQuade on? She needs work, oh, very much! She'll do her best."

Mr. Bell's smile was swallowed up in a return of his manager air.

"She's not an efficient clerk," he said shortly. He dropped the three coins into Cynthia's lap, and as she gathered them into her hand, added: "I'm sorry she's presumed upon your being in the store. I told your father and Miss Meredith this morning I regretted it. We don't mean to hire such girls."

Cynthia shrank away from the curiosity under his heavy eyebrows.

"They spoke to you—father and Rachel Meredith?"

"Just a word."

Cynthia stumbled to her feet.

"She must have work. She hasn't done anything." Did she say the words or only attempt them?

"Don't you bother your pretty head about her, Miss Bates. You can see it isn't fair to our patrons or our other clerks."

Then with a little nod he had dismissed her. Her furtive glance as she hurried from the store disclosed no glimpse of Queenie. Ducking across the street, she stopped in the shelter of the wooden Indian in front of the tobacco shop. No Queenie stalking her. Slowly she walked on in the swimming heat, the world and her own inner self swooning in a sort of suspended life.

When she dragged herself into the house, the glistening pallor of her face brought a sharp order from her mother.

"You lie down. I shouldn't have let you traipse downtown in this heat. This is the last bit of your foolishness."

She lay on the couch in the library. The shrill of locusts outside and the clatter of dishes in the dining room seemed remote and unreal.

Doubling down the crooked ways of sleep, she sought for Queenie, while something formless and horrible pursued her. Its tentacles reached for her at her very heels. She tried to scream. It clutched her shoulder, and she wrenched herself free of dream and sleep, to find her mother looking down at her.

"You'd better have some lunch, Cynthia. It's late."

The rest of that day Cynthia gave herself with wistful docility to her mother's suggestions. She stood before the mirror while her mother knelt to adjust the folds of the white dress, a tall, thin girl with drooping shoulders.

"There, that's the best I can do." Her mother rose stiffly. "You don't seem to like it."

"Yes, I do, Mother. It's pretty." Cynthia let the dress slide to the floor and stepped out of the white pile, a flush touching her cheeks. She felt the somber weight of ingratitude that her mother should kneel there, working for her, while she had no joy even in the dress.

"If you'd just fill out a little—" Her mother's eyes were on her shoulders. "After the wedding you've got to rest up. You're like a rail."

Cynthia drew her gingham dress hastily over her head.

After supper, to Robert's glee, she offered to play checkers. Something inside her lay numb, with faint pricklings, like a cramped foot. As she bent over the black and yellow squares she heard her mother say:

"After the excitement of the wedding she'll be all right."

Rachel's lover had come that afternoon. Cynthia was full of fierce relief that there was no chance of seeing Rachel again.

But at last she walked slowly, in order that she might not grow warm and red, under the elms and up the path to the Meredith house. Mrs. Meredith herself opened the door. Unexpectedly she kissed Cynthia, sighing, "Your turn someday soon." For the first time Cynthia saw her as Rachel, faded and hardened by the years. She led Cynthia into the parlor, heavy with the sweetness of many roses. Cynthia was the only outsider. She sank into a chair, pulling her feet close to the rockers; Rachel's aunt, in stiff gray silk, her father, florid and strident, the minister in formal black, regarded her solemnly, almost hostilely. Then, after a long moment, Rachel stood between the curtains. Her eyes sought Cynthia's over the great cluster of roses in her arms, caressed her swiftly, and lifted to the man beside her. Back flooded the beautiful mystery, and Cynthia abandoned herself to it. She scarcely saw the man, after one glance at his blond head over Rachel's. She saw only Rachel's face, the rise and fall of the lace at her breast. Incredibly soon it was over; Rachel lifted her face to the man, and a jealous ecstasy racked Cynthia at their grave kiss. Rachel turned to her people, laughing; her arms held Cynthia for an instant.

Presently the machine whirled up to the door, and in a flash Rachel was gone, slim, tailored, beside the straight, proud figure of her husband.

Cynthia started slowly toward home, Rachel's roses filling her arms, their fragrance swimming up in the heat. Insidiously another odor mixed with theirs, until, with a shiver, Cynthia halted. Stripped quivering from her, naked, rose the hidden impulse. She must see Queenie. Unless she did, she couldn't endure this beauty. It wasn't fair. Forgetting the heat, shaking away the little thought of her mother waiting to hear about the wedding, she turned down the long street to the river.

Even at the entrance to the alley she did not hesitate. The third house, Queenie had said. It stood nearer the river than the others, down a sloping bank. Cynthia walked straight to the door, the roses drooping against her dress. Scraggly hens scurried off the doorstep. Inside, at her knock, came a scuffling sound, a smart slap, followed by a child's cry. The door opened, and a woman, wiping reddened arms on her drab wrapper, faced her.

"How do you do?" Cynthia peered past her into a room full of the sour smell of wash-water. "I'm Cynthia Bates." She tried to smile against the woman's grim stare. "Is—is Queenie here?"

"What do you want of her?"

Cynthia shrank back, her roses and white dress suddenly strident with mockery. The woman snatched at a buzzing fly, and shook her skirts clear of the clutching child who had crept to her feet. He pursed his dirty little mouth for a cry, and she jerked him into her arms.

"What you want?" she repeated.

"I knew her in the store."

"Oh, you're that one! Well, she ain't here."

"Is she working somewhere?"

"Working! Her! Folks won't keep her. Expectin' us to feed her—a grown woman."

The woman returned to her tubs, setting the child on a

chair. Cynthia saw round eyes, pale like Queenie's, staring at her from behind the tubs.

"She isn't here?" she persisted.

"I don't know where she is, and, what's more, I don't want to." The woman broke into irritated volubility. "I says to her, if you can't work, you needn't eat. Crazy about the fellows she was, wanting to dress up fine and run with 'em. I stood it till she mixed up with a married man; then I says, 'This is enough of you.' "

"Where did she go?" Cynthia asked slowly.

"She ain't been here since yesterday morning. She needn't show her face here again."

Cynthia climbed the slope, the roses slipping from her arms. She glanced back once. The baby had crept to the step, and sat gravely pulling the red petals from one of them. She felt curious eyes nibble at her from the other shacks.

As she entered the alley, she looked back at the river, catching a sob at the sight of a bit of white. Only a paper sluggishly drifting; not Queenie's round, pleading face.

In the alley the air hung stagnant, rotting with the old buildings. Queenie was gone, Rachel was gone. She came out to the glare of the street, and after a second's pause went on to the bridge. Leaning on the railing, she forced her eyes back to the squalid shore. For the first time she saw it without a hovering vision of herself as ministering angel. There it lay. Somewhere else Rachel was hurried off to shining happiness. And Queenie—

A grinding moment, and stark and undisguised that dormant thing within her stood up. They had done it, Rachel and the rest—pushed Queenie back into her mud. Under goodness lay that festering.

She would confront them with that terrible accusation. Her head high, she started swiftly toward her home. Presently her steps lagged again. The hard brilliance of her judgment dimmed. They would only repeat things they had said. With her white skirts swinging limply about her ankles she came to the quiet, comfortable houses, in one of which she lived. A strange aloofness filled her. If she tried to tell them, her father and her mother, they would drag her back, shut her in safety, keep her cabined, *good*. She would keep silent.

She came to the steps of the house, a pale light in her tired face. Her quest had begun, secret, bewildering.

The Cat
and the King

Jennette Lee (1919)

She had been up this morning at four o'clock, and had crept out through the gate, almost guiltily, and off across the fields for a long walk. There might be nothing wrong in taking a walk at four o'clock in the morning; perhaps no one would have stayed her in her flight through the college gates, munching her bit of crackers and cheese, had they known. But no one knew. She had carefully *not* inquired . . .

She had had her walk, with the freshness of the spring luring her on, up Redmond Hill, down the slope by Board-man's and along home by the road, gathering from the bushes on either side the great masses of trailing vines that draped her head and shoulders and hung swaying from her arms. It had been a wonderful walk—pulling the vines from the bushes, shaking the dew from the clustering blossoms and drenching herself in freshness.

The blossoms were a faint, greenish white and, with her green-and-white-striped skirt and white blouse as she stood in the gateway looking in on the college halls, the flowers and the twisting stalks of leaves twined about her and framing her in, she might have been the very spirit of the outdoor world peeping shyly in at the halls of learning, curious, wistful and on tiptoe for flight.

She stood a moment gazing up at the great masses of brick and stone that made up her college world. The side of the buildings nearest the lodge gate was in shadow and the vines and the dull red of the bricks seemed to hold for her something mysterious and strange. She went slowly up the brick walk, holding in check a sudden longing to turn back, to flee once more to the fields and the little brook that ran gurgling by Boardman's and make a day of it out in the free world.

It was mysterious and wonderful—this college where her name was enrolled: "Flora Bailey, 1920." But there was something overpowering about it. The great walls that looked so gracious in the fresh morning light had a way of shutting one in, of hampering and binding the movements of freshmen. There were so many things one must and must not do within the gracious walls! Her eye glanced up to a tower of South Parker, high up to a window where silken curtains hung in even folds, and a sigh escaped her lips. One must not make friends with seniors, for instance, except by invitation—and a senior was very high up!

The curtains parted a little. The girl's eyes glanced quickly. A firm hand pushed back the curtains and a figure stood between them looking out on the morning. The lifted head bore a mass of reddish hair gathered carelessly, and the light that fell on the tallest peaks and gables of the college touched it with gold. To the freshman, gazing from her walk, it was as if a goddess, high-enshrined and touched by the rising sun, stood revealed. She gave a gasp of pleasure.

It had been a glorious walk out in the dew and sunrise, and now Annette Osler was gazing from her tower window—not on the girl on the college walk, to be sure, but on the world of wonder.

She looked up adoringly at the figure in the tower of South Parker. And the girl high in the window turned a little and looked down. There was no one in sight—only the quiet light of morning on the campus and the wind rippling shadowy waves in the ivy leaves on brick walls. A little rippling wave seemed to run from the walk to the high tower window, and with a gesture of happiness the girl on the walk turned toward the entrance of Gordon Hall. Her pulse sang as she went, her step danced a little, hurrying up the stairs and along the corridor to her room. She opened the door quickly.

Across the room by the window, her roommate, surrounded by books, was taking notes, dipping in here and there with an alert pencil. She looked up in swift surprise. "Why, where have you—oh, how lovely!" Her eye caught the green-and-white blossoms and she sprang up. "Here—I'll get the pitcher!"

She brought a pitcher from the bedroom and Flora placed the vines in water, standing back to survey them. They trailed down over the windowsill and onto the seat below. She touched them with quick fingers. "That will do. We'll arrange them after breakfast."

Her companion had gone back to her task of scooping up notes with flying pencil. She suspended it a minute and looked up. "Do you remember Bainnuter?" she asked absently.

"Bainnuter?" repeated Flora. "I don't seem to remember—was he on the Yale team?"

Her roommate stared. Then she chuckled. "He's ancient history, Flora dear! Early Egyptian. I was wondering if Doxey would ask us about him. Do you suppose he will?"

Flora wheeled. She regarded her with startled eyes. "History exam! This morning!" she gasped. "I forgot—oh, I forgot!" She seized her books from the table, hunting out a stub of pencil in haste. "I hate 'em all—everybody that's had any history done about 'em. I hate 'em!" she said savagely.

"Why, I thought you liked history! You did splendidly in the February exam. You're such a clever thing! I wish I were!" She sighed deeply and returned to her scooping and dredging.

The roommate's name was Aspasia—Aspasia Elton. That was another of the perplexing things about college, living night and day with a girl named Aspasia. It made life topsy-turvy. No one at home had names out of history books.

Aspasia glanced at her casually. "Better cram on Rameses II," she said kindly. "They say he's dippy on Rameses!"

The room was quiet. No sound came from the corridors or from the rooms above or below.

The two girls turned leaves and crammed notes. Now and then one of them sighed. Sounds began to come from the corridor—hurried feet in slippers, and splashings and calls from the bathrooms, and bits of conversation floating over transoms.

Flora closed her book with a little shrug. She put a pencil carefully in the place. "Doxey gave me warning last week," she said.

Aspasia looked up. "What a shame!"

"No-o. It's all right. I knew I wasn't doing anything; only I hoped *he* didn't know. I thought the February exam had fooled him—maybe."

"Anyway, you don't need to worry. Your February mark will carry you through."

"Yes; but it won't put me on the team. That's all I care about, all I've ever cared about," she said slowly.

Aspasia nodded. It was sympathetic and vague. "Well—you can live if you don't make the team. Other folks do."

"I can't!" said Flora.

Her roommate looked at her reflectively. "It's Annette Osler," she announced. "Just because she's captain, you want—"

Flora's face was scarlet. "I don't care if it is!" she murmured.

"Be a sport, Flora! *You* can't have a crush on a senior—"

"It is not a crush!" said Flora vehemently. "I just want to know Annette because she's the kind of girl I like. And if I get on the team, she'll notice me; she'll *have* to notice me! There isn't any other way to get to know a senior, is there?" she demanded.

"You're too aspiring," said Aspasia. She gathered up her

books and notes. "Come on to breakfast. There's the bell."

"I'm not going to breakfast," said Flora firmly. "I've got to study."

Her roommate reappeared from the bedroom. "You're a weak, sentimental freshman!" she remarked casually.

"I am *not* sentimental! I want to know Annette Osler because she's a great, glorious creature! So, there! Let be teasing, Aspasia."

" 'Let be teasing'! I must save that for Professor Goodwin. Funny English! Did you get it from your grandmother, honey? He'll be sure to ask the 'source,' you know."

"Go along!" said Flora crossly.

She was left alone and there was only the sunlight falling on the green-and-white vines in the windows and traveling to the scattered books on the table. She looked at them a minute; then her arms dropped to the table with a little gesture of defeat and her face dropped to her arms. . . .

A bumblebee hummed in the window and went away.

It may have been the blossoms.

She lifted her face and looked at them balefully. If only she had known enough to get up at four o'clock to study instead of going off for that miserable walk! And suddenly the sunrise as it came over Redmond Hill flashed back to her; it brought the song of a bird that trilled softly out of the woods.

Her face seemed to listen to the fluting call. Then it grew thoughtful. If there were some way, some legitimate way, of attracting the attention of a senior! Annette liked the things she liked. Often she watched her setting off alone over the hill that led to the fields. And because she was a freshman she might not hurry after her and say: "Come for a walk with *me!*" . . . And suddenly she looked at it. Why not? Why not go to her, this very morning, and lay the case before her and *ask* her to go for a walk? Why not? . . . The history exam might as well be cut; she was bound to flunk anyway!

She pushed the books aside with a look of distaste. She would do it—and do it now!

There was a sound in the hall. She picked up her book and opened it swiftly to Rameses II.

The door swung open on Aspasia, one elbow holding careful guard over a glass of milk and two large slices of bread and butter.

Flora sprang up. "You dear!"

Aspasia set the milk on the table and turned a little breathless. "What do you think? Annette Osler has sprained her ankle! They're taking her up to the infirmary now!"

And Flora looked at her with a foolish, half-startled smile. "Now isn't that a stupid thing to do!" she said slowly. "How long do you suppose she will have to stay in the infirmary?"

"Oh—ages!" said Aspasia carelessly. "A sprained ankle isn't a thing you get over in a day, you know. She'll be there weeks maybe."

And Flora looked down at Rameses II. "How stupid!" she said to him softly.

It had seemed so simple this morning to go to Annette. And now she might have been a thousand miles away, for any chance there was of getting at her.

The history examinations came and went in a maze of gloom. She had flunked of course. She did not care particularly about the flunking, but it was embarrassing to meet Professor Dockery on the campus next day; and she made a little skillful detour to evade him—only to see him coming toward her along the path by the elms.

He stopped as she came up and looked down at her consideringly. "You wrote a good paper yesterday; a very good paper indeed!"

"I did!" cried Flora.

"I shall withdraw my opposition to your being on the team," he said kindly.

Flora gazed at him mutely. "Now isn't that a shame!" she

said swiftly. And she hurried on to the fields, leaving him
to extract what sense he could from the wail.

She tramped far that afternoon. A new bird lured her on;
and she found a curious hummocky nest on the ground, with
a breakfast of shining roots spread out before it. She went
down on her knees—a field mouse probably—or a mole
perhaps. She wished there were someone to share it with—
the delicately lined dome that her fingers explored and the
shining roots at the door. . . . Her thoughts traveled rebel-
liously to the infirmary—"weeks perhaps," Aspasia said.

And then, as she knelt by the hummocky nest, the idea
came to her. She got up from her knees, smiling down on
the little brown dome and the breakfast of roots, and nodded
to it slowly and happily.

"I'll do it," she said softly. "I'll do it—right off."

When she came in from her walk she went directly to the
library and asked for medical books. The librarian bent a
keen, spectacled inquiry on her.

"I want them for fiction purposes," explained Flora, "for
local color."

But when the musty books were laid before her, she had
a period of depression. She attacked them in a little gust of
discouragement, selecting the most modern-looking one with
colored plates and diagrams and opening it at random. The
charts and plates held her. Next to outdoors could there be
anything more fascinating and mysterious than the human
body? Why had no one ever told her about these things!

She looked down curiously at her own hand resting on the
book. It seemed to her a new hand, one that she had never
seen before. The network of blue veins fascinated her; they
were little branching trees or the delicate veining of leaves.
She had not guessed people were like that, with all those
branches of muscles and nerves and veins.

Perhaps they *were* trees once.

Her mind dreamed on happily. She knew how it felt to be
a tree, swaying in the wind, with the rain on your leaves.

Perhaps she *was* a tree once, and grew on a hillside, and the squirrels ran up and down and nibbled at branches. She gave a little chuckling laugh in the silence of the library, and the librarian looked over reprovingly from her platform.

Flora made a gesture of apology and plunged again into her search. But it had changed now from seeking to dallying enjoyment. Why had no one told her? And she read on till the librarian touched her on the shoulder and she looked up, blinking.

"The bell has rung," said the librarian reprovingly.

"Oh-h!" breathed Flora. "Yes; I want them again, please!" and she hurried off blithely.

It was only as she was making ready for dinner that it occurred to her she had not found what she started out to seek.

But in the evening, in the library again, she came on it. She had almost given up her search and was only looking idly at the oldest of the brown books when her eye fell on "The Curious Case of Prudence Small."

She began to read. And as she read her cheeks glowed and her eyes danced. She looked speculatively at the librarian. The librarian was a small woman, and there were only two other girls in the room. Better wait? She shook her head. She would never have the courage if she waited! She opened the book again to "The Curious Case of Prudence Small" and read the details once more—and looked up.

The green-shaded reading lights in the dim room made little ghastly circles about the two girls bending over their books; and the librarian, mounted on her platform, seemed like some priestess of knowledge waiting for mystic rites to begin. Flora fixed her eye on her and stood up. The librarian went on counting out cards. Flora scraped her chair a little on the floor; and then, as no one paid attention, she gave it a shove that upset it with a clatter and brought the spectacled glance full upon her and a look of annoyance from the girls across the room. Flora lifted her arms slowly. She gave a long, low moan and subsided gently to the floor.

There was a flurry of green-shaded lights, a glimpse of the librarian's startled face; then the sound of running feet and the two girls were bending over a rigid figure and lifting it from the floor.

Five minutes later, in the consulting room of the infirmary, the college physician, summoned from a comfortable game of whist, bent above the rigid figure.

Flora's eyes rested trustfully on the physician's face. She had recovered consciousness almost as soon as they had deposited her on the infirmary couch. Five minutes the book said; she judged it must be about five minutes—and she opened her eyes and gazed pensively at the perturbed faces that surrounded her.

The physician dismissed them all with a curt gesture. She brought a basin of water, with a bit of ice tinkling in it, and began to bathe the girl's forehead with swift, sopping strokes.

"I fell," murmured Flora dreamily.

Doctor Worcester nodded. "You will have a good-sized lump, I'm afraid." She went on sopping with skillful strokes.

Flora's eyes closed meekly. She felt a little thankful for the bump. She had never seen Doctor Worcester before, near to, and there was something in the face bent above her that made her wonder how "The Curious Case of Prudence Small" would come out. "There!" The doctor put aside the basin. "I don't think it will be discolored now. How do you feel?" She was looking down at her critically.

Flora's face flushed. She recalled how she felt—and stretched out her arms and rubbed them a little. "I feel better," she said slowly, "only there is a little buzzing in the top of my head, and the soles of my feet are slightly paralyzed, I think."

She said it neatly and glibly and lay with closed eyes, waiting for what might happen.

The doctor's swift eyes studied the passive countenance. "I think we will keep you here tonight," she said quietly.

She touched a bell and gave directions to the nurse. Her fingers rested lightly on Flora's wrist. "We will put her in the ward," she said, "next to Miss Osler." She started and glanced sharply down at the wrist under her fingers and then at the girl's placid face.

She held the wrist a minute and dropped it slowly, her eyes on the face. "I shall look in again before I go to bed. She may need a quieting draft to make her sleep."

From her desk on the platform, the librarian peered over at the doctor, who was standing looking down at the green-shaded, quiet room.

"Tell me just what happened," said the doctor briskly.

And while the librarian recounted the meager details of the story, the doctor's thoughtful face surveyed the vacant room and the table where the brown books lay.

"It might have been studying too soon after eating—don't you think?" inquired the librarian helpfully.

"I don't think anything," said the doctor. "I'm puzzled." She walked across the table and picked up one of the books. "What was she reading?" she asked.

The librarian flushed. "She said she wanted them for fiction purposes; 'English A' I suppose, don't you?"

But the physician did not reply. She was looking at a page that had fallen open in her hand, perhaps because an energetic elbow had held it pressed back for half an hour. "The patient said, on inquiry, that her head still buzzed a little, and the soles of her feet were slightly paralyzed."

She shut the book with a laugh. "I'll take this along with me. No, I don't think it's serious—a case of nerves maybe."

Her face wore a thoughtful look as she gave directions to the night nurse in the infirmary and looked over charts. She did not go to the ward, and she left no directions for a sleeping draft for the new patient.

The nurse wondered afterward if the doctor could have forgotten. But there was no sign of restlessness in the ward when she went in a little later. The new patient was asleep. There was only one other patient in the ward, a senior who had sprained her ankle a few days ago. She had been asleep when the new patient was brought in. The nurse stepped very slowly and passed out of the shaded ward, drawing the door to behind her.

Flora opened her eyes. Through the chink of door the moonlight streamed in. The infirmary was at the top of the building, and she could look down on the sleeping world and off at the great clouds drifting and swinging against a blue-black sky. She turned her head a little. The senior was asleep, one hand tucked under her cheek, the reddish hair gathered into a quaint cap; the moonlight touching the quiet face made it seem like a child's. Flora gazed with devoted, happy eyes. The little pricks of conscience that had stirred in her under the doctor's inquiring gaze subsided. She felt happy and at home for the first time in her college life.

Something flew across the window, shutting out the moon, with great flapping wings. She turned quickly; a bat maybe —no, too large for a bat! The doctor's keen eyes flitted before her, and she sighed a little and moved restlessly and caught a glimpse of her hand lying on the coverlet. How pale it was in the moonlight! She lifted it curiously and gazed at the delicate strangeness of it—all the little veins and bones and tissues. They were made of moonlight! Charts and diagrams floated before her—filmy lungs, delicate branching nerves, all the mysterious network of wonder.

Then her mind flashed to the mole's nest and shining roots. And she gazed again at the pillowed head in its cap. To-morrow she would tell Annette! Tomorrow—and a whole week to come! She was not sentimental! She only wanted to know Annette—and take long walks—with Annette. Her eyelids drooped a little. She tried to prop them open, to gaze at the beloved face. She wanted to show Annette the mole's nest and the breakfast—of—roots. . . . And she trailed away into a dream world, carrying the mole's nest and the little roots with her far down into her sleep. . . .

When she opened her eyes they were gazing straight into a pair of gray ones framed in a curious cap. The gray eyes smiled.

"Hello!" said the senior. "Did you drift in in the night?"

And Flora smiled back shyly. No need to talk or make advances now. There would be a week—a whole week—

The senior sat up and reached for a purple robe that hung at the head of the bed and drew it about her. It was a gorgeous robe with tracings of gold running over; and, as she gathered it about her shoulders, a lock of the reddish hair escaped from her cap and fell across it. She made a royal picture for watching eyes.

She tucked in the escaped lock with half-apologetic fingers. "Stupid, to wear a cap! But my hair tangles so!"

"I like it," said Flora promptly. "I think it looks—quaint!"

"Thank you!" said the senior. She turned a smiling glance. A little look of surprise touched it. "Why, you're the wood nymph—green and white!" she exclaimed. "I saw you the other morning, didn't I, coming in, before breakfast!"

"I'd been for a walk," said Flora.

"You were a little bit of all outdoors!" said the senior laughing. She stretched her arms in a restful gesture and looked about the sun-filled room. "Glorious day, isn't it? Perfect for the game!" She glanced at Flora kindly. "Too bad you'll miss it. Are you in for long?"

"I don't know," said Flora happily. "They haven't found out yet what's the matter with me." She stopped short.

The senior had thrown back the covers and was sitting on the edge of the bed, gathering her robe about her.

Flora's startled gaze held her. "You'll hurt your foot!"

"My foot?" She glanced down at it and thrust it into a purple slipper by the bed, and stood upright—on both feet. "I didn't hurt it at all—not really. But they thought I'd better be careful. Rest for a day or two on account of the game. Too bad you can't come!"

She had knotted her girdle about her and was moving toward the door with vigorous stride.

"Oh-ah!" gasped Flora. She waved her hands in a helpless gesture.

The senior glanced back. "Yes?" she said.

"Did you—did you ever happen to see—a mole's nest?"

asked Flora. It came in a little jerk, almost a cry of pain.

"A mole's nest?" The senior paused doubtfully. "I don't think so. It sounds interesting!" But there was a laughing note in the voice that brought a quick flush to the freshman face.

"It might have been a field mouse," said Flora weakly.

The senior's eyes were laughing now and she nodded kindly. "I hope you won't have to stay in long. But they're awfully good to you here—take the best care of you!" And she nodded again and was gone.

And Flora gazed for a moment where the purple cloud of glory had been. It vanished into a misty blur; and she subsided, a bundle of sobs, under the tumbled clothes.

Doctor Worcester appeared at the doorway. The hunched-up figure in the bed by the window was very quiet. Only a damp handkerchief pressed tight over two eyes was visible, and a tumbled mop of hair.

The doctor came in, glancing about the sun-filled room with a look of pleasure. The infirmary ward was always a cheerful place, but never so attractive as when all the beds were vacant—or nearly all. The fewer heads on pillows the better, to Doctor Worcester. She was a tall, motherly woman, with snow-white hair and a little stoop of the broad shoulders that seemed to take something from the keenness of the straight-glancing dark eyes. She wore a white dress of soft material and in her hand she carried a book, an oldish-looking book in brown covers.

She sat down by the bed and the brown book rested unobtrusively on her lap. For a time there was silence in the room. The doctor's chair creaked a little as she rocked. Outside the window great white clouds were floating; the sunshine in the room had something of the same cloudlike quality of ethereal lightness. Only the huddled figure on the bed was darkened with grief.

"They tell me you didn't eat your breakfast," said the doctor tranquilly.

"I didn't want any." It was muffled and subdued.

"It would have been better to eat it," said the doctor.

"How long do I have to stay here?" asked the voice from the clothes.

The doctor's chair creaked. "Well, it depends. I have to find out first just what's the matter with you. It seems to be—a curious—case."

The words came slowly, and one small ear emerged above the bedclothes and cocked itself with almost startling alertness.

The doctor gazed at the ear attentively. "If you get on all right, of course you will not have to stay long, not more than a week or so—"

There was a movement of the clothes and a muffled sound from beneath.

"But of course if you are foolish and cry—"

The handkerchief moved briskly and drew back from one eye, and the eye gazed out at the doctor intelligently. After a moment it dropped and traveled downward and reached —the brown book. "O-h-h!" said Flora. She sat up swiftly and wiped both eyes and gazed at the book.

The doctor's hand rested on it. She nodded quietly. "Wouldn't you better tell me all about it?" she asked.

Flora gazed from the window at the great clouds traveling by. Her short upper lip trembled. "I just read about her— in the book." She waved her hand. "And so I—I did it."

"Yes; I'd got as far as that myself," said the doctor. "But why?"

The two souls were silent. The doctor had brought up three daughters. There was something about this alert-eyed freshman that touched her interest—and her sense of humor.

"You didn't do it because you wanted to meet me, did you?" The shot was closer than she knew, and Flora cast a quick glance at her.

"I didn't know about you. If I had, I'd have done it maybe." Her eyes had a look of shy pleasure.

The doctor laughed out loud. "Pretty good—for a freshman!" She held up the book. "Was it reading this put it into your head?"

"I thought of it first, and then I hunted in the library. I didn't know she was there. I was just looking for a disease —a disease that was quick and easy to have, you know— and I came on Prudence."

"I thought so," said the doctor with a look of satisfaction. "Go on, please."

So, little by little, the story came out, sometimes in bold sweeps and sometimes with Flora's back half turned and her eyes following shyly the great white clouds that went billowing by in the sky. She told it all—even to the catastrophe of the mole's nest, Annette's laughing exit and her own tragic grief.

But a little smile touched the words as she ended. "And that's all," she said.

"You're not looking at it sentimentally anymore," said the doctor practically.

The face flushed. "I wasn't sentimental," swiftly; "not exactly sentimental, I guess. Only it's hard sometimes to tell. Your feelings get mixed up so."

She glanced inquiringly at the doctor, who nodded with amused face. "That is one of the discoveries of science," she replied.

Flora looked at it. She shook her head. "You're not making fun of me?" she inquired timidly.

"Not in the least!" said the doctor.

"Anyway—that's the way it was. I wanted to know her. She's so beautiful! Don't you think she's beautiful?"

"Yes," said the doctor gravely.

Flora nodded. "And she likes walks, the way I do. But it was the mole's nest. Maybe it was a field mouse," she said reflectively. "Anyway, I wanted to show it to her. It was so wonderful!" She sighed softly. "It seemed as if I couldn't stand it not to have her see it. And I was lonely, looking at it all alone! You see it's all mixed up." She looked appealingly at the doctor.

"I see," said the doctor.

"The little roots were shiny and laid out for breakfast, as if somebody was coming back in a minute. And it was all still around, and the light in the sky just growing pink. It almost hurts you when things are like that. You can't help being lonely." She had forgotten the doctor and the infirmary. She seemed to see only the shining roots and the little nest on the ground. "I guess it's because it's like me inside," she was saying softly, "the way I am inside—all little branches and bones and shining things."

The doctor leaned forward to catch the words. Perhaps she asked a question or two. Her steady eyes watched the girl's face as the story went on—the discovery of the charts and diagrams, and the swift response and delight in them.

The doctor sat very quiet. This was the sort of thing one sometimes came on, once in an age! And the child had supposed she was playing a prank—getting to know a senior! And the books she opened were life! The doctor had watched girls come and go, reaching out to choose some nothing. And now and then it seemed to her a gentle hand reached down and touched the chosen nothing and it became shining, a crystal ball holding life in its roundness.

The doctor was a scientist. To her also the human body was mysterious and wonderful, and often she seemed to graze the edge of truth and catch a glimpse of the unity that binds life in one. She looked at the girl, who had finished speaking and was lying back watching the sky and the clouds moving in it. "Which of your studies do you like best?" she asked gently.

The girl turned. "I hate 'em all," swiftly. "History's worst, I think—studying about Rameses II and mummy things!" She threw out her hands. "It's wicked—when there's all outdoors and all the beautiful things inside of us!"

She had spread both hands across her chest, as if to cover as much territory as possible; and to the doctor there was something almost tragic in the gesture. Her eyes dwelt on the small figure—the disheveled hair and round eyes and reddened lids.

"You'd like to study biology, I suppose," she said reflectively.

"Everything that's alive," said Flora promptly.

"Perhaps you'd better have your breakfast now—and keep alive yourself."

And Flora ate it, propped against the pillows, the brown book lying on the foot of the bed. Now and then she cast a swift, resentful look at the book. But she was hungry and the marmalade was good and it was a wonderful day.

And then she glanced at the window and remembered suddenly the game that she was not to see!

The doctor had returned and was standing by the bed, looking down and smiling. "All through?" she asked serenely.

Flora nodded. "I was pretty hungry," she acknowledged.

"I thought so." The doctor removed the tray.

"How long do I have to stay here?" meekly.

The doctor sat down. She seemed to ignore the question. "I've been thinking about a biology course for you. There isn't any class you could go into just now."

"No," Flora sighed. "I didn't suppose there would be. Perhaps I can do it after I'm through being educated." She said it with a gleam of mischief, and the doctor laughed out loud.

"How would you like to work in my laboratory once a week?"

Flora leaned forward, breathless. "To study—with you!"

"Well—study, or call it what you like. I am working there Saturdays, and I generally have a student with me to help and look on. Sometimes she experiments a little herself."

"Oh!" It was a sigh of pure joy.

"It's usually a senior of course. In fact, I have a senior now." She was watching the glowing face. "Annette Osler is helping me this year."

Flora's face flushed; then the joy in it laughed out. "I don't deserve that, do I?" she said softly.

The telephone sounded in the next room and the doctor left her a moment. When she returned she glanced at her with a little smile. "Do you think you are feeling well enough to get up?"

The girl sat up with a swift glance of hope.

The doctor nodded. "It's from the team. Someone has given out. They are calling for the next reserve. I thought of you"—she looked teasingly and dubiously. Then she smiled. "Well, go along! And remember you're to come to me Saturday."

She went toward the door. She turned and looked back. "I forgot. You are to report at once to the captain—in her room."

Ten minutes later, in the morning of clouds and wind, a small figure in knickerbockers and blouse, with hair in a braid down its back, was scudding along the walk that led to South Parker. The braid of hair was tied with green-and-white ribbon and it swung gaily behind as the figure scudded on.

Miss Russell

Cherry Muhanji

Miss Russell dips snuff and spits in a can. Sometimes she forgets, stalls, then spits, missing the can or ignoring it, and that's what the Hollyhocks hated. It was like, they murmured to themselves, she made a special effort to spit on the hem of their dresses. "Heifer!" they said. They were dependent on winos' pee for a good growing season. And they were doin' good, ever since the war was over, and so many of them who went away came back flinchin' in their heads— wind-up toys with broken springs, oilin' themselves with Cask 59, maybe some Muscatel. And the Hollyhocks wanted to keep it that way. Winos can be choosey where they pee, they knew—exchanging privacy for a clean spot in the alley. They wouldn't pee on no ugly snuff stains if they could help it.

The Hollyhocks stood ready. The pee makin' a difference between pretty red flowers, or fadin' pink ones. They grew just at the edge of the alley where the cracks were widest. They would tunnel up through the concrete despite the best efforts of the people downtown, who felt that their good and loyal coloreds should have decent alleys to connect their neighborhoods. The record books downtown listed this alley as Sherman Street, so any summer week jackhammers could be heard cuttin' into the underskirt of the alley, gettin' it ready for a new pour of cement. The coloreds of this city were gonna have decent "streets" for their children to play in. "Or else," this administration said, "heads will roll."

Miss Russell had taken up crazy just in the last few years, the Hollyhocks knew. Before that, she had been a real Southern Belle. But now . . . collectin' bottles, sellin' all exceptin' Coke, the ones with the fragile green tint, countin' and re-countin' them. People was reluctant to take up with an ol' lady countin' and collectin', sellin' and savin' bottles. Smart thinkin' ones knew that folks who was "tetched in the head" best be left to they own musings.

"She ain't that crazy," the Hollyhocks argued. "She ain't got no reason." None that they was gonna accept, anyway, for spittin' on the hems of they dresses, and not in the Max-well House coffee can she carried for that very reason, or so she say, they said, she say. "Why," they asked, "don't she just spit in the alley?" Not take the time to find them to spit on. Who did she think she was, anyway, movin' down the alley just like she owned it? No sir! She never own nothin' acceptin' that old house on Maybury Grand, the one she had kept closed up all the time, the one nobody went into and she, the onliest one ever came out of, the one the people downtown never checked into. Instead, they preferred to keep tearin' up the alley every time the sun got hot—but we knew some very strange stuff was goin' on in there. Yeah, she was a sly one all right, even the Willows, with they worryin' self and all, knew she used to only come out that house for bottles and then sold all of 'em, exceptin' Coke, and was heard at odd hours cussin' and laughin', hummin' low and singin' inside the old house on Maybury Grand.

The Poplars told everybody who would listen 'bout her comin' up from Luzana after the first war, with her Southern ways and it-si-bit-si manners, wipin' her mouth on a napkin (and a cloth one at that!) after each bite. Why she even drank wine at breakfast! They had heard her clinkin' glasses, but with who?!

One day she just pulled down the shades and that was it. No more nothin'. Laughin' and cussin' sometimes, hummin' low and singin', but no more nothin'. Still, she wasn't so hot, and besides she didn't own nothin', not anymore, acceptin' all the Coke bottles in the world and that old house on Maybury Grand.

"Where is she now?" one of the young Hollyhocks asked.

"Child, let me see, if memory serves me right that was in 19 and 50. I hear tell she down in that ol' shack by the railroad tracks. Been there fo' some time. At least if a body can put any stock in what dem uppity Elms say."

Annabell Lee Jones Russell *did* like Coke bottles, the ones with the fragile, green tint. After all, in 19 and 50 fragile was very necessary. There was talk of another war, and she hadn't got used to the last one ending. Joe had left soon after that. And Jessie . . . what could she really say about Jessie?

Yeah, she liked Coke. The glassy green tint reminded her of magnolia trees—her daddy sipping mint juleps high up on the veranda, while she, home from college just for the summer, was seen, regarded and duly noted by her family. What would they have said if she had said straight out what she wanted? No. She couldn't. But it hurt to leave Jessie alone in the hot dorm all summer, with no place she could go. What else to do? They both needed to finish. Then Harlem, Chicago, Detroit—some place North—a place to get lost in. But it didn't happen, it just didn't happen.

[What to call it? How to call it? No good-byes. No ending. No way of saying now what you meant to me. You opened me up, Jessie. Made it all happen. I remember. Still, it was so long ago. So very long ago. But Jessie, I remember. I remember touch. And what touch is. And what it is not.

I couldn't get up before ten. You up working. The sun spilling through the doorway. Warm. As you were. Bent over your work. Frowning. Trying to make it work. Never thinking it did. But it was working, Jessie, and we were, we were working. But it was you. It was. Risking. Patient. Thinking I'd catch up. I was young. You were the artist, not me. I was all you. And couldn't understand why you couldn't be all me. And Bapu, your African elephant, was being born. He grew up between us. Munching sweet grass, etched on an African savanna, patterned in zebra stripes with ears that tricked the eye. You asking me what I thought, how I felt about an elephant in zebra stripes, with ears that waved. Me, not aware of just how good you were. Bapu, our elephant. I can still smell the cypress, sage, and sweet grass— and you, Jessie. And I learned. But not for years and not before Joe.]

Jessie made Millie Jones uncomfortable. Why, she didn't know. After all, she was a well-bred Negro woman. Her family was "niggah rich"—not like white folks, but better than the better part of most coloreds. Her daughter at Spellman. She had gone there herself. It was not a place for the coloreds. So why had her daughter brought home this strange, dark girl, much too dark, who made her perspire —no, sweat. And that girl knew it. That smug smile. That niggah! How dare her!

Yes, Millie Jones understood college. Nice Southern girls went, some until they finished, knowing they had a better time of it than many men. But most stayed only until they could meet and marry well. And she, Annabell Lee Jones, knew what "well" meant. A nice hi-yellah husband, with nice, dull hi-yellah manners, and they would have nice, dull hi-yellah mannered children, and all live together in a nice, dull hi-yellah, well-mannered house. So when she saw her mother was serious, she exchanged the yellow and dull for the black and gold.

Joe was black as a raven with one gold tooth in the front of his mouth. Like a beak, it filled his face and set her focus. How to live with Jungle Boy, for that's what he called himself. Marry him? Why would she do that? Well, she would if she had to. He was, he said, going North. She casually mentioned it to her mother who screamed at her when she announced his intentions and she declared hers. *What* career as an artist? Where *had* she gotten such a notion? From that dark girl, no doubt. And who was Joe Russell? What family? Do we know them?

[Maybe Joe just got tired of Detroit, the ghetto, the neighbors—me. He knew I was an artist. What kind, he never cared to know. Can I paint? Not like Jessie. But maybe.]

Joe had been in the first war. In Paris, France. Such stories. Nobody believed all those stories. But he had been to Paris, France. He finally came home with the flat hard helmet he wore in the picture. America, he said, was no place for colored people. But if you had to be here, let it be in the North. God, let it be in the North. He stayed, longer than he would have in Louisiana, because of her. But then, he said, "Come, Annabell, let's go."

And after they married and moved into Black Bottom, he whispered, "I am the man, man," and spoke obscenities under his breath as he went down between her legs.

"What are you looking for between my legs, Joe?"

"Hush, Annabell. Women ain't s'pose to ask questions like that."

"Why?"

"A woman is a woman and 'why' ain't what they needs to know."

"My ass."

"Annabell Lee Jones! (He never called her Annabell Lee Russell.) I don't like no talk like that comin' out yo' mouth."

"You cuss, Joe."

"Ya mean when I . . ."

"Yes, when you fuck."

"Annabell! Besides that's diff'ent."

"How?"

"There ya go again."

"Joe, at least I know what I'm looking for."

"When?"

"You know when."

"Not that again."

"Yes, that again . . . when I slide . . . down between the ridges . . . inside the fragile, green . . .."

"Now ya hush, Annabell! That's crazy talk! Nobody can git inside a Coke bottle."

"How many times do I have to tell you, I do? What's more I know what I'm looking for. Not like you—struggling between my legs—looking for something you can't name."

"Annabell, what do ya feels when I does go down . . . between yo' legs?"

"Curious. What, I repeat, are you looking for?"

"Annabell, ya sick."

"No, Joe, you're sick because you keep looking for something you can't name."

"Can ya name what's inside of a goddamn Coke bottle?"

"See, I knew you believed I could get inside—when I wanted."

"No, Annabell, I know ya cain't, and I know you speaks sorta crazy sometimes, but I be lookin' for . . .."

"Something you can't name."

"Naw. That ain't right. I can so name it."

"Is it feeling, Joe? Why do you look for it between my legs?"

"Because that's . . . where I find it—sometimes."

"Did it ever occur to you that good feelings can come from other places?"

"Like inside a goddamn Coke bottle?"

"Yes, Joe. It's like finding . . . finding God."

"Annabell, you a crazy screwed-up bitch."

"Joe, you get a feeling you can't name, a feeling some people kill for, themselves and others, a something they won't name, that is beautiful with so much feeling and love and . . . I know what touch is . . .."

"Annabell, nobody finds God in a Coke bottle! Nobody!"

"But it's all right for you to find Him between my legs?"

"Annabell!!!!! Stop yo' blasphemin'."

"Joe, you're an asshole. Just like most people."

Joe left just as the second war ended. At first, she was angry, then silent and finally, indifferent. What could she tell the neighbors? She couldn't just say he had gone somewhere. Where exactly was somewhere? So she said nothing and, finally, they stopped asking. Northern coloreds, she learned, after they see you're gonna survive, accept silence. Survival was the thing, the one sign that everythang gon' be all right! And that's the only real miracle they knew about in 19 and 50, in the ghetto, in Detroit.

Joe, she remembered, was always mumbling about "the man." "The man" this, "the man" that. "The man ain't never gon' give nothin' he didn't take back. Ten, twenty years down the road. Shit," he'd hiss, "we still ain't got our forty acres and a mule."

Joe didn't wait for "the man" to take it all back. He did. All the War Bonds he bought at the plant. Well, not all. He thought he took them all. He stopped counting after the first ten or so. For every one he got after that, she'd hide one. But he did take her two good pieces of jewelry and three foxes with the rhinestone eyes all clumped together and each other's tail still in the mouth.

Money was a problem now. Now that the second war was over. She had had money during the war. Everybody did. Now her shades were down and she was quiet, the silence so real sometimes, she could hear it. And she laughed. And kept laughing. And when she felt the deep hum in her throat, she laughed again.

[Jessie see! My lips are making your name. See my lips. Jessie, darling, good morning. I've been up for hours. Such a sleepyhead you are. Coffee? Bacon, warm toast and marmalade. Eggs, sunny-side up, right? See, I remember. Come, sit. No, the paper isn't here. And yes, I love you before you ask. We went to the summer country last night, don't you

remember? Before sleep—high on a hill we were—the stars
peeked at us . . . me, intoxicated, drunk inside of you. My
eyes, flame . . . you, all in velvet, ran your tongue along the
edge of me. I could not breathe.

You did not move after the last star burst. Your sleepy
mouth found my nipple . . . and you slept. And me? I slept.
Finally, but not before I reached again, inside the warm well
of you. Suddenly thirsty, I drank again. You came. And I
grew like a flower.]

The day dawned hot in 19 and 50. And good, green and
fragile were very very necessary. The sky heavy. Haze. Haze
that held the sunshine in. The sun would finally free itself
but not before it took revenge.

It's hot as twin bitches in here. Better not work so long
on top of the ladder. I'm getting kind of dizzy. If I fall . . .
but it's almost done. Jessie, you proud? You damn better
be. I'm working my ass off. So, what do you think, Jessie?
Yeah, I think so too, I'll get the glasses. Hold on a minute.
I know you're excited. But wait. Let's do it right. It deserves
a toast. Wait till I pour, will you.

The doorbell rang, Is it Saturday, Jessie? It is? Damn, I
forgot. I didn't hear them blow. Did you? I didn't think so.
You laughing? I love to hear you laugh.

"Hold on, I'm coming." Miss Russell raced for the door,
reached for the knob. It moved. The bell again.

"Yeah, I'm in here, wait a minute."

Where did he think she was? She went every second Saturday to the market on the neighborhood bus with these
nosy neighbors.

It was not the time to be careless and let him in. He had
once—well, he had looked in once. No more. It wasn't time,
yet. Where was she working then? In the living room? No.
The dining room. She had pressed the door shut leaving him
in and out, stuck like an animal caught in quicksand, with
terror and the scream still stopped in the throat. He was
careful after that and so was she. She reached for the knob
again. This time it turned, but now there were three knobs,

now five. How could she be sure she had the right one? There were so many of them—bobbing and weaving up and down, up and down just like the buoys on the Detroit River—moving all the time but going nowhere. Nowhere . . .

"Was that the bell again, Jessie? Shhh!!! Stop laughing, he'll hear you. God, how I love your laugh."

The door flew open. And that's the last thing she remembered. And *this* was 19 and 50 and all she knew . . .

Stories traveled fast in Black Bottom. The local coloreds, high up on they own porches, could spin a yarn faster than Miss Nitty could bake bread. But the Hollyhocks down by Maybury Grand still tell the story best.

"G-i-irl, they finally had to take her away."

"Girl, hush yo' mouth. When?"

"Kickin' and screamin', I bet."

"Ya kiddin'? Not that Southern Belle."

"Who took her out? The cops? The white folks downtown—who?"

"That Danny boy, the one use ta live near dem uppity Elms, the ones still got all that sickness, who keep they noses in a pinch, anyway. Seem like they woulda got off they high horse by now, seein' they ain't nevah got much bettah. Must run in the family."

"Will ya git on with the story. A body ain't got all day."

"Well, ya can try and tell it yo'self. Ha! But ya cain't. Ya grew up in the neighborhood later. After she done already left. Ya don't know it all after all, do ya, Miss Fast? Well, like I was sayin', fo' I got so rudely disrupted. Danny went in."

"What ya mean went in? Blossom tell me ain't nobody ever been in that ol' house since fo'ever."

"Blossom? That strumpet in the streets? She don't know her ass from a hole in the ground. Danny got in, I tellin' ya. And I don't know how. Do ya wanna hear the rest of this story or no? Well, Danny blows and blows. No Miss Russell.

So he goes in. Well, Sam, who tended to dem ol' and slow folks down in the hollow on Maybury Grand, gits tired of waitin' in the bus, so he hops out to see what done happened to Danny. If ya ask me, and nobody ever do, Sam was just 'bout the nosiest man I ever knew. Always tryin' to git in other folks' bizness. I can still see how his tongue used to slide over his lips when he finally done got a chance to see what got Miss Russell so holt up in that house. Well, ya know what Danny be doin'?"

"No, I don't. Remember I weren't there. Blossom say all y'all been tryin' to look up under the shades fo' the longest kinda time."

"There ya go again, bringin' that strumpet into decent folks' bizness. Danny lets up the shade I tells ya—that's when we seen the holy ghost got a hold of him."

"Have mercy! Was he jumpin' and shoutin'?"

"Honey, hush! I'm here to tell ya that's just what he was doin'. Then he stopped. Looked up and went to rockin' back on his heels. Callin' on the Lord. Hummin' 'Deep Jesus.' He a preacher man to this day. Do ya know that song? Learned it as a girl."

"Will ya *please* git on with the story?"

"Sam stop too, and was lookin' up, and then went tearin' through the whole house just like somebody half crazy, shoutin' fo' everybody to git outta the bus, and come see what been happenin' in the ol' house on Maybury Grand. Well, wouldn't ya know it, Big Bertha was the first one off the bus, Sam's wife. That heifer! Always lookin' fo' somethin' to see. Well, when she swung dem big hips through the do', Big Bertha stop dead in her tracks too. There was Miss Russell out cold on the flo' with everybody steppin' over her and dem three gon' to glory. Well, not Sam exactly, fo' he un-glorified hisself and was runnin' from attic to basement, basement to attic just like some rat spinnin' in a cage. Which caused Sam's wife to commence to movin' faster than she ever done done in her whole life. Upstairs, downstairs— nippin' at Sam's tail all the while."

"Girlll!! What be the mattah with 'em?"

"Well, we heard her shoutin', 'Looka here! Look yonder.' And then she started testifyin'."

"Testifyin'! Have mercy! Was she speakin' in tongues?"

"Let me finish. First of all, I ain't one to believe everythin' I hears, like so many other folks 'round here. So I peeks in real good and I just be damn! There we all was—on ever-thang."

"What ya mean on everthang?"

"We is on the ceilin' and on the walls and in the bathroom and in the kitchen and on the kitchen cabinets and, and . . .

"She paint us on everthang I tells ya. My flowers coverin' the whole ceilin', even when I don't look so hot. Ya know, like when they was all gon' to the big war and then the bigger one, and we ain't gettin' no real good waterin' then."

"Yeah, I heard tell them was some hard years fo' y'all."

"Yeah, but she paint us real pretty when we was high on the hog *and* when we wadn't. Ya know how I am. I ain't nevah cared fo' them uppity Elms, and I ain't nevah thought they looks so hot. Not as hot as they always thought they was. But shiiit! Even they looks good. And the Poplars, with all they talkin' and givin' way other folks' bizness, look real sweet—sweeter than the Lord at His last supper. And the Willows that be teary all the time. Even they look like they finally got it all together. Birds be comin' and goin' out they hair just like they does fo' real. We all touched by the Lord Hisself! She paint us friends, the winos, too. Even paint Melvina, with her mumblin' self, cuttin' through the alley on her way uptown to visit her sistah Grace. Ya know Grace? She give her money fo' that cheap wine she drink all the time. Ha! Mumblin' Melvina drinkin' her Silver Satin."

"Get down, Melvina."

"But it kinda funny when I commence to talkin' 'bout them ol' days—19 and 50, huh! But we all looked just fine. Somehow. Real fine. Huh! Now that we talkin' real honest. We did look kinda funny all over the ol' house. Ya thinks that's what she mighta been laughin' and cussin' 'bout at night inside the ol' house?"

"Well, I don' know. I weren't there, remember?"

"She even painted herself up there."

"How she do that? She cain't tell what she look like. Could she? 'Less she painted while she looked in the mirror. Can ya paint yo'self? To hear ya tell it, she musta lay on her back to paint y'all on the ceilin'."

"She wadn't the first ever to lay on her back to paint towards the heavens."

"How she do that?"

"All I know, she done it. And naw, I cain't paint myself. I ain't no painter, but I pretty 'cause I sees myself fo' the first time, like I seen by others. And I ain't nevah knowed I looks so."

"How a body look like anythang on the ceilin' and the walls?"

"Miss Russell musta thought so. 'Cause she be workin' on us fo' a long time."

No one saw Miss Russell rise from the floor and leave. After everyone went inside the house "Amens" and "Yes Lords" were heard when they entered Jessie's room. Where the altar was.

They all stopped suddenly when they saw all the Coke bottles. Jessie loved Coke—their long slow afternoons filled with each other and Coke with the fragile, green tint . . .

Jessie, stop, I'll get the Coke. Why don't you come in before your arthritis starts acting up? What? I know the light is good today. Are you ever going to get used to working up here and so close to the railroad track? You've been working all day. It's getting cold outside. You want me to bring your shawl? Better yet, I'll start a fire. Besides, I want you to come see what I've been doing. Is it that late? You're right. Here comes the five o'clock right on time . . .

Eating Wisdom

Jesse Mavro

If it feels like it's been a year since anyone's touched you, here's something to try. There's a coffee shop, Goodie's, not far from Lorraine Street, near the river. Go to the Central Artery, keep walking down Lorraine, past the methadone clinic, the boarded-up stores and the fender lot. When you come to the fallen bridge, take a sharp left. You'll see it, next to the barber shop peppermint stick sign, on the first floor of that building painted candy red. A waitress named Connie works there. She never calls customers by their first names. Instead, she says, "Hon," "Darlin'," "Sweetie . . .". You might think at first, as I did, how sour it tastes for a stranger to address you with endearments. But believe me, once you've made that walk, you'll take what you can get. And once you've ordered, you'll know the only thing that truly tastes sour is the food.

There are certain people you trust from the get go. And they're rare as a pie crust that melts in your mouth. The first time I went into Goodie's, Connie said those magic words that told me I could trust her. "Darlin'," she said, "I've never seen your face before, but something tells me you're low as a marsh in dry weather and I'd bet my last dollar it's love that caused the drought." It took me a moment to

answer. "More like lack of love," I said. She smiled her
"Connie-knows-what-you-mean" smile and we took off from
there. Some folks pay plenty of hard-earned money to see
someone who will help them understand their droughts. I
have to admit, I've done the same thing. Some of those
people are pretty good at what they do but Connie doesn't
charge a dime and truth be told, she does as fine a job.

About five months ago, I was having a recurrent nightmare. I was in a car, sitting in the passenger's seat. The car
was driverless, speeding along a dark road. It went faster
and faster, until it reached the crest of a hill. It began to
race down; just as it came to the bottom, someone would
step off the curb into its path. Since neither I nor anyone
else was driving, there was no way to stop the car. I would
always wake up a split second before the collision. When I
told this dream to Connie, she stopped drying the cup she
was holding and stared at me, hard. "Hon," she whispered,
"you gonna dream that dream again. When you do, look at
your hands." "My hands?" I wondered. "Go ahead," she
repeated, "look at 'em. Then, move over to the driver's seat.
Put those hands on the wheel. And drive that car, darlin',
just the way you like, not too slow, not too fast. Now drink
your coffee, sugar; it's the best tastin' thing we got and it's
gettin' cold."

The next time I had the dream, that's what I did: I looked
at my hands. The car slowed, almost to a halt. I looked from
my hands to the wheel and back down again. Then I awoke.
The time after that, I looked at my hands, the car slowed,
and I moved to the driver's seat. The third time, I repeated
all of it, and I actually began to drive that car. I drove it
just the way I liked: not too slow, not too fast. And I awoke
feeling totally calm. The hill disappeared from the dream,
and so did the person on the curb. The light surrounding the
road seemed to brighten. Remarkably, the nightmare had
become a good dream. I never knew that I could make such
a thing happen.

Of course, I told Connie. She smiled and said, "Same with

me, sugar." "You had that dream?" I asked. "Yes, hon," she replied, "and Charlie told me what to do. It worked for me; I figured it would work for you. Eat your muffin, sweetheart, it's gettin' dry."

I didn't ask her about him right away. I just waited. Sure enough, one day, she mentioned him again.

"Who's Charlie?"

Connie took a long, deep breath, let it out slowly and said, "Darlin', Charlie's one o' those folks God left behind to remind us what bein' an angel is all about."

"Your lover?"

"No, honey, no," she said quietly.

"Who then?"

"A friend. As special as rain in the desert and just as rare."

"Hmm," I mumbled.

"Hmm?" Connie repeated. "You sound like a doctor unsure of a case."

"It's just that I haven't met many men I'd call angels."

"There aren't many to meet."

"Tell me about him."

"Not much to tell. Charlie appeared when I needed him, and he's still appearin'."

"Needed him? Why?"

"Same reason you need me, child."

It was the first time Connie had called me that: *child*. And I didn't feel put down when she said it; I felt cared for. But I was embarrassed and needed to resort to some semblance of maturity, so I said, "I'm not exactly a child. I'm twenty-seven."

"We were all children once, honey. All of us. And that child's still there. We show it, beneath the beard and the boots. No matter how tough we try to make out, that child is there."

At that point another waitress approached, nudged Connie and said, "You gonna help me dish out these meals? Or are you too busy dishing out wisdom?" She said it kindly, so that I knew she'd had her share of similar talks with Connie.

I returned about a week later and struck the same chord. "Tell me more about Charlie. I'm interested."

"Ask me more, sweetheart, and I'll tell you. Don't let this soup get cold. It ain't good when it's hot, but it's lousy when it's cold."

"Exactly how did he help you?"

" 'Bout two years ago, I was feelin' low, real low. Like you were feelin', first time you came. Maybe lower."

"Lonely?"

"That and worse. Someone I loved had died, unexpectedly. Before I had the chance to tell 'em what I felt."

"How did it happen?"

"Hit by a speeding car."

I breathed in sharp and quick.

"It's like you're thinkin'," she went on. "The dreams started. Only, in my dream, that person who stepped off the curb was my friend."

"But you weren't in that car. Not really."

" 'Course not. Didn't stop the feelings, though. It was Charlie who came in—listen! Did you ever trust a person from the get go, just because?"

I stared into her pea green eyes and smiled.

"Charlie told me to do what I told you to do. I did it again and again. I looked at my hands, I moved to the wheel, I drove that car. Just the way I liked it."

"Not too slow, not too fast."

"You know what? Last time I had it, I was drivin' an' Carol, that's my friend, was sittin' in the passenger seat. And I turned to her and I said, 'I love you, sugarpie. I just love you to bits.' That Charlie helped me through an awful loss."

"He sounds like a guru."

"Don't be jealous, darlin'. The wisdom's gotta come from somewhere. We don't keep the chickens on the premises: our eggs get delivered. Everything come from somewhere."

"That's true," I sighed. "And you got yours from Charlie."

"Remember that child? She's showin' her face over that cold soup that's congealin'."

I stared into the bowl of brown mass, thinking how to broach my question. "Connie," I asked, "have you ever loved a woman?"

I noticed the man, two seats down, looking up from his newspaper, turning to us. Connie turned her back to him, planted her elbow on the counter and leaned forward. "Have you ever loved a man?" she returned, raising her eyebrow.

"Not fair. I asked you first."

"And I just told you about a woman I loved, very much. In fact, if you keep comin' in here, with that stray dog look you carry on your face, even when the sky's blue, and all your questions, plus your constant refusal to eat what's placed before you"—she took a deep breath—"you may become a candidate for the position that's opened up." The heat rose to my head and I felt my face becoming, like that building, candy red.

"Say what's on your mind, child. Say it direct."

"You know."

Connie didn't like going around the barn to get in the front door. Whenever I'd try to do it that way, she'd pull me back. "Yes," she said, "I know. But you learn to say it. Another thing, Cornelia: does it matter whether I ever scrambled eggs with another woman? What matters is how you feel about what you do."

Connie was very frustrating that way and very cagey. Often, when I wanted to find out something about her, she'd switch the question; she'd end up finding out something about me.

"And another thing," she continued, "when was the last time *you* got your eggs scrambled?"

"Connie," I said, blushing a second time, "do you really think that's any of your business?"

"You seem to think so. Or am I mistaken 'bout why you brought the subject up? Refreshen your memory. When you first stepped through that door, you said it yourself: 'low from lack of love.'"

"When I first stepped through that door, I was hungry. Period."

"Why d'ya think we get so hungry, Cornelia? Why d'ya think people eat when we're down? Food can help for a while. Sooner or later, no matter how much we eat, we're still hungry. Ready to answer my question?"

Connie had called me by my name twice. She'd never done that before, though I'd told it to her the first or second time I'd come in. It was clear she meant business. Before I answered, I looked to my right, to see if the man with the newspaper was listening. He was gone.

Returning my gaze to the muddy substance only a senseless person could continue to call soup, I said simply, "Shit."

"Just as I thought," she sighed. "Darlin', the next time you come, I want you to order coffee. Only coffee. Catch my drift?"

"What if I want some soup?" We both cast a disgusted glance at the bowl sitting in front of me. "Well, then," I amended, "a muffin."

"Nope."

"What if I'm hungry? Do you expect me to come here and not order food if I'm hungry?"

"You won't be hungry. I don't want to see your droopy face in this place until you've taken care of business. And, Cornelia Hammer Holden"—my eyes widened at the complete reference—"once you got the wheel in your hands, drive that car the way you like it."

"Not too slow, not too fast?"

"Now beat it. I'll be here when you get back. Go ahead, time's marchin' on, get going."

I felt like a schoolkid given a difficult assignment: one I had no idea how to complete. I stood up, put my money on the counter. As I opened the door, I turned to look at Connie. Her back was to me; she was scraping the grill. Without turning, she said distinctly, "Just coffee." Feeling exposed, I stepped quickly into the gray October afternoon, closing the door behind me.

It was a tedious, boring three weeks, until I went to some friends' house for dinner. They'd invited another woman I'd never met. Her name was Lorny. She looked like Shirley Letier, the actress who starred in that movie about women pilots. After that, in a matter of days, I saw her three more times. The third time, as I was about to leave, she asked if I had truly liked her cooking. "The matzo balls are a new recipe," she said. "Are they good enough to make again?" "Yes, do!" I responded, a bit too eagerly. And then, forgetting myself completely, I said, "I really like them: not too slow, not too fast."

"What's that?" she asked, tilting her head to the side, exposing her swanlike neck.

Recovering, I said simply, "They're delicious." Then leaning from the waist, as dancers do, she lightly brushed the corner of my mouth with a kiss. Straightening, she murmured, "Thank you."

"Thank *you*, Horny," I slipped. Immediately realizing my error, I felt a spark shooting from her emerald eyes. Bury me here, I thought, I'm ready to go. But then, with that gift she has of rescuing the most needy, she began to laugh. In tremendous relief, I joined her. And I was still laughing as I stumbled out her door.

When I returned to Goodie's, a week later, Connie was at the grill, flipping an egg. Assuming my position on a stool behind her, I announced, "Just coffee."

Without turning or losing a beat, she asked, "How do you take it? Black with sugar, right? Or don't you take sugar anymore?" She faced me smiling.

"I still take sugar. All needs can't be filled in one night."

Leaning on the counter, Connie said, "Welcome back, hon. What's her name? Give me all the ingredients."

"Just what the doctor ordered. Like chicken soup," I sighed. "Some of which I'd love to indulge in right now."

"I thought you said, 'Just coffee.' Did you or didn't you do as promised? Not to me, mind you, to yourself."

"In my humble opinion, I did," I proudly retorted.

"Then you can have whatever you want. Chicken soup, comin' right up. Drink that coffee, darlin', it's starting to freeze."

Feeling the pleasure of having accomplished the impossible, I began to sip at my coffee. Then, I glanced to my right. The same guy who had overheard our conversation a month ago was there, reading his newspaper. As Connie returned with the soup, he got up to leave. After he did, I said to her, "Ever notice how that guy is always sitting there when we're talking? I think he's trying to overhear our conversations."

"Of course he is, sweetie. Charlie's always trying to listen in. How do you think he got to be so wise?"

"So that's the wise guy Charlie," I said, dipping my spoon into the greasy soup.

"That's him. Doesn't keep his chickens on the premises. Gets the eggs delivered, just like we do. You see, sugarpie, everything comes from somewhere."

Tracking Down Vivienne
Carolyn Weathers

I smell like ink from Center Press. That rackety press and I had war again last night, until I shut it off at six this morning and stomped out on a carpet of ripped and inky waste paper. I try to write when I get home but am soon dozing on my typewriter instead, dreaming of the green Puloxi River in Texas; minnows appear on the bank, warning me the old swimming holes are now polluted and to go back.

Awakening, I climb the narrow stairs to the roof. Below, red roses bloom by the apartment building. In the distance, white houses hang on the hills of Silverlake and Hollywood. I see her for the first time, walking gingerly, with half-steps, down the sidewalk toward the Boulevard. She is old, frail and carries herself with such pride and presence as though she has a board at her back. Carriage, my grandmother called it, and instilled it in her daughters and granddaughters till we knew that to have carriage was to walk courageously, and with pride, to the guillotine, to walk barefoot over hot coals, as though to tea. Down on the sidewalk a kid on a skateboard roars past the old woman, and she jumps, startled. Immediately after, she draws herself to attention and inches on into the distance.

I go in, flip the cover off my typewriter and work on my

poetry for ten hours, till my mind feels like bugs are crawling on it. Brenda's drinking again in that New Hampshire haunted house. She sees shadow forms, not human, moving on the crooked hall door. I want my sister out of there. Kate calls at dinnertime. The gallery that just hung two of her paintings burned down, paintings with it. My solar plexus buckles up. My ex more sickened than she lets on, hangs up the phone to play her Rev. Terry tapes, insists that her good will come if she believes it will. I fix a mustard sandwich and think, yeah, sure.

The manager said she lives in #202. From out in the hall I can hear her tv blasting the evening news. I bang repeatedly on her door like it was the press. Eventually, she hears me, cracks open her door and says, yes? I'm Carolyn from #111, I say. Do you want to have coffee?

Her name is Vivienne Valle, and she is eighty-nine. She keeps up with events. What do you think of the steelworkers' strike? she asks. I don't know, I mumble.

The room is weighted with decades, heavy as brocade. A clock ticks among art deco and lace doilies. Vivienne sits straight in her chair, her white hair carefully set. I came here in 1917, she says, and worked as a scriptgirl for the silent movies. Oh, I remember the groves of orange trees and the scent of them. I knew I must be coming to Shangri-la. Did you know I once got to star in a silent? Yes. Oh, it wasn't much of a movie, but what a lark. A western. No, a jungle movie. Well, the star got sick right off, and everything was ready to roll, so the director looked at me and said: Send Vivienne. What good times we had. We had an art group, too. Anyone could join as long as they behaved.

Sepia photographs, memorabilia and original paintings cover Vivienne's walls and tables. She tells me it was forty years ago her friend Grace painted the still life in the hall. Grace is dead now, but twice Vivienne has seen Grace smiling to her from the hallway. Would you like some wine? she asks me. I help her get it. It is cranberry juice cocktail. Does she really think it's wine?

We sink into overstuffed chairs. Vivienne shows me two of her poems, written on yellowed stationery years ago. One is about her tiger cub she walked on a leash and let swim in her pool. The brittle papers slough off at the corners in my hands. The second poem is about her husband and their beloved hillside home and her wishing this could be heaven forever. He died young in the thirties, she says; and in the twenties, her sister just disappeared. Devastated, she survived both. I think of Kate and our beloved home and garden in the same hills, where we don't live anymore; of this in fifty years receding into the haze of them that were real and are become dreams. Vivienne sits composed, her eyes wet, her rosary hanging.

Center Press makes me nuts. Press war, machine war. Mustard sandwiches. Donna has the temperature for it; I don't. Twelve years of libraries and presses, of night and weekend writing. The anthology falls through; three other poems are accepted. The novel is finished, not as good as I want. Boozer, wastrel; charming, kindly. Try harder and shut up.

A package comes for me from Mother and my stepfather. It's my Native Texan T-shirt. Mother's handwriting is spidery and slants down the box. Her eyes are worse. I cry quietly over the clacking machinery, the ink pots, then on Donna's shoulder. She calls me Cryptic Carolyn, who somersaults across the lawn, then replies to her admirers that ultimately nothing matters. Go home, she says; I do, to the roof.

There's a letter from Brenda. She's coming back. Now there's a smell of excrement in that foul house. Kate will be as glad she's back as I am. She wants to play Rev. Terry tapes for Brenda. But damn these balmy nights, roof winds, this full, pungent air, stirring up. I want to pop, and it's not all bad. On the roof, in the air over the grounds, the winds hold life, meaning, eternity, blowing over us and on.

Like Vivienne's orange groves, the smell of patchouli incense was to me, sixteen years ago, the scent of Shangri-la.

Vivienne is packed for San Jose, to move in with a friend there. She tidies her desk, feeling for the objects. Like Brenda, she is cheered by adventures. Did you know, she says, that I once had a trapeze installed in my living room, just for the fun of it. Yes, I did. Amelita Galli-Gurci loved it best of anyone I knew. When she was out West, away from the Met, she'd sashay over to my trapeze and swing and laugh so hard my china would rattle. Vivienne runs her hand across her wall, plucks off fans and feathers, drops them into her suitcase.

A week later, Vivienne sits among her boxes, completely at sea. Her friend died. I unpack Vivienne's things and sort out her checks that she can't see anymore. She fingers her rosary, talks of divine will. I hold her close, and she grips my jacket. She says, may you have God's blessings always.

Brenda is back, shaken, haunted, she says, by evil forces from the house. But beneath the horror in her eyes still shows integrity and the ingredients of carriage. Kate's house of plants buoys us up. Kate's face is as pinched as the curled paint of her burned paintings, but her eyes gleam like sunlight striking blue water. I tiptoe across the floor, miming walking on the eggshells of life, but they break anyway, so I stomp on them, jump up and down on them, smash them up, hurry them along. The three of us fall back in chairs and laugh. Who do we think we are, we mock, asking the big questions. Even as we speak, there's someplace on earth it's yesterday and someplace else it's tomorrow.

Vivienne disappeared, and I tracked her to this rest home on Highland. Very old people sit under blankets in the sun, gazing at their thoughts. Of all of them, she is actually looking out to the street, though she can't see it. I touch her shoulder and say it's me. I bend down so she can see my face. She takes my hand, says she was afraid I was lost. Her thoughts are unsettled, she twists her limp hair.

She wants to walk and clings to my arm as we half-step from the terrace into the gray foyer, where cracked plaster statues lean in corners under low lamps, shaded by plastic orange trees. A woman, whose pink scalp tints through her soft white hair, bobs back and forth across the foyer, wringing her hands and saying, hello, hello, hello, to the hollow-eyed, to the cracked statues, empty air and dusty oranges. All answer with silence. Hello, I smile, hello. Vivienne straightens up, my hostess. She says, that woman is such a pleasant person; always a smile and a cheerful greeting for everyone. Vivienne nods in the woman's direction; Vivienne, on an afternoon's stroll, reclaiming her carriage, her eyes gone opaque.

Now she's moved again, to a dim, noisy, dirty place on Fountain near Western. A stick-figure man, bent in half and clasping the railing, grabs my arm, asks me to help; his eyes are wild, he wants to be free. Vainly, I shrug, turn this way and that. The doors have bolts, they lead to closets, halls, mazes. Someone in white comes and takes him off. Thank you, he mumbles, anyway.

Vivienne sits in the dayroom, one of the few not tied into her wheelchair. An ancient woman, who is tied into hers, spins around and around and screams for her ultimate bearings. She knows nothing of dayrooms. She only knows she is lost. Around us, others wail. Vivienne is oblivious. I grit my teeth. Mercy on them, on us all.

Next time I come, Vivienne is rasping in bed. We draw close, clasp hands. She's wasting. Carolyn, she whispers, Carolyn: don't tell anyone this. They'll think I'm crazy. I almost passed over last night. I lifted up. I floated away. Oh, such peace and beautiful music. It was hateful to come back. I want to go back there. I want to go home.

Vivienne looks at me but sees something else. In my hand, hers loosens its grip.

Marian, Vivienne's friend of sixty years, leans on her cane and on her friend Pearl, who only knew Vivienne ten years. Marian came from Seattle, on her third pacemaker, to be here. She ponders Vivienne's casket, on this green hillside, and places a small bouquet of yellow daisies on it. For several moments she stands here in homage and memories. At last, she steps back, swallows and says: Vivienne was so damned independent. She stands fixed in place. I guess that's it, she says. She turns away, and we face each other, not quite strangers. Tears roll down her cheeks and mine. The casket flowers receive the long, late afternoon sun; the metal chairs are slanted and empty on the hillside. Briefly we hesitate, then hug across the sixty years.

One More Time, Marie

Madelyn Arnold

12:30 A.M., Thursday

Opening the cupboard, Claire took down a can of soup, a box of crackers, and a tin of Spam. Where were the pans . . . ? Marie kept them . . . must be in the oven. She removed a skillet and saucepan and set them down on the rickety little table that served for food preparation. She found the can opener. Surprisingly, it was hanging on a nail. What to do first? No, not open a can, heat the skillet. Should she grease it? She couldn't remember. It had been too long.

Claire hauled open the refrigerator and stared at the too-many things inside: mayonnaise, milk, ketchup, sour wine, two cans of beer, bologna, cheese, wrapped things . . . (what?). Some sort of pickles. She was still perfectly capable of cooking for herself or a family (when she had been young all girls cooked) but why not wait?

She left hanging the question, *Wait for what?*, ate a cracker and drank half a beer, then lay down, suddenly sick to her gut, and was out cold.

What had happened was that they hadn't liked the movie and so had decided to have a drink, had parked in exactly the same place they always did. Their nights at the bar were infrequent. Was that incautious? People didn't know you that way. . . .

They had always stayed away from police. The times when the shop was broken into, they had always tried to avoid calling the cops, but this. They called, and the cops afterward told Claire what she herself had said, but in fact she did not remember the blows, how Marie had been—but thank God, thank God, no thanks to the goddamn SLPD—then all the questions and Marie's crying out. A heart attack. A heart. And what do the sons of bitches want to hear about but money. That's a hospital for you, like those, that piece of filthy—only without a gun!

The questions. About Claire's relationship to Marie, to that old woman in Surgery, she had snapped, "Business partner." And the ER people had written, *none*.

"None?" This to the Bright Young Man who worked in Intensive Care. This after she herself had been released from treatment. "What do they mean, *none* down in that looney bin? They get nothing right. I say she can't take that Lasix, her doctor says so, and I come up and if they're not about to give it to her! Said there was nothing against it on her chart. *No* relationship. Did anything else get wrote up right?"

After which the Young Man typed in *Friend* on Marie's papers for whatever. "Next of kin?"

In fact, Marie did have a next of kin, a brother in Chicago Marie hadn't seen in thirty years—a short, prognathic little thug of a man, who made you think of Mafia. Years ago he had said, stay out of his way. Which eventually had faded. He'd just got too tired to hate and gave it up; sent them a picture last Christmas of himself dressed as a silly imitation of a young buck, marrying again. The girl not quite half his age. What if he was ready to be the next of kin, decided to crowd her out, make the bad decisions? And Claire felt like hell, herself. Her face hurt.

"Next . . . ?"

"Wait, just wait, dammit!" she snarled, but he was not even mildly put out. Waited patiently, casually, helpfulness in the flesh. Of course if she didn't tell about the brother or even Leon they'd probably tell her more, but right's right, blood's thicker.

And this was the last time this could ever happen. That much she knew without being morbid, or superstitious, or boastful. St. Louis was rough—but always before they'd been lucky. Maybe they had thought by now their age would actually protect them better, but the charm had worn off; they were both too old and this was the very last time.

"Me," she snapped.

"Relationship?"

"Sister!"

"You must understand. We need a next of kin for legal matters."

How have a man for such a job? A clean job—cheat some poor girl out of a decent job. How old was he, twenty? She wouldn't explain. This was Missouri, and charity didn't mean herself and Marie.

As kin, she gave their lawyer's name and the smiling boy typed *friend* about her. *Friend.*

All that had gone on was that they hadn't liked the movie and so had decided to stop at the Karavan, had decided to have a drink. The Kar was exactly the same as it had been for years (well, with new decor), the same as back when the bar was Zenobia's and before that, the Alakazar. They had parked in exactly the same place they always did, exactly the same distance from the door (and the bouncer) and in clear sight of the bar, but statistics had caught them. Muggers, the cops had called them, but she called them filthy cocksuckers. She called them worse. Fury tore in, but its force rent only her because she was herself hurt, her nose broken and her face bruised, which was why the packed ice, and her padded wrist actually was broken. But Marie . . . Marie, Marie.

As if Claire herself didn't look like hell. Dried blood all over her face, swollen blue-black—white bandages across her nose like a bandit, the adhesive pulling loose on both sides. Except where blood had glued it to her skull, her hair stood straight up. Hadn't there been a time when a hospital cleaned you up? Or maybe that was only in the movies.

She ran water into the basin and, finding the sound intensely comforting, wetted a towel and began to gently, carefully, pat the bloody night off her face. No, she had told the police, she had not seen them clearly, but not one of them had been black, or not very black at least, and she would have scratched the memory out of herself. If somebody in the bar hadn't screamed to high God—

Look at that hair. Thin and coarse like a Brillo pad, always had been thin; well, now it wasn't thin but sparse, and one day from behind her Marie had said, "I tell you what, honey. The day you turn sixty-five we're going to chop off all of that fringe and I'm going to get you a real nice Elvis wig. You always did look cute in a DA."

In spite or maybe because of her appearance, the Intensive-Care young man bent the rules and, only for a minute, she was inside. Which restriction might have been pronounced even for family.

Walking into the room Claire had most been aware of a gentle sort of *shh-click, whiiii*, from a dozen sites, in random order around the room. In front of, behind curtains. With difficulty, she recognized Marie against the far wall, and frowning to clear her eyesight she could not be rid of the sense that Marie had a trunk like an elephant. Marie liked the zoo, she would think that was pretty funny. Wait till she heard—

Someone kept trying to ask Claire what she was doing. She was breathing.

12:30 P.M., Thursday

Claire found herself on her feet, answering the heavy banging down the hall, aware that it was not broad day—shambling to the door in an undershirt over a sundress, leaving her glasses on the back of the commode and her teeth in a jar by the bed; Claire did not realize that she was in fact awake and the knocking door would likely have somebody on the other side. She was never the one to answer. As she opened the door full out to let in the light from the hallway, she heard rather than saw the dumpy person in front of her, heard that little "oh!" delivered for nearly all occasions around Claire, knew it was her sister's girl, Janine, who blew hot and cold on saving Claire's soul. As if it helped, she usually brought her kids.

Miss Kitty Kat must have thought she brought them too, skittering past Claire's huaraches in a Great Escape. Without her glasses Claire lurched into the hall after all that she was capable of seeing, which was a black streak against a red rug.

"I'll get her, Aunt Claire," sighed Janine, and down the hall there was a squeal as her little girl spied the nice kitty and grabbed, unfortunately with real good aim.

Claire carried in the spitting Miss Kitty and dumpy patient Janine carried in the screaming child, raked across both hands.

"I'll stick her in the back," yawned Claire, continuing down the hall. She meant Miss Kitty. "You stay with your ma," she said firmly to the boys, who, abashed, hung back a full second. About this point she realized how her own face looked, that they were horrified.

Once in the bedroom, Claire kissed the cat on the ear, squeezed her and bowled her under the bed, from which she glared as the now shoeless boys tore in and out from the hallway, sliding on Marie's waxed floor in stocking feet. Claire was now awake to the way she looked. No use looking jakier than your fate. Bending over the Jacobean nightstand, she fished her teeth out of their jar, and making horrible faces, thrust them into her jaws—jerked them out—shoved them in—to the horrified delight of her grandnephews.

And having done the right things as soon as she could find

the tea, she demanded, "To what do I owe the honor, anyway?"

Janny wouldn't drink her tea; it was what she gestured with. "It's about last night." She sighed.

"What?" snapped Claire. "What do you mean, what do you know about it?"

"Dear. Well. The eleven o'clock news? Right after the Cardinals . . . I'm so sorry about—"

"What goddamn news? What in hell are you—"

"Please . . ."

Janny meant, of course, the little angels—two of whom had collared some of Marie's figurines, of which several hundred were arranged upon frail maple corner-brace shelves. Seeing Claire's face, Janny made the kids put down a shepherdess and several slightly sticky lambs.

"About the mugging," she resumed, forgetting to sigh. "Channel Six said this strong-arm ring that preys on . . . I called the hospital and they told me you were out. I didn't know if you needed anything. Maybe I could cook you a meal."

Claire was blowing smoke out of her ears, furious.

"Hmm," sighed Janny. "I wanted you to see that you can call on your family to—"

"My family! There's cabs, they're cheaper, and there's takeout Chinese, too. Family! I don't need any help from you. I've been lower than Satan's spit to my family for forty years—" Her blood pressure. She slowed herself. "*Family* told me in 1945 to get blanked and they won't get a goddamn out of me. If you think I'm giving up and giving you the store, you got one other think coming, you hear? I've left the kids a little something and there's *nothing* for your ma and *nothing* for you and George, and you tell your ma that. It won't work, and we don't need help—" The words hooked in her throat.

["Up, Marie. For God's sweet sake, get up—"]

3:45 p.m., Thursday

By the shouting, she knew it was Leon downstairs. That boy could not ask nor answer a question in a reasonable tone of voice, not once in the last forty years. It came to her that she had not been down in the shop all day, and that buyers were coming around to look at some new estate stuff. *Estate.* And for some of the auction stuff, she had a warehouse full, and here came Marie's idiot nephew. Marie, diplomatic Marie, Marie took care of the talk part. . . .

Claire shook off the robe and the Mother Hubbard and slid on some slacks and a blouse. It was almost four, but she stopped and again called the hospital—no change, no anything. She made to leave, still wearing the huaraches.

Instead of walking down the front stairs, onto the street, and hauling herself in the front doors of Marclar Antiques —as she customarily did for the simple reason that her baby-elephant entrance gave Pat and Louey the time to snap to and look intelligent—she climbed out the kitchen window onto the fire escape and stepped down onto the office window ledge, practically onto the old black Standard. She squeezed her bulk in the big window, over the ledge and onto the floor, and in the next second or so Felix, one of the movers, the part-timer, stuck his head in under the curtain and stayed to stare, bug-eyed. Not at her entrance. For a moment she entertained the notion that they were all doing something illegal or expensive out in the showroom. Then Claire remembered her face.

"What are you gawking at?" she croaked; not her usual bark.

"Hell, Claire—what the hell? You okay? You have an accident? You call the cop—"

"Say," she snapped, "you doing the news?"

She did not have to look in another mirror. But with the way her clerk and the movers kept looking at her, she finally, huffily, moved into the lavatory she and Marie had declared

was for women, and surveyed the taped nose, bruised eye
(it wasn't going to shut, she thought), the small bruise on
the point of her chin—that shouldn't have happened. She
hadn't been that easy to deck, not ever. Time was—drake's-
tail, jacket, scar next to her eye (from barbed wire when she
was about six)—nobody screwed with this one. Assholes at
the station, ugly mugs on the street. It helps to be *ugly*. But
hurts your feelings sometimes.

The last time anybody'd cold-cocked her was her brother,
in '45; their only real argument. He had brought Marie home
a few times from the Wayne Avenue USO, but she'd kept
coming out to the pantry. The giggles . . . That was a fight.
Before that, everybody knew Claire as just ugly, unmar-
riageable. . . . In 1965 he had died of cancer. No, it was
later.

Actually she was never much of a fighter, she was just
ugly. Nothing to be done with *this* face. But that nose. She
had always hated that dough-lump German nose. Wouldn't
it just be great if it healed distinguished? Marie would
say—

[Get up, honey. Marie . . .]

Claire headed out of the small room dizzy, but straightened when she saw they were all staring at her. Mournful
to make her crazy. Louey, Pat, Felix . . . the bookkeeper,
Alice—behind her that ape, Leon. Hell, couldn't he learn
to smile? Or get himself glasses? Not a bad businessman in
his own right; owned a hardware store up north. Reasonable
type, but what did he know about auctions? About styles?
And what was he messing with that estate junk for?

"Well, what do you want?" This to Leon.

"Wanted to know, do you want that shellac. Got a half
drum. That and I was in the area—" He was looking around;
crates in the middle were opened. "Aunt Marie go out?"

The veins swelled froglike in her throat, in her temples.
"Don't play dumb with me! You could have had the decency
to wait. She ain't dead yet!"

His jaw dropped.

"I don't believe that innocent act! Not for one moment do I believe that innocent act! Wait—damn you, wait! You're the heir all right, but wait!"

Oh, he would inherit. They had never been able to work around the "unsound mind"; if they had anything a will would go to court and the family would win; survivorship had seemed too far away. And you couldn't borrow money in both names—not until you already had a *business* partnership. Besides, it was Claire and her blood pressure scheduled to ship out first; and the place hadn't been supposed to do that well. Because they had bought into the building and fixed it up; then bought out the store, and before their handling it had always lost money. That part of the block would be a tax writeoff, but they worked too hard. First Marie had quit her job and filled in—her mom and dad had been in the furniture business. Marie knew all about styles, the fix-ups, the polish—then Claire had quit the railroad—did minor repairs, putty and shoe polish, built the inventory. They had so well absorbed their losses that the insurance two years in a row actually *dropped*. Marie knew markets. . . .

But auctions: Those were Claire's. Shoving through, hat over brow—she loved her effect on the thick-headed farmers. Gab and grab—*no*body elbowed Claire out. She got just about anything she had ever set her hat for.

Maybe Leon *didn't* know, and she should say. Maybe Leon really didn't know. It was his right. And he would inherit half; maybe she should say—

No.

He can have the place, but her grief . . . No, the *hell* he could have this place!

5:30 P.M., Thursday

They had parked in exactly the same place they always did. Though the place had changed, Lord. The Mafia used to

keep it safe. Making it legal, now *nothing* was safe. The bars
were different. It used to be, at the bar you dropped your
outside mental clothes and were easy in yourself. This was
your home. Now bars were just a place you went when
you needed to remember you were garbage. Lower-class.
(Equals butch and femme—equals old.) Their old bar at the
same place had had a pink neon parrot and a sign that said,
"We made an agreement. The bank don't give drag shows
and this bar don't cash checks." Now these new bars with
the cute ways, the ferns and loud music so you couldn't talk
but you didn't need to try to. Nobody to listen, couldn't find
even half the friends you had known all your life, and the
men and women were strictly separated. And the ages too.
Bartenders didn't see you even if they knew you had good
money, not if you're no spring chicken. Better to be a pretty,
young deadbeat. But it always had been better to be pretty
and young. She herself had been privy-plain, while Marie—
    We were so hot, then. Oh, it was bad of course, but back
then they were actually afraid of us, stayed out of our places.
Queers had their sections; dangerous for us down certain
streets—but me and that haircut. Bull dagger, bull dyke,
butch, *Les*bian . . . *Gray* Panther.

    She smiled her most horrible smile at the mirror, giving
up on her hair, and stepped out into the muted lighting of
the unit, where the first thing she noticed was the *shhhh-
clicking* around her.
    "Ms. Kohler?"
    He was either from deeper south, or women's lib had made
him hypocritical.
    "How's she doing?" Claire mumbled. Her mouth swollen,
the cheap teeth hurt her.
    "No change," said a brisk nurse.
    Said the Young Man, "Well, she might have been briefly
conscious. It's hard to say with—"
    Claire froze. "She said something?"
    "She isn't able to say anything. She has a tracheal tube,"

corrected the nurse. "What she was probably doing was an involuntary—"

"You mean she *tried* to say something—did—"

"We were clearing the trach and Dr. Findalito said it looked a little like she was moving her eyes. That was about . . . half an hour. . . . Please understand that this is not the same thing as her being conscious, of course, but there were some indications. We haven't been checking any electrical functions but cardiac—"

"Take it out. Take that tube out of her—"

Objections.

"For a minute. Just for a minute so I can ask her about —" What. What do you say. "Business. She's my— We own a store. I've got to ask her about some business—" Ask her about Leon's cut. Something.

"It's not a matter of simply removing the tube." They spoke slowly, evenly. Teachers of the not-too-bright. "She cannot talk or move. She has had medicine that completely relaxes her muscles. When a patient has been intubated, the curare—"

"That's poison." She had read this in a Perry Mason novel. "Curare, that's a suffocating—"

"Without the relaxed breathing muscles, she might waste the strength she does have fighting the respirator. Mrs. Kohler—"

"Ain't she doing bad enough already, and now you go and *poison* her?"

"It is only given because—"

"She can't talk with it. She can't talk. Is she going to live? Is she going to get better? Is she going to get to say anyt... ng first?"

Silence.

"Take it out then! Maybe she wants to talk!"

"Ah, with permission of the next of kin—"

"That's me! I give permission. I—that woman has just spent the last forty-two years of her life with me, nobody but *me* in the same bank account, in the same damn bed. If

there's anything she's got to say, it's to me. *N*obody, *no* kin
is as close, nobody in this world—take it out!"

"Well, you see," they said politely.

Which meant, Nothing. They probably understood, but
what of it.

7:00 *P.M., Thursday*

She couldn't stay long.

She had guessed that you could visit only one at a time,
so the very first relative visiting would displace her. That
would be Leon. He'd get off work, go to supper, drive down
to the middle of St. Louis. Down to displace her.

Wake up.

By now everybody would know what had happened;
they'd be rushing forward with sentimental claims, grasping
fingers.

Claire had spent the last hour and a half shaking violently
through her thoroughly imperfect memory, trying to think
what were the last words she had heard Marie say. About
the movie? Neither of them had liked it. . . .

[Head ringing with how dangerous you are. Marie was the
girl in the dark pique and Claire with her brother's massive
old Dictator with the muffler that fell off in the middle of
the night out in front of Marie's. So much for elopement.
How dangerous they were. (And there had been others before and over the years, and for both of them, but they never
except once discussed it. Claire had cried that time, cried all
night. That wasn't like her.) When it had all come out, Marie
had lost her ticket-selling job downtown—which was just as
well. Too many rumors. When everybody'd found out,
Claire was banned from her mother's house, her little sisters
looking through the fence. Didn't look back. She had dis-
ciplined herself to think how she was lucky to keep her job
with the railroad, growing a fine crop of ulcers wondering
when it would all fall in. What attention she and Marie had

commanded, for nothing much. Never thought dangerous now. Now dykes and queers gave sucker lines on sitcoms. Only one way to command much attention now.]

At the store, as she was leaving, she heard Leon asking what shape the books were in.

In and out with that elephant thing, Claire was breathing with her. *Shhhh . . . click! Shhhh . . . click!* [—Open your eyes. Open your eyes and show me who I am. Say my name. Only one more time.]

Monster

Michelle Cliff

My grandmother's house. Small. In the middle of nowhere. The heart of the country, as she is the heart of the country. Mountainous, dark, fertile.

One starting point.

My grandmother's house is electrified in the sixties. Nothing fancy. No appliances. A couple of bare light bulbs sway on black queues in the parlor, dining room, cast a glare across a moonlit verandah. Now scripture can be read at all hours, no fear of damaging eyes.

There are only two pictures on the walls of the parlor. Two photographs—hung so high the images are out of reach, distorted as they rest against the molding, slanting downward. Her two living sons. Each combed and slicked to resemble a forties movie star. The one with blue-black hair and widow's peak thinks he favors Robert Taylor. This alone will draw the gals to him, he thinks, somewhere back in time.

Today he is bald and rubs guano in his scalp over morning coffee, to ignite his follicles. His wife belches loudly and slaps her feet across the tile floor, her soles as wide as a gravedigger's shovel.

Pictures taken in a studio in downtown Kingston, where

touched-up brides (lightened to reflect the island obsession) grace the window.

My grandmother's faith is severe and forbids graven images (she makes an exception for her sons), dancing, smoking, drinking (except for the blood of the Lamb, bottled and shipped from another end of the Empire).

Does she look the other way when her boys take a dark girl into the bush? Does she object? I have no way of knowing and wouldn't dare to ask.

Graven images include motion pictures, of course. Although she has never seen a movie, she has seen advertisements for them in the *Daily Gleaner*, right next to the race results. Nasty things.

Like most evil, brought from elsewhere.

My father loves the movies to death. As do I. Some of our best times are spent in the dark, thrilled by the certainty that in the dark anything can happen. It's out of our control. The screen says: Sit back and enjoy the show.

We lived most of my childhood in New York City, visiting Jamaica once or twice a year, down the way, where the nights are gay. These are the fifties, sixties. In the city we go (at least) twice a week to the local movie house, the St. George, where we escape, comforted by the smell of popcorn mingling with disinfectant.

We are comforted also by the name. We live in America, as we always call it, but are children of the Empire. St. George is our patron, his cross our standard. We are triangular people, our feet on three islands.

The interior of the movie house is overwhelmingly red, imaging Seville, Granada—the St. George sports no dragon, no maiden chained to a rock, no knight in shining armor, but is decorated as if a picture book of Spain, sometime after 1492. A *trompe l'oeil* bullfighter makes a pass outside the men's room. Señoritas with mantillas and filigreed fans hang above our seats, gossiping across wrought iron balconies, duenna watchful.

Built in the heyday of the movie palaces, the delicacy of
the Alhambra arches across the screen—whose dream was
this?

"Some day, Nell, some day, when we're long gone,
and people—archeologists—dig this up—like Schliemann at
Troy—they'll think it was one of our cathedrals. You mark
my words."

Against his projection of the future our time spans come
together; the barest ellipse separates us. We're practically
contemporaries. "When we're long gone." Imagine saying
that to a child.

"Our lives are written in disappearing ink." I lie awake
terrified.

I am about nine or ten, but know all about Schliemann
and the four levels of Troy; in the time before the theater
darkens, my father instructs me in things that fascinate him.
Victoriana. The ripping. "From crotch to crown, Nell, from
crotch to crown."

When the chandelier in the ceiling begins to blink off and
on, signifying the start of the show, we fall into silence.

We prefer mysteries, war movies, westerns. Love stories
and musicals are for girls. Like my mother—who never joins
us in the dark.

Science fiction is our absolute favorite, with horror close
behind. The disembodied hands. The man with the x-ray
eyes. THEM!

The redness of the Forbidden Planet.

"You must make allowances for my daughter, gentlemen.
She's never known another human being except her father."

At night all hell breaks loose.

"What do you think they eat, Nell?"

"Vienna sausage and asparagus straight from the can," I
respond with my favorites.

We dare each other to eat raw meat—like "cannibals,"
he says. Slice the muscle which protects the littleneck, and
devour him whole; "in one gulp."

In my mind, my father and the movies will be forever joined. Dana Andrews in the Flying Fortress graveyard. The decorated boy.

My father found himself in the Army Air Corps of the U.S.A. They filled his teeth with carborundum, something to do with non-pressurized planes. Up there, in the wild blue yonder, flying high into the sun, he heard music in his head and thought he'd been shot down and gone to heaven, until—and this is a true story—until he heard:

> "Oh, Rochester."
> "Coming, Mr. Benny."

And he realized that it hadn't been an angel singing, but Dennis Day, the Irish tenor on the Jack Benny show—and my father's teeth were behaving like a Philco, as he told the story.

My father would like to be an exception like my grandmother's sons, and hang in the parlor on high.

My father tries to tell her that Cecil B. DeMille's *Ten Commandments* is a work of devotion and respect and could be used in Sunday School to illustrate the wonders of God.

She only smiles.

As if to say, when you need a graven image to perceive the glory of God, you're as bad as Aaron and them who worshipped the Golden Calf. She doesn't even have a cross in her house; Jesus is in her heart.

Is he Black in there?

When she dreams of him, who does he favor?

I don't know why she agreed to it, probably for the sake of her daughter, but on a Boxing Day (called by some "*their* Christmas"; in answer to the childish question: "How come Lillian isn't with her children today?" "Don't fret; Boxing Day is their Christmas.")—Anyway, on a Boxing Day in the

seventies, the last time I was on the island, she allowed my
father to show a movie, casting the images on a white sheet
spread across the verandah, straining the Delco almost to
the point of collapse.

She sits on the verandah behind the sheet, to the side of
the mouth of the parlor. Night begins to come on; she rocks.

The people in the surrounding area look to her for judgment, guidance, the food she generously gives them, and if
she has let her big, strong, American-sounding son-in-law
bring a movie to them, how can it be wrong?

At dusk they begin arriving. Trudging up the red clay hill
(vainly assayed for alumina by my uncles), dressed in almost
all-white are the women, looking as if they are headed for
a full-immersion baptism.

They come out of curiosity, respect, but not all are convinced of the rightness of the occasion. Some of the women
nestle asafoetida bags between their breasts, just in case,
acridity rises in the heat, damp from Christmas fat (as De-
cember rain is known), of the evening. A woman in the line
has sewn pockets into her Sea Island cotton underpants, in
which she has placed chestnuts, one in each pocket, so when
he sleeps with her tonight, her husband will not impregnate
her.

My father has planned the evening carefully. He is ring-
master, magician, the author of adventure. He is eager, nervous. He is to reveal the world beyond their world—of red
dirt that sticks in every human crevice, teeth darkened by
cane, loosened in the dark, eye-whites reddened by smoke,
rum. He wants to become crucial to them.

He's lost interest in me; given me up. He began to lose
interest in me when I grew breasts, kept secrets in a diary.
Bled. Not an unfamiliar story, I imagine. He tried to harness
me, driven to extremes that I now regard as pathetic, but
then. Then I recalled the reins they held me by when I was
two, three. He eventually realized it was no use, but not
without World War III.

Still, I was there that evening. The last time I spent on the island.

Before the picture show, there is a short display of fireworks, a taste of magic, unfamiliar, before the greater magic. Fireworks bought from a Chinese shopkeeper, a man from Shanghai, for whom there wasn't enough room in Hong Kong. Bought behind the colored strands masking the storeroom. The island is ripe for explosion, people crave gunpowder. But for American currency, caution is suspended.

The sky lowers over us, black. The promise of magic is everywhere, natural, unnatural. Magicians, natural, unnatural. The woman with chestnuts in her drawers. My father, a pint of Myers' in his back pocket.

An *otaheite* hosts the sputtering end of a St. Catherine's Wheel. The virgin/martyr/scholar pinned to a tree *tapu* to the South Pacific islanders. How'd it get here?

You might well ask. Krakatoa? High winds?

Captain Bligh. The one and only. 1793. When he brought the breadfruit trees to feed the slaves. The purpose of his earlier voyage interruptus.

The sputtering wheel is the only light but for the bulb of the projector. My father threads the film, fitting into the sprockets the Hollywood version of *Frankenstein*. One of the greatest movies ever made, he tells them, a classic like the book, he says, written by the wife of Percy Bysshe Shelley, the great Romantic poet.

"Me preffer Byron," a voice breaks in.

My father makes no sign he has heard.

It could be worse, will be with any luck: "Me preffer McKay." "Me preffer Salkey."

"Me preffer Michael Smith."

"Me seh me cyaan believe it."

My father doesn't mention that the author of *Frankenstein*—since we're identifying her through family ties—was the daughter of Mary Wollstonecraft.

The night is alive with the scent of women. Asafoetida.
Sweat. The ash of St. Catherine. Talcum powder.

My father wouldn't know Mary Wollstonecraft from Virginia Woolf, nor know they had more in common than some
stones in their pockets, nor know the significance of stones,
nor care.

Shelley is far more to the point. They have memorized
"Ozymandias" in school. Most of them. Or had their knuckles split across. Their own people came from an antique land.

Most of the ships landed no more than fifty miles from
here, in either direction.

The sound of the projector. A soft rattle across toads,
insects. Night-flyers. A family of croakers, somewhere,
ghost-white in the middle of the night. Lizards who mate for
life, and walk upside-down on ceilings. Sucking the white-
washed plaster to their feet. Moon rises, grazing the screen.
The doctor throws the switch. Caliban stirs. Peeniewallies
are attracted, their luminescent ends flashing past the black-
and-white.

My grandmother's shade.

I use the light cast from the projector, the images on the
sheet, the lurching monster, to glance across the audience.

On a girl apart from the group, unto herself, is an ancient
dress of mine. What was once called "polished cotton," blue
with a pink rose in the center of the bodice, pink streamers
sewn at the neck cascade down the wearer's back. Colors
faded to paleness by now, from sun, riverwater, the battery
of women against rock. I remember trying it on in a dressing
room in Gimbel's. I must have been about eleven, worried
about what I'd heard in the Girls' Room, that department
store dressing rooms were equipped with two-way mirrors.
Right now a stranger was scanning my undeveloped chest,
my panties, baby fat. I got it for Easter. Now it reappears
on the body of the daughter of the butcher's wife, apart from
the group. Reddish skin. Almond-shaped green eyes.

Her eyes could make her my sister. Stranger things have
happened.

It is not uncommon here to be strolling down a dirt road and come up against someone who is your "dead stamp."

While I stare at the girl, while the gathered company watches the progress of the monster, a Roman candle has settled into an eave on the roof of the house, nestling between mahogany shingles. Slowly the fire takes root. Slowly at first, then gathering frequency and height, sparks shoot into the night sky and fall on our shoulders like shooting stars.

The monster is talking to a little girl at the side of a lake.

FIRE!

Someone yells.

The little girl is gone.

My father is wild.

"Nell, take over!" he shouts, as if he still trusts me, then runs toward the house.

"Whatever happens, don't stop the movie!" he shouts back to me as he runs toward the house.

The mob is chasing the monster by firelight, torches raised above their heads, as sparks cascade across the sheet, across my grandmother's silhouette.

The people know they are out of doors; this is not their house. No one stops watching.

What happen to de lickle white gal, eh?

Him nuh kill she?

My father has vaulted onto the roof, is stamping out God's wrath with his tenderized American feet.

Night Life

Naomi Holoch

By one a.m. the temperature has dropped to who the hell knows where. It's like all of a sudden someone has opened giant freezer doors over the city. The garbage lying in the gutter, soggy from a day of steady drizzle, is icing up into some kind of sick art form while the sidewalks are already a slick death trap for the elderly. The cab's okay though. Late-night traffic has dried off the streets at least on the main avenues and I figure the deep freeze will drive a couple of extra fares my way. Assuming they don't notice right away that I have zero heat working in the cab. "You're young, kid," Oscar said, slapping me on the shoulder when I complained more than a month ago. "The cold air's good for you; it'll keep you awake." A real joker. "And what about the passengers?" I asked him. "What kind of tips you think I'm gonna see with them freezing their asses off?" "Don't sweat it, kid. I'll get Jimmy to take a look." Yeah, right.

I slam the thermostat lever up and down a couple of times pretty much the same way I used to ask God every night during all of fifth grade to make Lynne Taylor's perfect blond locks fall out: on the one hand, you know it won't work, on the other, it's worth a try.

At the corner of Tenth Avenue and 48th, while I'm waiting for the light to change, a guy limps out of the shadows toward me. He's got some kind of quilt wrapped around him. The couple of days of beard covering his face in dirty patches does nothing to hide its end of the line boniness. He bangs on my window and points a skinny finger at his mouth. I roll the window down.

"Hey buddy, help me get something to eat?"

I fish a dollar bill out of the box on the seat next to me and give it to him. He grabs it and crumples it up in his hand.

"Could you give me some more? I ain't had nothin' to eat since yesterday." He starts to shake or maybe I just notice it. I fork over another bill and roll the window back up as he mumbles "God bless you." Then I step on the gas, wondering how come I gave this guy two bucks when some other Joe Schmo wouldn't even see a dime.

I can barely feel my feet by this time, and I think about heading down to 23rd and the Tiffany. The bar will be pretty quiet about now, and what with the cold, I could use a pee. I flick my penlight on the little round stick-up clock pasted on the dashboard. It would be after 11 on the coast. I could try Richard again from the bar's pay phone. As I imagine the monotonous ringing I know I'll hear, I'm already pissed off. No answer, no machine for the last three weeks. And it's not like I haven't tried at every possible hour. The guy has just disappeared off the face of the earth. I could have rested okay thinking that he'd finally found the love of his life and moved in with him, too head over heels in love to worry about phones, machines, or friends. Except for the conversation I had with Harriet right after Thanksgiving when she was just back from California.

"He's too damn thin," she told me. "I don't like it."

After that, neither of us said anything. We just sat there peeling the labels off our beer bottles until Harriet thought to tell me about some shit she was going through on her job.

The Tiffany is not only quiet when I get there, it's dead. Shirley, who must have been dozing behind the bar, jumps up like a startled rabbit as I cross the room.

"Jesus, you could give a person a heart attack."

"Next time I'll knock."

Shirley snorts, and tugs on her sweater which is so tight it must be as hard to grab hold of as her own skin. I leave the meter on the bar and head for the ladies' room.

When I get back, she's wide awake. "So whaddya' want? Maybe a hot toddy now that the ice age has hit?"

I pretend to think about it for a minute. It's a standard game between me and Shirley. She believes that some day she'll get me to order something besides a Bud. I figure one day maybe I'll surprise her and let her convince me, but not tonight.

"A Bud, Shirley. When it's cold, you're supposed to drink cold, when it's hot, you're supposed to drink hot."

"Yeah. Remind me to warm up your beer come July." She yanks a bottle out of the cooler under the counter, pops the cap, and slides it across to me.

I ask her for change for the phone. She tells me it's out of order, but if I want to, I can use the restaurant phone.

"Unless you're calling Hawaii."

"Actually, California."

So she withdraws the offer, and I'm relieved. For tonight, no empty rings, and no bad news.

Back on the street, I have to heat up the car key with my lighter to get the door unlocked. A couple of minutes standing there, and the inside of the cab feels warm. I slip the meter back in place and think about where I have the best chance of finding the remains of some night life.

I turn east on 23rd, almost burn a light but don't when I see a patrol car hanging out at the corner. The woman in the driver's seat is young and good looking. We stare at each other through our rolled-up windows. My smile doesn't seem to register with her at all. Probably she's trying to decide whether she should check my hack license. I can't see her partner, but figure the driver's a rookie and nervous as hell about making her weight felt. The light changes, I move out slowly, they stay put.

I head downtown a few blocks so that I can come back up Sixth and check out the Limelight. Not a single hack waiting in front, and no sign of life by the doors, so I keep going up the empty avenue. The best bet now is the Red Parrot, which usually can be counted on to spit out a couple of boozed-up yuppies. The cold has gotten to me again. To entertain myself, I try out different formulas in my head to put a bomb under Oscar's butt so he'll pay attention to the heater. Maybe a surprise one-woman walk-out; he's too small an operation to get another driver for the graveyard shift just by picking up the phone at the last minute. And he likes me.

Further west, in spite of the cold, the hookers are out. The younger ones, whose age can make up for less exposure, have covered themselves with skintight jeans. One has even sacrificed her stiletto heels for some puffy-looking ski-lodge type boots. Looking at the others, in their tiny skirts and open jackets, you would think it was positively balmy outside. I wonder how long it takes them to defrost when they finally get a john, and if maybe even the unknown flesh, in whatever form it takes, feels good just by virtue of being warm.

I've already signaled to turn on 57th Street when I see a guy half a block ahead waving at me. I drift a couple of yards past him and stop. A white guy in a camel hair coat, carrying an attaché case. He looks steady on his feet. Better than I could have expected this time of night. He tugs open the door and slides inside. I hope we can get where he wants to go before he discovers that he's traveling in an icebox and walks out on me.

The guy still hasn't said anything. In the rearview mirror, I see that he's stuck a hand inside his coat. For a crazy moment, I think he's going to pull a gun. But all he does is take out a pack of cigarettes.

"You know how to get to West 243rd Street?"

"You mean Riverdale?"

"Yeah, Riverdale." The guy sounds testy. Like I've just asked a dumb question. I'm thinking this one could do with a drink.

"Yeah. You want me to take the West Side Highway?"

"Unless you know some way to do it by air."

I glance in the rearview mirror. The guy has changed his mind about the cigarettes. He's stuffing them into a coat pocket.

"Sorry, lady. I got no call to snap at you."

I am completely thrown by his apology. In the two years I've been driving, no one, but no one has ever said they were sorry, even after they've upchucked their dinner all over the backseat.

"It's okay. But you're gonna have to tell me how to go from the exit."

"Yeah, sure."

End of conversation.

So I head for the highway entrance at 58th Street. In the back, everything is quiet. I'm waiting for him to start complaining about the cold, but he doesn't say peep.

"Listen," I tell him, slowing down just before the ramp, "you should know that this cab doesn't have any heat." Why I'm telling him this I haven't the faintest idea. The guy hasn't noticed anything, and it's a great fare, maybe the last one in a real slow night.

"It's awright. Just get me there."

"You got it." In the rearview mirror I see the guy has started to chew on his fingernails. From the way he's going at it, I imagine they'll be in one sorry state by the time we hit the Bronx. Or maybe they already are.

It's when we pass the 96th Street exit that I hear these strange little sounds from the back. It makes me think of my sister's litter of newborn pups falling all over each other in a race for their mother's teats. As I'm wondering if I should say something, the noises escalate into up-front crying.

"You all right, mister?"

"I'm fine," he says, then starts to sob so hard, he has to catch his breath in big scratchy gasps.

I flip open the glove compartment and dig around until I find a package of Kleenex some passenger had left behind. I hold it over my shoulder for him.

"Here, take these." I always use handkerchiefs myself, but I'm not too crazy about handing them over to strangers, particularly in this case, when there's no way it could stop the flood.

"Thanks."

He keeps crying and pulling the tissues. He sounds so bad, I almost have tears in my own eyes.

Until the turnoff for the GW Bridge, all that happens is more of the same, with some loud nose blowing in between. Then things seem to get quieter in the back, and I begin to relax.

Just as we're passing Fort Tryon Park, the guy says in this miserable, squeaky voice: "Why didn't she tell me? She could have told me."

I hesitate. I've learned that sometimes they want you to ask, sometimes they're just talking to the shadows. And sometimes things get a little nasty if you pick the wrong direction.

"Why do you think she didn't tell me?"

At least this guy's signals are clear.

"Who's that? Your wife?"

The guy starts to cry again, and I wonder if I've pushed the wrong button.

"No, not my wife, Teresa, my daughter."

Right away I know the scenario. From the age I figure the man to be, he's probably got a daughter in her early to mid twenties, and she got knocked up. Either she snuck off and married the happy papa, undoubtedly a deadbeat, or went and got herself an abortion, or has decided to keep the baby and go it alone. I've already put my money on the first choice, since I don't see why she would have told him about the abortion, her not being a minor and us being in New York State, and not back in the Middle Ages where some people would like to see us. And I can't believe that her keeping the baby and getting rid of the deadbeat boyfriend would break the guy up like this. Having figured all this out in a flash, I'm all set to impress him with my powers of detection.

"So she ran off and got married?"

He sobs harder, which makes me believe I've hit the nail on the head.

"Jesus, if only she would," he gasps.

So I fall back on my third choice. "Do you know who the father is?"

This time the guy sounds really pissed.

"What father? What the fuck are you talking about? I just found out my daughter's a goddamn dyke, and she never even told me."

For a second, I'm all out of breath wondering how come I didn't even think of something I should think about at the drop of a hat. Then I'm ready to stop the cab and push the guy out right into the left lane of traffic for his tone of voice and maybe do his daughter a favor. While all of this flashes through my brain, I hear him begin to moan again.

"What did we do to her, what did we do wrong? Me and her mother, we was always there for her. She's my little girl, my best little girl. Her hair, so soft and curly, you should have seen her. Like a little laughing angel she was."

He says all this like he's looking into an open grave. Then he cries some more, only softer.

"Every Saturday we'd go to the candy store around the corner, just her and me. She'd take my hand as soon as we got out the door and wouldn't let go of it till she was sitting on top of the stool at the soda counter. 'Two black and white sodas, if you please,' she'd say to the soda jerk like it was this fancy restaurant. And Tessie'd talk and talk. Everything that happened in the week she'd tell me. And she'd make up stories and I'd ask her questions like I believed her. And when she was all done, she'd say, 'The check, if you please.' Where'd she get that, do you think, 'if you please'?"

He's almost laughing to himself. Then he remembers.

"She used to tell me everything. Why didn't she tell me? Why'd she lie to me?" he says in almost a whisper so I can hardly hear him.

"Maybe she was afraid."

Suddenly, he's roaring like a lion.

"Afraid of what? What the hell's she got to be afraid of? When did I ever raise a hand to her? When did I ever touch a hair on her head?"

"This is different," I kind of mumble.

He smacks his fist into the seat. "I don't give a shit if it's different. I don't give a shit if she fucks a turtle. I just want her to talk to me. She's my little girl."

Now I understand. This guy is from another planet. He's an alien.

"Sometimes," I say real slow like maybe he won't understand the language, "people throw their kids out for stuff like this."

"Whaddya mean?" He's so puzzled he's stopped crying.

"Happens every day."

All of a sudden the backseat gets real quiet.

"You mean she was afraid I'd throw her out, like I never wanted to see her again?"

I don't know how so many different things like hope, surprise, sadness, could be crammed into one little sentence, but this guy did it. I turn my head this time to get a look at him. He's staring at me like I had just brought the dead to life.

I shrug. "That's what I mean."

"You know some of these girls, these lesbians, I mean?"

"Yeah, a few," I say. "In fact"—I tap my hack license with a finger—"here's a picture of one."

This piece of information sends him right back against the seat.

"Okay if I smoke?" he asks.

"Fine by me." I understand we're settling in for the duration.

I smell the sweet fumes as he lets out his first puff of the cigarette and think about bumming one from him. And flushing six months of struggle down the toilet.

"So you wanna give me the money for the toll or pay it at the end?"

He hands me a five dollar bill, and we head over the
Dykeman Street Bridge.

"So your folks know?"

"Yeah, they know."

"You told 'em?"

"Who else was gonna tell them? The man in the moon?"

He doesn't pay any attention to my sarcasm. He's a dog
after a bone. "So whaddid they say?"

"Nothin'. My mother cried. My father left the room."

"That's it?"

I'm mad all over again. And the guy in the back is only
a stone's throw away from joining me in the kitchen of my
youth where the walls almost came tumbling down. But I
collect myself. For his daughter's sake.

"I left my mother sitting at the table, rocking back and
forth, and went after my father."

"Did he throw you out?"

Now I'm really mad. I raise my voice.

"He didn't fuckin' throw me out. I fuckin' left. The son
of a bitch never listened to me, anyway. All he could hear
this time was that his daughter was queer, a disgrace to the
family, a neighborhood joke waiting to happen."

Wild honking is coming from behind me. I come to, and
realize that I'm in the left lane, creeping along at thirty miles
an hour. I speed up and swing over to the right. A black
limo goes by, its headlights flashing its fury. My passenger
doesn't seem to notice.

"But you see 'em now, don't you?"

I can practically hear his future hanging by a thread. I'm
all of a sudden real tired.

"Yeah, I see 'em now. Not a lot, but I see 'em. My mother
got to him. 'She's your daughter, Herb, she's family. We
gotta stick together, no matter what.' "

"You bring your . . . uh . . ."

I'm not helping him out of this one. I'll answer him if he
finds the word.

"You bring your partner home?"

I debate whether this is satisfactory as a term. It could be better. On the other hand, it could be worse. He hasn't buried me in a flurry of one-night stands. He hasn't ruled out a Relationship.

"No. I tried. My father had an emergency call to go bowling, and my mother was so nervous it was like being in the room with a trapped bird."

By this time, we're almost at the exit, and as far as I'm concerned school is out. I ask him for directions. He gives me the first installment, and I ease off the highway. At the light, he starts in again, his voice all mushy.

"I had to hear it from her sister. Her kid sister. Who's known forever. Who even used to hang out with her and her"—he's definitely lost in new meanings of old words—"her girlfriend. One of 'em anyway."

"So how come this sister told you anyway? How come now?"

"You got any more of those Kleenexes?" I see his reflection bunching up the used ones into a big ball. Reluctantly, I hand him my handkerchief. He doesn't even say thanks, just blows his nose twice hard. I can kiss that one good-bye.

"Because of the wedding, that's how. Her kid sister's marrying this Jewish dentist in April."

I wait for him to decide if he's going to sidetrack onto the Jewish dentist, but after a short pause he leaves the switches in place.

"So she comes to my office tonight—Marianna, that is. We go out for a nice dinner, just the two of us, to talk about the caterer, the bridesmaids, the best man, all that stuff. It's gonna be a big do, you know what I mean? I mean finally one of my daughters is getting married. I wanna do right by her, even if she's breaking our hearts with this no church ceremony. Just some kind of minister or judge or something, she says. So okay. If she's happy, me and her mother, we'll survive. Then I say to her, 'There's still your sister Teresa. If she ever makes up her mind, maybe we'll get her into church.' "

I'm afraid he's about to start sobbing again at the memory. I snap to it and tell him I need to know which way to turn.

"You take a left, then another left over the bridge, and go straight down the hill." He lights another cigarette.

"So Marianna gets mad, I don't know why, and she just barks at me, 'Oh, yeah, the only kind of marriage Teresa's gonna have won't be in any church I know of.' So of course I wanna know what the hell all that means. She tries to clam up, but I tell her she's not leaving the restaurant until she explains. So then she starts to cry and says, 'Pop, don't you know that my sister only likes women?' Only likes women. I turn that one over in my head. 'What's the big deal,' I say. 'You mean she hasn't met the right man?' 'No'—she practically yells at me right there in front of all those people—'I'm telling you Teresa is a lesbian.' I can't believe it. 'What are you saying about your sister?' I'm yelling too by then. 'Are you telling me that all those years she lived in our house, when she said she was going out with Tony or Johnny or who the hell knows who, she was lying to me?' Marianna just nods and grabs her bag and rushes out, leaving me sitting there feeling like I'd been run over by a truck."

I've followed his directions. We've come to the bottom of a long hill. I think I see the glimmer of the Hudson River between some of the houses. My passenger is crying quietly again. I pull up to the curb.

"Listen, which is your house? Is it on this street?"

He tells me to make a right and stop at the third house.

"Maybe you could try talking to her. Tell her you figure maybe her life is very different from her sister's, and that's okay by you, that kind of stuff."

"You think she'll tell me anything?"

"Just don't yell at her. Maybe she'll listen. Maybe she'll hear what you're trying to say."

The guy pulls out his wallet. He hands me the fare plus a $20 bill.

"You don't have to do that," I tell him.

"Lady, you earned every penny." He holds up my handkerchief. "And you're gonna want to replace this." He shoves it in his coat pocket, for which I am grateful.

I watch him as he walks away from the cab, pulling his collar up against the cold. He seems to flex his shoulders as if he were taking a deep breath. Then he strides up the walkway to an ornate wrought-iron door. I sit there for a minute, wondering how it will all go. Whether he'll get lucky and say it right, whether he'll really mean it, whether she'll be able to hear. After a while, shivering, I pull away and head back to the city and think about how tomorrow I've got to get on Oscar's case.

Be Still and Know

Brigitte M. Roberts

"Child, what are you doing? Don't you hear that thunder and lightning? Turn off that tv and be quiet."

"But, Momma, I want to watch *Dobie Gillis*."

"I'm going to 'Dobie Gillis' your behind if you don't do like I say. You know better than to be carrying on when it's storming like this. The Bible says, 'Be still and know that I am God.' Girl, you best to be still and give God praise, for He is a mighty God, a powerful God, a fearsome God."

"A noisy God," I said under my breath, turning off the tv. Bye-bye Maynard G. Krebs.

She wanted me to see God's magnificence in sound and fury. Wanted me to fear the Lord of Sodom and Gomorrah, the God who turned Lot's wife into a pillar of salt. She wanted me to cower before the Father who so sorely afflicted Job. I believed in another God. The God of lute and tambourine in David's Psalms. I trusted and abided in the God who provided manna to the children of Israel. I was still and reverent in the magnificence of rainbows, waterfalls, mountains, a baby's cry, my aged dog's gentle passing from this place to God's bosom.

"Be still and know that I am God." Whenever it rains I hear Momma's command. Did she think she was God? I turn

up the stereo, or wash my dishes, or read *On Our Backs*.
Occasionally I reach for my pocket-sized *Gideon's New Tes-
tament* (with Psalms and Proverbs) and read of God the
Father, the Son, and the Holy Ghost.

>For God so loved the world
>that He gave His only begotten Son
>that whosoever believeth in Him
>should not perish but have
>everlasting life.
>
>For God sent not His Son
>into the world to condemn the world
>but the world through Him
>might be saved.
>
>JOHN 3:16,17

Whosoever, Momma, not just the straight, childbearing,
churchgoing folks. Whosoever. The pussy loving, clit licking
bulldaggers and dick sucking, ass fucking faggots who believe
in Jesus will walk beside you and rest at His feet in heaven.
I think this and a righteous clap of thunder lets me know
Momma is reading my mind and disapproves.

I remember when that thing with Linda blew up. Telephone calls at two, three in the morning. Hangups when
Momma answered, whispered arguments when I picked up
the receiver. I trusted Momma, but at least once she listened
in. One night she reached the phone before I could.

"Girl, you better stop pestering me and my daughter. You
best to pray and get yourself right with God. Don't you be
trying to teach my child your funny ways, them unholy
things. I ain't got but one child and God knows I will do
anything to make sure that we will be rejoicing in heaven
together, so you best to get over whatever is possessing you.
Call here one more time and I will call the law on you, you
child molester. Damn you, damn you, damn you . . ."

She called Linda everything except a child of God.
Momma was so enraged, so blinded by her tears of shame

and the knowledge that she had begat a Sodomite that she could not hear me cry, didn't feel me grab at her shoulder, didn't feel me pry the receiver from her hand. She did not respond to my own tears, choked breath, did not recognize me until I had slapped her soundly across the face and still, she shouted at the phone, "Damn you, damn you, damn you," as if that would correct me, make me desire men, make me the hapless victim of the butch on the other end of the line.

"Funny," she said, "I will not have anyone say my one child is funny. I'll have Deacon Carter pray about this. You will fast. Mother Robinson will counsel you. You can't be too far gone. I would've known. And I know it wasn't your fault, baby. We'll take it to Jesus."

I was black, twenty-one, but far from free. I knew the truth but was too frightened to tell her. I wasn't "funny." I was quite serious in my adoration of the clit, vulva, the taste of female sex in my mouth. Linda hadn't taught me a thing. She was my first serious affair, but sex partner number ten or twelve. But if prayer and fasting would make Momma feel better, so be it.

I allowed Deacon Carter to counsel me. I studied Leviticus 18:21–24, Deuteronomy 23:17,18, 1 Kings 14:24, 2 Kings 23:7, and Romans 1:27. But I refused to allow him to lay hand on my breasts, my ass, slip his tongue in my ear or mouth. When he threatened to reveal "my sin" to the church I promised to cry rape and named four less determined victims of his godless counsel.

Mother Robinson smelled of Cashmere Bouquet and lavender. She was deaf and nearly blind and requested only that I praise Jesus as she rested her arthritic hands upon the crown of my head. She kissed me on the cheek, and as she left said, "Child, all you got to do is trust God to make it right." I did. I do.

Momma, you taught me to see an image of God when I look in the mirror. You taught me to see God in all things, in everyone. How could He be absent in the faces of the women I've held in my arms? You taught me that God will never forsake me, that He is everywhere. How can He not be here, in a bed I share with another of His daughters?

A crack of lightning illuminates the sky and I know Momma hears me. I know she can feel me questioning, stirring, arguing against those things she thinks are fundamentally true.

Well, I'm still black, closer to thirty-one, and finally, finally free. I'm still her only child and, admittedly, "funny that way." Unless I make a turn for the worse, I'm confident of where I'll be come judgment day. Momma doubts, says I'm proud of my sin, declares that I mock the Lord. I say I praise God in every cunt I've known, tasted heaven most times I've made love.

Lightning followed by thunder. Crashing rain. I close the windows. All right, I will turn off the television. I will be quiet, be still, and know that it is God who put the love for women in my heart.

Past Sorrows
and Coming Attractions
Edith Konecky

Brenda Fiebleman, dreaming on the stoop, saw her mother turn the corner into their street. It was a long way from the corner to their front steps, perhaps an eighth of a mile, but she knew it was her mother because she had twenty-twenty. Her mother took credit for her eyesight.

"You think it's easy to raise an intellectual Jewish girl with twenty-twenty?" Having learned from Dr. Brady's newspaper column, she saw to it that the light was always angled over her left shoulder. "The heart side. To save your beautiful studious eyes."

She watched her mother's slow, spunky progress. She was a squat woman with a functional build and, though her arms circled huge shopping bags stuffed with provender hard won from her sly enemies, the Avenue J merchants, she didn't appear to be weighed down. The bags were extensions of herself, as natural as plants sprouting from an urn. Still, Brenda knew that after walking eight blocks, her arms would be aching. She considered going to help her but sat on, immobilized by her nervous breakdown, now in its fourth month. Besides, what about the shopping cart, her present to her mother three or four birthdays back, a simple mechanism, lightweight aluminum, big balloon tires. Other women took readily, delightedly, to shopping carts. A boon. Not her mother. Too much trouble shlepping. Unnatural. She, the daughter of peddlers who had wheeled their wares in gutters.

She turned her attention from her mother's progress back to her contemplation of the dead summer, the early Flatbush autumn, the changed air, the sharp new light, the shadows so different this morning from yesterday's shadows. The leaves on the maple trees, the sun-brittled grass of the small front lawn, looked tired, limp with disenchantment, echoing her. It was her twenty-fourth autumn. Her shoulders sagged, her hands dangled. Though the summer had been hot, it was months since she'd had her hair cut, and it hung limp and dispirited. Her fingernails were bitten and ragged, her sneakers filthy, her jeans frayed at the knees. For a moment she saw herself as her mother saw the neighbors seeing her: she was a disgrace.

It was only ten o'clock. All summer she had slept till noon but the changed air had driven her from bed. Now, faced with a lengthened day, she had only the shards of the night's dreams to play with. Her shadow self had wandered in sleep from terror to terror, from symbol to symbol. She would spend the endless hours ahead translating the night's rubble into the solid bricks of cliché she was learning from Dr. Shapiro. Dear Dr. Shapiro, recharger of failed batteries, restarter of stalled engines.

Her mother clumped up the walk, passing her wordlessly, leaving in her wake an agglomerate smell, microcosm of her morning's travail: the bakery, the appetizer, the delicatessen—the baked, the smoked, the cured—the bloodless perversions of field and sea and orchard. So her mother wasn't talking to her today! Bewildered, she reacted to Brenda moodily, one day with anger, the next with passionate concern, occasionally with disdain, never with fear. Nothing was ever more or less than she expected; life held no surprises. What could happen that could be worse than she'd already lived through: nursing her husband through two

years of cancer to the grave, her mother and brother and
most of her cousins dead in concentration camps, the years
of struggle, Sharon, now twenty-one, with her seven-year-
old mind. What could happen to her that could equal her
dreams: herself tall and slender and bejeweled, her older
daughter a professor, but rich and married and the mother
of fat pink babies, and, finally, a brilliant surgeon who, with
a simple operation, would correct Sharon's defect, then fall
madly in love with her, his creation, like a prince with a
sleeping beauty.

Without turning, Brenda listened to her mother's struggle
with the front door, heard the slam of it behind her and, in
the shattered silence, saw her safe in her lair, the white
kitchen with its new wallpaper, a dull dazzle of cups and
saucers and teaspoons repeating themselves with geometric
whimsy above the tile and around the breakfast nook. She
would spend the next half hour happily sorting, repackaging,
filing her purchases, humming and thinking menus, close to
the source of things important and necessary—dead husbands, retarded and nerve-broken daughters forgotten.

Brenda looked up and down the quiet street, thinking of
the fled companions of her childhood: Lincoln, Stanley, Ace.
From the age of six, she had, against great odds, played only
with boys. A natural athlete, coordinated and strong and
quick, she had had little use for most of the pursuits of the
girls on the block: jacks and rope-jumping and dolls. Because
she was as good as the boys at their games, they had grudg-
ingly admitted her, nicknaming her Bink. Brenda was an
impossible name.

Lincoln was now a pencil manufacturer in Mount Vernon;
Stanley a high school math teacher in Merrick; Ace in his
father's advertising agency; all three of them married, Lincoln already a father. Except for themselves and the Kauff-
mans, three doors down, there was no one left on the block
from the old days. They were still there because the house,
long since paid for, cost only taxes and heat, and because
she, Brenda/Bink, after the years of Brooklyn College and

working after school in cafeterias, libraries, photo dark-rooms, had failed to begin. She had achieved her BA and her MA and, all confident, had embarked on her Ph.D. only to wake one morning knowing, without surprise, that she had died. Respectfully, she had stifled the alarm clock and closed her eyes. Time passed. Her mother came and went many times. Her sister Sharon stumbled in and spoke her name. A doctor was summoned. Her response to all callers was minimal. She heard, she understood, but she no longer cared enough even to open her eyes.

"There's nothing wrong with you," her mother shouted at her as though, instead of dead, she was merely deaf. "Heart, lungs, stomach, reflexes, all shipshape."

Ukrainian borscht, dense with meat and bone and marrow (her mother never skimped), appeared at regular intervals at her bedside and it was this that finally roused her. On the fourth day, starved, she knew that she couldn't be all dead. Later, she learned from Dr. Shapiro that it was her ego that had nearly perished, her id that had responded to the soup. The doctor was convinced that the cause of her failure of ego went deep but that overwork had triggered the crisis. She'd been pushing herself too hard. She must take a rest from her studies and slowly, together, they would "set her house in order."

For weeks, she had languished like a vegetable, fingering dreams, except for two crazy weeks when, taking the doctor's injunction literally, she'd plunged into a frenzied campaign of home improvement, climbing onto the roof to repair a leak, replacing the cracked toilet seat with a gleaming new one, papering the kitchen with paper of her mother's choice, repainting Sharon's room. She had always been the family handyperson, by default of its other members. She ripped out leaky plumbing and, with the aid of a manual from the library and tools borrowed from a hardware store, replaced it with expert proficiency. She painted the outside wood trim, bound up frayed lamp cords, fixed the venetian blinds, and silenced the refrigerator. Then, when there was nothing more she could think of to do, she went to her mother and said, "I'm finished. I'll be leaving now." She meant it. She had set this woman's house in order and now she could leave it. But the woman at the sink said, "Go wash up, Brenda darling, it's time for supper."

Summer had come and gone. Thrice weekly she took the BMT to Manhattan, to Dr. Shapiro's dimly-lit cave where, supine on creaking leather, she mumbled nonsense through her disarrayed hair, distracted by the doctor's collection of treasures. The doctor was a cultivated man, no Spartan single-minded scientist, but a man of parts, proud of the diversity of his interests, the latitude of his libido. His walls were covered with second-rate contemporary paintings, surfaces littered with pseudo-primitive wood carvings, a jungle of knicknacks, mementos and conceits. Also, the doctor was a dandy dresser. He was a homburg man, but otherwise his clothes were too original, too lovingly inspired, to have been merely purchased. Brenda suspected that the doctor made them himself. And when Dr. Shapiro spoke of sex, as he often did, his eyes glowed with such pleasure, remembered and anticipated, that Brenda, sallow and apathetic, was devastated by her own indifference.

What had they in common, these two? There were only differences between her and the worldly doctor before whom she was endeavoring to peel off the layers of her pale Flatbush soul. Language was the most immediate difference, not that Brenda was unfamiliar with the jargon; on occasion she'd used it herself. As abstraction it was convenient, but applied to herself, the words were transformed into rigid nonsense, or too easy sense. She was a bundle of ambivalence and ambiguity. She was id, ego and superego besides being oral, anal and, with luck, genital. What had become of the comforting complexity of life? Where were good and evil, where were human values, where were justice, compassion and mercy?

She had it all balled up. She wasn't there to discuss philosophy but to be psychoanalyzed. Why was she wasting her money and his time? A form of resistance, a way of avoiding the unpleasantness involved in stripping away the neurosis. It was a way of sealing off the unconscious where the trauma lay. Back to beginnings. Back to mother and father. Back, back, *back!*

But it wasn't *back* that worried Brenda. It was the future, not the past, that haunted her. There was nothing unusual in her past, nothing she hadn't long since come to terms with. Just the usual odds and ends: a strong, outspoken mother, the death of a gentle father, a mentally crippled sister, her own escape into books and studies. So what if her toilet training had come too early, or she had been ashamed of her sister, or her mother often got on her nerves? These were only the ordinary currency of life, humdrum. The future was another matter. How could she tell Dr. Shapiro about the future without running the risk of being considered a nut?

Her first encounter with the future had come not long after her mother's borscht had raised her Lazarus-like from bed. She was sitting in the armchair in her room, looking out the window at the sunlight on the Spanish tile roof over the kitchen just beneath her, thinking of nothing in partic- ular. Afterwards, she couldn't tell if she had fallen asleep or into some kind of trance. Roof and sunlight disappeared as though a dial had clicked from one television channel to another. She was lying in bed, drugged and exhausted, and at her bedside sat a strapping middle-aged, anxious man, a little thick around the neck. "It's all right, Mom," the man said, clasping her hand. She tried to pull her hand away but she was too weak. Looking down, then, at her free hand, spotted and veined, she saw that she was an old woman and she understood that she was dying.

"You have the key to the vault?" she said with an effort. "Don't waste time crying. Go straight to the bank."

"Don't worry, Mom, I know what to do. And you aren't dying. The doctor says you'll be as good as new in a week."

She was annoyed that he should lie to her even while she

understood that the lie, if it failed to comfort her, comforted her son. Her irritation with him was diluted by a peculiar tenderness. She wished she could remember his name.

"Sell the house," she said. "Take whatever you can get for it."

"All right, Mom. Don't *worry* about it."

There was something else she meant to say but while she was trying to think what it was, her son launched into a speech, a testimonial. "Listen, Mom," he said, and there was no stopping him, "I want you to know. Whatever. I forgive. Might not always have understood. Inspiration to me. Love:"

It was the kiss of death and she woke on it to the present, to her twenty-four-year-old self in March of the year 1952. She was shaken, knowing that she had neither dreamed nor hallucinated, that the vision she'd just lived through had happened just as surely as yesterday had happened. It had happened in some future past, a past that needed only some five or six decades to be shaped. She would have a son, God knows how, who would look like that, talk like that. Did it mean that she would marry? Or, since she couldn't imagine that, would there be some sort of unimaginable upheaval in the near future to change the condition of women like herself? And, less surprising, she would die. Her last concern would be for material things, the house, whatever it was she had stashed away in the vault.

Good God!

Having come through two deaths, the neurotically inspired and the previsioned, she realized that she was condemned to a long and ordinary life. The earth would not be blasted away, at least not for a while, and she herself would not wither of inanition. She would breed and she would accumulate. How? And more important, *why?*

The front door opened and closed behind her. She knew by the sharp brisk steps that it was Sharon negotiating the length of the porch. Because walking was one of the things Sharon could do, she brought to it the full measure of her unspent purpose and efficiency; she walked like a drill ser-

geant. She sat beside Brenda on the step, leaving room between them for the huge brown paper bag in which she
carried her knitting.

"Mama says you'll catch cold sitting on the stone," she
said, emptying the contents of the bag onto her lap.

"I won't catch cold."

She watched Sharon position the knitting needles with her
long thin hands. Attached to one of the needles was the fruit
of two years of labor, neatly folded. She had begun with
what was meant to be a scarf, but she had gone on and on,
unable or unwilling to terminate it, so that yards and yards
of the stuff, all of it bright red (she would have no other
color) lay mountain-high, folded in her lap. She worked
slowly, taking great pains with the one simple stitch she'd
mastered, and the work was tight and perfect, an eternity
of diligence.

"What are you doing, Brenda?" Sharon always asked her
that.

"Nothing? What's that you're making?"

"It's knitting."

She watched Sharon's laborious pursuit of another mean-
ingless row of locked yarn and wondered at the circuitous
tissue of her secret, damaged brain, this odd Penelope (faithful to what?) spinning forth the patient, patternless, useless
fabric of her days. She wished she could risk the danger of
pitying her, but she had rarely pitied her. She had been
ashamed of her, sometimes even hated her, but she had
protected her. She saw in Sharon's face her own eyes, nose,
coloring. Sharon was neat, her hair was always combed, she
dressed carefully, she bathed as often as she was allowed,
sometimes twice a day. Brenda had rarely seen her cry. Papa
had called her "God's child, an angel," and, dying, wept for
her daily.

"Why could I never pity her?" she asked Dr. Shapiro.

"Guilt, Brenda?"

"Why guilt? Because I wasn't the one? I don't recall ever
feeling particularly blessed."

After Sharon's eighth birthday, they had risked sending

her to school. Brenda was ten, in fifth grade, and every morning her mother said, "Look in on Sharon. See what she's doing." On her way to gym or the auditorium, passing the kindergarten room, she would peer through the glass panel in the door and find Sharon instantly, so conspicuous among the five-year-olds. She was always at the rear of the room peacefully scribbling with her crayons, and even then she would only use the red ones, as though blind to other colors. "She was okay," Brenda would report later to her mother. "She was drawing."

Her mother, exasperated, would snort, "Again with the drawing! They call that a school?"

The next year, because of her size, they advanced her to first grade and when Brenda looked in she was still in the last row, still too large, but with her hands folded on the desk, wonderfully quiet, her lips parted, her eyes serenely empty. There was never anything on her desk but her clasped hands.

"She was okay," Brenda would tell her mother. "She was listening."

But that year, because Sharon was at school for the full day, Brenda would have to meet her in the schoolyard and walk her home. Once, Brenda found her backed against the chain fence by Allan Bernstein, a sickly grin on her face. Allan Bernstein's hand was up Sharon's skirt.

"I was scared to death of Allan Bernstein. He was a bully," she told Dr. Shapiro. "But I screamed at him to quit it."

"Ah, she don't even know what I'm doing," Allan had said.

"That makes it *worse*, you shit," she'd screamed, and head lowered, she bulled into him, knocking him down.

"Did a boy ever put his hand up your skirt, Brenda?" Dr. Shapiro asked. Brenda sighed.

"I didn't wear skirts."

"What did you wear?"

"Jesus, what do you think I wore? Pants. Jeans. I was a tomboy."

"Yes."

"And I didn't *like* boys. Not that way. I liked girls." She blushed and hated herself for it. "I had crushes on girls."

"All girls do," Dr. Shapiro said. "It's normal. At that age."

"Maybe. But I think"—she was finding it difficult to breathe—"I'm pretty *sure* I still prefer them."

"Nonsense," Dr. Shapiro said. "There's nothing in your Rorschach, nothing in your dreams, nothing in your transference, to indicate that you're a lesbian, if that's what you're trying to tell me you think you are. Did you ever have *your* hand up a girl's skirt?"

"Of course not!"

She hadn't even heard the word "lesbian" or known there was such a thing until she was fifteen and someone had thrust *The Well of Loneliness* at her, commanding her to read it. Valerie something, in her French class, an overdeveloped girl with short yellow hair and bangs who sat on Brenda's desk before class and talked about books, a little too intensely.

"I was fascinated and repelled by the book," she told Dr. Shapiro. "And that's how I felt about Valerie. I took great pains to avoid her after that."

"Too bad. You should have gotten it out of your system."

She looked at the doctor with disbelief. He was the one who was crazy. "I'm not talking about salmonella," she said.

But she wanted to believe Dr. Shapiro. It was always possible that he was right, that it wasn't just wishful thinking on his part. And she *had* begun to like boys when she was in high school, and to date them when she was a junior and senior. She was a good dancer and, after her early teens, she began to be good looking—even, in a way, or so boys told her, beautiful. When they necked and, later, petted, it was a relief to discover how much she enjoyed it. Later, in college, she had twice fallen in love, first with Andy for two years, a surprisingly passionate sexual relationship, and later with Ben, who was cerebral and gentle and who had gone

to graduate school in California and married someone else.
She was surprised, when she learned this, not to have felt
more pain.

Yet even while she was in love with Andy and Ben, there
had always been this other thing, some woman she felt
strongly attracted to, unwelcome feelings she had tamped
down as though they were shameful and disgusting. The
doctor knew all this.

"So you never did anything with a girl?" he now asked
her. She felt herself redden again.

"Well, yes," she said. "Muriel Kauffman. When we were
about eleven, I kissed her. I put my tongue in her mouth. I
don't know what made me do it, we were playing some kind
of game. She lived on the block."

Muriel Kauffman had laughed, then run away. After that,
they had stopped being friends. Some invisible line had been
overstepped and she couldn't be sure if she or Muriel was
the more embarrassed.

It was around that time that her father died. She tried to
sum up what she had felt for her father. Relief, mainly, when
he had at last died. There had been so many months of
knowing he was dying, of watching him shrivel and shrink
and suffer. She'd wept when her mother told her, "Papa's
incurable." Afterwards, she had scarcely been able to look
at him without thinking of what his skin contained, the inex-
orable growth that was devouring him. Her father no longer
belonged to them, his family; he belonged entirely to his
cancer.

Still, she had loved him. Twice a year, she drove her
mother to the cemetery, an outpost at some muddled point
where Brooklyn became Queens. She would stand in an
island of silence, though airplanes droned overhead and children played across the street in the yards of shabby houses,
while her mother walked the aisles of the cemetery hunting
for some ragged, bearded old man with egg stains on his
lapels, a death bum, who, for a couple of dollars, would
chant the mandatory prayers over the grave. Brenda would

stare at the simple headstone that bore only her father's name and the years of his life. That stone, and her own standing there with her mother, were almost all that marked the passage of Sam Fiebleman through the long history of the world.

"Hello, Muriel," Sharon called, returning Brenda to the present. As if evoked by Brenda's thoughts, Muriel Kauffman had turned the corner and was heading up the street toward her house, three doors beyond theirs. She would have to pass them and, though she was still too far to have heard Sharon's greeting, Sharon's face was lit with happiness. Brenda watched Muriel's leisurely, regal approach. Her mother had often said that Muriel "carries herself like a queen." It was true.

"Hello, Muriel," Sharon called again. Smiling, Muriel turned up the walk and stood at the bottom of the steps.

"Hello, Sharon," she said. "What are you making?"

"I'm knitting."

"What are you knitting?"

"This."

"Hello, Bink. Brenda." Her eyes did not quite meet Brenda's. For a dozen years, Muriel had neither spoken to Brenda nor looked her in the eye. Today it made Brenda angry.

"It was your idea in the first place," she said to Muriel.

"I know it was," Muriel said angrily, in a rush, knowing at once what Brenda meant. "But I didn't mean like that."

Brenda began to laugh and after a moment Muriel laughed, too.

"You look like a couple of kids, sitting on the stoop like that," Muriel said.

"We *are* a couple of kids," Brenda said. "What are you doing home this time of day? Did you lose your job?"

"It's Saturday."

"Oh."

"I love your shoes, Muriel," Sharon said. Brenda looked at Muriel's shoes. They looked expensive. So did the rest of Muriel's outfit. She knew about clothes.

"Thanks, Sharon," Muriel said. "I hear you've been having a nervous breakdown, Brenda."

"Who told you that?" Brenda said, furious. Her mother, soliciting advice, must have told her, probably because Muriel was a social worker. Brenda could imagine her mother's train of thought: Muriel works with people. She helps them. Maybe she can help my Brenda.

"Are you better now?" Muriel asked. Her face was all kindness. Brenda's anger receded.

"You want to go to the movies?" Brenda heard herself ask.

"What?"

"Tonight. If you haven't got a date?" Brenda loved movies; she hadn't been to one in months.

"I haven't got a date," Muriel said. "I'd love to go."

"I'll come by for you around seven-thirty."

When Muriel had gone, Brenda sat on, amazed at herself. She'd never thought of Muriel as a possible friend, not after all this time. Muriel was a fixture in her life, entirely peripheral to it, like the street lamp across the way, like the six-cup percolator that had sat on the back burner of the stove for as long as she could remember, like the Avenue J druggist who had never handed her a filled prescription without saying, "Use it in good health." Muriel, a social worker, chic, with her regal walk, was everything that she, Brenda, was not. It would be a deadly evening, boring, boring, boring.

But Brenda was used to boredom. There was little in her nervous breakdown that hadn't been boring. Maybe boredom had been its cause. It had certainly been the theme, the heart of her second prevision, which had visited her a month earlier.

She was on a camping trip with two women. The campsite, in a state park, was a rounded clearing in a wooded hillside that circled a crystal lake and, though it was hung with oaks and beech and pine trees, the smell of the sea was sharp in the air. In her years of lived life, Brenda had had little contact with nature—occasional excursions to Rockaway Beach for the day, and twice to Bear Mountain on the Day Line. There hadn't been money for summer camp, or for a rented cottage in the mountains, or even a room in one, though her mother would never have tolerated a shared kitchen. The closest Brenda had come to camping out was one summer when she and Lincoln spent a number of afternoons crouched under a bridge table draped with blankets, eating Fig Newtons by flashlight. Yet here she was in this remote woods fiddling with fishing gear in the shadow of a well-pitched tent.

One of her companions was small and misshapen, virtually a dwarf, and the other a tall thin Southern woman, the trip's organizer, familiar with the complicated workings of the paraphernalia they had assembled to house and feed them and illuminate the night. Neither woman ever stopped talking. The dwarf was a pedant, unable to accept the least part of this experience, new to her, too, until she had approximated its literary equivalent. Wordsworth had been credited with portions of the landscape, and Defoe and Hawthorne shared responsibility for several of their endeavors, some of which were also obviously Thoreauvian. Brenda couldn't decide which of the women was the more tiresome. While the little woman sat smoking on the sidelines, offering comments, Brenda helped Marysue erect the tent, a complicated affair with outside aluminum poles of varying widths and heights, with stakes and zippers and ties and cords. Instead of the ten minutes touted by the catalog, erecting the tent had taken them an hour and a half, with Marysue chattering on about her expertise, about earlier tents she had known and places where she had thrown them up and the women lovers who had accompanied her and who had since betrayed her despite the idyllic times they had shared in nature's bosom. Still, Brenda felt a thrill of triumph when the tent was at last standing and their gear stowed within. The site was solidly theirs. But she knew that this was merely the beginning. There were still food, drink, warmth, and sewage to be dealt with, nature to be outwitted, wood collected and kept dry, water fetched, food procured and prepared and prevented from spoiling, insects and raccoons kept at bay, and darkness penetrated. At the moment, however, she wanted to go off into silence, to absorb nature through her pores, and in solitude. She wanted to go fishing. Alone. But the dwarf, like the Ancient Mariner, had her pinned where she stood, with her incessant talk, her beady eyes, her words sent forth on clouds of smoke, inhaled through a long cigarette holder clamped between her teeth, an arrangement that in no way hindered speech.

"You're a traitor to academia," she was telling Brenda. "It's unconscionable. I can't believe that you're really going to do it."

"But I am," Brenda said, oiling her reel, trying not to listen. "I've contracted to do it, and in good faith."

"With sixty-seven percent of the American dollar going into space, you don't need experts to tell you where the economy is headed. What goes up may never come down, not from space. It's money thrown into the black hole."

"Smell that air," Brenda said, inhaling.

"Naturally they grumble, why wouldn't they? What does interstellar communication mean to the average person? What do they care about swapping beeps with some pointy-headed counterpart in another galaxy when they can't even communicate with their kids?"

"They care," Brenda mumbled, spinning the reel.

"You'll see to it that they do. You'll sell it to them, like an adman, a PR person, like it was laundry detergent or toothpaste. The commodification of space. With your talent! Aren't you ashamed?"

"I came here to get away from space," Brenda pleaded, backing off, "and out into the *air*."

"What I want to know is, are you sincere? Do you really believe in the product?"

Brenda began to walk away, out of the clearing, toward the lake. There wouldn't be any fish in the lake. And if there

were, she'd never catch one. And if she did, it would be full
of poisons.

"I'm going fishing," she said.

"Jingles will come next, I can see it now," the dwarf's
shrill voice pursued her. "The poet scientist! Don't you think
it falsifies to versify?"

As she emerged from the clearing, Brenda came out of
the vision, out of the future, completely baffled. The nameless little woman, so deadly dull with her clever little face
and her chain-smoking, had spoiled it all in the way that
uninspired academics so often demystify what is romantic,
profound, beautiful. And what were they talking about, anyway? Who was she, *that* Brenda? "I came for the trees and
the sky and the lake and the earth," she heard herself shout
back over her shoulder into the future as it dwindled into
the present, as her voice faded. "It isn't often I can come."
And why *had* she come, with those two women who obviously meant nothing to her?

At the movie house that night, Muriel Kauffman smelled
wonderful. "Ma Griffe," she said, when Brenda commented.
"D'you like it? I'll get you some."

"I don't use perfume," Brenda said, "though I appreciate
it."

It was a double feature, both films with Peter Sellers, and
they laughed a lot. Between films, during the coming attractions, Brenda offered to go for popcorn.

"Don't go," Muriel said, laying a restraining hand on
Brenda's arm. "This is the best part."

She sat still, watching the previews of forthcoming movies.
The first was about interns and nurses, hospital scenes filled
with blood and sex. The second dealt with a turgid marital
triangle, good man strong in riding boots, knocking down
his blind wife's punk nymphomaniacal sister. Muriel giggled
throughout the brief film clips while Brenda stiffened, feeling premonitions. "She knows," Brenda thought. "Muriel
Kauffman is telling me she knows." But how could she?
Nobody knew, not even Dr. Shapiro.

"Isn't it great?" Muriel said. "They give you these bits they think are provocative and you can figure out the whole plot, and then you can choose. You can choose to stay away."

"Oh, God, you *know*," Brenda said. "But how?"

"Know what, Brenda?" Muriel asked, covering Brenda's hand with her own. In the flickering, reflected light, Brenda searched Muriel's pale face, surprised that she hoped to find confirmation there. But there were only Muriel's features, the questioning eyes, the strong bridge of her nose, the soft uncomprehending mouth. Brenda shook her head, embarrassed, and they turned back to the screen where the second film had begun to unfold.

Afterwards, because it was just down the block, they went to Sidney's Versailles Snack Palace, a glittering eatery featuring waffle-based banana splits. They sat on crimson naugahyde, their elbows on pink Formica, and saw themselves repeated at a dozen different angles and removes in cracked and bronzed mirrored walls and columns. In the brilliant garish light from a ceiling cluttered with fluorescent chandeliers, Muriel's unretouched nose developed a slight shine. Brenda relaxed, feeling strangely happy.

"Will it embarrass you if I have one of the house specialties?" Muriel asked, while the waitress stood poised, waiting for their order. "I'm around deprived kids so much that I've acquired their gluttony."

"Have two," Brenda said.

Muriel described in careful detail exactly what she wanted.

"One scoop or two?" the waitress asked.

"Two. Both chocolate. Hot fudge on one, strawberry on the other."

"Strawberries on chawklit?" the waitress said, making a face. "What about whipped cream and nuts?"

"Yes. Everything."

"I'll take the same," Brenda said. "What the hell."

"Though the truth is," Muriel said when the waitress had departed, "I can't remember ever seeing a kid, given a choice, order anything he couldn't smear with ketchup." She scanned the room. "Only middle-aged women with long-departed waistlines," she said glumly. "Consoling themselves."

"We can cancel the order if it's going to depress you," Brenda said.

"You, of course, don't have to worry. You look as if you haven't eaten since you were twelve. Tell me about yourself, Brenda." Her eyes shone across at Brenda. Was Muriel flirting with her, or was that her way? But before she could answer her own question, or Muriel's, the waitress was there with their order. It was only with an effort that Brenda could bring herself to look at the vulgar confections she set before them.

"They look like Miami Beach motels," she said. She had been to Miami Beach once, the guest of her father's rich brother.

"It's vanilla," Muriel said, looking beneath the strawberries, her mouth grim.

"How can you tell?"

"Waitress!"

There was going to be a scene. While the waitress sauntered back, Brenda prayed that she would be one of the gracious ones, a philosopher.

"It's vanilla," Muriel told her. "I ordered chocolate."

"The other one is chawklit," the waitress said.

"Both," Muriel said. "They were both supposed to be chocolate."

Brenda steeled herself as she had so often done in similar encounters where her mother played the lead. They were both women, Brenda's mother and Muriel, who knew their rights as American citizens.

"Vanella, you said."

"Never. Chocolate. I said it twice. Clearly. Distinctly. Emphatically."

"That's right," Brenda said. "She said it twice."

The waitress looked at Brenda with contempt before turning back to her true adversary.

"With all that gook on it," she told Muriel, "you won't

even *taste* the ice cream." Brenda squirmed. The air was charged.

"Take it back," Muriel said.

"Be reasonable," the waitress whined. "Whaddyew expect me to do with this?"

"I am being reasonable," Muriel said in the most reasonable of voices. "You have many flavors of ice cream here, don't you?"

"Fourteen."

"And I chose chocolate. I was given a choice, I chose, I am entitled to my choice."

Defeated, the waitress took Muriel's dish back to the counter and shoved it across to the fountain boy.

"I ordered chawklit," they heard her say. "You put vanella."

"What about yours?" Muriel asked. "You probably got vanilla, too. Send it back."

"I don't mind," Brenda said, smiling. "But bravo. I don't think I've ever sent anything back in a restaurant."

"Do you want me to do it for you?"

"Please, Muriel, let's stop talking about flavors."

"Then tell me what you meant in the movies." She leaned forward. "When you said that I knew."

"It was nothing."

"It wasn't nothing. It was something. I could tell. Something important to you."

Brenda felt both tempted and trapped. "It was about the coming attractions," she mumbled. "About the future, about choosing to go into it or stay away. I'd rather not talk about it now."

"It's different with life," Muriel said. "How can you choose when you don't know what's there?"

But she did know. Fortunately, the waitress was back with Muriel's corrected sundae.

"Chawklit," she snapped, setting it smartly down.

It was after midnight when Brenda got home. From the hall, she saw her mother in the kitchen, hunched over the kitchen table, her rimless spectacles steamy from the tea she was drinking. Except for the circle of light in which she sat, the house was dark and silent. Her aloneness unnerved Brenda. Her mother had always been the president, the commander-in-chief, a *shtarka*. She was one of the angry old women, though she was not yet old. Life would never defeat her because she had never promised herself anything, not absolutely. In time her body would betray her, hardened arteries, arthritis, a stroke, but she would go down fighting, cajoling doctors, berating nurses, clutching at life to the last gasp. What courage. What tenacity. But at this moment, Brenda was touched by her solitude. She went into the kitchen.

"Have a nice cup of tea, Brenda darling."

"I'll get it," she said. "Don't get up. Mama, don't get *up*." Firmly, she pushed her mother back into her chair and fetched a cup and saucer from the cupboard, then sat at the table opposite her mother.

"There's plenty," her mother said, filling Brenda's cup from the teapot. "I made a full pot. You want some cake?"

"No."

"There's some nice sponge. Or a small piece of crumb I could warm."

"No thanks, Ma, I just came from Sidney's."

"You had a good time? She's a nice girl, Muriel?" Earlier, she had jumped for joy when Brenda mentioned that she and Muriel were going to the movies.

"I always liked her," her mother said. "She's kind to Sharon. Even as a little girl, she was never mean to her like the others."

Brenda sipped her tea.

"And she's smart, too. She has a good head on her. Like you, Brenda."

"I'm not so smart."

"You always got good grades. The highest."

"Anyone can get good grades."

"Don't talk foolish." She sighed. "Tell me, Brenda, heart

to heart. Do you think you're getting better? Is Dr. Shapiro doing you any good?"

"I don't know, Ma."

"Because the money isn't going to last forever."

"I know. I think I can stop with Dr. Shapiro pretty soon."

"So what will you do? Go back to school?"

"Maybe. I don't know."

"Because you're already a master. I don't want to interfere, it's your life, but what's the good of being a doctor if you can't hang out a shingle? How much education does a person need to teach a bunch of schoolkids?"

"I'm not going to teach. I don't know what I'll do."

Her mother sighed. "I'm not really worried about you, Brenda darling. I have faith. But I don't understand these breakdowns."

"These? It's only one, Ma."

"A gorgeous girl with education, perfect eyesight, practically no cavities, excellent health. Your entire future is ahead of you."

"Everyone's future is ahead of them," Brenda said, wincing.

"Don't talk foolish. With me, my whole future is already behind."

"You should get out more, Ma. You're not old. You could do something."

"What about Sharon?"

"It's not fair for you to spend your whole life taking care of her. You're entitled to a life. There are places where she'd be better off."

"How could she be better off than here in her own home with her own mother? And what would I do, tell me? Go dancing? Go to the racetrack like Mrs. Persky and bet on horses?"

"You could go to Florida and visit Uncle Jacob. You could meet a nice man, a widower. You could get married again."

"Sometimes I think that," her mother said. "Poor Papa." She sighed again, then her mouth tightened. "Is that what you'll do when I'm gone? Put Sharon in one of those places?"

"I don't know, Ma. You're not going to die for a long time. You'll live forever, if necessary."

"God forbid! Promise me, Brenda."

"All right, I promise."

"So what will you do with her?"

Brenda shrugged. "I'll buy her a mink coat and teach her to play canasta," she said. "Then I'll go to Seventh Avenue and find her a husband."

"Why are you talking nonsense? She has a child's mind."

"Lots of people have, Ma, and nobody notices. Sharon knows how to dress herself, she can count change, and she knows how to hail a taxi. All she needs is a rich husband."

Her mother took the empty teacups to the sink. She stood there deep in thought.

"Canasta's complicated," she said. Brenda went to the sink and kissed her on the cheek.

"Good night, Ma."

For the first time in months, she fell asleep almost instantly. She awoke some hours later while it was still dark and lay comfortable and at peace, realizing that she hadn't dreamed. Maybe it just goes away, she thought, the way it comes. Still, the absurd, impossible, boring future lay before her, an undigested mass, booked as the next week's movies, coiled and immutable in their cans, were booked by the Midwood Theater. Was time an illusion and the future, as her mother had said, past? As a child, she'd been given a toy movie projector that cranked by hand and had a weak, battery-powered light. It wasn't much of a toy but, crazed with science fiction, she had made it the instrument of a complicated game. She had chosen a distant star, dreamed it rich with all but human life, named it the planet Brendith, surrounded it with an atmosphere that gave substance to shadow. Then, in her imagination, the projector grew enormous, its tiny bulb became a sun. She pointed the toy at the star and cranked it, unreeling the film, and said, "Five hundred light years hence, Donald Duck will live on Brendith and do these things and I, Brenda Fiebleman, long dead, am God of the planet Brendith." The responsibility was overwhelming. In time, she promised herself, she would make her own films, better ones. Sharon, her parents, one or two of her teachers, the kids on the block, she would beam them all at Brendith. She would give them immortality.

But the game turned on her and, in terror, knowing God was a child like herself, the earth his toy and Brenda his fiction, she hurled the projector to the back of a closet. Gradually, reassured by the quiet confidence of her arithmetic teacher and by the sound of her mother faithfully chopping liver in the kitchen, her voice quavering over some half-remembered song from her Russian childhood, Brenda watched the stars recede and time again became tick-tock, tick-tock, yesterday, today, tomorrow.

She lay in the dark. Between the rooftops a street lamp shone, trembling like a star. She groaned and turned in her bed, the sheets twisting around her legs. "Let there be a third vision to give me the answer," she prayed. Three is the symmetry of religion, of fairy tales, of magic. She would wait for the magic third. And if an answer came, how would she know it, if she didn't know the question? She fell asleep.

In the morning it was raining. A wind had risen, driving the rain against the windows. She felt shut in and restless. It was Sunday, a long day, yet no longer than all the days of her recent idle past. There would be no Dr. Shapiro to break the pattern of emptiness with their mutual consideration of the furniture of Brenda's psyche: her feelings, her lack of feelings. But yesterday the pattern had been broken. Muriel Kauffman had looked her in the eye, and they had gone together to the movies. Muriel had made a scene and Brenda had actually admired her for it, even liked her. They had become friends. And who knows? Muriel had touched her a lot, her hand, her arm, had seemed to be flirting with her, had wanted to know all about her.

Her restlessness grew. After breakfast, she took her coffee into the living room and read the paper. On the sofa beside her, her mother picked up sections of the paper as Brenda discarded them. The radio was on and she sat, half-listening. A sermon. Ethical culture. Finally, driven from the living room, she prowled through the house.

She went into Sharon's room. Sharon was sitting in a straight-backed chair, still in pajamas and bathrobe, her hands cupping her small breasts, her mouth quivering, her eyes closed. Brenda stood in the doorway, afraid.

"What's the matter, Sharon?" she asked.

"Oh, Brenda!" She had never heard such sorrow in Sharon's voice. She came all the way into the room.

"What, Sharon? What is it?"

"I love him so much." Tears trembled in Sharon's eyes, waiting to fall.

"Who, Sharon? Who do you love?"

"Ben Casey."

Brenda tried not to smile. Until he had ridden off into the sunset, Gene Autry had been Sharon's love. She had remained faithful as long as he was there to remind her, dozens of his pictures adorning the walls of her room. Now it was Ben Casey, dark and taciturn, whose photos were everywhere.

Brenda sat on the neatly made up bed. Three dolls, carefully dressed, their hair neatly combed, like Sharon's, sat propped against the pillow sham.

"Why Ben Casey?"

"He's so handsome. And he . . . he helps people."

Brenda felt her heart turn. Should she tell Sharon that Ben Casey wasn't real, that he was a shadow on the television screen, an actor speaking written lines, that Ben Casey wasn't even his real name? No, of course not. What do people love, after all? Ben Casey wasn't real, but Sharon's pain was. What did it matter what it chose as object, as long as it chose . . . this child's mind trapped in its hungry woman's body?

"I'll teach you a card game, Sharon, okay?"

"Old Maid?" Sharon said eagerly, her face lighting. "I know how to play Old Maid."

"No, a new game. Canasta."

The third, and what was to prove the last, of Brenda's previsions came to her an hour later. She had lost Sharon's attention for the dozenth time and had finally released her from the card table. Alone, she gathered up the cards. On the radio, the Philharmonic played the Sibelius First Symphony. The bass thumped a stacatto warning while the strings strained toward a passionate crescendo. Then click! The radio went dead, the cards, table, room, vanished, and she was in a small kitchen. It was night. There was another woman, young but out of focus, blurred, so that afterwards Brenda couldn't identify her, standing at the sink. Brenda stood, conscious of her hands dangling at her sides, and of a trio of conflicting emotions battling for ascendancy.

"May I take out the garbage?" Brenda asked.

"No," the other woman said without turning.

Her heart beat in its cage. She was wild with fury. Of the three emotions struggling for dominance, it was anger that won, but even as it did, she knew it was transient. Still, she stood trembling with it, battered by it.

The scene clicked off; that was all there was. She had missed only a few bars of the Sibelius, but there were tears in her eyes, real tears, and her head ached. She pushed away from the card table and went to the window. The rain fell in a straight, steady downpour. The wind had died. She looked up at the leaden, monotonous sky, the sky that would darken into night and brighten again into tomorrow and all the tomorrows of her ridiculous, impossible future, the years gathered there waiting for her to live them. If she chose.

What kind of woman says, "May I take out the garbage?"

Who was that other woman and under what circumstances would she answer, "No." To such a question!

She was dying to know.

And what had she been feeling? Anger, yes. Abjectness (how had she failed the woman at the sink?). But what was the third thing, so strong, so vital, the thing that made the other two possible? Was it love? She was dying to know that, too.

She was dying to know. She thought she was weeping, still, but then she heard what was bubbling and growing in her throat: that dark twin of tears, laughter.

Snake in the House
Gail Shepherd

Mama said to tell a lie was the worst thing you can do, so
I'm going to tell the truth as far as I know it. She was raised
in a convent which had been converted from a nineteenth-
century "chateau" that the people of Saigon called Mondor's
Folly. The hapless millionaire Mondor disappeared on a
clear morning in 1957 after going to confession, and the priest
he'd confessed to soon afterwards produced a questionable
will which left everything Mondor had accumulated in his
tempestuous career to the Saigon Mission. So it happened
that every morning the convent girls lined up in their white
dresses to one side of the grand ballroom underneath the
old Louis Quatorze chandeliers and under the domed ceiling
painted with garlands, and the rosy cherubs looking down
and laughing at the ridiculousness of human ways. The girls
lined up and waited until the sisters floated in and settled
down on the opposite side in an arrangement of blacks and
purples and maroons whose color depended on how the sun
was falling through the high windows. Their habits smelled
of starch and jasmine-scented soap, their faces were smooth
and as full of possibility beneath their wimples as was befit-
ting the Purest of the Pure. Then one by one the girls would
cross the great emptiness of the parquet floor spattered with

sunlight, and Mama says she can still hear the sound of their footsteps, how it seemed an interminable length of time and full of echoes. She learned then that no action we take in this world is discrete, but is like a stone tossed into still water with circles that radiate outward and put motion into everything.

Every morning the girls had to kneel down at the feet of the sisters and they had not just to think and speak the truth but to become the Truth itself, keeping as still as possible. There was no room in the convent at that time for any degree of uncertainty. It might be that Chaos paced all day and night outside those high windows and pressed its dark face against the leaded glass panes, but through those panes only the light of Truth would pass, and that light broken down into all the colors of the spectrum.

The thing to do, Mama said, was to try to *become* that light, kneeling there under the beautiful and direct gaze of Sister Luce and Sister Claire and Merciful the youngest, who had known no pain but the pain of her own birth and that she had long since forgotten. Oh, to turn that undiluted red, that deep and static blue, that yellow of honey spilled out in a patch of sun! Mama said she never tried to think of God, who she guessed had her father's face and her father's tendency to distance and complexity, a large man brooding over the messes and turmoils of the world He'd made. Anyway, her father was dead, which complicated his memory in a way that made her breathing come fast and set her heart to fluttering, just the opposite of the state of grace she was trying so hard to achieve. She'd look down at Sister Luce's foot, so poised and self-contained in its cotton stocking and supple leathers, and she just let her head fill up with the apprehension of texture, as if her mind had been overlaid with the intricate weave of cotton stretched thin over what she thought and saw, and over who she was and what she would become.

What she became in the end was not much different from what happened to a lot of Vietnamese girls at that peculiar juncture of history: she married a Navy man, and he brought her to America. I am the product of these two versions of the truth, the one on its knees trying to adjust its vision to the lay and pattern of a parquet floor, and the other with its eyes on the horizon and its back to the known landscape of home.

Old habits die hard, and Mama is up every morning at 6 A.M. and throwing open the sash windows so that the weather can have its way with me. I open one eye and the dresser mirror is etched with the lacy scrawl of winter's signature, and the perfume bottles and silver brushes and the Chinese bowls full of hairpins are dusted with a light snowfall, like a miniature town in a Christmas display window. Depending on the season, I'll wake up with red and gold leaves stuck in my hair or the wasps looting the dregs of last night's Coca-Cola from the glass on the bedside table. It makes me jumpy, the way the outside never seems to stay in its proper place but is always pressing in at the edges of me. One time I found a baby raccoon hid in between the folds of my dirty laundry, and the birds often enough swoop in and beat themselves to death, so the wild rose wallpaper is sticky with fluff and old bloodstains.

Mama pulls back the coverlet and finds me naked, last night's sweats still drying under my arms and between my legs. She thinks I am no child of hers because I am long and golden and she is small and dark, because I am sleepy and she is perpetually waking. She has little feet and black hair and tear-shaped breasts with drawn out nipples almost purple in color. I could put my two hands around her waist. When I lift her up sometimes to tease her, she's light as if her bones were hollow and her heart made of dust and feathers.

Mama is the first thing I see in the morning and the last thing at night, her face bending over me, and her voice rubbing along my skin. She lost her native language but not the accent that makes her American speech seem full of small

holes, like a knitted scarf in which many stitches have been
dropped.

According to Mama, the color of a person's soul depends
on the work they have to do and what Fate has decreed will
be their great and decisive action. She says my soul is red-
orange because I will have to fight for something and hers
is blue-black like the South China Sea. Her dreams are not
varied and surprising like other people's; mornings she has
nothing to tell over the breakfast table but what she's told
a hundred times before. Every night she closes her eyes and
makes the crossing over water to the country of her childhood, and she finds herself standing outside the convent and
looking up at the terrible angels nesting in the eaves with
their great wings folded as if in prayer.

But in the early hours of morning when things get bad she
will slip into bed with me and pass her arms through mine
and rock until we both go back to sleep. She has waking
visions. Pretty often her dead mother arrives with a suitcase
full of mud and her wet hair streaming down her back from
her long fall through the river of time, still wearing the
Mildred Pierce tailored suit she designed from memory after
seeing Joan Crawford in the movie of that name. The suit
has smooth pebbles for buttons and is stitched together with
weeds and fishtails. Along the edges of its notched collar
and roll-back cuffs, paper-thin shards of mica shine like se-
quins.

Mama lost her entire family in a flood during the season
of rain. The river rose up and swallowed her little white
house and everything and everybody in it: the French porcelain tea-service and the clay pots filled with spices, the
wooden dining table in which she had carved her little sisters'
and brothers' names and dates of birth, the kerosene lamps,
the bedcovers appliquéd with scraps of taffeta and velveteen
left over from the party dresses my grandmama sewed for
the wealthy ladies of Saigon. Mama washed up four miles
downriver in a tangle of old fishnets, and the nuns came

down from the convent and took turns breathing into
her mouth and nostrils until she woke up as if from a
deep dream. They carried her uphill with the fishnets drag-
ging behind her like the train of a wedding gown and laid
her out on the massive four-poster in what had been Mondor's bedroom, where they spent many hours untangling the
nets that had woven themselves together with her long black
hair.

When Mama lies down with me these early mornings I
hold as still as possible so as not to frighten her, like you do
when you stand still in the woods sometimes and the deer
come up and put their velvet noses against your shoulder
and breathe in your ear to find out if you're one of them. I
want her to know that I'm of her likeness. I want her to
know that her holding me is not much different than if she
were touching her own body. I try to make my face a mirror
for her to look into and find out what she's always known
about herself. I put my mouth on her thin shoulders and run
my hand along the soft insides of her knees. Mama, mama,
mama, I want to tell her, I am your daughter, the end of a
long line of daughters that runs like a steel cable through
the years and wars, that moors together continents to keep
them from their slow drifting.

During the war the sisters and the little girls had hardly
anything to eat except for the few pale and twisted vegetables
that grew in the convent garden. Their arms and legs got
thinner and thinner under their white dresses until it was
like if you looked hard enough, you could see the bitter
sunlight shining right through them. They were like pieces
of paper on which a few words had been scrawled: a name,
maybe, and a line of made-up poetry. They made bread flour
from ground-up roots and split each dark and heavy loaf
sixteen ways. When Mama got sick with a fever, Sister Luce
put the bread in her own mouth, and held it there long
enough to let it soften so Mama could swallow it. Luce fed
her the bread in little moist balls, pushing them down her

throat with fingers that tasted sweet as the rationed sugar they never had any of.

Mama's treasured possession was a small fragment of mirror she had saved from when her house was washed away. When the sisters finally got her untangled from the fishnets, Luce pried open Mama's fist and found this shard of broken glass which, when she bent over to see what it was, reflected her beautiful, sad face through a film of Mama's childish blood. Mama still has a star-shaped scar on her palm; the raised lines of flesh are rough against my cheek, my tongue. She keeps the piece of mirror propped on her dresser.

Sometimes I look into this mirror, and I see Mama disappearing under the overlay of Daddy's stronger features. I see that there's hardly anything left of her in me but what pushes through at the last moment, almost on the edge of vision.

Daddy keeps his tools under my bed: an Indian ax with a painted handle that depicts scenes from the Fetterman Massacre of 1866, a Smith and Wesson rifle, a small handgun of uncertain origin that looks like something Bonnie Parker might have used to rob banks, a silver knife inlaid with ebony, a Japanese Seppuku sword, a pair of metal balls attached to a leather thong, a spur with chestnut horse hair still stuck to its iron points. Many times I have asked him to remove this cache from my private premises; I feel like the princess with the pea under her mattress and have had many a sleepless night listening to the metallic conversations of these instruments whispering to each other their sad and violent histories. Daddy pontificates that in the event of total warfare I will be able to hold off the barbaric hordes for an indefinite period and perhaps survive to repeat the tale to my grandchildren. Failing that, I suppose, I can always commit seppuku with the Japanese sword, as women do in foreign movies when all is lost but their honor. Personally, I have no taste for suicide, and from what I've read, seppuku is no fun. Maybe you die in an hour, maybe it takes a day or two for your bowels to poison your system and your lungs to fill up with blood. Besides, whatever I once had to protect got lost one night a long time ago in the woods, with Betsy Sawyer experimenting to find out if there really was such a thing as a hymen or whether this was a myth. I assume the barbaric hordes would be disappointed, since we never could find it.

In the morning when I go to brush my teeth I hear Daddy rooting around under the bed and counting his things to make sure none of them has slipped away during the night. Sometimes he takes them apart to inspect their interior functioning and I come back to find little bits of unidentifiable metal scattered around on the floor like jewels from a broken necklace. It takes him a long time to take everything apart and put it back together because he has only two fingers on each hand, which makes him clumsy and vulnerable, and it could be this sense of his own imperfections accounts for his obsession with routine. Every day is the same. First thing each morning, he does his pushups. While I'm still rubbing the sleep from my eyes I can hear him in the next room yelling:

"eighty eight,
eighty nine,
ninety,
ninety one,
ninety two,
ninety three,
ninety four,
ninety five"

and these numbers push all memory of pleasant dreams out of my head. I blame Daddy for my fear and hatred of mathematics in school, and my general inability to think clearly or remember what happened from one day to the next. How easy is it to know what the Truth is, when any remembrance has to squeeze itself out between columns of numbers that run in both directions all the way to infinity? And each of these numbers divisible into smaller and smaller parts? Winter mornings are crazy like this with noise and interference. Then his rituals start way before dawn. By the time the sun comes up he's done the pushups and scrounged his gear out from under my bed and he's out of the house and the air is clotted with the sound of gunfire repeating and repeating.

What do I want? I would like to lie there with the sun in my eyes. I would like to study the hum of silence rising and falling in waves like the sound of bees' wings. I can imagine myself, in another existence, drowsy and enlightened, filled with the peace that passeth understanding.

I go downstairs to eat my cereal in the parlor, thinking about how if it were just me and Mama living here things would be different. It seems like where she goes, objects just fall into place around her. When she settles down in her wingback chair next to me, the plates and cups and polished silver spoons arrange themselves around her in a perfect order, and if I were a painter I would show her like this: the criss-cross of shadow in the nap of her sweater, the blur of potted begonias casting their pink light on the planes and angles of her face. She turns her head to catch their scent. The bare trees outside are a rush of motion, a brushstroke. Maybe love is about nothing so much as a power to apprehend what's different from yourself, which is why a painter would spend time as though time were as plentiful and endless as the air. How many hours and days to get just right the curve, the color, of that mouth, or the blue-black hatch of darkness under those eyes? How many mornings spent with a stiff back and aching wrists to cross the shining expanse of wood floor between the unfinished canvas and her distant and imperturbable being?

But Daddy comes in with a brace of birds and Mama is at the kitchen sink up to her elbows in feathers and entrails, cutting the bullet out of a slick heart so warm you can still feel the ghost of its beating. Daddy comes in and there's venison to be divided into steaks and wrapped in paper and the kitchen floor spread with tarp, with hooves and antlers and pelts. The smell of time which is not plentiful and endless, but bound like precious marrow in the bone, the smell of the world confined as we are in this kitchen in rural Tennessee, and the first snowflakes falling around the house like in a glass ball which someone has shaken, once, twice.

One thing I try to do: to make myself strong and quiet for the great battle I will have to fight. Winning anything depends on timing and your ability to wait in silence while the enemy thrashes around in the underbrush making a fool of himself trying to kill you. Maybe you make yourself a tree. Maybe you stand out all night in the snow with your mind slowly emptying, and when the sky finally clears, the last stars burn through you as if you were made of glass.

During the war, they burned the villages and everybody in them. There was suffering. The villagers turned into smoke to escape the cruelties and drifted among the swaying palms and then out over the open plains and into the mountains. In Saigon, monks set themselves on fire. The burning pagodas lit the faces of students chanting in the streets. The walls of the convent shook and big cracks spread across the painted ceiling and through the gold filigree; the stone faces broke from the angels and fell into the dirt.

I read in a book I had to report on for American History that the U.S. First Infantry Division carved its divisional insignia with defoliants in the jungle before they shipped home; the writer called it a "giant, poisonous graffito."

I remember it all as if I had been there.

The night Mama left the convent for good she walked down to the river. She tells me the river talked to her and she answered it. Daddy calls this story one of Her Delusions, like we're all supposed to take it with a pretty big grain of salt. But she says the river talked in Vietnamese and she answered it in the English she had learned from phrasebooks

at the convent. Mama is good with details this way. Whatever
it said she took as a warning, but she didn't follow anybody's
advice at that time because she was crazy with grief over the
terrible thing that had happened to Sister Luce.

I think about Sister Luce a lot while I'm standing in the
snow or out under the stars, because Mama says she had a
strong body like mine and her own way of doing things. She
had an unshakable belief in herself right up until the end. I
am a girl, and my skin is yellowy gold and sometimes brown
in summer, but when I have to walk through town to school
the kids throw rocks at me and call me nigger-boy. No matter
what happens, I will not hate myself. I get to school on time.
I sit straight at my desk. My homeroom teacher Miss Sea-
graves often says that I am a "good citizen." I whisper her
name over and over under my breath, "Sea-graves, Sea-
graves," and I think about boats going down in the Gulf of
Tonkin. I think about Mama's family, which probably
washed out into the China Sea along with Grandmama's
French tea-service, and imagine their bones bleached white
as porcelain cups.

Early in the morning when Mama comes to me and curls
around my back like a blanket of bones, it is because the
voices of her ancestors whisper in her ear how she abandoned
them to the river, and this makes me think that the force
that breaks things apart often wins out over the one that
would keep them together. The voices remind her how she
went away to live in the American South, a place where she
is despised by her neighbors and by her husband's family
because of her coffee-colored skin and her halting speech.
Now she is a stranger to her own people as much as she is
a stranger to these great, pale, ham-fisted relations who say
how my Daddy married beneath him, isn't it a pity. Somehow
she got unmixed from everything she was bonded to, like
some chemical element in a laboratory experiment.

I have no comfort to give her but what my own body gives,
never enough.

The moon hangs in the window without moving. What we
do feels like the Truth, my hand in the small of her back

and her tear-shaped breasts pressed up against mine. The brine taste of her and me, and the watery darkness, like we are swimming, swimming back to Vietnam.

Here is one of my most important memories, and if I don't write it down I will surely lose it. One time a pair of black-snakes came down our parlor chimney and plopped down on the brass andirons. I heard Mama yelling. When I came in the snakes had slipped across the floral rug Mama had bought from Luria's and gone on down the hall, trailing each other in and out of all the bedrooms and nosing along the quarter-round with their pink tongues flickering. They were maybe four feet long and as thick around as my wrist, and they looked so strange and seemed so delicate in their slow perusal that I hardly felt at all scared, but took a kind of interest in their progress that was half scientific, half pro-tective. They seemed like a pair and who knows, maybe even felt a snakey kind of tenderness for one another. So Daddy goes down to the basement and sharpens up his axes for what seems like two hours before he comes back up and corners them in the bathroom. I hear the ax ringing on the bathroom floor tiles. When I go in afterwards, I see he's cut each snake clean in two. The four black snake halves on the powder-blue tiles are perfectly symmetrical.

I stand there looking down at the dead snakes on the powder-blue bathroom tiles and I notice how their skulls are fragile, they are like birds' eggs. Their long, smooth bodies are very flexible, as if they had learned to go around things the way a river does. Daddy has lined them up head to tail and head to tail, like you might do with a cut length of rope. I take them out to the woods and bury them under my big oak tree.

I think of the place where I buried those two blacksnakes as my place of past and future because it has something to do with family and something to do with what happened to Sister Luce that ought not to have happened but was somehow inevitable. Mama tells me that the Vietnamese think of family as a tree—each person is a leaf, and when someone does something bad, or even fails to do something good, the whole tree withers up at the root and dies, and all the leaves fall down in a big shower.

When the soldiers on leave from the U.S. First Infantry Division came up to the convent that night, maybe even they didn't know what they wanted. They were dream-walking. They walked in a black line that snaked its way up the hill from the river. The girls looked out from their gabled windows and saw that the soldiers' faces in the moonlight were blank, and their big hands hung open at their sides as if they had had enough of holding on to anything that mattered. The soldiers stepped over the fallen angels delicately in spite of their boots and walked in the dark, slipping up the grand staircase whose wrought-iron lamps had long since been shattered. They were dream-walking and I know what that feels like. It's when you can't remember how you came to be where you are, but you wake up in blankness, floating and disconnected, divided from what you used to be.

You are very free then, and you can do anything.

Now even Saigon is divided this way into two parts. There is French Saigon with its long avenues and villas and then across the river there are the slums of Bui Phat where the refugees live in the dark because they have no electricity. They make up their own laws as they go along, there in the dark, and each day is different because there are no fixed rules. Sometimes the gangs of boys will come and steal your money, sometimes they will just sit around taking heroin and talking nonsense among themselves. You never know. There is room in Saigon now for all kinds of uncertainty. The tree of the Vietnamese people has shaken down its leaves.

Is this a bad thing? I don't know. Part of myself is always wanting to fix things so they don't change, but more and more these days I feel another part of me that thinks I can live and move in the dark. I am like Saigon, one side of wide streets in sunlight and pastel houses, the other side a tangle of alleyways and tin-roof shacks. Every day a new shack or a concrete apartment building is added in Bui Phat. Every day a new footpath carves itself out between the sewage lines and clutter. The jungle will one day swallow French Saigon, with all its pretty gardens and balconies and lengthy traditions.

In French Saigon, you get on the smooth-running escalator of life with your Mama and Daddy in front of you and your babies behind you; you can go so high or so high but your place in line never changes. In Bui Phat, any mean-enough kid can be king.

The bomb craters are filling up with paddy silt and the burned-out villages are full of living children.

From what Mama's told me, it seems like the sisters were on pretty good terms with the American GI's, who liked their soft ways and French manners; it was like a tentative association between separate but equals. The sisters truth to tell were not so pure as they looked, and the GI's were not all bad but had a little God in them now and then. This is the way of the world, is it not? The GI's brought up American magazines and Milky Way bars for the girls, and in return the sisters would sit with them and try to shake the loneliness out. Mama sat between Luce's knees and heard everything while Luce braided Mama's hair. She thought the GI's were handsome enough, but nothing so nice as feeling Luce's fingers weaving and weaving on the back of her neck, not so nice as the soldiers going off for the night, and Mama and Luce walking down with them as far as the river.

One of these times they sat on a stone and then they lay down for only a minute, and when they came to it was morning, the dew in the folds of Luce's habit and her veil pushed back from her broad face, her hands open on the wet grass and little pools of moisture in her palms.

Luce must have been very young then.

But there was something frightening about the way the soldiers came on that last time, late at night, without talking or laughing or passing each other cigarettes and candy bars, sliding along in single file like that. Luce and Claire and Merciful smelled trouble. They got the girls up in their night-gowns and hustled them along the halls hung with threadbare tapestries and upstairs past all those dozens of closed-up rooms that no one ever set foot in. The girls had to make their way between heaps of tarnished candelabra and old Chinese lacquer trunks and stacked-up portraits of moldy French aristocrats. They left a clean trail of polished floor behind them where they moved through the dustbunnies by candlelight. Finally the sisters pushed the girls up the tiny secret staircase into one of the high turrets, and then they put a big bookcase full of Bibles in front of the little door.

This is the reason why Mama wakes up in the middle of the night saying Luce's name over and over. I put my mouth over hers and she lets the name slip into me and run its dark whip around my throat, until I can feel the pressure of my resisting heart. The wind which rattles through the open windows fills the lace curtains with ghosts. Her hands are so small and cold on the back of my neck I wonder if she is dying.

There are some things that someone or something has carved into your heart and which poison you. Sometimes you can get this thing very young, like Mama who was only sixteen when she lost Luce. She was sixteen and she felt her soul turn as blue-black as the bruises which were draped like a necklace on Luce's breast when they found her, a dark chain of hurt spilling down the length of her body.

When Mama married my daddy she looked into his face through her white veil there at the altar and she saw nothing at all, like the nothing that was in the faces of the soldiers coming uphill in the moonlight. Do you understand? In some way, I think this very blankness in his eyes reassured her.

La Ofrenda

Cherríe Moraga

Strange as it may seem, there is no other way to be sure. Completely sure. Well, you can never be completely sure but you can try and hold fast to some things. Smell is very important. Your eyes can fool you. You can see things that aren't there. But not smell. Smell remembers and tells the future. No lying about that.

Smell can make your heart crack open no matter how many locks you have wrapped 'round it. You can't see smell coming so it takes you off guard, unaware. Like love. That's why it can be your best friend or worst enemy depending on the state of your heart at the time.

Smell is home or loneliness.

Confidence or betrayal.

Smell remembers.

Tiny never went with women because she decided to. She'd always just say, "I follow my nose." And she did, and it got her ass nearly burned plenty of times too, when the scent happened to take her to the wrong side of town, or into a bed of the wife of someone she'd wish she hadn't in the morning.

She hated to fight. That was the other problem. She never stuck around for a fight. "The only blood I like," she'd say, "is what my hand digs out of a satisfied woman." We'd all tell Tiny to shut her arrogant mouth up and get her another drink.

Christina Morena stood in front of me in the First Holy Communion line. Then by Confirmation, she'd left most of us girls in the dust. Shot up and out like nobody's business. So, Christina, who everyone called Tina, turned into Tiny overnight and that's the name she took with her into "the life." Given her size, it was a better name to use than Christina and certainly better than mine, Dolores. Dottie, they used to call me years later in some circles, but it never stuck cuz I was the farthest thing from a freckled face bony-knee'd gabacha. Still, for a while, I tried it. Now I'm back to who I was before. Just Lolita. Stripped down. Not so different from those holy communion days, really.

When we were kids, teenagers, we came *this* close to making it with each other. *This* close. I don't know what would've happened if we had, but I couldn't even've dreamed of doing it then. Yeah, I loved Tiny probably more than I loved any human being on the face of the earth. I mean I loved her like the way you love familia, like they could do anything—steal, cheat, lie, murder and you'd still love them because they're your blood. Sangre. Tiny was my blood. My blood sister. Maybe that's why we didn't do it back then. It'd be like doing it with your mother. No, your sister. Tiny was my sister like no sister I've ever had, and she wanted me and I left her because she'd rather pretend she didn't and I was too stupid to smell out the situation for what it really was. I kept watching what was coming outta her damn mouth and there wasn't nothing there to hear. No words of love, commitment, tenderness. You know, luna de miel stuff. There was just her damn solid square body like a tank in the middle of my face, with tears running down her cheeks and her knees squeezed together like they were nailed shut on that toilet, her pants like a rubber band wrapped down around her ankles, and I ran from her as fast as my cola could take me.

"Fuck fuck chinga'o, man, fuck!"

"Tina . . ." I can barely hear myself.

"Tiny. The name's Tiny."

"What're you doin' in here?"

"I'm crying, you faggot. That's what you want, isn't it? To see the big bad bitch cry? Well, go get your rocks off somewhere else."

"I don't have rocks."

"In your head."

But I never loved anyone like I loved Tiny. Nobody. Not one of those lean white or sleek black ladies that spread their legs for me and my smooth-talking. There was blood on my hands and not from reaching into those women, but from Tiny's hide. From my barrio's hide. Cha Cha's Place, where you only saw my ass when the sophisticated college girls had fucked with my mind one too many times. That's something Tiny would have said. We weren't meant to be lovers, only sisters. But being a sister ain't no part-time occupation.

"Lolita Lebron," that's what they used to call me at Cha Cha's. Of course, they didn't even know who Lolita was until I came in with the story of her with the guys and the guns taking on the whole pinche U.S. Congress. They'd say, "Hey, Lolita, how goes the revolution?" And then they'd all start busting up and I'd take it cuz I knew they loved me, even respected what I was doing. Or maybe it was only Tiny who respected me, and all the others had to treat me right cuz of her. Tiny used to say her contribution to La Causa was to keep the girlfriends of the Machos happy while they were being too revolutionary to screw.

But it was me she wanted. And I needed my original home girl more than I needed any other human being alive to this day. Growing up is learning to go without. Tiny and me . . . we grew up too fast.

"Do you think Angie could want me?"

So there we are, fifteen years later, me sitting on the edge of her bed, playing with the little raised parts of the chenille bedspread while my sister there is taking off all her damn clothes, tossing them on the bed, until she's standing there bare ass naked in front of me.

"Look at me."

I can't look up.

"Lola."

I'm still playing with the balls of the bedspread.

"Look at me. C'mon, I gotta know."

"Tiny, give me a break, man. This is too cold. It's fuckin' scientific. No one looks at people this way."

"You do."

She was right. So, I check her out. There I am, staring at her with my two good eyes, the blue one and the brown one, and I knew she wanted my one hundred percent and honest opinion, that she could count on me for that since we were little . . . so I sat there looking at her for a long time.

"C'mon, man, does it hafta take so long? Jus' answer me."

The blue and the brown eye were working at this one, working hard. I try to isolate each eye, see if I come up with different conclusions depending on which eye and which color I'm working with. Figure one is the European view, the other the Indian.

Tiny goes for her pants, "Fuck you."

And then I smell her, just as she reaches over me.

Her breast falling onto my shoulder, something softening.

A warm bruised stone.

I inhale. Grab her arm.

"No, wait. Let me look at you."

She pulls back against the dresser, holds the pants against her belly, then lets them drop. She's absolutely beautiful. Not magazine beautiful but thirty-three-years-old and Mexican beautiful. The dresser with the mirror is behind her. I know that dresser. For years now. It didn't change, but Tiny . . . she did. The dresser is blond. "Blond furniture," very popular among Mexicanos in the fifties. We are the children of the fifties. But the fifties have gone and went, and in the meantime my Christina Morena went and changed herself into a woman. And in front of this blond dresser is brown

Christina. Christina Morena desnuda sin a stitch on her body, and she looks like her mother and my mother, with legs like tree trunks and a panza that rolls around her ombligo como puro miel. And breasts . . . breasts I want to give back to her, compartir con ella que nos llena a las dos.

"Well . . . ?" she asks.

And it had never occurred to me that we had grown up. The hair below her belly is the same color as her head. A deep black.

Denso.

Ocolto como un nido escondido.

Un hogar distante,

aguardándome.

It didn't stop there. She needed me to touch her, that's all. Is that so much to ask a person? Angie and her wouldn't last long. Tiny didn't let her touch her. She never let any of 'em touch her.

"Never?"

"Never."

"I don't get it. What do you do then?"

"I do it to them."

"But I mean do you . . . y'know?"

"Get off? Yeah. Sure."

"How?"

"Rubbing. Thinking."

"Thinking. Thinking about what?"

"Her. How she's feeling."

"You ever think about yourself?"

"No one's home."

"What?"

"I don't gotta picture, you know what I mean? There's nobody to be. No me to be . . . not in bed, anyway."

So, I put my hands inside her. I did. I put them all the way inside her and like a fuckin' shaman I am working magic on her, giving her someone to be.

"Fuck fuck chinga'o, man, fuck."

"Shut up," I say.

"What?"

"Don't say shit."

"But . . ."

"Shhh." I press my fingers against her lips.

"Don't say nothing, Tiny." Open your mouth and tell me something else . . .

She smells like copal between the legs. Tiny, Tina who stood in front of me in the first holy communion line smells like

fucking copal
sweet earth sap
oozing out of every pore
that dark bark tree
flesh kissed
I couldn't kiss her, only between the legs
Where the mouth there never cussed
where the lips never curled
into snarls, smoked cigarettes, spit
phlegm into passing pale stubbled faces
mouthing dagger
dyke
jota
mal
flor
I kissed her where she had never spoken
where she had never sung
where . . .

And then we are supposed to forget. Forget the women who we discover there between the sheets, between the thighs, lies, cries.

But some things you don't forget
smell
I close my eyes
and I am rubbing and thinking
rubbing and thinking
rubbing and remembering
what this feels like, to find

my body, una vega
anhelosa, endless
lleno
de deseo
Donde 'stá ella
que me regaló mi cuerpo
como una ofrenda a mí misma?
Ella
Lejana
Una vez . . . mía
I open my eyes
. . . Desaparecida.

I would've married Tiny myself if she would've let me. I would've. I swear to it. But, I was relieved when she put on her pants and told me to get out. I was relieved because I wouldn't have to work for the rest of my life loving someone. Tiny.

But I was willing to stay. This time I wasn't going nowhere. I mean, where was there to go, really? The girl was family and I knew her. I knew her and still loved her, so where was there to go? You spend your whole life looking for something that's just a simple matter of saying, "Okay, so I throw my lot in with this one." This one woman y ya!

Tiny knew she wouldn't last long.

She was already telling me in her thirties how tired she was fighting. And then I read it, right there in the *L.A. Times*. All these women, lesbians, who never had babies, getting cancer. They never mention Tiny's name, but Tiny was there, among the childless women, among the dead.

I thought, what's this shit? Women don't use their breasts like biology mandates, and their breasts betray them? Is this the lesbian castigo? AIDS for our brothers, cancer for us? Hate thinking like this, hate thinking it's all a conspiracy to make us join the fucking human race.

I burn copal.

Her name rising up with the smoke,

dissolving into the ash morning sky.
Her flesh, softening like the sap
turned rock, returning liquid
to the earth. Her scent inciting . . .
memory.
I inscribe her name, too.
Tattooed ink in the odorless
flesh of this page.

I, who have only given my breast
to the hungry and grown,
the female and starved,
the women.

I, who have only given my breast to the women.

The Waking State

Gerry Pearlberg

She had a reputation. Even now, when I say her name, people tell me how terrified or obsessed, repulsed or fascinated they were by her. Everyone knew about her back then, everyone but me. When we danced that night, she was lewd. I wasn't sure I liked the way she touched or talked to me. It wasn't disrespectful, just sleazy.

Her dormitory cubicle was like a little church, a shrine to perversion. She caught me scanning the titles on her shelf: all sex books. Some I recognized by a kind of sexual osmosis. Others were new to me, like a neat row of distant, wriggling mirages capable of doing damage, but also holding promise.

We showered together down the hall, and when we returned to her room, she told me she'd be right back. "Check out the books," she said, "and see if anything strikes your fancy." Her brief disappearance was calculated. It gave me time to absorb the implications of being in this room, wrapped in her towel, reading her well-worn copy of the *Leatherman's Safety Guide*.

When she returned, she showed me her black velvet "bag of tricks," explaining the purpose of each exotic or mundane item it contained. As she spoke, my mind began ticking like a logic clock. Fantasy was one thing, but what did I really know about this person, anyway? I had work on Monday. Dinner with Mom on Tuesday. Who I was and what I was doing here did not seem to reconcile, yet I was transfixed. She must have known she did not need to push. We climbed to the top bunk of her double-decker bed and had vanilla sex. I came hard just feeling her fingers gliding on me and thinking about that velvet bag lying like a wishing well on the floor below us.

Early the next morning, we lay in bed together, chatting before she left for class. She told me about her lovers, women in Boston and New York who'd ask her to tie their hands above their heads, make them panic with longing, and eventually, if they were lucky, to fuck them, let them fuck themselves, make them fuck her. "I admire bottoms," she said wistfully, "I really wish I could trust someone enough to let them do those things to me." I rubbed the thorny crown of her new crew cut, her warm and vulnerable head like a bird's nest in my hand, and wondered what it would be like to take control of someone that way, to set up the field of their fantasy, plant its seeds, nourish its crops, and finally plow through its maze of delicate but deeply set roots, nerve endings of desire.

"I want you again," she said, breaking in on these new thoughts, "but not like last night. Can you meet me back here at lunchtime?"

I arrived promptly at noon. This time, fear competed with anticipation. I could claim no excuses for being there: it was, after all, the middle of the day, and there was no loud music, no bar atmosphere, and no beer to create a ready context for this visit. My erotic intentions were undiluted. I was there in the full bloom of the Waking State.

She was wearing a black leather jacket. I wore a chain necklace with delicate multicolored metallic links. Anywhere else, it would have seemed innocuous, even cutesy. Here, it was loaded. She noticed it instantly, fingering it in a knowing way. We started necking. The smell of her jacket was a fetish cologne. I ran my fingers along its snaps, buckles, and loops.

This simple paraphernalia created an ambivalent, insistent friction between my body and brain.

After a few minutes, she stiffened and, taking my wrists in her hands, planted my arms at my sides. "I'm famished," she whispered, staring me down, "but for what, present company excluded?" She bit her lip in mock concentration, running her fingers lightly up and down my forearms. "A hero would suit the occasion, don't you think?" she said at last, her eyes twinkling, "Go and get me a hero, a hero with everything on it."

I asked if I could wear her jacket, feeling able to leave only with this part of her, a part of this. I wanted her skin on me when I exited her domain to fulfill her wish. I would wear it like a visceral embodiment of her command. She obliged me, lifting the heavy coat around my shoulders, kissing my throat and the base of my skull. I ran my hands along her bare arms and white cotton T-shirt. She seemed so fresh and naked this way. When I leaned into her, she sent me out with a caustic smile.

I felt conspicuously queer and overtly aroused walking down the sunny New England street to the sub shop across the square. I glanced in store windows, catching quick reflections of myself. It was like seeing another person there, someone familiar, but not quite known. In the glass I witnessed the physical embodiment of a deeply planted wish, a tulip bulb blooming in the dark. My heart was a bright penny twitching at the bottom of a fast-moving stream. I wondered if anyone on this all-American street could read the hidden meaning of the jacket and this errand, or whether they perceived the reconstruction of mundane experience that these things implied.

I wore the jacket while she ate her hero hungrily, tearing off pieces of bread and meat and cheese and feeding them to me as if I were a tender creature of metal and hide sidling against her for sustenance. I too felt hunger, but mine bit well below the belt. I wanted more than meat from her hands; I longed for her blood on my lips, her fingers in my mouth, her knee between my legs, unlikely things in unexpected places bringing pleasurable discomfort and reassuring dissonance. Watching her eat, wearing her leather skin, the experience of waiting became a sexual entity all its own.

Eventually, she pushed the hero aside, pulled me slowly toward her, and kissed me again, erotically aloof. Once more, she touched the chain around my neck, coolly signaling that the games had officially begun. We deep kissed, and when my tongue found its way into her mouth, she held it firmly between her teeth. Till it almost hurt. Till it hurt a little. Till it really hurt. She looked me in the eye while doing this, till I began to hum, to moan, resonating like a tiny bee hanging on an orchid's blazing crimson cliff. Her hand went down my pants and began stroking my clit; all the while she restrained my aching tongue in the prison of her white hot teeth. Throbbing hard, my mouth became a second vortex of sensation, shimmering against a perfect moment of intimacy, stillness, and possession. A sudden orgasm bit through me like a steel-jawed eel. She held my tongue till the pounding subsided, then released, generating a second dose of sharp decompression. I slumped against her, exhausted. Running my teeth lightly over my tender tongue, I pressed a long string of bright aftershocks through my blasting cunt.

I was late for my ride back to the city. She watched me collect myself. She watched me pee. She took her jacket back. We exchanged telephone numbers, smiles, and a long kiss in the doorway. She plucked gently at my collar before I turned to leave. Genius of the small, irrevocable gesture.

A few weeks later, she called me at work. I told her I'd bought myself a motorcycle jacket. She sounded flattered when she congratulated me, and advised me on its proper care and treatment. She mentioned a special cream that would soften the leather. "You'll appreciate the way it tastes when I make you lick it off *my* jacket," she said, inducing my first long-distance blush.

She was coming to town for the weekend. Did I want to get together? She could bring her bag of tricks. Two sides of an alarm clock went off inside me, tiny hammers rapidly banging opposing bells. One was desire, a flash flood between my legs. This I had expected. The other was fear. Fear of her, fear of the feelings she aroused in me, and fear of her intrusion upon my "real" life. Her offer was an earthquake, dislodging the bridges between awake and asleep, good sex and bad. My inner fault line tore open before me, violently dividing my body's terrain from that of reason, intellect, and self-restraint. It cut right through the Waking State which I'd called home, and which had somehow accommodated within its generous borders both the instinct toward and the terror of the sexual end of the world where mythical beasts take mysterious forms, churning whole oceans to fire. I bit my lip and chose my ground. My apartment had such thin walls. My mother would die if she ever knew. My roommates would never let me live it down. Besides, the things she did were well beyond illegal in the Waking State to which I pledged ambivalent allegiance when I told her "No."

How the Butch Does It: 1959

Merril Mushroom

1. The Butch Combs Her Hair

The butch combs her hair. She combs it at home in private. This is the functional combing. She stands in front of the mirror. Holding the comb between her thumb and first two fingers, she slaps the flat of it against her other palm, then places the comb down on the edge of the sink.

She leans forward and peers at her reflection, flicks her first three fingers through the front of her hair, pulls a curl down over her forehead. She tilts her head sideways and looks at her reflection from beneath lowered eyelids. The butch is sultry. The butch is arrogant. The butch is tough. She picks up the bottle of Vitalis and pours a generous amount into her palm, rubs her hands together, and strokes the lotion through her hair, rubbing carefully to be sure that each strand is well-coated, yet not greasy. Then she turns on the water and wets her hair with her hands. Now she is ready to begin.

The butch lifts the comb from the side of the sink. She stretches both her arms forward, then bends her elbows. Now! One-two-three-four, she strokes the comb carefully through one side of her hair, following the path of the teeth with the flat fingers of her other hand, barely touching herself as she smooths. The pattern of hair wings back above her ears, back, back, all the way to the middle of her head. Then five-six, the sides are lifted on the comb to fall in a wave over the top.

Okay, one-two-three-four, comb the other side in the same manner, five-six, over the top. Now back to the first side again, going straight up to the top this time, seven-eight-nine-ten; then comb the other side in the same pattern. The butch pats her hair as she combs it, pressing it gently into place. She admires her reflection, tilting her head this way and that. Then she lifts the comb to vertical, places the edge of the teeth carefully at the top of the middle of the back of her head, and draws it precisely down the center, pushing the ends of her hair into the furrow, creating a longitudinal cleft above her neck—a perfect duck's ass.

Now the butch concentrates on the top of her hair. She uses the comb expertly to settle the waves into a pompadour. When she is finally satisfied with the effect, she pulls the teeth of the comb carefully down through the center and over her forehead, then uses her fingers to push, pull, and tease the front into one very casual-looking lock that curls over her brow.

The butch makes eyes at her reflection. She is ready to go out. She is satisfied with her appearance.

2. *The Butch Combs Her Hair*

The butch combs her hair. She combs it in public. This is the "show" combing, done primarily for effect. The butch shows off. She draws the comb from her pocket smoothly, holding it between the thumb and index finger of the dominant hand. She stretches both arms out forward, then crooks her elbows, ready to begin.

The butch spreads her legs, balancing her weight on the balls of her feet. She holds the comb ready to her hair, the fingers of her other hand extended, ready to smooth stray ends if necessary. She leans over to the side, bending away from the side she will be combing, tilting her head toward the comb. Her elbows jut until they are almost horizontal. She squints, concentrates, and then she lowers the comb. She will not comb her hair just yet—there is something more she wishes to do to show off:

With the first two fingers of the hand that does not hold the comb, the butch pulls a cigarette out of the pack that is either in her breast pocket or rolled up into the sleeve of her T-shirt. She places the white cylinder between her teeth, closes her lips around it, and rolls her head back just a little. She pulls out her Zippo, flicks the flame on and ready to the end of the cigarette in one expert motion, inhales deeply, then snaps the Zippo closed with her thumb, palms the lighter, and curls the index finger of that same hand around the cigarette, withdrawing it from her mouth. Still holding the cigarette, she slips the lighter into her hip pocket, pushing it down with her thumb, then grasps the cigarette firmly between her thumb and index fingertips. She places it back between her lips, then swiftly combs her hair, four strokes on each side, then two, then the top. Skillfully, seemingly carelessly, the butch fingers her pompadour and casual curl into place. Then, with a flourish, using her comb followed by the fingertips of her other hand, she creases the duck's ass down the middle of the back.

All this time, smoke from the cigarette in her mouth has been curling up into her face. Although she has squinted her eyes, it was only done in concentration for her task. At no time did she close her eyes against the smoke, nor did she cough or gasp for breath. The butch is tough, stoic. Only at the completion of the combing does she remove the cigarette from between her lips, and she does not draw in a deep breath immediately thereafter.

Now the butch returns her comb to its pocket. She does not reach up to check on her hair, to make sure that all is as it should be. She trusts that she looks wonderful, that her hair is impeccably in place, perfectly styled. She is satisfied with her performance.

3. The Butch Plays Pool

The butch selects her cue. She eyes the sticks that line the wall, looking every one over from end to tip. The four fingers of each hand are thrust into her hip pockets, thumbs resting outside the fabric beneath the swell of her belly, causing her elbows to jut out from her sides. She tosses her head and throws her shoulders back, nods once, then pulls one hand from her pocket to reach, grasp, and take the stick of her choice from the wall. Now her other hand comes up to stroke fingers down the length of the wood. She feels the weight of the stick, tests its balance. As she sights down it, she strokes it along her cheek. She smiles, moving her tongue slowly back and forth behind her slightly parted lips.

Now the butch sets the butt of the stick against the floor and straightens out the elbow of the hand she holds it with, turning her arm slightly so that her triceps bulge and ripple. Then, giving the stick a little toss into the air, she catches it neatly at the middle and strides over to the pool table where she picks up the little cube of blue chalk. She blows across the top of it, looking around the bar, lips pursed into a kiss for the one whose eye she catches. She lowers the chalk deliberately, grinds it suddenly and intensely across the end of the cue stick, rubs it around until tiny blue grains shower from it. Gently, she blows away the excess, then leans the stick up against the side of the table.

Now the butch reaches into her breast pocket and pulls out a half-full soft pack of Camels. She gives it a sharp flick of the wrist, and two cigarettes shoot out of the pack ½ inch and ¼ inch respectively. Raising the pack slowly to her mouth, the butch takes the end of the longer cigarette between her lips and pulls it free. She tucks the pack back into her breast pocket; then pulls her Zippo from her hip pocket. She crooks her elbow, raising the lighter. Slowly, deliberately, she flicks open the lid so that it rings, thumbs the wheel smartly, and dips the end of her Camel into the flame.

Inhaling deeply, loudly, she snaps the Zippo shut and returns it to her hip pocket. She grips the cigarette between her thumb and first two fingers and takes several more deep drags, blowing smoke out sharply. Then she places the cigarette on the edge of the pool table.

The butch bends and lifts the wooden rack from beneath the table. She runs her fingers suggestively around the lower point of the triangle, grins, raises one eyebrow. Suddenly she flips the rack into the air, catches it, raps it against the palm of her other hand, and sets it down smartly in its proper place with the top point just touching the silver mark. She picks up her cigarette again, smokes some more, then drops the butt to the floor and grinds it out with the toe of her boot. She places her middle finger on the quarter that her challenger has placed on the edge of the pool table, hesitates for just one moment, then slides the quarter off the edge of the table, snaps it up against her thumb and spins it smoothly into the slot.

The balls crash down. The butch pulls them from the tray quickly, four at a time, two in each hand, banging them onto the tabletop inside the rack. She plucks a few of the balls out with her fingertips, swiftly, setting them down with sharp noises, expertly rearranging them so that they alternate striped and solid with the 8-ball in the center. That done, she grips the rack, pauses for a moment, then snaps the balls into place with a sharp crack and smoothly lifts the rack up and away, leaving the balls in a perfect triangle on the surface of the table.

The butch picks up the cue ball and carries it to the other end of the table. She spins about, bending backward slightly and leading with her shoulder. She sets the white sphere down with a flourish, holds her stick out at arm's length for a moment, then takes her stance. Turning sideways toward the table, she spreads her legs, bends her knees, and finds her balance. She raises her stick, sights along it, then lowers it. She rearranges the cue ball, then rearranges her stance, aware of the many eyes on her. Aware of the women who are watching her every move, she poses, then turns back to the table and, quickly, gracefully, projecting all strength and energy, she places her left hand on the tabletop, bends at the hips, rests the cue stick in the crease between her thumb and forefinger, and wallops the cue ball with the end of the stick. The cue ball plummets across the table and smashes into the side of the triangle of balls just next to the upper point. With a tremendous crash, pool balls scatter across the table, and two solid-colored balls with low numbers roll into the corner pockets.

The butch looks over at her opponent, her face expressionless except for one slightly lifted eyebrow. She casually picks up the chalk, and rubs it over the end of her cue stick. She does not smile, but she is very pleased with her performance. She nods magnanimously to her opponent, then turns back to the table to take her next shot.

But first, she lights another Camel.

Mighty Muff

Mary Wings

You're good at it.
You know it.

You're good at it. You know it. It's not just that nobody
has ever complained; it's that you like it so much yourself,
you get so charged you know that every thrill communicates,
streaming out your pores and jiggling through your fingertips, an exciting addition to your well-developed technique.
She's almost always as wet as you are.

Your batteries never run out, although one-night stands
hold no more interest for you. It's the second time when you
hit your stride, and the third time when you know how to
hit the surprises. But there's no second time without a first.

She saved you a lot of guesswork the way she looked at
you across the dance floor. You had heard stories about her.
She was a great guitar player. Her last lover was a lawyer,
a plumber, a Girl Scout leader, a film distributor, an heiress,
a political heavy. It didn't matter. A mutual acquaintance
said that she came here often. She danced with her feet in
one place, moving her arms like a woman treading water,
her head tilting back occasionally, her mouth gulping for air.

Until she started eyeing you. It was no problem dancing;
you could do a disconnected swim and close your eyes to
match hers. It was no problem going to bed together. It was
late. It was a turn on it was her house.

It's winter and you wrap yourselves in parkas and scarves walking out the door. She lives on the ground floor.

She's poor and beautiful, a fairy-tale princess fallen on hard times. She's proud; she's patched a hole in the sofa with matching material. Her kitchen of mismatched cups is clean; she offers you fruit. She's washed the underside of her garbage can lid.

Her living room features a mahogany highboy, a raised chest of drawers, veneered with inlaid rosewood flowers, drawer pulls in the shape of lions' heads, the whole thing resting on turnip ball feet. It was my grandmother's, she explains, walking past the monstrosity to close the curtains.

She talks about herself. She worked in the library and lost her job. She has unemployment insurance. Reading materials are piled on her desk. She takes her time with life, with you.

You ask her. She doesn't play guitar. Let's cut the small talk, she says, and get to bed.

You're thin, a muscled reed, you climb on top of her and you're not heavy. Your hips move and something in the middle of her responds. Your hips dance and her skin comes with you a quarter inch and when you don't expect it she's crying out and grabbing you so you ride her harder in response; she's clutching you and something like a wail emerges. A sound too big. It's almost empty. A sound like a siren on its way to a patient. It makes you feel alone. Her fingernails retract from your skin.

Afterwards you look at her head on the pillow. Her face is pretty. Like a picture, like a present.

It's morning and you're not in bed together anymore. You get up and she's shorter than you remembered. You sit on a stuffed vinyl chair and wrap your feet around the chrome legs and watch her make coffee.

She's from New Jersey. Her father lives in Idaho. She has a useless master's degree in ancient history. She has two sisters and an allergy to cats. She broke the lawyer's heart; she became bored with the plumber. The Girl Scout leader was a figment of misinformed gossip. The others were just pit stops along the way. She doesn't play any stringed instrument. And . . . she doesn't come. She doesn't have orgasms. Never has had. She knows there are techniques, devices, masturbation groups, guided fantasies, vibrators, sexual aids. She's never tried them. She's satisfied unsatisfied. She says.

You don't know what to say at first. Then you say all kinds of things. You say it's an opportunity for sex without beginnings or endings. You say you sort of knew anyway. You say that it doesn't matter. But you think you can fix anything. You like women who are flawed.

It's time for you to go to work. She walks you to the door; you leave each other with kisses that are now open-ended promises. You wonder at the softness of her brown eyes. You wonder if she masturbates.

The next day she calls you. Before she hangs up she breathes in deeply, a question she doesn't want to ask. Instead she tells you it was a wonderful night. She never felt like that before. Quite that close. You feel her waiting on the phone; a silence travels over the line.

You say, "I'll see you tomorrow. And I plan to keep you busy all night." No beginnings, no endings. But before you go to her house you hit a sleazy side of town and walk into a store that only displays plywood in the window. You choose from among many devices that are mostly made in Taiwan.

It's small. It's big. It has a handle. It's handleless. It's hard plastic. It's soft rubber. It's black, white, pink, flesh colored.

It's shaped like a teddy bear, like a Virgin Mary, like a penis. It comes with and without veins. It coughs and throttles like a motorcycle. It hums like a sewing machine. It purrs like a honeybee making its way between your juicy lips. You buy the abstracted penis model in soft rubber, black, with the honeybee song. There's an extension cord and remote control with three speeds. The batteries are not included.

You go to her house. The curtains are still open. To the

right the mahogany highboy is topped with a blown glass vase and badly bunched white iris buds. She opens the door wearing a jogging suit. In no time you are both on the floor. There you take off your parka and scarf. She's easier; there's nothing under the jogging suit. You're sure she hasn't been jogging at all.

Your fingers are a melody, traveling up and down her sides, just deciphering ribs under her smooth, light skin. Tempo is picked up with breathing. A pinched nipple is a surprised counterpoint and then a contrast of tone in the sweetest of kisses on her neck, a verbal suggestion to move to the bed.

Once there you prime her slowly; she's tired, a massage that starts at her fingertips and ends at her toes where you suck the tiny digitals one by one. She's moaning.

You turn her on her back and as her head rolls over, her face gives you a confident knowing smile. You lean back until her lips wobble and then you start again. You are having a wonderful time. She is too.

You tell her about the toy you've bought. Crinkle of plastic bag, memory of mom with paper cut-out dolls on a rainy Saturday afternoon.

But this doll is different; it hums, and after you've sucked her sufficiently, between her legs, you let her lips accustom themselves to rubber.

When you turn it on you both laugh, but her smile disappears as her hips move and try to place the thing where she needs it. She concentrates, you see it between her eyebrows, you feel it in her legs. It's a Zen mathematics problem, it doesn't add up if you look at the numbers. She's working it out. Seeking, giving it up, it comes back by itself, she looks it in the face, it dives away.

Then she just wants the vibrator inside and you guide the rubber tip but it's big and you can't find her hole, so your fingers go looking first, and slowly push the rubber thing between the folds and just past the taut spot where it seems to sink and be swallowed inside her. You work it carefully, following wordless instructions of her voice.

You turn it, teasing the entrance which grabs or pummels the interior; she tries to spit it out. Then a spasmodic speed develops, your hand jerks, fusing with the thing, beating inside her soft cylinder.

She's getting her fingernails into your back again, and then she's yelling. Like a witness to a traffic accident. Like a woman who's about to miss the bus.

In the morning you sit on the stuffed vinyl chrome-legged chair and she makes coffee and you get the same mug. She's depressed about finding a job. She's getting cold. Auto exhaust from the street coats her windows and she must clean them often. She wants to go to the country. She wants a job, a faculty position in ancient history. She wants a lot of things she can't have.

It's time for you to go to work. She walks you to the door, her hands riding your ass, your buns moving back and forth across her palms. You earn many kisses in the hallway. The sun is shining and you realize that her first-floor apartment gathers no sunlight.

Outside, a wind works its way down the front of your parka. It can do that because you've forgotten your scarf. You start walking back to her, your legs enjoying memories that grow stronger as you approach her front window.

She's drawn the curtains already. You can see the white irises on top of the highboy and her black bathrobed figure underneath them. You think she's going to rearrange the flowers; you think they were grouped too close together.

You consider tapping on the window, but you notice that she's not reaching up, but bending over slightly at the waist. She has the vibrator and you think, she's going to use her grandmother's highboy as a hiding place. And you're right.

You watch as she slowly slips a lion's-head drawer pull from one of the veneered drawers between her fingers. You see her elbow jerk; the old mahogany has warped and shrunk, the drawer has stuck. But she gets it open with a sharp pull. She will put the dildo in it, you're thinking.

But you don't know what to think when she opens the drawer. Her windows are clean enough of exhaust to afford you a perfect view of the contents and your eyes are sharp enough to see what lies waiting inside the drawer.

There are an assortment of things. They are small. They are big. They have handles or are handleless. There are teddy bears, Virgin Marys and penises with and without veins. They are pink, black, white, flesh colored. Soft plastic, hard rubber, hard plastic, soft rubber.

You don't need your scarf anymore. You hurry down the street, hoping not to miss your bus.

Dry Fire
Cathy Lewis

At night I lie on the couch in my polyester blues and I dry fire. I stare down the stainless-steel barrel and line up my front sight. *Southern Living* loses its *i*'s, *Emergency Medicine* its *e*'s and the tabby in the Morris chair loses her tail. I turn to the TV and shoot Road Runner. I want Wile Coyote to hold up a sign saying *Thanks Officer* but he never does. Five days ago I shot at a man who robbed a convenience store and missed. Now I dry fire and hope for a second chance. Maybe tonight.

Nine o'clock check-on Sergeant Bollero pulls his waxy mustache while reading *BOLOS*. Today's bulletin sheet has an assortment of twelve robbery, rape and shooting suspects. My zone partner spits tobacco juice in a Styrofoam cup then tosses an envelope across the table. This came for you, he says. It's a paper target with holes, but not on the silhouette: Swiss cheese on white. *Not bad for a girl* is penciled in on the top. I ball it up and shoot it back in Camp's face. A roomful of laughs and whistles ricochets. Red-faced, Camp spits in the cup then looks back up at Bollero. Keys are flying through the air as he assigns vehicles. After the last toss, Bollero twists his mustache and shouts *Cuidado!* Arrive alive.

———

At the beginning of each shift I stop at a convenience store for candy. Fifty-nine cents for cherry Life Savers. Little black threads on the clerk's lip quiver as she stuffs my dollar bill into the register. She asks if I'm surprised to see her back so soon. At all, I say. Fading shades of purple surround her left eye. She hands over the change and calls as I'm walking out the door. You will catch him won't you? Right then I'm sorrier than ever that I missed him. I visualize his ruddy face as I'm lining up my sights dead center in his forehead—click.

I chomp on the Life Savers while en route to an accident with injuries. As I step out of the car the radio on my belt clanks against my aluminum nightstick. Immediately, I'm reminded mothers' screams are more piercing than sirens. My baby she wails. That man ran over my baby. I pat the man down then take his license. On or about his person is the odor of alcoholic beverage so I put him in the back of the squad car then get my jump bag from the trunk. Upgrade that ambulance I tell dispatch. The nine-year-old boy is posturing like a penguin, rigid limbs, hands and feet rotated outward. I open his airway with my finger and clear a clump of phlegm-filled blood. I look beneath his eyelids. Pressure from escaped blood forces them to pop up like spongy marshmallows. Cerebral fluid is dripping from his ears. Paramedics arrive and pack sandbags around him as if his head might pop and flood delta style. They tape his forehead to a long spine board, load him and go.

Camp is directing traffic while I canvass the area for witnesses. Traffic homicide arrives taking pictures and marking off paces. Two witnesses say he lost control and drove up on the sidewalk hitting the boy. In the back of the squad car I shake the guy's shoulder. Wake up. He starts to cry. I didn't see him he says. Then he asks me for a cigarette. On the first sobriety test he wobbles down the line and falls as he tries to pivot. You're under arrest.

Miranda sounds like a childhood prayer I know by heart and recite, cuffing him as quickly as I used to cross myself before dinner blessing as a child. I take his keys and impound his Mustang. Come on honey, he cries, give a guy a break.

The bicycle I load into the trunk is twisted geometry. It's necessary evidence if the boy dies. In seconds the entire vehicle is rocking. Sober truth has sunk in and my new arrest, my 10-15, starts banging his head on the Plexiglas. Stop it. I slam the lid. Camp lets traffic roll again. Appreciate the assistance I tell him. He nods then spits tobacco juice on the prisoner's window.

Hands tell me everything I think as I uncuff him. Watching hands can mean your life. Ink rolls smoothly onto his fingertips and just as fluidly onto the card. It's the signature of a nail biter who doesn't trim his cuticles. The interdigital pads of his palm are soft and pink. On his finger is a white line where a wedding band used to be. He's probably a middle-management type who can't handle stress or change. Hard copy I pick up in dispatch shows it's his second DWI in three weeks. While I'm still flipping my traffic template trying to reconstruct the accident on paper, he'll have bonded out with the plastic in his wallet.

I feel the promise of another humid night as I lie on the couch taking aim at the ceiling fan, firing upon the blades in rapid succession. I simulate a reload and drop five feet to a new target. Dan Rather gets it in the forehead. A clean Hindu-red hole. Philodendron leaves fall as I fire. They join the dead ones on the floor. Goldfish in the Matisse print float belly up and the tabby loses her tail for the nine thousandth time. Lowering front sights to the coffee table I shoot: white ice in a glass of Mountain Dew, a granola wrapper, the popcorn kernels left from dinner, *The Color Purple*.

9 P.M. check-on, Bollero points at me. Your robbing rapist struck again early yesterday morning. My throat goes dry. All of me feels dry except for the space between my breasts where a cold sweat can't be absorbed by my vest. Bollero passes his picture and rap sheet around again. Maybe he's

trying to rub our faces in it. I look at the ugly mug and scraggly beard that does a poor job of covering up acne scars. He's got the vapid look of someone who did too many drugs in high school. Twenty years later he's the guy tearing up our zone. I toss the photos to Camp who's busy tugging on his briefs. Every time his wife goes out of town and leaves him with laundry he shrinks his BVD's and comes to work especially testy. He yanks a pen out of his pocket and pokes a hole in the forehead of the picture then tosses it back to me. That's where I would have hit him, he says. Pressure is where you separate the men from the girls.

Of the fifty reasons why I might have missed, Camp attributes it to my sex. Bollero's voice seems like a distant buzzing in my ears until keys come flying toward my face. *Cuidado!* Arrive alive.

Is a .38 special a good gun? The clerk's thinking about buying one. Next Tuesday she starts her first judo class. I look at her greenish-yellow wrists and hands, as I drop change into them. Ecchymosis to the mid-forearm, the doctor called them at the hospital, four quarter size marks. What they really are: the outline of a stranger's hand pushing until her wrists hemorrhaged from the inside. She hesitates, her eyes moist as she looks down and drops the change into the register. I never really thanked you, she says, for how good you were to me that night. I pick up the Life Savers and touch the tip of her fingers lightly. It's okay.

Between the *Play Lotto* and *Ice 99c* window signs, I see Camp sitting in the parking lot. He drives up as I'm walking toward my patrol vehicle, his hairy arm out the window. A brown stream lands on the pavement in front of me. Getting yourself a new girlfriend, he asks. Hey, she just might swing your way after getting the hell banged out of her.

I turn, lean in on the driver's side until our noses touch. I hear him swallow some tobacco juice. Camp, I whisper, buy some boxer shorts.

———

Outside the emergency room is a deserted hallway leading to the morgue. I shake out my raincoat, then sit on my briefcase to finish an attempted robbery report. Two juveniles broke a seventy-six-year-old lady's hip, shoving her down in hopes of getting the six dollars and twelve cents in her purse. Honey, I just wasn't gonna let those thugs have my bag. Don't care if there weren't nothing but a dime, those hoodlums weren't gettin' it. And they didn't. She lay there clutching it to her bosom with pain and dignity. Her suspect descriptions were sketchy and the sad thing is we probably won't catch them, I think, as I'm writing the report.

Squeaky sounds of a gurney arouse my interest so I stop writing and look up. Slowly it comes toward me. The lump under the sheet becomes more defined and it's small, child size. It seems like a dream, sounds of mechanical whimpering and deliberate slowness becoming real only when I grab the aluminum rail. Officer? The orderly stops and waits for me as I lift the sheet and look at the poor boy's head. His eyes, devoid of swelling, lie beneath flat closed lids. The rigid little hands are now loose and there's a secret plastic decoder ring on his finger, like the kind you get from saving Bazooka bubble gum wrappers. I drop the sheet and walk into the wet night. Rain seems to have picked up and I feel it on my face and try to wipe it away. But it keeps falling.

I shoot Gilligan's hat, Lovey's pearls, Ginger's mole. Mary Ann's coconut cream pies are filled with lead, so is Skipper's belly. Waiting to terrorize the *Brady Bunch* I dry fire the *T* in *Time*, the double *i*'s and *z*'s in *Jazz Musician*. Propped in the corner is my saxophone and I zero in on the keys. Next time I won't miss. I visualize a clean shoot, steady arm, smooth trigger, pull—click.

In 9 P.M. check-on, I visualize again the face I'll convert to Hinduism. Bollero starts reading. He's picking hairs off the tip of his tongue, the result of a biting habit whenever his mustache gets too long. Camp scans the room for something to spit in and directs a stream into a recycling bin next to the Coke machine. He's got a cranky look, and it's evident his wife is still out of town. Bollero tosses me a set of keys. *Cuidado!* Arrive alive. We hit the streets.

She reaches for a roll of Life Savers. Not tonight, I say. Give me those Dutch Masters cigars. The Cadet pack. She tells me she bought a .38 last week. Been to the firing range in the national forest twice already. She asks me if I'd like to see it but I don't have time. Dispatch is holding a Signal 7 which means Bollero's en route also.

Instead of the Dutch Masters, she hands me Middleton's. They're ten cents cheaper, she says, and cherry flavored. As I'm leaving the guy behind me lays his Cheese Doodles and pink sno-balls on the counter. It isn't enough for them to have a man's job, now they want a man's cigar.

Cigars make me cough but anything's better than the smell, especially when it's summer and the body's been cooped up. I'm puffing and coughing as I drive up and step out of the patrol car. There's a neighbor standing outside the house in Bermuda shorts and I ask if he's the key holder. He hands it over. Used to feed the cats when he and Maggie went out of town on weekends. Maggie, that's his wife, or was until a few weeks ago when they separated.

Bollero walks up, biting and twisting. A stinker? It's been a few days I tell him. He takes one of the Middleton's out of my back pocket. Deeply he breathes the smoke, allowing it to ride up over his mustache into his nostrils. We go inside.

The guy is hanging in the living room like a dang piñata, bloated and ready to pop. The breeze from the open door causes him to turn slightly and I recognize his face. Right at eye level hang his soft pink hands, with a line where a wedding band used to be. No sign of forced entry is present; Bollero says to write it up as suicide. These aren't bad cigars, he says and takes another before driving off. ID takes photographs while I talk with the neighbors. Mr. Bermuda Shorts rambles on until the hearse arrives. A somber-looking man and woman step out in navy suits, trailing a stretcher behind them. I escort them inside then stand on a coffee table to cut the nylon cord and guide the body onto the stretcher.

3:30 A.M., I'm dog tired and sick to my stomach from the cigars but it's better than the first time without them. Crawling over a fly-infested windowsill, buzzing everywhere and the memory of it lingering in the hallways of my mind. I lived that lady's death, smelling and seeing her on the floor. For three days it was like a broken rib, reminding me of its presence every time I inhaled. She must have lain there a while too because there were lots of balled-up Kleenex. Scratch marks on the back door. Nearby, an empty water dish and stiff schnauzer.

Suddenly I need fresh night air. Parked in a strip center in my zone, I start walking. I've written about a dozen business checks when the emergency tone cracks through the silence. A robbery in progress at the same store hit three weeks ago. All I can think about is that poor lady being victimized again. Camp is already en route. As I'm running back to the car, I picture the suspect in my mind, visualizing the two holes I'm going to add. The back tires fishtail around the corner and I compensate at the wheel.

Camp radios in his arrival and I tell him my location. Six blocks away I run over an opossum. Bollero calls them road pizzas. Camp is calling for an ambulance when I pull into the convenience store parking lot. Sprawled out on the floor is a lanky kid, maybe sixteen. There's a knife next to him. Behind the counter stands the clerk with a state of shock calmness about her. I look at Camp who's plugging up the wounds with napkins. There's a .38 special tucked in his belt next to his service revolver. She emptied the entire cylinder on him. Placed five of six at point blank. Camp spits across the floor. Hope to hell this joker don't have AIDS.

You okay, I ask the clerk. I grab a bag from behind the counter and walk over to the knife, quickly tracing the outline on the floor. Using my pen I scoot the knife in the bag.

No one, she says, her voice starting to quiver, will ever do that to me again. Do you understand? I nod.

Between the *Play Lotto* and *Ice 99c* window signs, Bollero pulls up followed by an ambulance. I'm taking her statement while Camp fills Bollero in. I can see the disappointment on Bollero's face as he looks at the kid and sees it's not the guy we've been chasing after for weeks.

An investigator will want to speak with you at the station, I tell her. The manager scuffs in with his slippers on and pajamas sticking out the bottom of his pants. He looks at the clerk and asks if any money got stolen. He punches open the register and fans a stack of bills. You're one sick puppy, I tell him.

You can't talk to me that way. I'm a businessman and taxpayer. Sergeant, did you hear what she called me? Bollero pulls on his mustache and finishes talking to Camp. As I walk to my car carrying the knife, I keep thinking if I hadn't missed none of this would have happened. I shut the backseat door for the clerk. Camp walks by on his way to the ambulance. So, you finally got her where you want her, in the backseat of your car. Don't do anything I wouldn't do. The problem is, I tell Camp as I open my door, you wouldn't know what to do. He laughs, then shoots a stream at the green *Democrat* news box as he walks toward the ambulance. Between the *Play Lotto* and *Ice 99c* window signs I see Bollero trying to appease the angry manager. He buys a cup of coffee and a five pack of Middletons. I drive away in silence.

A Bicycle Story

E. J. Graff

Three weeks after my grandfather died, almost a year ago already, something happened. I'm riding my bike along the Charles, a battered old Fuji I got just after I moved in with Enrique and Stacy. I got it because Enrique invited me to go biking with her. I was working as a grill cook for just about nothing a week, but when I told Gramps I needed a bike to get to work, he found one and fixed it up for me. Which makes me feel like shit that day on the bike path— practically his last gift to me was because of a lie, a lie because of Enrique. I never rode it to work. I took the T to work.

It's a gray day, no one else out. A dog loping along, sniffing for piss in the cattails. A middle-aged rower, hauling at those oars like he's going to save his life. The sky so low it's leaning on your head, so dark you can hardly breathe. You have to keep blinking to be sure you can see. And not because it's late—it's early July, only seven o'clock, plenty of time before sunset.

I'm rounding the curve just before Harvard, under all those sycamores with their skin peeling off, pumping as fast as I can, trying to get away from that green hospital smell that I can't get out of my head. It was worse than the sweet-smoky church smell, with the priest talking about Gramps like he knew him personally, and then swinging incense into every corner like he was banishing evil spirits.

Ahead of me there's a woman walking in the middle of the path, wearing a pseudo-designer sweatsuit, white with black wedges on the shoulders. She's walking deliberately, feet going down like they're planted, probably a dyke. Which used to be such a thrill. But my legs are flying, the sweat flinging off me, and she's smack in the middle of the path. So I call out, "Passing on the left!"

She turns around and gives me this blank look. Spiky black hair, crooked nose. I arc around her—not too far, I want to shave her just a little so she'll get the fuck away next time someone's passing her.

She holds her arm out full length, stiff. Her fist slams right into my neck. On purpose.

It doesn't knock me off the bike, I don't even wobble. But it throws me, inside. I just keep pedaling, bumping over the curb into the intersection. This jerk in a Chevy tries to turn right into me, I swerve and yell at him to fucking watch where he's going, asshole, I'm standing up so my bike wobbles from side to side while I pedal, I'm back on the sidewalk where the branches scrape my hair, pumping, pumping, barely stopping at River Street, bursting past the BU Bridge where I meant to stop, gasping past the river littered with sails, straining over the Mass Ave Bridge and onto the Esplanade where the whole city jams in.

All the time I can't stop thinking about that bitch. She didn't hurt me—I feel my neck a couple of times, and there's no bruise. But she could've knocked me right into Mem Drive traffic. She had this psychotic look, like her soul was missing. Like she would've left me bleeding to death without looking back.

I get so pissed I want to kill her. How can you let someone get away with that? Ahead of me there's a tall woman with a halo of curly black hair, stooping just a little. For a minute I could've sworn she was Enrique. I zoom right past her, close enough to bite her hair off. Rounding the Hatch Shell

I swerve past these flat-topped black guys rollerskating with attitude, blasting their boomboxes, and I grit my teeth and haul ass back to Harvard Square.

Of course she's gone. I go up and down all the little streets off Mem Drive, up toward Harvard Square, even across the bridge to Harvard Stadium where Enrique loved to tell visitors they shot *Love Story*. The sun drops below the clouds, stabbing orange across the buildings. I can't see in that light, everything a weird muddled gray, like being swallowed up into nothingness.

So I give up and go home.

And Enrique's still there, the stool I gave her tucked under her arm, talking to Stacy in the front hallway. Even though she said she'd be all moved out by seven. It's the stool I found for her at Gramps' and painted cream-green to match her bedspread. Gramps' apartment turned into a junkyard after Grandma Mae died when I was ten. Everywhere you looked he had stacks of things he was fixing up to sell— broken toasters, cribs with missing bars, twisted charm bracelets, you name it. After he got off his day job doing appliance repair for Sears I'd skip out of the motel to help him glue and sand and stain. Sometimes I'd just sit there watching him tweezing some tiny bit of wire with his needle-nosed pliers, his place so dusty and quiet after the motel it was a relief. You never knew when my folks might give me shit for skipping out of my shift, so I stopped caring. The hard part was not showing up at Gramps' again until the swelling went down, so I didn't upset him.

Enrique's hair is in a bandanna, black curls spilling through, her armpit hair looking like a snakepit. Although if I said that their faces would squeeze up, annoyed. I never could be politically correct. That's one thing I learned, living in that perfect dyke house.

My legs are shaking after riding so long. My stomach feels like a rag someone keeps wringing. I grab a beer and shove through boxes of her books piled in the hall, past her room gaping with dustballs. In my room I drop onto the futon, face into the pillow, belly coated with sweat, sweat stinging my eyes.

Enrique sticks her head in. She asks if I'm okay.

Yes, of course, what the hell does she think, I say, and start to cry. Not like real crying. More like dry heaves.

When she starts stroking my back I could cry forever. But I don't. My nose keeps running, my breath keeps shuddering, but my throat tightens up. I grip her thigh so hard it feels like I'm biting it.

"I'm getting your chinos all full of snot."

"That's okay, hon." She strokes the back of my neck, right at the soft spot. Like she used to when we were making love. That starts the shuddering again. I want to kill her.

She leans over and kisses my forehead, like I was a little kid.

I sit up, wiping my nose on my hand. I tell her about the woman hitting me in the neck.

"You're kidding," she says. She peers over to look, black eyebrows knitting together so close they look like one. When she's worried, her black eyes are soft as a nest, her little mouth purses up, a red bruise.

"I want to kill her," I say. I tug on Enrique's shirt. It's her sailor shirt from the Army Navy store, hard white cloth with a flap in back. I grip it tight.

"Stop, hon," she says quietly, putting her hands on my hands.

"I'm going to go back every day at seven until I see her again," I say, looking at her shirt bunching up in my hands, starting to expose her soft belly that she's so ashamed of. "And I'm going to fucking kill her."

"Arlene." It's her warning voice. She tries to push my forearms away, but I hang on. I stare at the scar on my right hand where I got splashed by grease when I was a kid. It happened by mistake, my mom told the guy at the emergency room. Enrique said she wasn't leaving on purpose to hurt me. Things just weren't working out, she needed to take care of her own life.

"Arlene, I have to go now."

I grab her shoulders. Something happens. It's not me. I keep staring into her eyes. Until I can't see anything.

I still can't remember what happens next.

Later I wake up. I lie there listening to the TV babbling in the other room. I can't make out anything it's saying.

In the shower I notice my knuckles are scraped up, a little bloody. Her smell is gone from the bathroom, the sandal-wood soap that used to scent up the whole apartment when she showered. Afterwards I come out and sit in the sagging chair. There's no light in the room except the TV and Stacy's aquarium, so it's like we're drowning.

Stacy bristles, fingers pressed together, righteous under her crewcut. Her pale eyes gleam at me. I cross my arms over my chest.

"I want you out by the end of the month," she says.

"What's with you?" I say. Wary.

"What's with you," she spits. Like I'm the scum of the earth. I turn away and pick up the paper, pretending to check what's on TV. I feel like I'm falling. I push my elbows down into the lumpy arms to try to stop.

She makes a disgusted noise, and stands up. "Get some help, Arlene. Take care of yourself for a change."

Two weeks later I lost my job. I just kept forgetting to go to work. I'd find myself staring at the ceiling, whole days blank—no memories, nothing. Maggie put me up until I got my act together—she was a waitress where I worked, she said I was good enough working a grill that she wasn't worried I'd find another job. When I finally did I kept living with her, but I started paying rent. The good thing about living with a straight woman is you don't fall in love with your roommate.

Meanwhile I looked after her kid sometimes. Not that Carla really needed watching, she was twelve, old as my brother Bobby, who by then was probably working the grill and the front desk both. When I found out Carla had a nature report to write I took her to Franklin Park Zoo and showed her the hoofed animals, my favorites—she loved the word for them, ungulates, she said it over and over until she couldn't breathe. It was a kick to watch her laugh like that, her freckles quivering, her hair staticky and red as the crackling fall leaves. That got me hanging out at the zoo again, like I used to—watching the monkeys scratching each others' behinds, scrambling up and down the branches, screeching like they were having a party for no good reason except they were alive.

Christmas Eve was the first time I tried to call Enrique in New York. I got her machine saying to leave a message and she'd call back after the holidays. Which meant she was visiting her folks. Without even letting me know she'd be in town.

So I'm wandering around Fields Corner on the coldest night of the year, so cold the hairs in my nose freeze, my mouth icy where I breathe into Maggie's wool scarf wrapped around the collar of my jean jacket. I want to call Gramps so bad it's like someone blasted a hole through the spot where he was. I finish my beer and drop-kick the empty bottle against the gutter. It explodes into bits of green glitter under the streetlights, the crash-sound frozen in the air.

No way I'm going up to my folks' motel, even to see my little brother Bobby. The wind's rattling through the leaves crumpled in the storefront grates. I stop walking. My stomach hurts when I think of Bobby alone with them, the rest of us gone.

My old boyfriend Ed and I always took Bobby to Gramps' on Christmas Eve. Then we'd spend Christmas Day with Ed's folks. Last year Enrique came with me to Gramps', and next day we went to her family's in Reading. We didn't take Bobby—I was too nervous about Enrique meeting Gramps. Like a jerk I was afraid Bobby'd be sulky. She brought Christmas cookies that she baked, with nutmeg and orange peel. Gramps pulled himself up on his aluminum walker and cleared away the junk on the coffee table so we could lay them out to eat. It was hard watching his thin hands shake,

I went into the kitchen to get a tray and napkins so I didn't have to see. I went ahead and ate some of the cookies, even though Enrique's look said we had plenty at home. I knew he'd stick them on top of the refrigerator and let the mice get them. Anyone could tell he forgot to eat, the way he was so tall and bent, even bonier than he used to be.

Usually Gramps had a long crooked wrinkle across his forehead, like he was concentrating on something just behind you. He didn't talk much, he mostly liked to fiddle with things. I liked it fine, but Enrique is the kind of person who talks about books and ideas, words come out so fast you feel like you're watching them fly out of her mouth. When I asked her what something meant she'd say, Look it up, you have a mind of your own. At first it pissed me off, but then I started looking things up, what the hell. I liked it.

But Gramps shut off his face if he thought someone was acting too good for him. He'd just nod, his eyes blank. And never mention them again.

When we got there Enrique walked around the apartment asking questions about where he found this or that. She got him telling stories, her mouth made little o's and her eyebrows went high when he talked about his best deals, like the time he fixed up an Empire wardrobe and sold it to a collector for $1300. She started opening the doors of some rusty bird cages stacked in the corner, telling him he must've been pretty careless to lose all those birds.

There it was, a little grin across the thin wrinkles of his jaw. I got up and adjusted his collar, I was so happy, standing behind him with my hand on his bruised, bony arm.

When we got up to go he said he wanted to give Enrique some spice balls for her closet. He must've got them from Mrs. Pennington downstairs, who always made them for the parish bazaar. He pulled himself up on his walker, breathing slow and hard. He reached over to Enrique—his hand so frail and blue I could hardly look—and took hers.

When I saw that look between them, I felt like he just passed me on to a new guardian angel. I almost cried.

Back in Maggie's apartment it's so dark you can hear the porch creaking in the wind. My teeth are chattering. I pick up the phone. My fingers are so frozen it hurts to punch the buttons.

Someone says hello. I can hear a lot of nieces and nephews squealing in the background. When I was there last year one of her aunts was getting on her case big time about settling down and starting a family. We kept giving each other looks.

Finally the guy on the other end hangs up. So I call again, only this time I manage to ask for Enrique. It's hard to get her name out of my frozen mouth. He has to ask me a couple of times before he understands.

By the time she comes to the phone my feet are burning with thaw. I'm stamping like crazy, trying to get rid of that half-dead feeling, wishing I had a beer. When I hear her voice, I almost hang up. But she says it again: "Arlene?"

I ask how she knew it was me. She says she just knew. For a minute we listen to the static, like ice cracking on the wires.

So she asks me is it snowing in Dorchester. I ask if she's had a lot of snow yet in New York. She says no, but it wouldn't matter that much anyway, she lives practically across the street from Columbia. She went back to school to get a Ph.D. in psychology. Social work made her miserable: all those poor people who hated her for trying to save them, and hated her for not being able to.

"So what's new with you?" she asks, flat and careful.

I stick my free hand under my armpit and look around the dark apartment. Red Christmas lights from across the street are flashing red shadows over everything: Carla's flute stand with the music slipping off it, the card table splattered with pieces from Maggie's half-finished puzzle, the wreath on the grandfather clock. No protest buttons, no mile-high newspapers, no posters shouting at you to do something. How can you explain to someone how different your life is?

So I tell her I'm working at the Milk Street Cafe, and living in Dorchester, and sometimes going to church with my roommate. I don't know why I tell her that. Maybe because she used to tell me I had a responsibility to my soul. Soul. That was the actual word she used.

But she's not listening. She says, "I'm not sure I'm ready to talk to you. You really hurt me, you know."

I feel like someone punched me. "I hurt you? Who the hell left who?" Maggie used to tell me not to waste my breath over someone who left at a time like that. And then she'd slap her hands together like she was getting rid of dirt.

"Arlene," Enrique says, like she can't believe this, "Stacy drove me to the hospital. Thank God there wasn't a concussion. You were—you lost your mind."

That shuts me up. In the background there's kids whooping.

"I couldn't believe you never wrote to apologize."

"I don't remember it." My fingers are burning where the feeling's coming back in. I bite them to stop the pain.

"You don't remember it." There's a big quiet, we're listening to the ice on the lines again.

There's a big cheer behind her. "Listen, call me in New York, okay? We're going caroling. I have to go." But she doesn't hang up. Her voice softens. "Take care of yourself, okay?"

I hang up. While the clock ticks, low and stony, I sit there on the couch, red shadows flashing on my Reeboks, wreath-smell filling my head. When he was five Bobby fell into the tree and got tangled in the lights, pine needles stuck in his eye. He just sat there blinking, he never cried once. The emergency room nurse looked me straight in the face and asked should she report my parents. And I told her no.

For a minute that's all I can see: Bobby on the green plastic seats in the waiting room, hands gripped between his legs, blinking, eye red and swollen, trying not to cry. My chest grips up, ready to kill.

Then I flash on my scraped-up knuckles that day in the shower. I buckle forward, terrified I'm going to vomit, head between my knees. I stay curled there, breathing the dust from the couch, alone in the blinking dark.

By the time Maggie and Carla come back from Pittsburgh,

I've been lying on my cot for two days, coughing through the fever and mucus in my chest.

Maggie sticks her head in on me, still wearing her electric blue beret, pale face flushed from the cold. "Look at this. I leave for four days and what happens—you turn my house into a pile of Kleenex. You need a mother, hon."

I prop myself up on the pillow. "Want to volunteer?"

There's a slam, and Carla's tape deck starts blaring, Janet Jackson pounding the walls.

"You crazy? Ask Carla there, maybe she'll take you on."

"Ha," I say, "I'll do it myself."

Maggie reaches in across my room—it's pretty small, practically a closet, they used it for ironing and storage before. Her fingers pull open the curtain, bumping off the sill some of the stuff I got from Gramps'.

I slap her hand away. She grabs the door and slams it shut behind her, so hard the cot shivers. I roll over, tangled in my hair, and stare at the bubbling wallpaper, which is supposed to cover up the cracks in the wall.

One Saturday in April there's an early fog, not too bad, just enough to warm things up a little. The paper says the Blue Hills Trail Center is leading a nature walk at noon. Without even thinking about it I go down to the basement and drag out my bike. It's been forever since I fixed anything up, so I wheel it down to the bike shop at the end of the street, and the guy shows me what I need to do. It's not hard—a little oil here, a little tweak there, some air in the tires. And I'm free.

That's how it feels—free. My legs are creaky at first, but once I get pumping I feel like I'm flying. I stop at the end of Dot Ave to check the map the bike shop guy handed me, and then I'm swooping over the river to Milton, where things are a hell of a lot prettier than Dorchester—winding past grand estates, past arbors, down the steely highway to the Blue Hills. All afternoon we follow a skinny uniformed guy who shows us green shoots folded like prayers. We breathe the dirty smell of spring.

At dinner Maggie and Carla tease me for riding that far. Next day my thighs and butt ache. But not much. One Epsom salt bath and you barely notice the leftover pain.

I really get into biking. Once I start I can't stop—it feels so good to have blood pumping through you, sweat pouring off you, skin electrified by the wind, alive again after the bitter winter. I ride to the Blue Hills, to the zoo, to the arboretum. Once I start it feels like nothing could hurt me. Like the whole world is burning off my back, my lungs a huge pump, breathing, breathing, ready for takeoff.

One morning, as I swoop back from the Milton hills and over the river into Dorchester, noon light's hitting the tripledeckers. It drops me into the time—before we were lovers—that Enrique and I went zooming up and down the hills of Somerville. We were racing like kids, her laughing and yelling after me not to go so fast, clutching her brakes while I flew. I spotted an arcade, leaped off my bike, and went in. She had to squeal to a stop to catch me. I got her playing video games, surrounded by teenage boys slamming themselves up against the noise. She honest to God never played before, a real library type. I made her put her hands on mine while I worked the controls, showing her how fast she had to maneuver. That got her laughing so hard she started to hiccup.

I was flushed when we got out of there. I knew what was going to happen. She'd been tutoring me in Spanish for two months, telling me I had to go back to college, it was a sin to waste my life. When she talked like that I could hear my heart beating against my skeleton. Like her voice was talking right inside me. I never felt anything like that before, it made me nervous, I'd scrunch down in the comforter bunched at the other end of her bed. She'd close her eyes and run her hand around her neck and throat. Something would leap inside me, like a fish hurling itself out of a river, a gasp. With her little red mouth and her serious black eyebrows, she was the most beautiful woman I'd ever seen in my life.

After the video arcade we put together a picnic and headed over to the Mystic River to watch the sunset, flamingo and pink, scalloped across the sky. What a gift you are, she said, so alive. That made me nervous, my butt squirming against the cold ground. When she leaned over to kiss me I was so scared I was dizzy. But I couldn't make myself stop.

I knew right then she would leave me. I'm not stupid—I know I'm no intellectual. That night after she fell asleep in my arms I stared at the sparkles in the ceiling, unbelievably happy, dread weighing on me like rocks.

I'm pedaling so furiously that I keep going all the way down Morrissey Boulevard, past the harbor speckled with boats, past the Globe where the presses are spitting out more greasy news, past stiff-necked Southie houses, out the spit to Castle Island. As long as I keep moving I'm all right, the feelings keep pumping through me, they don't bite or twist. It's just like breathing, in comes the ocean air, out go the bad thoughts, I'm racing out the spit like I'm being chased. But it feels good, salt spray filling my head, wind sending goosebumps inside my windbreaker, the sky so huge and blue I'm riding right through it.

Then I notice the sun slipping down, and I ask a tweedy old guy for the time. Sure enough, it's nearly my shift, so I haul ass downtown.

Riding my bike in traffic I'm exhilarated, I don't know why. I weave around the glinting cars, I'm like a ten-year-old popping wheelies in the crosswalks, I wave at a school bus full of kids giggling against the window. One of them gives me the finger, and I don't even care, I feel like a parade. I'm whistling when I lock my bike against the grate in the back alley, I call out as I slam the screen door and come inside.

Then I figure out why. I rode my bike to work.

In my head I get this picture of him fiddling with it, needle-nosed pliers in his hand as he squeezes on the chain. Standing there unwrapping wax-papered slabs of hamburger onto the spitting grill, it feels like he's fiddling inside me, with his halfway grin.

I burn my finger in the grease. Heading into the restroom

I'm almost giddy despite the pain, like someone just took a block of cement off my chest. When the chilly water rips into the angry red bubble, I start to sob. Silently at first. Then in huge gulps, so hard one of the waitresses, Diane, steers me out to sit on the back step. It's shaking me from inside, making me gasp for air, I'm praying to him to hang on to me, seeing things I forgot. His knobby pink butt sticking out from his hospital gown, flickering under the blue lights of the ICU monitors. His transparent blue eyelids fluttering. His breath wheezing under the green mask like a building caving in. His waxy hand in a white fist impossible to untwist. Me unpeeling from the chair in the ashy waiting room, stopping mid-breath when the nurse's face came clear in the dull red dark. Hands gripping me when the gurney rattled past, white hollows draped over his skeleton.

I must've raced out of the hospital, because next I remember gray light slanting through his place. I was scooping up anything that lay around, terrified my mother would gut the place and never let me near him again. When I spilled out my pockets and laid it on my windowsill in Somerville, it was a hopeless collection: tarnished medals from half a dozen wars, a broken watch, bent spoons, foreign money, a dented Christmas ornament.

Next time I went by his place there were yellow gingham curtains in the windows, and a staring cat.

My mother hadn't waited a week to rent it out.

I'm rocking in the café's back alley, holding onto my knees. The jerky sobbing's starting to slow down, leaving my heart pinched with missing him. A hand brushes back my hair, and I startle—like he's come to say good-bye. But it's only Diane, checking up on me. She steers me to the washroom where I splash my face and try to settle down. Looking up from the sink, my cupped hands leaking water, my breath makes a little mist across the mirror. So I must be alive after all.

Pain slices my hand. I suck on the blister that got popped where I was twisting my hair. The washroom door bounces and slams behind me, I'm pulling open the freezer for a piece of ice.

"That's going to be one nasty scar," Diane says, pulling glasses out of the dishrack.

"No problem," I say, "I've always wanted one to match." I hold up the back of my other hand to show the old wrinkled triangle of skin. It used to feel creepy when someone touched it. Now it just feels numb.

"Ow," she says. "How'd you get that? Wake up, Arlene, take better care of yourself." Which makes me want to slap her. But she's filling up the glasses with Diet Pepsi, wiping off the foam at the top and tossing the towel back over her shoulder.

It's creepy: that's my mother's gesture, a towel over her shoulder, part of the way she rumbled around the motel. Like her huge laugh if you could mimic a guest. Or her thumbs rubbing your temples when you were sick. Or her sneer, worse than her fists, letting you know you were shit.

For a minute I grip the thick edge of the counter, holding on. That's when I remember the feeling of shoulders gripped in my fists. Her black curls smashing flat and fanning out the white wall. Her pale cheekbone catching against the brown shelf, smashing the radio to the ground. The red dents in the plasterboard where my knuckles hit.

All of a sudden the restaurant noise is loud as a jackhammer: clattering silverware, the blurred roar of voices, a laugh high and angry as a parrot's. I pull on the mitt to pick up the wire mesh basket of sizzling french fries, and drain the grease into the steel sink. All my life I've been trapped in this smell of rancid grease and frying hamburger. Carla turned vegetarian a few months ago. Now she wrinkles her nose and hides behind her magazines when I get home. As if it would be that easy to change someone like me.

What Has Been Done to Me

Jacqueline Woodson

Mama is sitting across from me sipping her third vodka tonic. She sips nervously, bringing the glass to her lips for quick tastes before sitting it down again—too far away from her so that she has to reach across the table to retrieve it. I stare at her dark fingers, nearly black at the knuckles and the thin gold bracelet steady on her wrist. Mama is not a slim woman, though she says there was a time before us, me and my sister and brothers, that she was as small as I am, maybe smaller. When she is reminiscing she warns me that there will come a time when I too will blow up like a balloon, too quick to stop the pockets of fat from collecting at the back of my neck and around my waist. It has not happened to me yet. But I watch for signs.

My seltzer goes flat in front of me now. In the quiet restaurant our conversation is filled with too much silence. We were and always have been, strangers.

"I'm ready to go home *now*," Mama says after a while and picks up her drink again. "Everyone talked about how fun this Mardi Gras thing would be. Just a bunch of noise and crowds. I could get that at home."

Mama has brought me here to celebrate our birthdays. We were born on the same day, twenty-five years apart.

Fifty is harder on Mama than twenty-five is on me. I see the worry lines that have creased a path across her forehead, the strands of gray hair braided into her cornrows. I did not want to come.

"I bought the tickets already," Mama said into the phone, the Saturday before my birthday party. "I've never been anywhere."

"I had plans with friends, Mama," I reminded her, hoping the sound of my voice would also convey the fact that we had not sat down to dinner together in five years and would have absolutely nothing to talk about. It didn't.

"It'll be real nice," Mama continued as though I hadn't spoken. "We can have dinner in those Cajun restaurants. Maybe hear some jazz somewhere. I bought everything for you, the plane ticket, the hotel room. It's all paid for. Happy Birthday."

When Mama looks at me now, I shrug. I had not expected anything from this trip so it is not a disappointing one. New Orleans isn't friendly to dark strangers.

"Maybe we could change our tickets," I offer. "See if we can leave tomorrow."

Behind me in New York, I have left a new lover. We have been in New Orleans two days now and I have refused to brush my teeth for fear that the taste of her might leave my mouth, the tips of my fingers. I have left a group of friends, who I have grown close to in the three years since I have been out. I have left an apartment I share with my best friend, Dana, nights in the lamplit living room drinking rum in intimate groups, potluck dinners with too much tabouli, couples evenings and evenings out alone. Mama has left no one and nothing but the familiarity of a house she has lived in for twenty-two years, a bookshelf of best-seller novels that she reads lying in bed on her side, and a living room full of plants that cover one whole wall. And a memory of us the children, who, one by one, left her behind. Each taking as we went, a different recollection of childhood.

"That man over there favors Joe, doesn't he?" Mama points and I turn in my chair to take in the man sitting alone at the bar. He is light-skinned with a beard. The man wears a jogging suit and sneakers. "You remember Joe, don't you?"

I nod. "You kicked William out because you were going to marry him."

Mama looks surprised for a moment then reaches for her drink again. "William shouldn't have been there in the first place," she mumbles.

"But he came back," I say and Mama goes quiet, staring down into her glass.

Joe was going to buy Mama a house if she married him. A big house out on Long Island. With a pool if we wanted. There were five of us in three rooms then. Mama and William sleeping in the living room on a convertible sofa. Me and my sister Pauline in the middle room on a double bed. In the back room, my brothers Raymond and Tyrone and my Uncle Michell when he was home on furlough or out on probation. The apartment was a railroad with a small kitchen and bathroom falling off like the bottom of an "L."

Years later, Raymond, because he was the oldest, would be the first to leave, marrying the first woman he made love to and inheriting with her, the five girls she had from a previous relationship. Then Pauline, moving at twenty-three to Hawaii where she hoped to grow her own pot because it was nearly impossible to buy the amount she consumed daily in New York on an office manager's income. I would follow behind her because I had fallen in love with someone Mama banned from the house, taking with me only the clothes I had bought working summer jobs between semesters at college and the books I had held onto through the years. Tyrone would be the last to go, following in the footsteps of my uncle, his favorite relative, ending up in Danamora State

Penitentiary with three years for possession and intent. I
never learned what he possessed nor what he intended to
do with it. Ours was not a family to process.

William and Mama had fought the day before Joe came
over to make his promises. Then William packed a small
suitcase and was gone. We waited. When Mama married
Joe, Raymond was going to ask him for a Lionel train set.
Pauline wanted a sewing machine. Tyrone wanted a box of
toys. And I, sitting in center of the circle of my brothers and
sister—was going to be the first to tell my best friend, Clarise,
that I had a father. A family. Like the Brady Bunch but
smaller. Like the Partridge family but without any music
except the saxophone Raymond played when the school let
him bring it home and the love songs he wrote in secret.
Years later, fighting the wars of adolescence with myself, I
would steal his songs and write the lyrics on the sidewalk to
amuse my friends, to embarrass my brother.

But Mama came home alone that night pulling Milky Ways
and Three Musketeers out of her bag. We huddled around
her, expectant. Tyrone had started packing. Two pair of
shorts and an undershirt were neatly folded in the bottom
of a small blue leather-like suitcase.

"I can't marry him," Mama said and I felt the chocolate
and caramel go hard in my mouth. "He's not my type."

Later, as we lay in our beds, I heard the wall being peeled
away in my brothers' room.

"Tyrone's eating plaster again," I whispered to Pauline.

"Mind your business and go to sleep," she whispered back,
then sniffed.

On the bunk bed above Tyrone's, Raymond lay humming
one of his made-up songs. In the cramped apartment, it was
hard not to hear ourselves grieving.

William came in near dawn, leaving the smell of stale
alcohol through our room as he passed.

That night Mama and William's bed moaned under the
weight of them. That night I dreamed of swingsets and swimming pools and families.

At school the following Monday, I am yelled at for wetting my pants and sent home. The house is quiet and empty when I get there. There is no shower so I run lukewarm water into the bathtub and wash my skirt and panties while I bathe. William comes home at one o'clock. When I come out of the bathroom, he is sitting on my bed, stroking his crotch and smiling.

"I saw him again after he moved out the second time," I say to Mama now. She has ordered another vodka tonic and her eyes are growing distant behind the tall glass. Behind me, I hear the restaurant filling up. There is soft laughter coming from the table next to us and when I look over, I see that two women are sitting there. I smile, hoping to convey to them our common preference. My smile is not returned. Too often now I am realizing race gets seen first. It takes a longer look to see queerness. Many of the white women in New Orleans, as the ones I've seen in South Carolina, Puerto Rico, Amsterdam and Brooklyn, just don't have the time.

"Where'd you see him?"

"Once, when I was in high school, I saw him coming around the corner on Putnam. He wasn't drinking anymore, he said."

"You stopped and talked to him?" Mama folds her lips into her mouth. She is not mad, just curious.

"What else was I supposed to do?"

"But that was the whole reason I asked him to leave. Because of you and Pauline. People were warning me that he shouldn't be in the house with you two getting older . . ."

I look up at Mama and for the first time in three days, our eyes actually meet. Then my head begins to move on its own accord, slowly, from side to side.

"You never asked him to leave, Mama," I nearly whisper. "He left on his own."

"Is that what he told you?"

"No! That's what I remember. I was there, Mama. I heard you beg him not to go!"

They had been fighting for a long time when William left that fall. From the shelf above the closet he and Mama shared, he took the duffel he had ordered from a Spiegel catalog the month before and a small suitcase. There were at least a dozen suitcases and bags on that shelf, none of which had been used by any of us.

"I'm tired of being here living like a roach," William yelled. "And these kids not even mine!"

And Mama, sitting on the edge of her bed, shooed us out of the room but not before the four of us, piled into the doorway, saw her there, tears smearing dark mascaraed trails down into her mouth.

"So what am I supposed to do here with this, William? Where you going to go? Why don't you just stay here until you get yourself situated someplace? I'm not asking you for anything else . . ."

In the next room, I climbed beneath the thin sheet on my bed. I would never beg. If I lived to be a thousand, I would never beg for anything.

Pauline sat down beside me and began stroking the bottoms of my feet with her hand. The sensation was strange, new and soft.

"I hope he leaves," I whispered to her. "I hope he takes the express train the hell out of here."

"Don't curse," Pauline whispered back. Then after a moment, in a voice I could barely hear, she added, "Me too." We stared at each other. Our silence revealing our mutual connection to William.

"You're misremembering," Mama says to me now, pushing her glass across the table like an offering.

I tip the slithers of ice into my mouth and get up to leave.

"No I'm not, Mama. I wish I could remember it differently though. I can't. And neither can Pauline or Raymond or

Tyrone. It's like a brick or something that somebody's tied around my neck . . ."

Mama shakes her head. "That's ridiculous. Nobody's carrying around any bricks. You were a lot younger then. You know how sometimes what happens gets mixed around a little over the years."

I reach into my back pocket, pull out the ten dollar bill I have there and place it on the table beside my empty glass. "I'll pay for my stuff," I say softly.

"No. Don't be sil—"

"I don't mind. I'll meet you later at the hotel."

Walking out, I pass the man who looks like Joe. When our eyes meet, he smiles and beckons me toward the seat next to him. I give him the finger and keep walking.

Outside, I push through a crowd of college-looking boys guzzling beer, then look back through the plate glass window and see Mama, staring off above her glass. I swallow hard and swear I will never let myself be broken.

I push through another crowd of tourists snapping pictures of a Commercial Street hotel and make my way toward the one queer bar I have found. There are no women inside, so I buy a beer and carry it across the street, to a dark alcove underneath an abandoned building. In the distance, I can hear laughter coming from both the bar and the other end of Commercial Street. There is a parade heading in my direction. Slowly, the bands grow louder. I guzzle my beer then run across to the bar for another one, walking back to the alcove slowly so as not to spill.

During the Mardi Gras people go out and do all the things they've wanted to do all their lives but couldn't because others were around cautioning them against making fools of themselves. Some dress up in outrageous costumes, often of the opposite sex. Still others find comfort in exposing themselves to the crowds. Standing there, I wonder what I would do if I cared enough about the event. There is nothing. What

I have done, and what has been done to me, is enough to make a hundred Mardi Gras.

I crush my cigarette against the cobbled street, light another one immediately, enjoying the sudden heat and light of the flame on my face. Across the street, the boys exit the bar in groups and pairs. I watch them for a long time, until the parade takes over the street between us.

You spend your life waiting for the moment when you are free of the history your life makes for you—the moment you can step outside of who you once were into the body of the person you have always been becoming. Then, from that point on, the things that have been done to you no longer matter. They become a part of a past . . . a past that you are no longer a part of . . . a past that never existed.

When I can stand the parade no longer, I fling my cigarette into the crowd, pop a breath mint and head back to the hotel. I know Mama will be waiting.

Invented Sisters

Annie Dawid

More than anything, she loved a horizon with nothing on it. Shadows cluttered York Ferry, memory occupying every corner and field. Out here, looking east over the Atlantic, she could testify nothing had ever happened to harm her. The gray sky offered no evidence of past acts, nor the gray sea, indistinguishable from air. Her father's absence bore a slow hole in her heart, but here even absence did not exist. Presence and lack alike, history evaporated at sea. Every sailor with something to forget or remember could see and sense only water, sky, ship. On the huge Coast Guard cruiser, the life of the shore diminished, sifted by salt winds, never quite disappearing.

Zoe Mae was spending her afternoon off, as she always did, on the foredeck with a book, today only half-interested in reading as she tried to clear her mind of business: the second mate's duties proved overwhelming at times—the tedium, drain, imagined and real responsibility for other lives. She studied the small print of the ratty paperback, willing her mind to depart the deck for the tidy, foreign world of Hercule Poirot's England, the mystery of place as alluring as the detective's task.

Suddenly Charlayne appeared, her sturdy brown arm sliding down the rail toward the open book. "Hey there, sweet. Thought I'd check to make sure none of the boys were coveting that delicious body." After checking to make sure no one could see them, she leaned over and kissed a freckle on Zoe Mae's cheek. "Well, coveting's okay in itself, but doing something about coveting's another story." She winked.

"Charlayne! You gotta be more careful up here!" Appalled and exhilarated by Charlayne's brazenness, Zoe Mae smiled nervously, her body aswim with the contradictory reactions Charlayne's presence elicited: longing, indifference, disgust, anger, desire. The older woman opened a pack of generic menthol cigarettes and offered one, as she always did, to Zoe Mae, who shook her head disapprovingly. "Cancer sticks. It's a shame—beautiful girl like you." She said that every time Charlayne lit up.

To Zoe Mae, Charlayne's beauty transcended all preordained categories. She stood five feet ten, with a slim bottom half and small breasts, but her arms were steel: solid biceps of a dimension Zoe Mae would never achieve. Daughter of sugarcane pickers from Florida, Charlayne worked in the engine room and took flak from no one. Four years ago she had adopted Zoe Mae into an intense and loyal friendship, protecting her as an older sibling would from dangers actual and impending. She was, in fact, ten years older than Zoe Mae, the same age as Dean, her oldest brother. For the last eleven months, they had been lovers, Zoe Mae slowly losing her resistance, slowly succumbing to Charlayne's tenacious seduction. Still, she didn't know how she felt about it from day to day, her desire for love crashing headlong into an idealized vision of some handsome man—white though faceless—whose arms opened toward her, encircling like a natural harbor. "Be mine," he was saying: "I'll never leave you." He would smell like a man, responsible, dependable, faintly sour. Charlayne—no matter how much she sweated —wore the aroma of talc, and told her, "I want you. Now and now." She never used words like "never" and "always."

"You on a cig break or what?" asked Zoe Mae, carefully

placing a letter from home in the second page to mark her place, then turned her back to the railing, facing Charlayne, and again she felt that ripple of awe knead her stomach and make its way up her throat. That past year she often felt this rush of amazement whenever Charlayne appeared and looked at her the way she did, the possessiveness and powerful love flashing in her eyes if Zoe Mae was talking with someone else.

"What're you looking at, Zoe child, huh?" Charlayne sucked on her cigarette, hands in her back pockets, one eye closed from the smoke. It was a cool, windless day in October, the kind most people found depressing, but which cheered Zoe Mae in her contrary way.

"What do you think I'm looking at?" Zoe Mae watched the broad callused hand that rose to grasp the cigarette and fling it over the side in one sure, graceful gesture. They both followed it with their eyes as it sailed in a falling arc. Once, Zoe Mae thought she herself was tough, someone to be reckoned with back in York Ferry, but she didn't know what toughness required until she joined the Coast Guard and met Charlayne and the other women. Zoe Mae was unacquainted with her own inadequacies and ignorance until that first year at sea when it seemed as if every man and woman wanted something from her: straight or gay, married, unmarried, old enough to be her father, or mother. And the physical exhaustion—she'd fallen asleep over dinner almost every night. But the rest were never too tired to want. She was confounded by all of it: the intensity of desire in men and women long confined on ship, the commonness of homosexuality, the vehemence of friendship. Loyalties galvanized in a week, a night. Hatred rose like sea foam, cresting into violence when communication failed, flinging itself flat on some port shore, spent only by fists and a last exhalation of energy.

"You best be looking at me. When I check out those freckled lips and think how long I waited . . ." Charlayne's smile lit her face like a line of sparklers against the night.

She laughed. "I just say to myself, 'Ms. Boyce, you are the patientest woman in the known world.' Don't you think I should get a purple ribbon or something?" Without waiting for a response, she whispered, "But you were worth every minute, Zoe child—every one."

In her white Coast Guard uniform, red braids pinned in a crown like her mother used to wear, Zoe Mae filled her eyes with Charlayne Augusta Boyce, registering everything opposite to herself: old, black, southern, wise, tall, formidable. She wore two gold studs in one ear, her fine hair cut close. In every port, Charlayne could cause a stir, even among sailors who prided themselves on their nonchalance. Zoe Mae herself was something to look at in a place like Biloxi: a too-short girl with more freckles "than the sea has salt in it," according to Charlayne, who had begun a scientific study of the spots on Zoe Mae's body. They took a sample square inch of representative areas (face, chest, buttocks, back, knees and elbows—highest density) and then actually measured with a tape measure the length and breadth of Zoe Mae's various parts. Charlayne never grew tired of it; every season they recalculated to account for the effects of sunlight.

"I'll see you suppertime. And later. Second mate, sir!" Laughing, Charlayne saluted her for the benefit of a few men who had appeared on deck. She pursed her lips and feigned a small kiss before heading below.

Zoe Mae watched impassively as Ensign Peter Blake dismissed the man he was speaking with and nearly jogged over, first holding up her book to read the cover. "You still reading that Agatha Christie junk, Zoe?" He pronounced it Zoe-ie, in two syllables. When she first entered the Coast Guard, Zoe Mae's name became an issue. Vera from Louisiana informed her that Mae was a middle name most eagerly stopped using after childhood. She gradually grew accustomed to answering to Zoe instead of her full name, but she couldn't get used to the diminutive pronunciation, which rhymed with Joey—a name her brother Joseph, who was also short and feisty, despised.

"Zoe," she said. "Just one syllable. Rhymes with no."

"Right. Got it." He pronounced it correctly, as if for in-spection. "Saturday night we pull in at Newport News," he said, rapidly tapping the toe of his white shoe against the deck. "What do you say you come to dinner with me? No seafood, I promise! Steaks maybe, or whatever you'd like." He looked at her hopefully, his clean, earnest face gleaning nothing whatsoever about Zoe Mae's situation. He was rel-atively new on ship and probably hadn't yet been informed by the rest of the crew, most of whom left the two women more or less alone.

"I'm sorry, Ensign, but I'm busy that night." She almost pitied his innocence. Since Zoe Mae joined the Coast Guard, she'd received the education she'd been waiting for while growing up in York Ferry. Although the ensign was older than her by several years and had been in the Coast Guard most of his adult life, he hadn't taken the course on Coast Guard women. He reminded her of Steve a little, her shy brother, with his stark cheekbones and military haircut, a runner ready to sprint. "Thanks for the invite, really, but I can't." She opened her book and pretended to read, deciding a little rudeness worked better than sympathy.

Hands in his pockets, lips in a pout, he shrugged, gathering up his confidence. "Another time, then. Okay? So long, Zoe-ie."

She was glad she had Charlayne now, glad she didn't have to deal every day with people pawing at her, wanting some-thing: sex, companionship, love, a shoulder, a lap, an ear. Zoe Mae surprised herself by yearning for the relatively uncomplicated attachment of her family. The love she shared with her brothers and mother—protective, unquestionable, unbreakable—would never be repeated anywhere, nor could she return such love without deliberation. Men were not like her brothers. They always wanted her to form herself around them, demanded, in the end, her body beneath theirs. Once understanding this, she could not help being suspicious of them all. Her father, who left when Zoe Mae was three, never wanted anything, though—never asked.

Unfolding the letter from her mother, Zoe Mae scanned

the familiar handwriting which, however neat and careful, slanted in opposite directions, the top half looking nothing like the bottom. The North Country changed little from letter to letter. It turned on its axis, shifting the angle at which it received the sun like any other place, people aging, withering, at times jolted by violence. Her grandmother died the year Zoe Mae left, plowed under a Northway divider by a drunken truck driver. Instantaneous death, the sheriff said, but Zoe Mae believed her grandmother knew fear before she died, the hollow terror of impending disaster. Zoe Mae remembered perfectly such fear: not long before graduation, she and Eric, her high school beau, had left a party drunk, she less than he, but he refused to let her drive. They weren't going far, so she didn't worry. Driving north around Elbow Curve, they crossed the yellow line into the lights of a pickup headed south. Only miraculous alertness on the part of the other driver had prevented all their deaths. She remembered most the silence: no horns, no screaming, just a split second of outrage passing in terrible quiet. She would never trust Eric again, and gladly broke off the relationship upon leaving York Ferry.

When Charlayne heard the story, she sighed loudly. "Men are always doing shit like that and getting away with it," she said. Nothing surprised Charlayne. "Never let yourself get flustered in public" was one of the Charlaynisms engraved in Zoe Mae's memory like Bible homilies. "Someone tell you something you don't know, you say: 'Shit! Didn't you know that already?' " Zoe Mae hadn't dared use that one yet. Grinning, she returned to the letter.

Dear Zoe Mae,

This'll have to be a short one because I'm so tired from looking after Robby and the baby, who doesn't seem to get any better no matter how much money and medicine they pour into him at Plattsburgh General. Fern gets so upset that she goes up to the Inn to have a beer, leaving me to watch them both. "For half an hour," she promises, then comes back two hours later, all glassy-eyed and happy, by which time Joe's back from work and either me or him better make dinner because I wouldn't trust her near a hot stove. Not good over there.

I still feel sad Herk isn't here to sit on my feet and drool. But I like to be alone in the farmhouse. Paul's out some-where—he's been gone three days. Thunder's rattling the panes. You know how I love storms like you do. Funny how the boys never did. I've built a fire in the woodstove, and I'm drinking tea with milk and sugar like Grandma used to make. It'd be nice if you were here. Sometimes I look in your room to see if old Ramona is stirring up any dust. Remember how long it took you to let go of that imaginary friend? I was ready to worry there was something wrong with you.

I wish you'd come home more often. Zoe Mae, I have tried to be the patientest mother in the world, but once a year seems to me way too little to see your own family. You mentioned that you and your friend Charlayne go exploring when you're on shore. Well, how about a little North Country exploration? I bet she's never seen this corner of the country. Bring her along—you know there's plenty of room for your friends here.

Averill asked me to marry him, again, and I said no, again. I don't understand why he can't be content with this nice thing we have together. He says it's for my benefit—that when he dies he wants me to be well taken care of, but I don't want to run my life that way. Besides, I'm just starting to get along with Simon, who I'm guessing will stay in his father's house a long time. He wouldn't like me to marry his dad.

Well, pumpkin-head, your old Mom's getting sloppy. The sound of the rain against the big window is putting me to sleep. Remember what I said: Christmas is still a long ways away. And I order you to telephone me the next time you're on shore.

Love and invisible hugs from me and Ramona,

Mom

When Zoe Mae went to supper, she remained silent while
Charlayne and the other four women talked about Newport
News, about dancing and good food and new clothes and
"finding some ass," as Sally put it. She meant guys. Of the
ten women on ship, only Charlayne and Jean were bona fide
lesbians—women who had been attracted to women their
whole lives and didn't try or want to change. The others
liked men. And then there was Zoe Mae. Once, she and
Charlayne had gone to a bar for women in some divey part
of Baltimore. Female bodies slow-dancing breast to breast,
womanly hip against womanly hip, moving as if in slow motion, as if to stop time. Zoe Mae tried not to stare, but it
was all so strange. She wouldn't dance and Charlayne got
mad, found a pretty black girl to make Zoe Mae jealous.
She kept peering over the girl's shoulder to register the effect. But Zoe Mae didn't care who Charlayne danced with;
she knew she had Charlayne's love. Bodies were irrelevant.
Exasperated, Charlayne left the very young woman in mid-
song and sulked back to the table. Jean was kissing someone
by the jukebox—a secretary type who kept playing with the
buttons on Jean's uniform. It made Zoe Mae a little queasy
since the scene was similar to what she'd seen in the straight
bars where she'd spent time with Jack during six months of
training.

"Zoe Mae, what're you thinking about so hard? I can see
those worry lines making grooves in that fine fair face of
yours." They had finished their fish and chips and moved on
to coffee and cigarettes. Again Charlayne offered a smoke;
Zoe Mae declined.

"My mother said in her letter that I'd better get my ass
up there. She invited you, too."

Coughing and laughing up a lungful of smoke, Charlayne
pounded the table as if Zoe Mae had suggested a dip in the
Arctic Sea. "You serious?" she asked between coughs.
"Right. I'll just be your regular black girlfriend waltzing
around this hick town where no one's ever seen anything
darker than a farmer's tan. No, honey, I doubt your mother'd
be real happy to see me with her prize possession."

Zoe Mae shrugged and returned to contemplating her stubby, ragged fingernails. She didn't want to take Charlayne home with her. Showing York Ferry to Charlayne—and vice versa—signified something major, an announcement she wasn't ready to make. At the same time, she didn't like hiding things from her mother, especially something so important. Kay knew all the details about Jack. How would she react to Charlayne? Although Zoe Mae had heard stories about parents disowning their homosexual children, she couldn't imagine that happening to her. As the youngest child and only girl in a family of five, she knew she'd received more than her fair share of attention and privilege. Charlayne would get along with the boys, but not with the sisters-in-law. Dean would admire her; Charlayne could meet him tit for tat. Smiling at the new, graphic image that expression called to mind, Zoe Mae announced she was off to write a letter. Charlayne's eyes met hers in tacit agreement to meet later. From across the room, Ensign Blake waved, his resigned smile following her out of the room.

Dear Mom,

I'd like to come before Christmas, but I can't say it's actually possible. I hate flying, hate being more than a mile away from water—on the ground, that is. But you succeeded in making the farmhouse appealing. I can't hear the rain fall from my cabin. It's too far below deck. I miss that.

Funny how you mentioned Ramona. I haven't thought about her for years. I guess I made her up because I felt deprived. The boys got to have a bunch of brothers and a sister too, but I had no sisters. So I invented a girl who would keep me company when I was tired of being with boys. She liked everything I did. Actually, Charlayne is fun to hang around with, though we're not alike at all. The other day she said to me at the exact time I was thinking the same thing: "It's about time for your mother to send you a long, juicy letter." And then the mail came, and there it was.

When I go to port this weekend, I'll check into flying home from the next port, which I guess is around Thanksgiving. I promise to call, but I can't guarantee a visit.

Why don't you find someone else to babysit at Joe's? I don't want you to get all run down because things are tough over there. I'm sorry to hear that Fern's drinking. And since when does Paul go off on a three-day binge? He's getting worse, isn't he.

Don't cave in to Averill, whatever you do. I mean, do what you want to do when you're good and ready. Grandma never let anyone push her around. I know she drove you crazy a lot, but she was a tough gal. I admire her.

I'll ask Charlayne if she wants to come at Christmas, but she'll probably want to be with her Mom and family in Florida. Hugs to everyone, esp. you and Dean.
Love,

Zoe Mae

P.S. If Joe needs help paying the hospital bills, let him know I have a lot of money saved that he could use.

Zoe Mae and Charlayne often slept in Zoe Mae's narrow bed together, but since they shared the room with two others, they refrained from making love unless they were alone. That night, however, Charlayne went directly to her own bed without even saying good night. The others hadn't come in yet. Zoe Mae tried to make small talk, but Charlayne wouldn't respond.

"All right—what's the matter? What'd I do wrong?" she asked the bottom of the mattress, which was not far from her head.

The bed squeaked, but Charlayne said nothing.

"Why're you upset with me?"

No answer. Charlayne was subject to spells of moodiness which descended like a freak storm off the shore. She wouldn't talk for a whole day or night, and then she'd go back to normal, as if nothing had ever disturbed her.

"You sure put up a fight when I said I wouldn't go home with you." Charlayne's voice, small and deflated, finally drifted down in the dark. "Big protest on your part, Zoe child. I didn't know you were so eager to show me off."

Swallowing hard, Zoe Mae knew she'd been caught in some kind of dishonesty, hung on her own ambivalence.

"I didn't mean to hurt your feelings, sweetie," Zoe Mae said. "I don't think I'm ready yet to take you home."

"Knock me over with a feather, girl. I figured that one out. At the rate you're going, I wonder if you ever will. You took Jack home, didn't you?"

Zoe Mae shifted uncomfortably. Jack had been transferred to Alaska, and the relationship ended abruptly. If Charlayne were a man, she *would* take her home for Christmas. She couldn't argue that Charlayne had done the same. Every month, Charlayne suggested a trip to Florida and repeated that her mother would be pleased to meet her. Charlayne's father had died not long ago, and her mother moved in with a woman friend. Charlayne thought they might be lovers, but nothing had been said.

"I'd bring you home 'cause I'm proud of you," Charlayne added. "But you're not proud of me, are you. Maybe it's fine to get your hands dirty at sea, but please, not at your white bread country house."

Furious, Zoe Mae wrestled with the sheets and scrambled up to Charlayne's bed. "That's bullshit, Boyce! It's not your skin color that makes me uptight."

"Oh, right. It's what's between my legs that's the problem."

Her legs dangling over the edge, Zoe Mae rested her head on her knees, embarrassed. "I wouldn't say it like that. It's not a problem what's between your legs—between my legs, for that matter, but I'm just not sure I'm a lesbian. I mean, I never thought about women until I met you." Lesbian. The word sounded so harsh, as if she'd named herself the victim of a disease—an epileptic or a diabetic.

"Four years this woman's arms been around you, comforting you, making love to you, and you're not a lesbian. Right." Charlayne had raised herself to her elbows and her voice to anger. "How long I spent consoling you over that dumbass Jack or those other stupid white boys you thought you wanted? Shit. I'm the dumbass here."

"Charlayne, we did not spend four years as lovers. It's been one year. Almost. You were my friend before that, doing what friends do for each other."

"Well, you got a loose definition of friendship, girl. 'Just friends' don't spend that much time together, don't stand so close together."

"I didn't know you were so resentful about it. Or were you just trying to get into my pants the whole time?"

Silence.

"You don't believe that, Zoe Mae."

"Maybe I'm filling the Coast Guard's female quota, and you're filling the black quota, and I fill your white girl quota." Zoe Mae trembled, her bare feet ice cold.

Charlayne's arm reached out and found Zoe Mae's knee, her callused fingertip drawing a slow spiral on her kneecap. It gave Zoe Mae the chills, made her stomach tense up, and as Charlayne's hand traveled lightly up her thigh, beneath her T-shirt to her breast, her nipples responded, hardened.

"But you like me getting into your pants, don't you."

It was not a question, and Zoe Mae did not bother to answer.

Charlayne pulled her down so that Zoe Mae was lying on top of her. She kissed Charlayne's tobacco-tasting lips, trying to take back her own words, kissing away the smell of coffee and old bitterness, swallowed one more time.

When 98.6 Is
Less Than Zero

Nisa Donnelly

When you meet her again, the woman you used to love—
and you WILL meet her again, for fate is easily amused by
chance encounters between intimate strangers—it will be
nothing at all like you'd planned: less awful than you'd
feared; less wonderful than you'd hoped. *(What did you
expect? This is real life, not the movies, where everything is
neat, predictable, where only the audience is surprised. That's
what you'll tell yourself. Later.)*

You will forget that you've been rehearsing monologues,
that she is the audience, that there's no soundtrack to take
cues from. You will wonder what music should be playing
in the background. *(You can no longer remember what music
she liked. Then. You cannot forget the songs she hummed
gentle in your ear the first time you took her hand and led
her to your bed.)* You will forget how you're supposed to
feel. *(Feelings are never right or wrong, they just are. This
from your therapist, the same one who said love is just a blend
of compatible neuroses.)* You will forget your new credo:
The Past Can No Longer Hurt You. *(It came to you one day
while you were riding the bus down Haight Street; you imagine
it's cosmic because you weren't even drunk when you thought
of it.)*

When you meet her again, the woman who is not quite your enemy but certainly not your friend, it will be a little better and a little worse than you'd imagined. You will pause and feel your breath catch and a smile will cross your face; you will forget, just for a moment, how much time has passed. *(Too much time. So much time that you are now only intimate strangers.)* You'll catch her hand in both of yours. *(It's a new, intimate gesture learned from another woman, when you were first alone and in the company of real strangers.)* You'll be careful not to hold on too tight, too long. *(You held on too tightly for too long. This from your best friend, the pragmatist.)*

"How good you look!" you'll say. Or "How wonderful to see you again!" *(The words don't matter.)* You'll be careful not to show emotion: no tears, try to make the smile genuine, remember your lines, remember the lies. *(You showed too much emotion with her, once. Remember what it cost. Too much.)* You'll hope the words sound the way they're supposed to: crisp, light, almost sincere, like woodwinds in the symphony. *(They'll sound that way to everyone but her. She will know the truth, she who could read your mind. You really were that close. Once.)* She will smile, too. *(Some things never change. Some things need no explanation.)* Now.

Nothing can help us now. You will remember saying that—or at least thinking it—when your life together was falling apart, when you realized some things broken can never be repaired. *(Totally destroyed. The newscasters say that. You wonder if there's such a thing as partial destruction.)* You won't allow yourself to wonder if she heard those words, those thoughts. You'll pretend to have forgotten that she could ever hear your thoughts. *(Coincidence. You tell yourself that's all it ever was.)*

Instead, you will offer up tiny worms of half-lies, seasoned with a tolerance you no longer feel, and uneasy smiles glinting cold against the afternoon. You will not ask about her lovers; she will not ask about yours, although her eyes will stray from time to time to the woman on your arm. You could introduce them, casually, smiling, the way beauty queens smile. Instead you'll wait for her to ask: "Who's your friend?" or perhaps something more direct. *(Introduce them. Watch them watch each other, the way women in such situations do. Smile brightly. Touch the hand of the woman on your arm, the one you're learning to love, the one with whom you share passion, but no past. "My ex," you might say later, inserting a small and exasperated sigh, as if two syllables can untangle, can tidy, can excuse the past. Although you've formed the words a thousand unspoken times on your tongue, they are still too hard to say, and you won't know why. "We were good at sex, just bad at relationships." You've practiced those words, too, but said them more often. When you say this, laugh, the way sophisticated women do in the movies.)*

You'll see the confusion in the eyes of the woman you once loved, and take some comfort there. You will not fall into the trap of her thirsty eyes. You'll be happy you're not alone; that the woman on your arm is grimly beautiful, the way she was grimly beautiful. *(Is, still; push that thought aside.)* You'll wonder if they see the resemblance, or if it's only in your mind, the little checklist you carry with you. *(Your taste in women hasn't changed: butches in leather, with sturdy thighs which hide warm secrets and stride long and determined through city nights; who find it hard to smile, harder to talk, but oh so easy to curl their fists deep into the furrows of your cunt, of your mind.)* Will she notice; will it matter if she does? You will focus on her mouth because it's safer than those eyes.

You'll try to remember the lies that spilled across her lips—not the way those lips tasted or how they were soft against your skin—that so often called you beautiful, that pulled you into her, leaving you wet and bruised, filling a hunger you'd never even acknowledged. Before. *(She said: "You're so beautiful when you come." Forget that you believed her, that she said that when her hand was buried deep inside you, giving you voice, but robbing you of reason.)* You'll forget that it's too dangerous to remember. Just like you'll forget that you sometimes hate her. Finally. Still. *(She said: "You act as if you hate me," when the pain was still fresh, when your mind was still raw and confused, when you still cared, when rage was your only reliable friend, when you wanted to wound her, as if that would cauterize your own wounds. "No," you'd told her. And it was true, something nameless stopped you from hating her. That is what you'd told her, the woman you couldn't quite stop loving. Yet. "Hate is a small and simple word. It doesn't even begin to cover what I feel toward her." This, you'd told your best friend. Later. For once, she didn't ask why. For once, she'd said: "My ex hates me and she has every right to." You were surprised at this admission, although it is probably true. Pragmatists so rarely bother with lies. You turned the words over in your mind: "has every right to." They sound like absolution.)*

You will wonder why you can no more forget her than you can forgive. *(She'd asked for one; she'd gotten neither. She said: "I'm sorry. I really fucked up with you." That from her when it no longer mattered. She'd cried and held your hand. She was asking for forgiveness. You had hugged her and pretended it was possible, even though nothing was possible then. "The bitch obviously has me confused with some old Polish guy in a white dress, who hangs out at the Vatican." This, you'd told your best friend. Later. Then you'd laughed. You were talking about absolution. Even your best friend hadn't understood.)*

When you meet her again, the woman who was the fabric of your world for so long, you'll tell her nothing important about your life; she will do the same. You'll be secretly pleased at the small omissions which crowd between you. She will dredge up memories from the far-distant past. *(The recent past is too painful, or perhaps she has already moved beyond that, into a time still soft and gentle, when you were first falling in love. Before.)* You will not follow her there. You know how the story ends. *("There are no happy endings, anymore." You say that too often lately, remind yourself whenever you are too close to falling in love, even with grimly beautiful women. "There are lots of happy endings, there's just no happily ever after." A woman you dated one empty Saturday night told you that. You don't remember her name. You do remember her dog, Dracula, a great woolly brown beast with yellow eyes. You weren't sure about the intentions of a woman who would name a dog such a thing. The woman on your arm keeps cats and a stuffed macaw. It isn't a real macaw, of course, just a collection of plaster and dyed chicken feathers, with a garish plastic beak. You aren't sure about the intentions of a woman who keeps a chicken-feather macaw, either, but it doesn't matter. Much.)*

The light will catch her hair, the way it used to, when you loved her. Just for a moment, you'll feel yourself curled warm and deep into her, warm against warm. Just for a moment, you'll feel the weight of her breasts under your palm, the taste of her against your tongue, feel your nails rake through the damp flesh of her back, the smell of her on your cheek, feel her tremble under your lips. Just for a moment. Then, your breath will catch and descend into a hard throb between your legs, because cunts have no time-table, because they remember what the mind chooses to forget. *(She said: "Cunts don't lie," the night you didn't want to make love, but did. You lied, then, hoping she'd never know. Lied because you loved her. And she pretended to believe you, for the same reason.)*

You will remember winter rain on the open windows of your mind, and Sunday afternoons stretching sunny and for-ever. You'll remember howling against the night, not caring what the neighbors think. Thought. Then. *(She said: "I've never made love to anyone like you." Before and then, later, long after you had learned to keep safe distance of strangers. You know that is one secret she does not tell your replace-ment.)* You will wonder if you should ask her for references; the idea will make you smile. You will be more careful with each other as strangers than you ever were as lovers. *(You have learned how to take a whisk broom to the dust-devils of*

*memories, tangled and untended in the crevices of the past.
Some things are better left forgotten. That is your mantra.
Now.)*

You will be careful not to expose the truth because details,
like the past, no longer matter (*call that freedom*); because
your life is no longer built around one woman or any woman.
*(You did that too hard, too long. Once. Your heart is still
wearing scars like looped hemp rope.)* You will remember
you don't believe in commitment; you don't believe in freedom, either. *(You won't tell the woman on your arm this.
Yet.)*

You will see her scowl, the woman whose words burned
you. Once. You will brace yourself for the attack that will
not come. It will remind you of how hands go instinctively
to protect scar tissue from another assault. *(You said: "I
deserved better," when you were still deep into the shouting
stage, when you finally understood there was nothing left to
lose. You meant better treatment. She pretended to misun-
derstand because she wanted to. She said: "Well, I hope you
find someone good enough for you. I really do." She spat
out this last. Curses have hard edges. You felt your face flush
to ice. Rage is hot only in the movies. You said: "I already
have," and were surprised at how cold your voice had grown,
how distant; surprised that you no longer cared; relieved that
you no longer needed to protect her.)* Now the past is your
only enemy. Friendly fire.

When you meet her again, the woman who told you often
but no more, "You're the most important thing in my life,"
you will smile and tell her you are doing well. *(Your best
friend said: "You're better off without her." And you agree.
Pragmatists believe self-reliance is akin to sanity; you aren't
so sure. You tell the woman on your arm: "You're the finest
thing in my life." And she smiles and pulls you too close,
tangling her fingers in your hair. She smells of well-oiled
leather and smoke, with a hint of sweat on her neck. She
wraps her hand in your hair, tilts your head back. You open
your throat to her and keep your eyes open. This time.)* Mem-

ories will send you stumbling through a minefield of gentle lies.

The woman you once loved will tell you about the minor inconveniences and triumphs of her life, all centered around your replacement, a woman you don't know and don't care to. *(You saw her once; you imagine she's nothing at all like you.)* You'll find yourself nodding. Smiling. *(You won't wonder if she tells your replacement "You're the most important thing in my life." You know she's a woman of few words; you don't imagine she's constructed all new dialogue.)*

She'll forget and call you "honey," then correct herself. Too quickly. The woman on your arm will not scowl; she will drop her hand on your shoulder lightly. You'll shiver, even though it's summer and already too warm. You won't shrug her off; you'd like to. *(You say: "Butches are so damned territorial," to your best friend, later. You know you don't mind. Much. She says: "Why do you suppose that is?" She's studying to be a psychotherapist. She asks why too often. You won't answer. Instead, you'll laugh and reach for one of her cigarettes. You quit smoking six months ago. For once she won't ask why.)*

Eventually, you will know there's nothing left to say. *(There is everything left to say. But it all belongs to the past; that's all you have left in common. Now. And you do not want to go there again.)* You will look at your watch; shift your weight (high heels are finally good for something); make any of the other tiny, polite moves people do at such moments. When you hug her good-bye, you'll be amazed at how well she fits you still. You'll feel yourself stiffen and pull away. *(First, so there is no misunderstanding. Be careful to appear strong and beautiful, to display your independence like a well-deserved medal.)* You'll pretend it matters. Pretend you are safe. Pretend not to see the sadness in her eyes. Pretend. You don't love her anymore.

After she's gone, leaving a wake of promises that are made to be broken—phone calls neither of you will make, invitations neither of you will ever extend—only then will the woman on your arm ask. The questions will not surprise you. *(Why are you no longer lovers? What happened? When?)* You'll wonder if it's fear or only curiosity in her eyes. You'll wonder if she really cares or if it's only the kind of idle excavations new lovers sometimes make. You'll decide the truth is too brutal. Now. You'll lie and it won't really matter. *(Even if she doesn't believe you.)*

You'll say: "Breaking up was the right thing to do." You'll remember how the woman you used to love too well spoke them first, long after it was over, how she had cried, the way she had cried the first time you made her come. "Keep telling yourself that, maybe one of these days you'll believe it." You can't remember if you said that; you know you thought it; know it's true. You'll wonder; you'll know. *(The woman on your arm will see none of this, of course, and she won't ask and you wouldn't tell her even if she did. New lovers tend a secret past. It's their only defense for the future.)*

When the woman you could love is finally draped naked and open across your bed, she'll pull you to her, under her, and you'll let her, you'll want her to. You'll close your eyes and design new memories. *(Later, when the night has finally crumbled against dawn, she'll ask: "Why don't you trust me?" You know it's all tied to an elaborate piercing fantasy she's constructed. You'll wonder if you should tell her flesh is cheap, easily healed. You'll hope she doesn't imagine claiming a tiny bit of flesh means more than that. You won't tell her you have been pierced too often, and only some of them show. You won't tell her you trust no one.)* You will let her spin her fantasy, until it reminds you of a great and beautiful web in the morning dew. You will not tell her reality never lives up to fantasy's expectations. Instead, you'll trace her breasts with your tongue, catching bits of soft skin between your teeth. You will feel it rise into goosebumps and then smooth, hot and wet and warm under your tongue. You will pretend tomorrow is not waiting outside the door. *(You won't mention your checklist; how you are attracted only to butches with magnificent breasts and sad eyes. She won't have seen the resemblance between herself and her predecessor—just as you imagine there is no resemblance between you and yours—and if she knows, she won't mention it. Some things are better left unspoken.)*

She will offer up her flesh, letting you ply her with your hands and your teeth, letting your eyes hide behind your hair, tousled and damp. She'll sink deep and swollen onto the sheets you bought for another woman and split the silence with her stranger's cries. She'll smile. *(She won't weep in your arms. She isn't that kind of woman.)* You'll begin to tally the differences. You'll call that progress. You'll take out the whisk broom, catch another dust-devil, banish it into the past. *(Maybe this time it will disappear; maybe this time there won't be another to take its place. But there always is. Another.)*

Later, you'll watch morning sift across the bed, across the bare and grimly beautiful woman sleeping there. You'll touch her arm lightly, amazed at the coolness of her flesh, careful not to waken her. You'll wonder if you love her. You'll wonder if it matters. You'll be amazed at the number of past lovers—yours and hers, as well—crowding your bed. You'll be more amazed at the similarities. You'll wonder if your therapist was right. Mostly, you'll wonder why it isn't like it is in the movies. You'll wonder if the woman you used to love sometimes ever thinks of you at all. Then, you'll remember all the things you should have said.

You will have forgotten to tell her you're happy. It wouldn't be a lie.

State of Grace

Lucy Jane Bledsoe

I.

When I was fifteen I believed that sex was nearly the same thing as softball. The feelings were the same, anyway. I fell seriously in love for the first time during a double play. Charlene played short stop and I played third base. We were ahead by one run, and it was the bottom of the ninth, bases loaded, one out. We had to win this game to go on to the State Championships, so you can imagine how I felt just then. The best hitter in the league, probably in all of New Mexico, stepped up to home plate and on the first pitch she belted a one-bouncer right between Charlene and me. Charlene called for the play and snagged the ball while she dove through the air horizontal to the ground. Even before her body thudded into the dust she scooped the ball to me at third. I tagged up and fired it to first base for a flawless double play. We'd won the game. I looked at Charlene and fell instantly in love, deep in love, and could tell by the fervor in her eyes that she had too, in the exact same moment. The next thing I did, after falling in love, was look for Michael in the stands. He was my best friend and primary coach and also happened to have been living with my mom for the past seven years. After scanning the bleachers for a couple seconds, I found him sitting alone, far away from

Mom, and remembered that Mom and Michael had broken up last week. A fireball of anger and sadness tore through my stomach, but I discharged it by thinking of Charlene and the double play. It was as if Charlene rolled like a boulder right into the spot Michael had been. All in about five seconds.

After the game, the rest of the team went straight to Galluchio's for pizza. Charlene and I lingered in the locker room, said we'd be right along, but didn't hurry. First I couldn't pull myself out from under the shower nozzle where the water slid down my body in dozens of hot rivulets. Then I wanted to take my time with the lotion, getting between my toes and behind my neck. Finally dressed, Charlene and I walked slowly back to the softball diamond, just talking, not planning to go there but that's where we wound up. We walked deep into left field where the grass became patchy under the pine needles of the piñon forest. Twice Charlene had slugged homers into these woods. I liked to think about those two softballs that no one had bothered to chase down and wondered where they were now. Coyotes might have carried them off. Or they could be sinking into the forest floor, slowly decomposing, the earth sucking them in.

Charlene dropped down next to the first tree in left field, placed her hands behind her, and threw back her head. I knew just how she felt. A hot dusk swelled up around us. The smell of fresh cut grass raked through my chest like some kind of ancient yearning. When I laid my hand on Charlene's thigh it was only to feel her short-stop muscles. Beneath her jeans her thigh felt warm and alert. Charlene picked up my hand and examined my calluses, touching them with the tips of her fingers. She said, "Here is the hand that can stop any hard-driven ball in the league. And you're only a sophomore." She lifted my hand to her mouth and ran her tongue along each callus, then licked the center of my palm, swirling her tongue in slow concentric circles.

I waited a long time, as long as it took the full moon to rise over the top of the backstop, expecting Charlene, being a senior, to kiss me. But when she didn't, I kissed her. Charlene was a loud, sturdy girl. She was tall, big-boned, and had long dark hair which she usually wore in a ponytail or a long braid. Her mouth and eyebrows seemed to jump off her face they were so aggressive, bold. She was the team captain that year, gregarious and so brassy that some people just couldn't quite take her. I could take all of her.

The funny thing about Charlene, though, was that when she wasn't cracking jokes and taking charge, she had a raw shyness. Hardly anyone knew that about her, but once you started looking closely it was obvious. Her brown eyes, for example, even as she shouted some obscene remark across the shower room, always had a tentative glint, like soil in spring where you never quite knew what was going to pop up. As long as we all kept laughing, Charlene kept performing, but she was ready, at any given moment, to back off. I was just the opposite. I was quiet most of the time, and people usually thought I was really shy. Actually, I'm not shy at all. I have a way of going for what I want. That night, out in left field, when I pulled Charlene's face to mine and kissed her, she folded right into me. The moon climbed higher and higher as we lay on the borders of the softball field and the piñon forest, its light sanctifying every touch. Still, even then, it was all softball to me.

From then on, every day after softball practice we walked home together. She wasn't allowed over to my house because of the lack of supervision there, so we usually went to hers. Charlene's mother never really liked me. My mother let me do whatever I wanted and I guess it showed. I wasn't wild or anything, just freer. My hair, I know, looked like straw, bleached and dry and nearly the same color. I didn't comb it enough. My nose was usually red and peeling, my continual softball sunburn. Besides the way I looked, I made Charlene laugh too much and we rarely did any homework. Also, when we walked home together we were often late because we liked to take the long woods route. The way we went, there wasn't even a trail, just dry pine trees and thick sweet air. One of us would always find a reason to start wrestling even though Charlene had already established time and again that she could whoop me. I liked lying on my back, afterwards, watching the clouds in the sky. I imagined they were giant beds and Charlene and I were floating on them. I didn't want to talk much at these times because I wanted to savor her salty softball taste in my mouth. Neither of us could wait until the middle of June when school would let out.

The last thing I wanted to think about that spring was Mom and Michael's breakup. But at home, it was always in my face. In the mornings, Mom didn't just leave toast crumbs all over the kitchen counter, she didn't even bother to brush them off her shirt anymore. She gained ten pounds, which was a lot of extra on Mom who was already big, and let her hair grow lank and long. She even canceled a class she was teaching at the junior college. Suddenly we weren't even saying hello and goodbye, just coming and going in the house like two stray cats. Michael had moved out (or was thrown out) and was sleeping in the back room of his auto parts shop.

I didn't need to tell Mom anything about me and Charlene for her to get the picture. She had to know by the music I played, by my face every evening when I came home, by the fact that I *lost* ten pounds. Besides, I had an attitude a mile high. I believed I had surpassed Mom in the realm of Knowing About Love. Mom had left Michael because she'd discovered he was having his second affair (actually, it was his third, but she didn't know this) in their seven years together. I pitied Mom for allowing herself to be abused like that. I thought I knew everything about love, especially that Charlene would never be unfaithful to me. I knew that. I knew that like I knew how to belt a ball into left field with the full force of my body. For the first time Mom's and my lives seemed to be forking off into completely divergent directions. I felt sorry to be leaving her behind.

On a clear Saturday morning in early June, Charlene's mother opened the door to Charlene's bedroom and found

me on top of her daughter—buck naked, the both of us. I
had been deep in softball at the moment, the smell of blue
sky lying against the back of my throat, the dampness of
spring soil between my legs, the strength of the best short
stop in the league surging beneath me. When I heard the
door burst open I flipped off of Charlene and looked her
mother dead in the eye. In that moment I learned that this
wasn't softball at all. This was sex. And I felt not fear but
an overwhelming sadness. My mother had raised me with so
much sophistication that even in the heat of that moment I
knew I was losing my innocence, that this was a Big Moment.
I would never again be able to confuse the sweetness of
softball with sex. Sex was fucking, and I was doing it with
another girl. I read all that information on Charlene's mother's face.

In softball, there is one perfect moment. You are standing
at home plate, the bat cocked over your shoulder, waiting
for a pitch. You watch the pitcher's feet, the scuffle of dust,
the strength in her calves as she winds up, then lets fly. As
the pitch comes your way, you feel a surge through your
groin, a racing of blood down your arms and into your wrists.
You lead with your left arm, pulling the bat even and hard
until that one perfect moment, exact contact with the ball,
the *crack* of a well-hit pitch.

Ever since I was eight and Michael began teaching me
baseball, that crack of the bat against a ball has been my
mantra, a sound I hear in desperate moments, at times when
I crave total satisfaction, a sound I hear over and over when
I want something very badly but can't express what it is. So
when Charlene's mom opened the door that Saturday morning and found me lying on top of her daughter (buck naked,
the both of us) my mind filled with the sound of bat-driven
balls, one after another in quick succession, as if I were at
some marathon batting practice. Like an alarm or siren,
perfectly hit balls flew from my mind, slamming across the
dusty floor into the astonished gut of Mrs. Duffy. After I
rolled off Charlene I couldn't stop staring at the woman in

the doorway, her stature filling the entire room. Charlene looked exactly like her mom, the same imposing presence, only Mrs. Duffy wore her hair in a French bun. The horror on her face showed me in one second what my mother had refused to teach me in fifteen years: that sex was an ugly beast, that sex was definitely not the same thing as softball.

Charlene's parents pulled her out of school that Monday. I heard the news from our coach, Mr. Kaufman. He looked miserable. "Charlene won't be with us anymore. She's taking her finals early and going on a trip with her parents. She won't play in the State Championships. Of course, we'll still go to the tournament. And," he added not at all convincingly, "we'll still win."

I couldn't quite believe what I'd just heard.

When I called Charlene that night, her mother answered. "You are not to call here anymore, Kathy." She hung up. I called back.

"You'd better listen to me carefully." This time it was Charlene's father. He worked as a missionary on the Navaho Reservation. The whole family used to live on the reservation until their home had been vandalized too many times and they moved to town. Mom thought trying to be a Christian missionary among Indians was as sick as making nuclear bombs or raping women, but she tried to keep her opinions to herself when Charlene became my best friend. Of course I agreed with Mom. But Charlene was different. Not many people got to see the authentic Charlene, she was buried so deeply under that loud voice and coarse language. The authentic Charlene knew remarkable things, but she carried her genius in her muscles. I could see it all when she played ball. I liked to think that one day Charlene would let the authentic Charlene take over all of her. I liked to think that one day Charlene would do this. With a father like hers, though, I understood why she kept herself a secret. He said to me on the phone, "One more call to our household and there will be serious repercussions. We've decided, for Charlene's sake, not to talk to your mother or the school officials. But that will become necessary if you don't understand that—"

"You can talk to whomever you fucking want to talk to," I interrupted. I knew the difference between whom and who because Mom was a writer. "Put Charlene on the phone."

He hung up on me.

I wished he *would* call Mom. I needed her. Until this spring we had always talked about everything. She treated me like another adult, not only because I was all she had until we met Michael, but also because she believed children should be treated as full people. Mom does just about everything by principle. Or at least she tries incredibly hard to. She'll do anything to avoid making a mistake. I always figured that was because of the couple big ones she made early on. First she married my father, and then she had me. She hates it when I remind her that I was a mistake because she says I'm the best thing in her life. I believe that because she says so, but that doesn't mean I wasn't a mistake. "There can be good mistakes," I used to tell her.

Mom was in the next room and must have heard me shouting on the phone, but if she did, she ignored me, something that never would have happened before Michael moved out. I kicked the wall a couple times and still got no response from her. It struck me just then that Michael was gone, Charlene was gone, and now even Mom was gone, way gone. I felt too alone to even cry.

II.

I met Michael when I was eight. He was driving a truck for Van Lines at the time and dating Sandra, another waitress at the truck stop where Mom worked. Sandra looked like those chrome decals on the mud flaps of trucks, big head of hair, size three waist, and huge pointy tits. She had about as much brains as those chrome babes have, too. But though

Michael was dating Sandra he always sat in Mom's station at the café because he liked talking to her. The first thing I ever heard Mom say about Michael was "He's so typical. Likes to talk to women with brains but have sex with airheads."

When Michael learned that Mom had childcare problems with me on Saturdays, he started taking me to ballgames. Mom wouldn't have ever given Michael the time of day if I hadn't adored him so much. But we started going out for barbecue on Saturday nights after Mom's shifts and Michael's and my ballgames, and before long they were sleeping together and I don't think I had ever seen Mom so happy. It was as if Michael had reached in and turned her inside out. He was pretty ecstatic, too. He'd never been with a serious woman before and Roberta—my mom—is definitely a serious woman. He said it was the first time, since he was sixteen, that he'd ever been really in love.

Then Mom found out he'd never quit sleeping with Sandra. She canceled out her relationship with Michael like a check she hadn't meant to write. She could be that methodical and thorough. After that Mom managed to take some Saturdays off and tried taking me to ballgames, but they were no fun without Michael. Mom had no idea how to keep statistics, and I hadn't yet learned enough from Michael to do it on my own. "We'll look for a class, Kathy," she had said. As if there were a class on baseball statistics out here in the New Mexican desert.

That was just the beginning. We ran into Michael in the grocery store a month after they broke up and I blurted out that I'd like to go to the ballgame. At that age I didn't understand faithlessness, and I pretty much blamed my deprivation of Michael and baseball on Mom. He instantly agreed to take me to a ballgame and Mom fired him a vicious look. I thought she was being a bad sport.

I began to realize the extent of my power over my mother's life when, after Michael and I had gone to several ballgames, she began seeing him again, too.

Mom's first novel got published the following year. She
began a second one right away. When that got published,
her publisher sent her off on a reading tour. That's when
Michael had his next affair, the one that Mom never knew
about, though everyone else in town did. I was eleven. Michael was living with us by then. He'd quit driving the big
rig and had opened his own auto parts shop. The whole time
Mom was out of town he moped, at least around me. I think
he wanted me to know how hurt he was that she'd left him
for so many weeks. As if that would justify his affair. I was
torn. I didn't think it was justified, but I loved Michael. I
pretended I didn't know.

This third time (second, to Mom's knowledge), there was
no pretending. When Mom found out in the early spring,
she remained calm. She announced that Michael's problem
was maintaining intimate relationships.

"Seems like he maintains too many of them, if you ask
me," I commented.

"Kathy, when a person is afraid of his own depth of feeling, he'll try to spread out his feelings so that he doesn't
have to feel so deeply."

Mom repeated her diagnosis every day for a week, then
she abandoned reason altogether and blew up. At first I was
relieved. All that psychology talk made me nervous. But
then I was frightened. Her rage hurled her into some kind
of Twilight Zone and I thought she would never come out
of it. But when Charlene's parents censored Charlene from
my life, I joined Mom, attaching myself like a caboose to
her rage at Michael. From what I could tell, it was all his
fault. If he hadn't cheated on Mom, I'd still have a family.
I blamed him for Mom's inaccessibility to me. It was his bad
luck that he chose the week following the Saturday in June
that Charlene's mother discovered us in bed to come beg
forgiveness of Mom. I heard it all because it took place in
Mom's bedroom which is next to mine. Michael was so quiet
through Mom's reasoned speech (she could pull off a show
of rationality even at the heights of her fury) that I wondered
if she'd killed him first. She finished in a low steady voice.

Michael had to know that that voice meant now and forever dead to Roberta. She said, "I've loved you more than anyone in the world, and I've given you every break I can think of. Now, I don't want to ever see you again. This is a small town, Michael. So I'm going to ask you to do one last thing for me: respect my feelings. Please don't try to see me or call me. It's over and this time it's so final you could be a lead weight dropped in the sea's abyss as far as I'm concerned."

Leave it to Mom to be dramatic and literary even while ending the love relationship of her life.

I snuck out of my bedroom to watch Michael leave. His face was gray and slack as he left Mom's bedroom. I'd never seen him cry, but I could tell he was going to now. "Michael," I said as he opened the front door. Michael is over six feet tall and he nearly cracked his head on the top jamb of the door I'd startled him so. A tiny burst of hope skidded across his face. How many times had I saved him from Mom's fury? But he had the wrong idea this time. I told him, "You deserve it, every single word. You're a slime bucket, and the whole fucking town knows it." Then I just stared at him until he got up the courage to continue out the door and leave. I watched out the window and saw him drop his head down on the steering wheel. His back started heaving. I have to admit a very big part of me wanted to run out there and throw my arms around him. I loved Michael. But he had hurt Mom so badly I didn't know if I'd ever see her throw her hands on her hips and die laughing again. Even a smile seemed damn near impossible at this juncture. And me, I had no one. Not Michael, not Mom, and now not even Charlene. So I let Michael cry. I wanted him to feel the full extent of the damage he'd done.

The next day I stopped by his auto parts shop on my way home from school. I had never felt more evil and venomous in my life. But when I entered his shop, he looked so pleased to see me that I almost couldn't do what I'd come for. "Kathy! Here, sit down. Want some coffee?"

Even then I knew my hatred was for Charlene's parents,

not Michael, but that didn't stop me. I snarled, "Since when do I drink coffee?"

"Well, it's all I have."

I said, "Michael, you are not invited to any more of my games, including the State Championships. I want nothing more to do with you." Then I waited to see the agony register on his face.

"Sugar." He'd always called me sugar. "This is between your mother and me. It doesn't have to have anything to do with you and me. We've always had a separate relationship." Since being with my mother, Michael had learned all kinds of relationship talk.

"It has everything to do with me," I said. "Roberta's my mother. You've cheated on her three times. You think I never knew about that second time, but I did. Everyone in town knew, except Mom. If you can't control where you stick your dick, then forget it. I don't want to see you at *any*, and I repeat, *any* of my games. Got it?"

Michael looked devastated. I was his only link to Mom, and I knew he counted on somehow working his way back to her through me. He always had. Sometimes I thought Michael and I had been closer than he and Mom. We were definitely more alike. He claimed he got involved with Mom, back when I was eight years old, because of me. He said, "Any woman who could raise a daughter like Kathy, I wanted to know." Besides being his link to Roberta, Michael had taught me everything I knew about softball. He'd bought me my first glove, showed me how to tie a softball in it and oil it for shape, and taught me how to keep statistics at games. He'd coached me for hours and hours and hours over the past seven years. I knew that my going to the State Championships was one of the proudest moments of his life. I intended to deprive him of it. For hurting Roberta. For hurting me. And because I missed Charlene so much even my toes ached.

"What can I do?" he asked. "For god's sake, Kathy, what can I do?"

"There's nothing you can do. You've fucked up royally."

III.

If I had known everything about love in April and May, I
began to know a lot about loss by late June. A week before
the State Championships I broke down. I called Michael at
the shop. When he answered, "Main Automotive. Can I
help you?" I just said, "Okay, you can come."

"Kathy!"

"Yeah."

"Hold on a minute." He must have put his hand over the
receiver because I could only hear his muffled voice say, "I
got to take this call. I'll be with you in a minute." Then he
was back. "To the games next weekend, you mean?"

"Yeah."

"Well, uh, great." Like, what else could he say? Then he
thought of something. "Does Roberta know?"

"Know what?"

"That you said I could come."

"I didn't mention it."

"Oh."

"She doesn't own the ballpark."

I could hear him smile. It was like I was dangling a bit of
bait. My power to grease his way back to Roberta, if I chose
to. "Right," he said. "You know I'll be there."

"Right," I answered, still all business. I wouldn't cut him
much slack. I needed to have the feeling he was wrapped
around my little finger.

IV.

"Kathy," Mom said the morning of the State Championship
finals. We'd already breezed through the quarter- and semifinals. "You're in some kind of trouble. I've been a bad
mother. I'm sorry, but I'm just cracking up right now."

"Then crack." Why was she laying all this on me now?
On the morning of the most important game of my life?

"You're in trouble, aren't you?"

"No more trouble than you're in." For the last two nights Mom had sat with Michael in the bleachers watching the quarter- and semifinals. Both nights she had come home, gone to bed, and cried. I'd never seen her so broken, nor so stripped of pride. Because Mom has pride even in private, even alone in her bedroom. I got the feeling she wanted suddenly to talk about my trouble now because hers had become so acute.

"What happened to Charlene? Why isn't she in the games?"

"Fine time for you to be asking now," I answered.

"I'm sorry I haven't been here for you."

What could I say? In a way, Mom and I were going through the same thing. Only Michael had been a shit to her. Charlene had no control over what had happened to us. I felt superior to Mom, for having sense in whom I chose to fall in love with. So I sighed and said, "You got your own problems, Mom. Deal with them. I have a game to play tonight."

Mom looked bad, sallow and puffy. I sort of hated myself for not caring, for needing Michael for my own reasons.

"Well," she said. "It's only right of course that Michael should come to the games." She said this as if it were a conclusion to the discussion we'd just had about her and me.

"It's the principle of the thing," I said sarcastically, tossing her one of her own favorite expressions.

Everyone turned out that night for the State Championship finals, which by luck were held in our town. The Lions were selling hot dogs, popcorn, and sodas. The fans in the bleachers began rhythmic stomping even before we started warming up. The local radio station was broadcasting the game for those who couldn't be there in person. I wondered if Charlene, who was back from her trip with her parents, would be able to listen.

Michael had painted an enormous purple and red (our school colors) banner that read, "Wildcats Shred the Trojans," which he hung off the railing of the upper bleachers. He sat next to Mom in the lower bleachers right next to third base. Mom had that brown and orange Navaho blanket, the one she brought to all my games, wrapped around her shoulders. During warm-ups, as I fielded grounders and tossed them to first, I could read the tension between them. Michael sat with his hands folded and dangling between his knees which he held humbly close together. He slouched a little as if to diminish himself. Roberta held the blanket around her like some kind of armor and wore her best "I don't give a shit" expression which was way too obvious to be effective. Both of them I could tell were trying very hard to let the game be the focus of the night, not each other. I also tried to let the game be the focus, not them and not Charlene's absence.

We won, of course. Not that it was an easy game. But I never questioned our winning. I felt as if everything rode on our victory. If we won that game, I had reasoned with myself, somehow everything else would fall into place.

The fans swarmed onto the field. They picked up every last one of us on the team and passed us over their heads shouting and singing the school song. Very corny, really. I didn't usually go in for that school spirit stuff, but it was fun for a few minutes.

I had plans, though, and needed to get out of there before the crowd thinned too much. I didn't want anyone to notice me leaving.

"Listen, Kathy," Mom yelled into my ear. The fans were still shouting and screaming. "Michael and I are going somewhere for coffee. I don't think we'll go over to Galluchio's. That okay with you?"

"Sure," I said, thinking *perfect*. "I'll see you later." I hardly had time to think about the significance of their going for coffee together, I was so glad to have them leave. My knapsack was already packed. I'd go right now, straight from the game. That'd be the best.

V.

Though ten at night, it was hot, around seventy degrees, and
I was still sweating from the game. I wore my uniform and
walked as fast as I could. Mom and Michael running off
together after the game made my getaway a cinch. Even so,
I felt funny about them not going to Galluchio's with the
rest of the team to celebrate. I mean, I wanted them to get
back together, if that's what they were doing, but couldn't
their stale old romance wait one more evening to get glued
back? After all we'd just won the State Championship! Yet,
it *was* perfect because I wasn't going to go to Galluchio's
myself and would have had to come up with some fantastic
excuse which I hadn't thought of yet. So I had no right to
be so hurt. Still, I was.

Soon though, as I drew closer to the Desert View Motel,
I forgot all about Mom and Michael. The anticipation of
having Charlene under my hands, under my thighs, made
me sweat more. She was supposed to arrive first because she
looked an easy eighteen, I barely looked the fifteen I was.
We chose the Desert View Motel, the last one on the highway
out of town, about four miles from my house, two from hers.
The place was a complete dump, from what I could tell.
We'd always wanted to go away together, to Alaska or Hawaii. A motel room, I thought, is a motel room. And tonight
we could be near the Arctic Circle or at the base of a volcanic
cone for all we'd know. I wanted Charlene, tonight, and
whatever was left in the world would radiate out from her,
a complete world in its own, a paradise, her father's god-
damned Garden of Eden. Tonight I would have Charlene
to myself.

My palms sweated, but despite the heat, my feet were icy
and damp. A car slowed and its driver asked did I want a
ride. I almost took it, to get there faster, but I knew she
wouldn't be there yet. I wasn't supposed to arrive first.

But a few minutes later, there I was, standing in the small
weedy courtyard of the Desert View Motel. I didn't know

whether I should hang around and wait or try to check in. If I tried to check in and they didn't let me, we'd be real stuck. If I hung around, someone might call the police or see me. A small breeze slid across the courtyard like a rat scuttling across garbage, sly and stupid. I felt exposed, spot-lit, and had to move, get away, so I walked into the office. A young woman who moved and looked as if she were eighty shuffled out of a doily- and afghan-draped living room adjacent to the office. She rubbed her hip as she walked, making sure that I knew I'd caused a woman with a bad hip to rise from the couch. She didn't speak and I saw that she considered asking for a room to be some sort of affront.

"Has a Cassandra Ogilvy checked in?" I asked. We'd chosen fictitious names. As I spoke, the nauseous smell of hot wool, a mixture of the woman's dinner and the afghans covering the surfaces in the front room, invaded me. If I wasn't tasting Charlene's mouth on mine, smelling her lotion in my face, I'd have left in a second. Nothing short of Charlene would have kept me there.

The woman looked me over a while longer before checking her book. I felt conspicuous in my uniform. "No."

I pulled out thirty dollars and laid it on the counter. "I'd like a room."

The woman was a pro at communicating without words. She shook her head with disgust and, gripping her hip, bent to open a drawer where she kept cash. After painstakingly getting her drawer open, she took my money and handed me the key to number six.

The room was dark, the light bulb over the bed was out and only the bathroom light worked. I pulled back the bed-spread and wadded it up in a corner on the floor. It was made of that plastic material that gets lots of little balls on it. The sheets were not a lot better, full of cigarette burns, but at least they looked clean. I sat down and bounced for a moment on the springs. I closed my eyes and imagined the Pacific Ocean crashing against a beach outside the window. Possible, but Charlene would never buy it. I tried alpine slopes, a sharp slanting roof overhead, icicles pointing off the rafters right out the window. But the sweat baking under my arms, running down the back of my neck, canceled that one out. *I* didn't mind that we were going to be right outside of town, in a creepy motel, but I thought that Charlene would. I looked around trying to figure how to improve the atmosphere. The rug was gritty with dirt and the green walls smudged. I stood up to pull the curtains shut but they pulled only so far, leaving a crack. Finally I decided that I would clean up myself. The shower head was a good one and the cold water a blessing. I let it leach the salt out of my hair first and then run down my front and back. I couldn't help touching myself, thinking that Charlene was walking toward me now. She said she knew a way to get here without walking the main road, like I did, and would only have to come into sight of the main road when she ducked into the motel. She'd like it, I thought, if I was watching for her out the window so she didn't have to go into the office and ask for me. We'd said midnight and it was eleven-thirty. So there was time to wait. And to shower. I thought of Charlene striding through the night heat, her big legs filling her jeans, her arms swinging wide the way they did. And I moved my fingers through the hair between my legs, let the water stream down my breasts. I thought of Charlene not wanting to be late, of her jogging a little, a light wetness forming on the back of her neck as I eased a finger up myself and then let it slide out and across my clit. I wanted her to taste like salt when she got here, I wanted Charlene to be flushed with anticipation. As I came, I saw Charlene's tongue, instead of my finger, sliding across me, easing into me. I fell back against the metal shower stall and moaned her name.

I thought I heard a knock on the door. She was early! I quickly toweled myself dry and shouted, "Hold on one minute!" Suddenly I was shy and didn't want to open the door naked. I pulled on my jeans without underpants and found the clean white sweatshirt I'd brought in my knapsack. My hair a wet tangle, I pulled open the door unable to control my enormous grin.

The proprietor of the motel stood on the threshold of my paradise. She wore pea green stretch pants and her hair in curlers under a plastic cap. "Your change, you forgot it."

I took the money. She and I both knew the price of a room was twenty-eight dollars, there were signs everywhere, but when she hadn't offered me the two dollars back I figured she was accepting some kind of bribe. I wasn't sure what I would have bribed her for, silence maybe, but I'd let her keep it. Why had she changed her mind?

"You say you have a friend coming?"

I nodded. What was it to her?

"I'll send him along when he gets here."

"*Her* and *she*. Cassandra, remember?"

The woman looked me over good.

"I'm renting a motel room, okay? Is it that big a deal?"

"I don't tolerate no drug dealing." Her eyes were keen, a metallic hazel. She could be as young as twenty-five, I realized, but she desperately wanted to be much older.

"I'll deal my drugs somewhere else, then." And I shut the door. I had to before I killed her for not being Charlene.

While I combed my hair I heard someone turning a key into the room next door. A bag was thrown against the wall, the TV clicked on.

I waited.

Being late was not unusual for Charlene. Who knew what she had to do to get away from her parents? Our plan was that she would go to bed at ten as usual, then slip out after they fell asleep. But maybe her father had a sermon to write, had to stay up late. She might not be able to even leave the house before midnight, in which case she wouldn't get there for at least forty-five minutes.

The heat pushed in on my head like a vise. I couldn't get the window open, so I opened the door. Between my room and number seven were two metal chairs and a man sat in one. "Who are you?"

"Ronald Sweisinger. You?"

"Laura Smith."

Ronald put out his hand. "Too hot for sleep, no?"

It was true. I fell into the chair next to him. I couldn't tolerate another second in that fetid motel room. This way Charlene could see me.

Ronald Sweisinger had a huge mouth with the largest and whitest teeth I'd ever seen. His hands too were very large and he combed them through his hair, over and over again, to keep the few long strands over his bald head.

"I used to be a carpet cleaner," he said. "What are you?"

"I'm a high school student."

"I'm unemployed now. Out of work and out of a family. Wife left me."

I looked at him carefully wondering if my room would be better.

"But I'm living it up tonight. A motel room. A bottle of rum. A six-pack of Coke. Join me?"

"No thank you."

"Good girl. I didn't really want to be corrupting youth, anyway. You hardly look old enough for high school. What are you doing in a dump like this? She your mother?" He pointed to the face pressed against the window of the room next to the office.

"No." I didn't want to talk about mothers. "I'm meeting a friend here."

Ronald leaned back and suddenly looked melancholy. "Savor it," he sighed. "Just savor it."

I tried to ignore him, but finally couldn't help asking, "Savor what?"

"Your sweetheart. Laura, you'll never feel the same again as you do now. Oh, god, do I remember my high school romance. Carla Remington. Homeliest little gal you ever laid eyes on, but what could I expect?" Ronald smiled apologetically and checked the hair covering his bald head.

"You're not bad looking," I said, surprising myself. I hated it when people didn't like the way they looked. Charlene always talked about looking horsey or being too fat. "You're kind," Ronald said. He dropped a few pieces of ice from a bucket at his feet into a Styrofoam cup. He poured a little rum into the cup and then pulled open a Coke and added it. "Carla had a head full of curly hair. Have you ever noticed that all Carla's have curly hair?"

I knew one and she did.

"Carla and I were madly in love. We actually eloped, but her parents had the marriage annulled. I'd hoped that she'd gotten pregnant in our two days together, before they'd found us hitchhiking to Michigan where she'd heard jobs were easy. But she hadn't gotten pregnant. So we were separated forever. I like to play a game with myself sometimes. I think of a certain juncture in my life and try to guess as accurately as possible how my life would have been different if I had done the thing I didn't do. There's a theory, you know, that every time you try to order something in the universe you simply set loose randomness somewhere else. For all I know, by keeping us apart, Carla's parents might have started a civil war on another planet, or caused the beginning of the greenhouse effect."

I smiled. I liked Ronald.

"Who's your young man, or do you mind my asking?"

"She's a young woman."

Ronald was quiet for a very long time. Then he said, "Is it, well, a romantic relationship?"

"I guess so." I was not one for much analyzing. Mom did enough of that for both of us.

"I never much understood that. You know, two gals or even two guys. But that sort of thing is big out here, in the West, I mean, isn't it?"

"Ronald, I don't know." I felt like a child just then and wanted him to treat me like one. Sometimes I acted too sophisticated for my own good.

"I'm sorry," he said as if he understood.

Charlene was supposed to have been here an hour and a half ago. I worried. I knew she would want me to be inside hiding now. After all, it could be anything. Her father could be on his way with the sheriff. But what did I care? I had absolutely nothing to lose. Every last thing I wanted would meet me in this motel room or would not.

Sometimes Ronald and I talked, sometimes we didn't. The

minutes passed like the growth of a plant. If I watched, which
I did most of the time, nothing changed. But now and then
my mind broke loose and rose out over the desert like the
moon, ethereal, light, and free. Then time grew and the
hours passed.

At three in the morning, Ronald offered me some rum
and Coke again and I took it. The night was cool now, the
moon had set, and the stars were dim. We sat silently for a
hour, Ronald having caught me up on his entire life since
Carla. I had told him the play-by-play account of the championship game, the account I had been preparing for Charlene. At four in the morning the phone in my room rang.

"Kathy. It's me."

I was amazed that my relief to hear her voice lasted only
a second. Then I was furious. "Charlene, where the fuck *are*
you?"

"I can't get out," she whispered, her voice barely audible.
"Tomorrow night. I'll try again."

"Charlene!"

She hung up.

I awoke the next day at noon and opened the door. A
couple Cokes and half a bag of sour cream and onion potato
chips sat next to our chairs from the night before. Ronald
had left. I popped open a warm Coke and slouched in one
of the chairs. As I finished off the chips, I began to doubt
everything that had happened between me and Charlene.
Who was she, anyway? Maybe I'd made it all up so I didn't
have to deal with Mom and Michael's breakup.

But I knew that wasn't really true. If nothing else, there
had been that one moment. We were at practice, about a
week before her mother found us in bed. I'd walked out to
my position, paced off a few steps from third base. An afternoon breeze came up, and I was a little hungry—I always
liked to play ball slightly hungry—and this peace came over
me. It was like complete happiness, steadiness, all the squig-
gles in my head lying down and relaxed. It was a clean and

spacious euphoria. I smiled at Charlene at short stop and she knew exactly what I was feeling.

"State of grace," she said.

"What?" I asked.

"It's a state of grace."

VI.

At six in the morning, after my second night in the Desert View Motel, I walked home. Charlene hadn't even called the second night. I felt like a dog. That loyal. That stupid.

The day was dusty and hazy. I scuffed along slowly wondering if Mom had sent out the police. I wondered if Michael would be there at the house. My eyes felt gritty, and there was Coke spilled on my sweatshirt. I wanted a shower, a good sleep, and then I wanted to toss the softball around a little.

The screen door to our place scraped the porch, as it always did, when I pulled it open. Mom and Michael jumped off the couch. Mom's eyes looked red and swollen. They both cried, "Kathy!" and fell all over me. For a few moments, as I clung onto Mom and Michael, I forgot all about Charlene. I finally cried.

That afternoon, after Mom called off the police and I slept, we barbecued some chicken and Michael made his special potato salad. I felt completely drained, both in the good relieved sense and in the bad empty sense. We didn't talk much, just sat on the porch together, the three of us, and watched it grow dark and listened to the crickets.

VII.

I saw Charlene a few times that summer. Around town. She had graduated of course and gotten a job checking at Safeway. She ignored me, and I never tried to talk to her. I didn't really even *want* to talk to her anymore. Oh, she was still the same old Charlene, shouting jokes to all the other checkers in Safeway, throwing the groceries in the bags without enough care for not bruising avocados or squashing strawberries. But I saw that the authentic Charlene had sunk even deeper into her body and that she wasn't going to even *try* to coax her out.

It's not like I just let it all go easy. Presto! I'm over her. I cried and sulked and pouted. I took long soulful walks out to the ballfield and lay on my back in left field for hours at a stretch. But I knew better than to try to find the Charlene I loved—the Charlene that knew the meaning of grace—in the Charlene who checked groceries at Safeway and wouldn't speak to me. I'm not stupid. I realized pretty quickly that surviving my sorrow over Charlene was just another way of beginning my life.

Besides, I had learned that softball and sex were two separate things. And understanding that distinction was a far greater loss than losing Charlene. For the rest of my life, I would be looking for the kind of sex that was synonymous with pine nuts and spring breezes, hardball and aching muscles. For love that was grass stains under a sky full of stars, the snap of my wrist and a hurtling softball, the taste of hard-won sweat. For the rest of my life, love would be letting go of Charlene.

Commercial Breaks

Cass Nevada

When Renny left me, she said it was because of the TV. I
admit it, while we were together I watched a lot of TV,
maybe too much, maybe she was right. But she watched it
with me, almost every night. Then all of a sudden, after two
years together, Renny up and left, just packed her things
and moved out. She didn't make a big scene or drag it out,
she was just here today and gone tomorrow.

It was right in the middle of *Hill Street Blues*, a repeat,
the one where Joe Coffey gets killed. Renny came into the
living room and stood between me and the screen and said,
"Either you turn this thing off right now or I'm leaving." I
stared at her, I thought she was kidding, but she didn't crack
a smile, not even a little one. Just then, shots rang out and
I knew Joe was getting aced. It was really a sad scene, one
of the saddest, so I tried to kind of see around her, I didn't
even think about it, I just leaned a little to the left so I could
see the screen and Renny said, "That's it! I'm out of here."
At the commercial I went into the bedroom to try and talk
with her but she just said forget it, no matter what I said,
she said, forget it. Then she said, "The commercial's over,
shouldn't you get back to your show?" And she was right,
so I did, thinking we'd work it out later. I never really under-

stood why she left. She wouldn't talk to me about it and what she did say didn't make any sense because from where I stood, if it weren't for TV we never would have even met.

It was the summer J. R. got shot on *Dallas*, the first time a serial ended its season with a cliff-hanger. It's done all the time now so you might think it's always been done like that but it hasn't. *Dallas* was the first. Personally, I was certain Sue Ellen shot him and I didn't blame her. I spent a good part of that summer explaining to my friends and really anyone who would listen that it was Sue Ellen. In fact, that's how I met Renny. I thought she was great. Renny, I mean. I never did like Sue Ellen. Shooting J. R. would have greatly improved her personality, as far as I could see. Anyway, my friend Teri had a potluck dinner the night of the season premiere and Renny, a relatively new convert to *Dallas*, was there. We got to talking about the show and I was filling her in on all the seasons she missed and I remember she kept saying over and over, "I never watch TV but *Dallas* is such a social event, how could I resist?" I thought she was kidding. She reminded me of Joyce Davenport on *Hill Street Blues*, cool and intelligent, beautiful and brainy, what a catch, I thought.

After a few dates, she started staying at my house most of the time and finally she moved in. By that time, I had introduced her to *Cagney & Lacey* and *Knots Landing*. She was impressed when I told her that Gary from *Knots Landing* was actually J. R.'s brother but he left *Dallas* a few seasons ago and moved to California where he started his own show. Incredible, she said. Still, I should have seen it coming, I really should have. After our first year together, she started complaining about the TV. She accused me of "indiscriminately watching anything that came across the screen," which wasn't true. I rarely watched sports, for example, and never football and I was kind of suspicious of women who did.

The show that really sent her over the edge was *Star Trek*. She would scream, really scream, "How many times have you seen this episode? Ten? Twenty? I've seen it twice and I never even watched this show before I met you!" She claimed I had something she called Star Trek Amnesia, she said I would purposely forget having seen an episode until the last ten minutes of the show, then I'd say, oh yeah, I remember this, but by then it was too late, I'd just go ahead and finish it.

Well, after Renny left, I thought a lot about my TV habits. I thought maybe she's right, maybe I'm becoming a total lowbrow imbecile. I mean, I'm a college graduate, I'm not an idiot. So, I unplugged the set and put it in the basement. I want to tell you, those were some pretty dark months for me. Not only did I lose my girlfriend, I lost Cagney *and* Lacey, Joyce on *Hill Street Blues*, and Sue Ellen on *Dallas*, not that I really missed *her*, I didn't but in a way I did because she was trying to get sober when I quit watching and I'd find myself at work or late at night wondering how she was doing.

About a year and a half after I quit TV, I met Mona. Mona reminded me a lot of Renny who I never saw again after the last time she came over to get the rest of her stuff. Renny was surprised not only that the TV wasn't on but that it was gone. I told her I had changed my ways but she just laughed and said, "Yeah, right, you and J. R." For some reason, her mention of J. R. made me feel hopeful and I thought for sure she'd come back. But she didn't and a while later I heard she hooked up with some ultra-correct professor from the Women's Studies Department at the university. Everybody said it was true love and what a perfect couple they made. Good for them, I said, maybe Donahue will have them on his show as America's only perfect lesbian couple. I was angry for a while, but I didn't go downstairs and get my TV which was what I felt like doing. No, I was going to prove I didn't need that TV. Whenever the subject of TV came up, I simply said, I don't watch TV. I loved the silence that always followed my pronouncement but when they finally went on talking, I felt starved for the details of J. R.'s latest schemes and Sue Ellen's relapse or recovery.

It was about the time that Sue Ellen's drinking took her
to some dark Dallas back alley, sharing her bottle with common winos, that I met Mona. I was certain that this was a
match made in heaven, that this was *it*. Mona was bright and
beautiful just like Renny with one major difference: she
loved TV. She watched it all the time, more than I ever
watched it. And she did something I never did—she watched
soaps. She was raised on them, she said. She used to watch
them with her mother and whenever she phoned her mom,
the bulk of their conversation revolved around who was
doing what to whom where. I loved Mona instantly and
devotedly.

The first night I had her over to my house I prepared
everything carefully. I brought the TV up from the basement,
dusted it and cleaned the screen and set up TV trays in front
of the sofa so we could watch during dinner. I was nervous.
I hadn't really told Mona I didn't watch TV anymore. I was
scared to. So I thought I could just fake it. I made sure
dinner was ready by seven P.M. so we could watch an old
B&W episode of Perry Mason while we ate. It was right in
the middle of a Toyota commercial where this guy drives his
red truck all over and finally ends up on top of a mesa in
the Grand Canyon that I told Mona the truth. I just blurted
it out, I couldn't go on living a lie. "I haven't watched TV
in over a year," I said. Mona looked at me like I told her
she had dandruff. Unbelievable, she said. And then she
started to laugh. Between laughs she said, "So, what were
you trying to be, one of those holier-than-thou-I-don't-
watch-TV types?" She burst out laughing again and I was
embarrassed because over the past few months I had in fact
begun feeling, well, special, I guess, because I had started
reading books and magazines again. When I told my friends
that I no longer watched TV, I felt proud, in a way. I started
wearing my reading glasses more often. But I didn't tell
Mona about all that, I just said I stopped watching because
I was depressed. Then Perry Mason came back on so I shut
up.

During the next commercial, I told her about my breakup with Renny and the TV issue and all and when I was done, Mona looked at me like I was an orphan and said, "Oh, you poor baby." She hugged me real tight and kissed me. For the first time in a long time I felt good, I felt relieved, like the time Cagney broke down and admitted to Lacey how angry she really was at her hero father, and Lacey just held her and rocked her and said it's okay. Finally, Mona leaned back and looked me in the eye. She said, "Girl, you're going to watch just as much TV as your little heart desires!" I thought, this is the beginning of a wonderful romance.

I loved everything about Mona. Her taste in shows was impeccable, I thought, the perfect balance between hard-hitting shows like *Cagney & Lacey* and just plain old funny shows like *Cheers*. And Mona could do this most amazing thing, she could remember all the shows she had seen a certain star in, like she remembered that the first time she had ever seen James T. Kirk was on an old *Twilight Zone* long before he was the captain of the USS *Enterprise*. Really amazing. She even got me started on those game shows that Renny used to scream about. Life seemed perfect and for the first time I felt really comfortable, really at home.

But, a little more than a year and a half after Mona moved in with me, something happened. It was just a little thing so I didn't pay attention but I should have because it was just the beginning. Mona and I were getting ready for work and were watching *Good Morning America*, like usual. One of the guests that morning was this woman who was talking about her new book on chocolate addiction. It was right at the beginning of the inner-child–outer-addiction wave that took over everything for a while. This woman was explaining how eating chocolate affects the inner child and what you should do about it. Then a commercial came on and it was one of Mona's favorites: the one where the woman is being driven crazy by her husband and children who make piles of laundry and mess up the house and burn things in the kitchen. She's worn out and has no life of her own but then her friend tells her about a new oven cleaner that will save her so much time she'll be able to take those tennis lessons she's been dreaming about. At the end of the commercial, she's on a tennis court overlooking the blue Pacific Ocean and she's really happy so you know that oven cleaner really helped her a lot. I don't know why Mona liked that commercial so much; she said she liked happy endings and I guess she's got a point.

Anyway, Mona was watching the commercial but I was still thinking about that chocolate addiction stuff, I was thinking about Mona. I don't know what got into me but it struck me suddenly that Mona ate a lot of chocolate and I thought maybe she was addicted, I thought maybe she was stuffing her inner child. I said, right in the middle of her commercial, "Mona, you eat a lot of chocolate." That's all I said but she looked at me like I had threatened to unplug the TV. I dropped the subject like a hot potato and was relieved that there was a different guest when the show came back on. But I still thought Mona should read the book, especially since she was so sensitive about the subject, but I didn't bring it up again.

A couple of months later we were watching the new series *St. Elsewhere*, it was our favorite and everyone else's too. Everybody at work watched it and every week we had pretty intense conversations about it. It had been a long time since there was a show that everybody liked. *Dallas* used to be like that but not anymore. No one I knew even watched it anymore because it was just getting sillier every week. I mean, what did they think we were, idiots? *St. Elsewhere* was different, it treated us like thinking adults. It wasn't afraid to deal with difficult issues like love and death and, oh, I don't know, lots of things. Plus, you got to learn about different diseases. That's where I first heard about Tourette's syndrome.

So, we were watching *St. Elsewhere* and we were really involved, too. When the commercial came on, Mona turned to me and just stared. It felt creepy and I thought I had done something but I hadn't done anything so that couldn't have been it. So, I just kind of smiled at her. Then she said, "I finally figured out who you remind me of. You remind me of Fiscus who works in the E.R. and tells stupid jokes to people who've been run over or shot. He's such a little jerk and that's who you remind me of."

I was completely confused. What had I done to her? I never told jokes to people who'd been hurt. I didn't get it so I said, "Mona, what did I do?" but that just made her madder. She threw her hands up and said, "You are *so* brain dead. How can you be so insensitive?" It was getting worse by the second. I was relieved when the show came back but then there was Fiscus telling jokes to an old woman who'd been hit by a bus after the brakes on her wheelchair had given out and she went careening into a busy intersection. Fiscus the jerk said, well, that's the breaks, and it was such an awful pun I couldn't help myself, and I started to laugh. I put my hand over my mouth but then I just laughed harder. I apologized to Mona for laughing but she just shifted on the sofa, a little farther from me.

I really wanted to talk to Mona about what she said but I never got the chance because the old lady in the accident died at the end of the show and Mona started crying and locked herself in the bathroom until the *Tonight Show* came on. By that time I was tired and wanted to go to bed. Mona stayed up and watched Johnny and in the morning I found her curled up asleep on the couch. I just let her sleep. I got the small TV out of the bathroom and set it up in the kitchen so I could watch the morning show before work. I closed the door so Mona could sleep but also I think I did it because I didn't want to face Mona.

That night Mona came home late and when she walked in she handed me a big bouquet of flowers. She looked at me and shrugged. She said, "I don't know what came over me, I'm sorry. I love you." I said, "I love you too, Mona." We went to bed early that night and turned on the *Cosby Show* but we missed most of it because we were feeling so romantic, which was okay with me because I'm not crazy about that show.

Everything was fine for a while but then the weirdness, I don't know what else to call it, started again. This time it was during *L.A. Law*, which was our absolute no-holds-barred favorite show. It was everybody's favorite show. It made *St. Elsewhere* look like a picnic, it was so tough. Every week somebody was dying or going to die or falling in love or breaking up, they just did every issue you could imagine. So, this week, it was another episode where Roxanne lies for Arnie and cleans up his shitty life and she does this because she secretly loves him even though everyone else hates him. At the commercial, Mona turned to me and said, "You know, sometimes I feel like Roxanne around you," and she got this disgusted look on her face and kind of squinted her eyes like she was trying to see through me.

Well, this just blew me away. I mean, it's bad enough that she compares me to creepy guys but then, it's not just any guy, it's the worst guy in the whole world. I couldn't believe what I was hearing. I turned away from Mona because I didn't know what else to do, I was so angry. The commercial showed a beautiful woman bathing and dressing for her handsome and successful husband who is pulling into the driveway of their expansive Southern California home overlooking the ocean. I had absolutely no idea what they were selling, everything, I thought. Suddenly, I realized that what Mona was saying was true. Not the part about me being like Arnie because I wasn't but the part about *her* being like Roxanne. *She* was a liar, she lied for her boss all the time when he came in late with a hangover. She even did some of his work. *L.A. Law* came back on but I could hardly follow it, I was thinking about what a liar Mona was. She and Roxanne were two peas in a pod, all right, and when the commercial came on I told her so. I laid it all out for her to see.

Our relationship went straight downhill from that night on. The next several months of our lives together felt like a flashback of every breakup that ever happened on TV. We still watched all of our favorite shows but every time a commercial came on, we'd pick up where we left off, punching, kicking and jabbing at each other until there was nothing left between us but bad feelings.

After more than three years together, Mona moved out, taking with her the small portable TV and the bedroom TV we bought together. I didn't try to stop her. The night she came to get the last of her things I was watching *Star Trek*. I didn't want to watch, it was my all-time least favorite episode, "The Trouble with Tribbles," but there wasn't anything else on and I didn't want to look like I had nothing to do when Mona came. After she got her stuff together, she waited around till the commercial came on and then she picked up the remote. She turned off the sound but I kept watching anyway, like I could hear everything the Isuzu guy was saying. Then Mona says, "You know, this feels just like Renko on *Hill Street Blues* who's just a donut-eating worm, essentially, but you really hope he might change, you really hope all these life and death situations might change him but they don't. Nothing changes. He just eats more donuts." And with that, she dropped the remote in my lap, picked up her last box of stuff and walked out. I yelled through the front door, "Oh yeah? Well, you're no Grace Van Owen, you know. Cool and beautiful? Ha! You're more like Sue Ellen, Mona, you're just like Sue Ellen!" She got in her car and slammed the door, skidded out of the driveway and down the street.

I turned the sound back on the TV right when Kirk was making his speech to Spock and Bones about the trouble with Tribbles. All of a sudden I hated Kirk and I hated *Star Trek*. I threw the *TV Guide* at the screen and thought, if I ever see another *Star Trek* again, I'll shoot myself, I swear I will. I decided I was through with reruns, *all* reruns, and I vowed I would never watch another rerun as long as I lived. I turned the channel to the public station and started watching a show on sea cucumbers and endangered sea life. It was fascinating and I didn't think of Mona at all, although at first I did, a little.

A month after Mona left, I was watching the public station

Cass Nevada

all the time and learning about everything: the stars, earth-
quakes, elephants, hormones, death. The more I watched,
the more I learned. After a while, I took the money I had
been saving for a vacation with Mona and bought a big screen
TV. I started watching British comedies and mysteries. I
began to feel at home with different accents and humor and
best of all, there weren't any commercials. I found a new
circle of friends at work who only watched PBS. They were
smart and worldly, sophisticated, I thought. I admit I felt
ashamed about my past with *Dallas* and *L.A. Law* but I
decided not to say anything. I just put the whole thing behind
me. I felt at last like I had found a way of life I could live
with. I met a new woman at work, Margaret, who was raised
in England and still had a little bit of an accent. She only
watched the British shows on PBS. "American shows are so
coarse," she said and I agreed. "They're positively boorish,"
I said and she nodded. I fell in love instantly and invited her
over to watch *Mystery!* the following week. I couldn't wait
for Thursday.

Alfalfa

Nona Caspers

It's 8:40 P.M. on a Saturday night and Ruthie Marie is not
out driving around the countryside with her boyfriend John
and her best friend Margaret in John's El Camino. She is
not squeezed between John's hard hip bone and Margaret's
fatted thighs; she is not lusting after either of them.

Ruthie Marie is at home, on her belly in the middle of
her bed staring at the mute TV. She couldn't tell you what
she's watching; she is trying not to think. Ruthie is supposed
to be reading her family's Bible and picking out the scripture
to be read at her wedding. The Bible lies at her side. Her
family waits downstairs. In one month, June 1, before the
Minnesota heat sets in full slaughter, Ruthie Marie Sand is
going to marry John B. Koltser. The couple will move into
the Koltsers' second farm about a mile down the road from
their first. John and his dad bought it for them. John will
leave his mother and father and cleave unto his spouse, and
Ruthie will do the same. This is as her mother and father
did, and as her sisters did when they were about Ruthie's
age, which is eighteen.

"Don't be a baby, it's all worth it," Ruthie's sisters assured
her after their special planning supper tonight when she ex-
cused herself with a headache. "You're gonna be a June
bride."

John and Ruthie will be married in the Melrose church by Father Lutkin, a friend of Ruthie's parents and the parish priest who married both of Ruthie's sisters. He also performed Ruthie's, John's and Margaret's first holy communions, and every winter since the third grade blessed their throats against infection. The bridesmaids will appear in Tiffany pink with big puffed sleeves and scooped necks; John will wear powder blue; and Ruthie will blind them all in high-waisted heritage white. Her mother and sisters picked out the patterns and the colors for all the dresses, except Margaret's. For Margaret's dress Ruthie picked a strapless curve-line, and a color the saleslady called *crimson rose*— Margaret is the maid of honor. Ruthie will walk in on her father's arm ten paces behind Margaret, who will lead the way for them down the middle of the aisle alone.

If Ruthie squints between the baby leaves on the elm outside her open window she can spot Margaret's silo over to the left. From Ruthie's barn to Margaret's barn it's a fifteen-minute hike through the alfalfa field. Ruthie shuts her eyes and takes a deep breath, but she knows it's too early to smell any budding plants. After the long winter the ground will need a lot of spring rain and softening for the crop to grow back as thick as earlier years. Twisting onto her side on the bed she switches channels on the TV, and her family's Bible slides to the floor.

Every once in a while Ruthie hears sounds from downstairs. She hears her mother's footsteps in the kitchen, opening the refrigerator—the gulp of suction before the door is yanked away from the frame. The family had already eaten supper by the time Father Lutkin arrived to allot the details of the ceremony, but Ruthie hears the distinct sound of a waxy potato chip bag being ripped open. It startles her. She twitches on the bed because she thinks the sound is springing from inside her. That her stomach or her heart is being grasped by two hands and ripped in half.

Ruthie imagines that her heart is a paper valentine with two identical halves—the kind she and Margaret used to cut

out in school. They folded the paper in half and cut out one
lobe, then unfolded it into a perfect crimson heart, like the
one in the breast of Jesus. Ruthie remembers the time in
grade school when Margaret was mad at her for something.
While the teacher faced the blackboard Margaret dangled
the valentine Ruthie had given her high up in the air, grasped
the two top lobes, and then ripped it in half.

In her room, Ruthie digs her thumb into her breast until
it hurts. She shuts her eyes again, and smells thick fields of
alfalfa. She is ten years old and the plants stand almost as
tall as her waist. She flops her small thongs across her yard
and toward the path she has carved into the field since the
beginning of summer. The corn and oats planted in early
May have sprung up tall and healthy; the second-year alfalfa
stems grow leafy and the tiny purple flower on the end has
just begun to blossom. In the breeze, the purple-tipped heads
bend toward Margaret's house. Ruthie knows tomorrow her
father will cut the field. She's been told that if the flower
blooms and goes to seed the stems won't make good hay.

In his sermon that morning in church Father Lutkin
preached about insides and outsides. He told them that on
God's scale clothes count less than skin and skin less than
what lurks under the skin.

Under her church dress Ruthie's freckled skin tingles over
her bones and though she took a bath that morning and
though the pure wafer-heart of Jesus rests whole in her stomach she feels grimy and excited. She's going to meet Margaret. In her plastic beach basket Ruthie has packed a cotton
blanket, a can of Mountain Dew, a pair of scissors, two of
her sisters' gold barrettes shaped like falling leaves, a pink
comb, and her sisters' *Bride's* magazines. The sun shines
bright and Ruthie sets her basket down to pull on her plastic
shades. It is part of the game she and Margaret play; they
come in disguise. Behind the dark lens Ruthie feels brave
and the world becomes muted and private; she and Margaret
are the only two on it.

The air in the field hangs damp and sweet with the smell

of blossoming stems—but broken plants can be sharp, and Ruthie must be careful. She sees Margaret's taller, thicker body hiking across the field toward her and she waves; Margaret is wearing her floppy hat. When they reach their spot, far from the road and the barn, they kiss on the cheek and cling to each other's shoulders, pressing their flat chests together. Ruthie's chest grows huge and porous as a saint's— she feels as if she would suffer anything for Margaret. She unfolds the blanket and they settle cross-legged on it. Ruthie digs for her scissors and cuts out pictures of brides to tape to her bedroom wall; Margaret reads the articles out loud in her low, singsongy voice. Later they comb their hair into the *Bride's* fashions. Ruthie sits perfectly still as Margaret's square fingers part her waist-length sandy hair into three strands and tickle her scalp. The back of her neck tingles, her mouth falls open and she shuts her eyes. She sees herself and Margaret walking through the purple field in white; the hems of their dresses are stained green and dirty.

Margaret teaches herself how to double braid, crown braid and French braid on Ruthie's hair; then she teaches Ruthie how to braid on hers. From the high heat of the Lord's day to the cool end when the sun turns white Margaret and Ruthie flatten the alfalfa and braid.

Braiding is as old and clean as the Bible, Ruthie has heard her mother say, but when she returns home she takes another bath. In the hot soapy water she scrubs off her top layer of skin to see what lurks under it. She sticks her finger inside herself and pushes it as far as it will go.

After John gives her the engagement ring Ruthie meets with Father Lutkin. They sit in the small triangular room built in a corner at the back of the church. The walls are paneled and a fluorescent light buzzes over their heads. Father Lutkin is a tall thin man with a sense of humor Ruthie doesn't understand, but she trusts him because he has a loud laugh that blocks out any doubt. His round gray eyes sit deep in his face as if protected by the folds of skin around them.

Ruthie tries to look right at him, but instead she looks at her own sweaty palms in her lap, and then at Father Lutkin's photographs of weddings and funerals taped on the wall.

Ruthie tells him she is confused about love. She tells him there are things inside her that no one ever mentions in the Bible. Her voice trembles when she speaks the words and Ruthie can feel Father Lutkin's round gray eyes stare at her small but growing abdomen and then at her throat which he'd blessed all those years. He thinks she is talking about the baby but she hasn't even thought about that.

"There's nothing you can't tell to God," he assures her. "Nothing's too hard for Him to hear."

Ruthie wants to touch Father Lutkin then because she knows he believes that; he can't imagine what she's talking about. She wants him to hold her. She reaches out and straightens the sleeve of her shirt. She wants to tell him that she would talk to God if she thought He was really listening. If she got any hint that He understood such things. There seems to be no way to get the words out of her mouth. Reaching over her to his desk Father Lutkin picks up a half-empty bag of potato chips. Ruthie feels his teeth crunch, as if they were crunching her heart. He watches her and after a long while he sighs. Then, as if taking his turn in an old game Ruthie didn't know they were playing, he reaches over her again and picks up the Bible. He reads to her Saint Paul's message to the Corinthians: "Better to marry than to burn," Father Lutkin reads, and then he wipes a crumb off his vest, and laughs.

The summer when Ruthie and Margaret turn thirteen the sun rises high and hot. Margaret drives tractor in her flowered halter top, tilling a fallow field for next year's oats. Ruthie perches on Margaret's barn fence and watches her. The steel blade of the till digs into bottom black soil and churns it to the top. Back and forth and up and down the field she drives. Ruthie swears she can see Margaret change color right in front of her eyes. The skin on her round arms burns from raw cream white to barn red and her long shaggy hair bleaches straw gold. Ruthie knows the feelings she has don't have anything to do with being fruitful; she knows she has to have her hand all over Margaret's burning skin.

One day they lie on their old red and white blanket in the middle of the alfalfa field. Ruthie combs Margaret's hair over to one side of her face. Strands fall into Margaret's mouth and she plucks them out and holds them up for Ruthie to grasp. Ruthie bends down to clip the hair at Margaret's ear and she dips her tongue inside it. Margaret giggles and bends her neck to Ruthie. Margaret sits still as the alfalfa while Ruthie giggles and licks her neck.

Ruthie thinks: chickens lay eggs, heifers give milk, cats chase flies and she loves Margaret Mueler from across the way.

When Ruthie's sisters turn sixteen they get boyfriends and when they turn nineteen they marry. They set up their own houses close by, with their own family Bible, and swingsets, and vegetable gardens, and Ruthie convinces herself that she and Margaret will set up their own house: Margaret and Ruthie together forever, like Martha and her sister Mary in the Bible. Even when Ruthie's older sister has her first baby, and Ruthie starts seeing John, she somehow thinks her and Margaret will have it all, and things will stay the same. John will be her boyfriend, and Margaret will be her best friend. She never really imagines a life without Margaret.

It is Margaret who first points John out to Ruthie, the day after Father Lutkin christens her sister's baby. John is in the eleventh grade and they are in the tenth. "John's growing up to be a real man," Margaret says with a laugh when they are walking to town and he passes them on his tractor in his swim trunks and waves. Ruthie has seen him nearly every day of her life, but looking is a different story. The tips of John's dark hair brush against the top of his back, which looks tan and flat as the road under her feet. That evening after supper Ruthie hikes across their empty cornfield to the edge of the Koltser barn. It is fall and the ground is just beginning to crackle. The lights are on. Ruthie hears top forty music on the barn radio and she unlatches the wood door and steps inside. When the heat of the barn mixes with the outside air, the hallway fills with a warm mist like a layer of fog or breath. Through the dirty window of the milk tank room Ruthie sees John. Across the barn he kneels in the corner of the calf pen near the open pasture door, bottle feeding a runty newborn heifer. He sings "Stairway to Heaven" out loud with the radio. He sings off-key and the notes float out with his breath.

John never pushes her in any way. They start going to the movies and to bars, and Ruthie is the one to get drunk and light her hand on his arm and on his knee. One night her hand drifts just close enough between his thighs.

Ruthie thinks sex with John will be hard but it isn't. It's as easy as stripping a field, she tells Margaret. When John is inside her Ruthie closes her eyes and pulls his hip bones close. She waits for the heat to reach her heart, the way it does when she's with Margaret, but John never goes that deep.

At school he is never one of the cool guys who brags and cruises around stoned in his car. He is always shy and steady with big warm farming hands. Ruthie watches him set up the volleyball nets in the school gym. He plants one pole on the floor and then untangles the net bit by bit until he reaches the other side. In her room, at night, Ruthie thinks about the family Bible, and about Margaret's skin, and John's goodness, and the tangled feeling in her stomach grows. Plenty of girls would like to date him, and John asks Ruthie a few times to tell him if she isn't truly in love with him, to tell him right away and he won't be mad but just to tell him before it is too late.

"It's already too late," Ruthie replies.

The whole town says John and Ruthie are good for each other. He's patient, Ruthie's not. He plans, Ruthie doesn't.

John is always good to Margaret. The three of them hang

out at the Greenwald bar or the sand pit or between the cornstalks when they grow tall. They drink Miller beer and talk. On the nights John picks up Ruthie and Margaret in his El Camino they all drive around and around the country and they talk about the world until midnight. After Ruthie's third or fourth beer she lays one hand heavy as sin on John's kneecap, and wraps the other around Margaret's ribless waist. They take turns driving fast in a circle from Melrose to Greenwald to New Munich and back as though someone were chasing them.

A week before the wedding John drives over to eat Sunday breakfast with Ruthie's family. After breakfast the couple takes a long walk down the pasture road. Not a drop of spring rain has fallen since the end of April so the soil lies choked and dusty and the oaks, elms and maples that line the road begin to look brittle. But the sky is one of those perfect skies, unyielding and blue, like Ruthie imagines heaven will be. She thinks how funny it would be if Jesus floated down over the pasture and scooped her up right then. Ruthie laughs out loud and John gazes shyly over at her bloodshot eyes and pale face. He takes her hand and says, "You want to marry me next Saturday, Ruthie?" Ruthie looks at the bulge of her stomach, at the ground, at the thirsty elms, at Margaret's silo and up at the sky. Her head hurts and she thinks about the passage Father Lutkin read at Sunday mass, about the Garden of Eden. She says out loud, "The Bible says, Ye shall not eat of every tree lest ye die."

The Wednesday before the wedding Ruthie's father cuts the field. That evening Ruthie hikes through the broken stubble over to Margaret's house. The baby will keep them busy at first, Ruthie thinks—and Margaret loves babies— she loves anything that grows. Ruthie imagines herself and Margaret fashioning the baby's hair and dressing the baby in pink and yellow outfits on Sunday. Margaret has said she doesn't want to marry and Ruthie imagines she can come live with her and John on the Koltsers' second farm, and help them with the fields and the kids. At night, Ruthie dreams she and Margaret stand in a clean long pantry lined with empty jars and they fill them with boiled corn, apples and tomatoes. In back of the house they plant their flower garden with nothing practical the way they always talked about: just rows and rows of zinnia, snapdragon, Crimson Glory and bloomed alfalfa.

Margaret is in her bedroom lying on her stomach on the floor. The bed lamp shines over her shoulder and her shaggy hair covers her face; a stack of papers sticks out from under her nose. "What are you looking at, Margaret?" Ruthie asks.

She hears Margaret inhale before she answers, quietly, "Applications for colleges."

Ruthie settles next to her on the floor and stares at her own sweaty palms and laughs. The room feels cold and she wants Margaret to put down the papers; she wants Margaret to hold her. "Margaret, who could teach you anything, you know everything."

Margaret doesn't say yes or no to that. She just wipes her eyes and sits up on the braided rug and picks up Ruthie's hand and kisses it. "You don't have to do anything you don't want to do, Ruthie Marie. It's all your choice. Everyone here has a choice," Margaret says. "Everybody has to find their own way to grow. You and me, we both have to grow."

After her sisters finish reading from the Bible they'll join her mom and dad in the first pew. When the ceremony ends John and Ruthie and their guests will drive from the church over to the VFW and hang one on. Her sisters say it will be the biggest party this town has seen since their weddings. They invited all the aunts, uncles and cousins from both sides plus neighbors plus school friends and John's baseball league. After the couple opens their presents everyone will dance. Ruthie's dad hired a local pop band that plays the old stuff and the new. John doesn't like to dance, but Ruthie will stand on the VFW stage just like her sisters did, and every man will line up to pay a dollar and whirl her dizzy.

Margaret and Ruthie love to dance at weddings. When her oldest sister got married, Margaret and Ruthie danced the polka and waltzed until Ruthie's feet broke out in blisters. Margaret practically had to carry her home. When the other sister married it was the same story.

Margaret says it wasn't the blisters; she says Ruthie always drinks too much at weddings.

Ruthie's mother and sisters holler up the stairs and ask her if she is ever going to be ready. Ruthie turns her white veiled head away from the mirror and hugs against her chest the Bible she's to hold during the ceremony. She opens the book and stares at the black print. Before she leaves the room to join them she shuts the light off so she can't see the words but only the promising glint of gold on the edge of the pages. It's another beautiful day and she glances out the closed window at the fields. June 1 and no rain means the crops will straggle up dazed and yellow. The first bales of alfalfa wait to be stacked in the barn. From where Ruthie stands, she imagines the smell of stunted, drying stems, and she hopes they'll make good hay.

Chelsea Girls

Eileen Myles

The waitress *was* cute. If you passed by that restaurant on a summer night you'd see all those tiny white Christmas lights in the trees in their backyard where we liked to eat. She was cute in an utterly conventional way—dark hair, very fair skin. No one ever really looks like Snow White but that's what I'm thinking of. And to go out even farther on that limb—the reason Snow White is so unreal and gorgeous for me comes from that description of her my mother used to read before I fell asleep: eyelashes black as black window frames. Imagine eyelashes that dark. No one has them, but my mother gave me women to love.

I was sitting in that twinkling summer restaurant with my girlfriend Tommy who was always trouble, but nights when I had money were okay. We were both sitting in that restaurant and I was writing poems on napkins: "like a fascist. Your/beauty, . . . our drinks . . ." Tommy's mind was wandering, so was mine. I had a shirt of hers on—I worked, but she had new clothes. It didn't seem right but it was absolutely right that I wear them. It was just that when she had money she knew what to do. Mary, the waitress, had blue eyes inside the powerful black Celtic eyelashes. She set our drinks,

vodka tonics, down with authority and no fuss. Having both
waitressed, we knew we were making her night better. Oh
this couple I really loved came in. Drinking a lot, kind of
bored looking. Tommy was tanning that summer and planning our next play. I was writing my poems on napkins and
making our living in a way I would never forget, cooking
French toast for Jimmy Schuyler. Then sitting down and
reading the books I would pick up off the floor in his messy
beautiful room in the Chelsea Hotel. I lived for nights like
the one I was about to have with Mary Turner. Actually the
Mary Turner nights sparkled best in the morning recitation
of events for the amusement of Jimmy Schuyler.

She *is* cute said Tommy—she was preppy looking, athletic.
She wore a white alligator shirt, without the alligator I
think—small tan, not too much, mostly the kind of tan you
get from sunbathing on the roof of the gym across the street
from the Chelsea where I later learned she went. She had
that fresh sort of sparkling all-American look which gets
subtly wild once you pick up that she's a lesbian because
then the strong all-American girl eats pussy which makes
her bad, and everything that's good be bad, and in cahoots
as she's putting your drink down on the round table with an
umbrella in the center and with her big blue eyes she goes
I want you too. It was swift, fast, the check, rrip. Tommy
saw it all. Why don't you get her number. Tsk, I went,
quietly. The tsk carried everything: disapproval, I wouldn't
do that, are you kidding, who cares? My tsk was as tough
and private as every one of Mary's solid little gestures that
led me toward being someone slightly drunker who would
sleep with her that night.

We walked down Bleecker Street, I smoked. Kept the
stubby blue pack of Gauloises in the pocket of the dark blue
cotton shirt that was Tommy's. Sometimes I could forgive
her for buying clothes because I thought in reality she was
buying me clothes. I felt like mother. I paid the bills. She
was the teenager and oddly enough she dressed me. Let's
go to the Duchess I said lighting another one. I slid my yellow

Bic into the small pocket of my orange painter pants. I had
such faith in things. I had a little notebook in my back pocket
where men carried their wallets. Firstly I was a woman, then
I rolled my cash and I put it in my pocket. It was impossible
to carry two square things. If you wanted anyone to see your
ass. And I did but I didn't.

What—so you can see your waitress? She won't be there.
Was she there? I keep seeing her in the second bar when I
was further along the glowing cord of drunkenness and sex.
I saw her in the Duchess and it was electric. I saw her among
the sea of leaning and dark bodies—just a peek. I put the
information away instantly. I was owing Tommy one—making me support her—being volatile so I had to be reliable,
being younger than me so I had to be old. Look who's here
Tommy said. I know I said. I didn't want it turned into a
mockery. Tommy was the boy in our relationship. Not the
butch. No, Tommy was the pain in the neck little teasing
boy—guess who's here means Eileen likes a girl. You know
it was like we were in fifth grade and I was doing something
really finky. There was something very sick about our relationship and to her credit Tommy always pushed it to the
surface as quickly as possible. Could we possibly be two boys
out cruising women together. But then why was I living with
Tommy? What did it mean? Was I that desperate? Tommy
was beautiful, I thought. But at this moment standing there
in the Duchess around quarter of one in the summer holding
a cold can of beer in my hand Tommy's beauty was less than
a fact.

Well go talk to her then! You must really like her. You
are really weird. I wasn't. Not if I was planning to do something, to go after the waitress. Was I planning to do that.
No I couldn't do that. I was the good one, here and everywhere. It was a private universe I assure you but there I
was—sort of a lamb of God or something. I secretly thought
even my poetry was a sign of my goodness. Wet words on
soft limp paper. Holy Holy Holy. All of my pants had a little
black circle, a mark that hit just above the patch jean pocket

of my ass. My life was a network of private signs. Leaking
pens. Stuff that stayed in place as I moved along. There was
lots of trouble but I didn't ask for it. I moved slow across
the dance floor toward Mary Turner who held her beer close
to her shirt and looked up at me unsurprised and said hello.

What a surprise I said, sounding tremendously stupid but
also picking up instantly that what I said didn't matter at all.
Where's your friend she asked. Tommy, I informed. She's
over there I said waving my hand. Can I get you a drink she
asked her tone ironically still implying she was still my waitress. Yeah I would love one of those pointing to the Bud
Lite she held against her breast. We both slightly twitched
at the suggestion that I would like one of her breasts and
the embarrassment loaded her brisk departure and she
smiled be right back with that wonderful natural toughness.

I think it gets learned in Catholic schools. Once a sado-
masochistic nun banished myself and four of my twelve-year-
old girlfriends to half an hour in the paper closet where we
awaited the smell of her soapy body and her middle-aged
teeth bad breath. It always seemed like nuns ate really
strange food. Our crime had been giggling uncontrollably at
her tales about martyrdom. It seems the Romans thought of
nothing all day but how to torture Christians and Sister Ednata did justice to that obsession with her ecstatic tales told
with her big lips of naked Christians tied up and left on the
silvery blue ice in ancient Rome. Women's tits were cut off
and served symbolically on plates, there were endless spank-
ings, rape, tearful pleas by virgins like St. Agnes that their
chastity be preserved and naturally it was not. They were
violated and then they were killed and all these people who
had suffered so much were now in heaven and hearing their
trials just made us laugh and we'd go make eyes at each
other in class and cough into our handkerchiefs such code
words as *ah-slut* which stood for us. Little whores who would
go to hell. Waiting for Sister Ednata in the paper room I
could smell girlfriends and Donna Murphy burped and Deb-
bie Considine's stomach was growling and we were laughing

so hard we were almost peeing and the nun flung the door open and we sobered up. I don't remember any punishment. I remember the riches of the piles and piles of unmarked paper, a heaven of sorts. I remember the shiny wood of the incredibly old lemony-smelling wood shelves. St. Agnes School was a huge old-fashioned box for sex and paper and prospective temptations. It made girls like me and Mary Turner and for that I am grateful.

I raced back over to Tommy, being good. What do you want she said, leaning against a pole. I was wondering what *you* were doing, trying to take on the role of a mild accuser. Really and what's your friend's name? I don't know. I was just telling her what a good waitress she was. Would you like another beer I asked, shaking her can. Tommy smiled. Up at the bar I ran into Mary Turner. Couldn't wait, she asked. Uh, I said. Everything we said went two ways. No I'm getting a drink for Tommy. Well here's yours she said with a smile, giving me a beer and her back, turning to a friend. I looked back at Tommy who had missed the whole thing, bent over the jukebox, undoubtedly looking for that song by Air Supply. She had the weirdest taste in music. She was like a redneck boy from the Midwest who looks like a god. He wore red lipstick. We were fags. These bands she liked told me all that. She should have stayed home and bought a truck. So what's her name, Tommy asked.

God I groaned. I was sort of praying now. Nothing had happened so maybe I should just ignore the whole thing. We stood there in that nook next to the jukebox facing the bar. I was looking at that blond bartender that Irene Young was all excited about. She was cute too. God I was bored. Mary Turner walked up with her blond friend from the bar. Hi she gleamed, aiming at Tom. I'm Tommy, this is Eileen. Sometimes she had excellent manners—it always shocked me. She was so competitive. I'm Mary Turner and this is Beth. Beth nodded and couldn't have been more bored. Maybe we'll see you girls later. We're going to The Club.

Streets were so dark that year and it was really the hottest

summer. I should have been drinking vodka all night, but I
was drinking beer. The smell of bread from the bakery on
Carmine Street spilled over to Bleecker as we were walking
by. I don't know why I was hungry. The sidewalks looked
like it had momentarily rained. Proprietors trying to cool
their sidewalks off and oil in the gutters that made those
teeny rainbows. Urban nothing—I liked it so much. Pizza
shops, all those dangerous boys roaming the streets who were
always trying to get into women's bars. There were tourists
too. Across the street was a bicycle shop where I would buy
a bike next year. Got a cigarette? I didn't bother to question
Tommy who'd been preaching that never again was she going
to smoke. I displayed my pack. I'll wait she said. That's right
I thought. She hates Gauloises. There was a diagnonal brass
bar on the big wooden door. We pushed it. The summer of
three dyke bars in the West Village. We were rich. This one
looked like a Chinese restaurant. Several stars were twinkling outside. The bartender waved. I owed her money. We
went downstairs.

You know we don't have to stay together tonight said
Tommy. Well sure I said. Do you want some money. Come
and get me when you want to go home. Give me five bucks.
I mean we don't even have to go home together. And walked
off. How can you punish someone who's pushing you into
doing something bad. She was Protestant. If anything. She
was like an animal that could sniff out my state before I had
even worked up the question of what I could or couldn't do.
I went up and got a vodka. Hello said Mary Turner. She
was sitting there alone. Where's Beth I nervously asked. Is
Tommy your lover asked Mary Turner. She's my roommate
I said pushing my hair out of my eyes. Between my words
and my gesture it was probably clear that Tommy and I were
having a fight. The best I could ever figure out about talking
to people especially other lesbians was that we were mostly
acting. Mary Turner put her hand on my shoulder. She was
playing with my hair. This was unbelievable. How did you
like your food, she asked. I liked it. Are you ummm. I was

making conversation. I used to be in a program for physical therapy but I dropped out, she replied. I'm a poet I said. She looked at me. I was standing there thinking I'm 29. I wonder how old she is. I sipped my beer. Let me buy you a drink, okay she asked. I nodded. Well what do you like she asked. Vodka tonic? That's what you were drinking at the restaurant. I was standing there praying I would get really drunk really fast. Out of the corner of my eye I saw Tommy strolling by. She looked okay. Do you like Stolly she asked. Sure I said. It's really better for you. Really do you think that way about booze. I don't drink much she said moving her glass around the bar, spreading the circles. I pulled out a cigarette. And I don't smoke. I do. I said. I love cigarettes. Finally I said something intelligent.

Tommy stood about three feet away from us. I turned feeling someone looking. She beckoned me with her index finger. God! You okay I asked. Was there a crisis? I didn't know. I didn't know how to be. I was wondering if you would loan me a couple more bucks. She looked a little sad and vulnerable and the word *loan* implied she had forgotten that we lived together.

The floors in my apartment are nice old wood. There's a tree outside the window and in summer its shaking green leafiness acted like curtains that softened the hungover mornings and allowed the darts of light in the later afternoon to illuminate my place. Sometimes in the afternoon friends would come by and we'd drink red drinks, hot ones. By the fall the leaves were down and I began to think of my apartment as blue. It's warmer now, everything having gone around twice. Tommy used to live here. For a couple of years. There's a character now called Eileen's apartment and perhaps she remembers everything I don't.

Well where are you going. Home. Well I'll see you in a little bit. What about your girlfriend. We're just talking. Maybe I'll get another beer. Oh God this was so awful. And what was on the jukebox. This place actually had one of

those rotating balls. Mary waved from the bar. Tommy
marched over toward her. Oh God. Oh no. Hi Eileen. The
woman I began talking to had big bags under her eyes, was
skinny but kind of powerful. Having a good time, Eileen?
She always treated me like I was drunk. Was she flirting?
Years later I learned she had a crush on me, at least that's
what she said, but at that moment I thought she was laughing
at what an asshole I was. I guess flirting often looks like sarcasm.

Looking up I saw Tommy drink her new beer and Mary
laughing and smiling. She did not have her arm on Tommy's
shoulder. Excuse me I said to the flirt, walking over. They
ignored me for at least three minutes. Can you imagine?
And I'm facing the bartender I owe fifteen dollars to, my
back is to the flirt. So I went to the bathroom. Then they
looked up and I kept walking. In the bathroom I leaned
against the cool tiles and looked at the flooded bathroom
floor. Two women were giggling in the stall. I smelled pot.
It's broken they yelled and broke into gales of laughter. I
thought of the paper closet. I should turn out the light and
fling open the door and I should be and am Sister Ednata.
I looked into the mirror at the dark blue shirt.

Tommy was outside talking to the flirt. I approached but
veered away at the last minute. Actually some really big
woman in a cap was moving at the same diagonal as me so
I chose to surrender. One of these really flowery femmy
songs was on the jukebox. One woman's humble voice rein-
vented and reflected one million times. Eileen Tommy
yelled. It was marshmallow music. I am going to leave now
she confided but I think you should go home with her. Maybe
she has a girlfriend I suggested. Just a roommate. Tommy
—Don't do me any favors, Eileen. *I'm* going home. The ball
turned a few times and I went back to Mary. She's nice, she
said. Listen do you have a girlfriend? I live with my ex-lover.
She's a go-go dancer. And we have a male roommate. He
cleans house. She smiled. Do you want another drink. Can
you handle it she said kissing my neck. I nodded.

We were going up Eighth Avenue in a cab. You know where we were going? We were going to the Chelsea Hotel. I loved the moment when Mary said should we go to a hotel. She kind of snickered like a dirty girl. I was glad I was not with a complete sophisticate. I was with another Catholic. This was unique. It seemed I never met them, or got this close. Well, I have ten I said. Keep it. I'll get it. She was only giving me profile now but it probably did bother her. They probably gave us the tiniest room in the Chelsea. We were on eight. Because of my job with Jimmy Schuyler I was very familiar with the place, its smells and sounds and the degree of dilapidation, the ugly art in the lobby that wasn't distractingly exotic or worthy of note at all. It was normal. It was like fucking at home. You know, like your mother's home. Mary lived nearby and had the cab stop at Twenty-first so she could run up and get a bottle of champagne. It was corny of course, but I had only been corny like this with men, men that I didn't like. To be with a woman who had such a mundane mind about what was sleazy or hot was really great. We opened the door and it was small. The bed a small one was immediately to the right of the door. Mary put the bottle on the night table and immediately began to strip down. She was a sport. She had an athletic body, she wasn't skinny at all, but she wasn't fat. She had a body basically like the women in my family. Most of the women I'm lovers with have bodies like my sister. Not Tommy, but I'm talking from the future now. Her athleticism made me shy and besides I didn't go to the gym and was really kind of scared to take off my clothes. I was drunk and was just more comfortable being dressed. So we rolled around the bed that way for a while, this crazy part of me shocked that I was making out with a naked woman and keeping my clothes on for a while made me a man, my big dick cunt. Please she finally said as if it were something we'd been discussing for a while and she began to unbutton Tommy's blue shirt and kiss my breasts which sort of looked like hers. Then it seemed that every time a woman kissed me and

touched was like something that had never happened before.
Still it's like that. Kind of a shock.

I pulled my own orange pants off. My sneakers I kicked
on the floor. I reached for my cigarettes. She said no. We
were kneeling on the thin bed at the Chelsea Hotel just kind
of facing each other. I kissed her mouth. I looked into her
eyes. The pale blue light flooded in from the back. She had
very round nipples. She would suck mine, I would suck hers
it was kind of like we had both just gotten this toy. She'd
take a sip of the champagne. Eventually she let me smoke.
She smoked too. Eventually she did everything. We rubbed
our bodies and breasts against each other till we couldn't
stand it anymore. She was so pretty. She was very strong.
We rolled around. We held each other down. Then we
fucked.

I had never been fucked by a woman before. It's scary.
You want to do something for so long. Anne Clarke had
black framed eyes. In high school in front of Brighams she
was dancing in front of everyone to a car radio blasting "Girl
I want to be with you in the daytime," except she would go
Beep Beep-Beep Beep Beep-Beep-Beep-Beep and wag her
knees and sway her arms slightly bent just for the absolute
delight of everyone standing there 16 17 18 sipping their
Cokes, watching this girl called Clarksey. It's like having a
boy around. And everyone laughed. We were twelve and
Donna was showing her padded bra in her basement to all
the girls and I was afraid to come in too close because I
thought so much about Donna Murphy and how beautiful
she was and now I would see her nipples. She couldn't handle
it either. We just couldn't handle that I was a lesbian though
no one knew it yet. I was like a boy, that's all.

The first time I was in bed with a woman it was also in
morning light and so was the first time Tommy had her head
between my legs. I was running my tongue along the lips of
the cunt of the first woman I had ever had my clothes off
with and this is what love felt like. One thing, not two. That
was it. With a woman I felt whole, not different. For instance

if I wanted to put a finger inside her vagina and she said not that, then I knew that maybe the new room wasn't as big as it felt and it went on from there, being diminished though never ultimately losing its glamour but being bound nonetheless by what each woman told me lesbians don't do. So Mary started fucking me. One finger two fingers three fingers. And her face all that strong part coming out, dissolving her prettiness and pale freckles and Celtic distance into force. I had really liked the thrusting presence of a man's dick inside of me. What I didn't know what to do with was men. Who would rub their beards against my cunt and up and down my clit for hours and I wondered what was wrong with me it was such a dirty thing. I couldn't get off. Only once or twice. The last man being such a pig that I couldn't believe I was letting him eat my pussy. I had a tremendous orgasm. He laughed. The first woman put her head between my legs and the complete sin, the absolute moment of sex came back and I was all in one piece coming apart. I was willing to sacrifice all for that moment. Even I guess my vagina, that jar. I thought I had to give that up but there was nothing like that at all.

I've gotta go to work. What are you talking about? She was holding my head on her chest. I told you this man I take care of who lives here.

Ten o'clock. I came into the world of 625. I was squinting. Hello Dear boomed Jimmy. O Shit I forgot the papers. I see. I'll go down. It's okay you can get them later when you go out. Are you sure? I'm quite all right. Jimmy was so big. He was like an enormous sunflower lying on the bed of his long skinny room with French windows that opened onto clanging noisy Twenty-third Street. It was a street I knew nothing about till I worked for Jimmy. The Chelsea was a myth loaded with old denizens, Europeans from the 60s, rock bands and then Jimmy and Virgil Thomson. He was so skinny when I met him and now he was so fat. You look a little weathered dear. I do! Well, I put the pan of water onto the stove. I've got a girl upstairs. A friend staying in the

hotel. No we're having sex, I met her last night. I was with
Tommy in this bar, she kind of forced me into it. I'm sure
she did. Actually standing in Jimmy's kitchen such a regular
thing felt strange in a way that fucking in the Chelsea didn't.
Now I felt I was doing the wrong thing. Well, maybe you
want to get back up there. Well, she's waiting but I'll make
you some French toast. That would be fine. I could still taste
champagne while the buttery smell of French toast filled the
pantry. I opened the applesauce and examined the dry stuck
applesauce coating the rim of the glass. I was wanting normal
now and normal was tawdry. What's her name, your friend
upstairs. Mary. She was our waitress. Whose? Me and
Tommy. You girls lead quite an exciting life. Yeah well I'm
sure she's home breaking every glass in the house or selling
my books. Oh I don't think Tommy would act that way. I'm
sure she'd do something better than that. Right. The light
flooded in through the windows as I placed the dish down
next to Jimmy on his bed. There was a little chair, salmon
colored, next to his bed with several packs of Export "A"s,
old coffee and rings on the orange seat from other coffee
cups. There were pennies, two prescription bottles of pills.
Oh God I forgot the pills. Now this really was bad. I was
standing in his room on the old green rug. The floor was
covered with books: Firbank, Virginia Woolf's diaries, John
Ashbery. *As We Know*. He was like a music box. As you
flashed each to him he was bound to respond in his type of
quip: He's writing in columns now. It's pretty good. Oh she's
much too interested in typesetting to really chase pussy. The
phone rings. Hello Dear. I think that would be very nice.
He has big lips. His lips are like some kind of fruit he
squeezes his words out from. I wonder if the drugs do it.
Make him slow and careful. The silences here in the room,
the spaces that linger and fill the air when we speak are what
I know about Jimmy more than the things he says. The room
is yellow. I come in babbling every morning—Oh God what
a night. But I must take care of him first. Once I do—he's
finished eating, when he's lying on his bed with the soles of

his bare feet facing me and I'm sitting in my chair by the
window reading a book I found on the floor—I wait for a
break—Tommy's really mad at me because—I would throw
her out, he advised solemnly. You would? Read my new
poem, Dear. It's on the desk. If you like. Jimmy was gay.
He went to dyke bars in the Village in the forties. The
butches would rise and bow when the femmes came in. The
first day I stood facing him, a thin man with long curly hair
rigidly lying on his bed I blurted out I love your poems. He
said thank you. His friends, a painter and a dealer were
standing nearby. They needed someone to spend some time
with him and give him his drugs. Say your favorite poet in
the world is lying there. Who you've always been told is
unmeetable, has nervous breakdowns, is a recluse into S &
M. Just out of a hospital, almost killed himself. Jimmy Schuyler was my new job. Slowly I moved his possessions to the
Chelsea from an Eighth Avenue flophouse where on the final
day among the dry-cleaned clothes still in plastic bags,
charred bits of poetry on papers, art prints books—I mas-
turbated because it was a filthy and interesting place and he
found out because I told one person who told someone else.
It's all right dear I don't need anything. Go have fun.

From his bed he ran the show. It's a talent a few people
I know have, mostly Scorpios which he was. You'd be hes-
itatingly starting your story, or like a cartoon character running right in when you realized the long wharf you were
taking a short run on, his attention, was not there. It was
hopeless. The yellow in his room became brighter, the air
became crinkly your throat became parched—you felt you
had simply become a jerk. The presence of his attention was
so strong, so deeply passive—such a thing to bathe your tiny
desperate words in that when it was gone you had to stop
and hover in the silence again. Then he might begin, or
perhaps you could come up with something else once the
brittleness, the void passed. You had to stay silent for a very
long time some days. He was like music, Jimmy was, and
you had to be like music too to be with him, but understand

in his room he was conductor. He directed the yellow air in room 625. It was marvelous to be around. It was huge and impassive. What emerged in the silence was a strong picture, more akin to a child or a beautiful animal.

Hello Dear. Sometimes I came in and he was sitting on his chair by the bright window. He got up early. He told me that, but I could also surmise it from the number of cigarettes in the ashtray which he never dumped, and how much spilled Taster's Choice was on the kitchen counter. (*John* says Taster's Choice is the best. The emphasis on John meant both that it was a funny thing to have an opinion on and a useful tip that one should take.) I saw his dick a lot. Probably more than any other man's in my life. It wasn't small, it was kind of large. As I would narrate my nightly voyage he would tell me about all his affairs in the forties and fifties and invariably these often very famous men who were practically myths now would be rated: He was like sleeping with a reptile. Really icky. Edwin. He had a lovely dick. I'd be standing over him holding a dirty dish and figured to leave the silence alone. Well yours looks pretty good I might say as it nudged out of his boxer shorts.

I ran up the two brown staircases to Mary. The firehoses were there. The Europeans were coming in and out of their rooms. I crawled back into the blue bed with her. She was slightly asleep. Not entirely. I don't love you I thought. I kissed her. I kissed her again. I thought of the big sunflower man downstairs. He was not sex. It was something else. I hugged her. She was everything else. It was blue. She was Mary the mother of God. Till checkout time I sucked on her tit.

I returned around 3 with his pills. I knocked. Jimmy I yelled. I had the key. He was sound asleep. I put the pills on the chair. Here's your paper I said to no one. He'd been up making coffee. The kitchen was a mess. I stuck his change between his glasses and this morning's coffee cup. I kept 3 bucks. I stuffed the bills into my orange pants and I felt something damp. It was the poem I wrote on a napkin last

night. The ink was kind of smeared but I could read it. Want
to hear my new poem, Jimmy. I wrote it last night. It's called
"Under My Umbrella."

> the old are very ugly.
> You know what I mean?
> When you see them
> smoking a cigarette, it's
> like the tip of the iceberg.
> And their boozy wrinkles
> under their eyes. You
> know I like this evening.
> I really deserve the leaves
> in the trees
> around this restaurant. I'm
> kind of overwhelmed by
> the beauty of things
> like a fascist. Your
> beauty, mine,
> our drinks, I wonder
> if I should catch
> up, you're drinking
> faster than me, Oh
> I guess I'll get
> another vodka tonic
> and see how the evening
> goes. Clink-Clink.

He woke for a second. Nodded. I'm leaving now. Did you
have a good time? Oh it was all right. Bye Jimmy. Then I
opened the door and stepped back out to the hall which I've
mentioned was brown. It was a hot summer day in 1979.

AmaizeN

Lexa Roséan

I'm sittin there satisfied suckin on cascos de Guayaba con
Queso Blanco n' you're butterin corn. On the cob. I forgot
it was boilin softly all through dinner, "Babe we're on dessert
you wanna go back an eat the corn," I say "Okay let's do
it. You start I'll let mine cool." I see your pearls goin round.
White on Gold. I'm ready. How do I start, like I write this
poem: from the left on in or in the fashion of my forefathers:
right to left eat the ancient script. Or do I anoint the center,
chomp on down, return to centerandslideup in the sacred
manner of the Arts? I think I'll begin at the left, spiral across
then from the right, spiral across again then return the carriage to center and carefully move down around then up
around sucking up the missed pieces.

"This corn is good" you said. I said. We both thought.
Yes. Been boilin a long time. You're done. Never picking
incessantly the way I do. Never quite stripping everything
of all its value the way I do. Almost purposely leaving over
whole kernels and pockets of juice. I am picking mine clean
and dry to the cobbone. "It's warm, wouldn't this be nice.
It would feel good inside," you say turning short of the trash
pail and fingering the cob. You catch me off guard. I'm still
munching. I tune into *Jeopardy!* not wanting to think such

thoughts at the dinner table. But now as I head toward the
pail I am overwhelmed by it, blown away, and melting into
the thought of the warm moist maize in my hand. My mind
is racing. I once went with a straight girl. Before she wrapped
her legs around my lips she told her husband to "fuck her
with a zucchini and save his strength." Yeah but didn't I
hear of some doll who ended up in the hospital with some
fungus of the zucchini growing up her—"What are you saying?" And what about the broad with the seltzer bottle. Geez
two liters. Bottoms up! And it broke in half. "Why are you
dancing with the cob between your breasts. Rising from your
cleavage. Right. I am not alone with Mr. Schweppes. It's
me and you and a hankerin to try something different something unknown. And what? Yes right. The corn has been
softly boiling for several hours. It is safe and organic and
my God you can read my mind. Fuck the dishes. Let's go."
I see your tongue flash between those pearls. White filled
with flecks of gold. "My baby needs some butterin up," you
say, movin in. "You're bad," I say. Movin in. My God I'm
already dripping. The thought of this is sending my skin to
heaven. Why didn't we ever think of this before? "You
know, a thought occurred to me. Something Pedro said.
Pedro in Puerto Rico. About his chickens. Remember. Yes,
he had forty chickens, right and then someone made a joke
about only needing one cock. One cock for forty—what do
you mean I'm spoiling the mood? No really listen this is very
intense. It's revolutionary. Now he said it was true that he
had but one rooster for forty hens but the fact of the matter
was that something in the feed made his chicks lay eggs. The
cock did nothing but doodle doo all day. Something in the
feed. Now what's in henfeed? No. Plantains. Don't be funny.
Be serious. This is serious. It's AmaizeN. I mean when we
were in Amish country you saw those big, ah, vats of corn.
And then they grind them up and feed it to the chicks. And
so maybe, just maybe, as a matter of fact I remember this
old Indian myth about the goddess making people out of
corn. And they were a very beautiful and intelligent race of

people. I mean this could revolutionize our lives and the
lives of all our friends. If you could love me with a cob a
corncob and I, we could give birth to a whole new race of
people. I mean I know it sounds corny, but just suppose we
had a little sheath of our own? What do you mean it would
be all ears? Why would it have bad feet? C'mon wait wait.
Where are you going? I—I spoiled the mood how could I
—I was just trying to get us in the proper holy fitting mood
for this for this new experience in dildo living. I I I love you.
You're my corn goddess. C'mere. I want you I want you so
bad. I want you all the time. Even when I'm on the phone
with my mother. I'm only listening with half an ear and both
eyes on you and I can't wait to get off—off the phone I
mean. And be with you. You're my goddess. My gift of God.
Okay. All right. I love you too. C'mere." (Now we're kissing.) "Hmmmmmm. Did I ever thank you for putting Paris
between my legs? Well I'm thanking you now. Hmmmm."
(Now we're really kissing a lot more and farther down.)

Whoosh. YUNAX. It's in. YUNAX. Yunax, the ancient
Mayan corn god, is with me. Is in me. The god of the mount
and the mountain. YUNAX. What do I think about as my
lover penetrates me with a moist warm ear of corn. What
would you think about? I am moved very deeply by her love
and devotion and the spirit of YUNAX the Mayan corn god
the god of the mount and mountain. I close my eyes and I
feel us together in Mexico. Under the hot sun we climb
together to the very summit of our love. And once there we
rest and rejoice, thank the gods and burn Copal to one
another and the sky. We laugh in the Temple of Venus and
tremble on the Pyramid of Kukulkan. CHAAC the rain god
descends upon us and we are and everything in us is WET.
Chaac it to me. Chaac it to me. Chaac it to me. Her lightning
touches my very core. She sends me into bold electric night.
UXMAL where wild dogs howl upon the wind while we cling
to one another. Dhingos dance down the steep steps of
UXMAL their eyes are crazy with colors and their sounds
are like whips of wind down my spine. I can only cling to
the woman I love. AmaizeN.

And then a surge. A silent surge soars through me. Renews me flushes and fills me and I turn into you needing to fill you too and open and prepare you for the entering of the God. He soars through me sending pulses of light out my fingertips. His fire dances off the tip of my tongue. And I see you roll over moaning, delighted, knowing I am possessed and will possess you. Both of us needing to belong to one another and the ancient god delighting in our resurrection of his power and the ancient goddess smiling through tears—allows all things to grow—including our love. "This corn is good." You say. You think. You know! I take you. Make you feel it. Make you say it again. "This corn is good." Yes. You're done. Filled with pockets of juice. AmaizeN, how hungry we can be. For each other and all we put forth. I am sucking every drop of you left on the cob. This harvest worthy of all praise. AmaizeN!

A perfect pyramid plants a kiss upon my lips
The evening ends like fall upon our lids
ushering in a winter's slumber.
Our blanket from the Guatemalan hills guarantees
to keep all evil out and sheaves us from the cold.
In the morning the gods whisper their assurances
that we will awake and spring forth, renewed in our desire.

A Good Man

Rebecca Brown

Jim calls me in the afternoon to ask if I can give him a ride
to the doctor's tomorrow because this flu thing he has is
hanging on and he's decided to get something for it. I tell
him I'm supposed to be going down to Olympia to help Ange
and Jean remodel their spare room and kitchen. He says it's
no big deal, he can take the bus. But then a couple hours
later he calls me back and says could I take him now because
he really isn't feeling well. So I get in my car and go over
and pick him up.

Jim stands inside the front door to the building. When he
opens the door I start. His face is splotched. Sweat glistens
in his week-old beard. He leans in the door frame breathing
hard. He holds a brown paper grocery bag. The sides of the
bag are crumpled down to make a handle. He looks so small,
like a schoolboy being sent away from home.

"I'm not going to spend the night there," he mumbles,
"but I'm bringing some socks and stuff in case."

He hobbles off the porch, his free hand grabbing the railing. I reach to take the paper bag, but he clutches it tight.

We drive to Swedish hospital and park near the emergency
room. I lean over to hug him before we get out of the car.
He's wearing four layers—T-shirt, long underwear, sweat-

shirt, his jacket. But when I touch his back I feel the sweat through all his clothes.

"I put these on just before you came." He sounds embarrassed.

I put an arm around him to help him inside. When he's standing at the check-in desk, I see the mark the sweat makes in his jacket.

Jim hands me the paper bag. I take his arm as we walk to the examination room to wait for a doctor. We walk slowly. Jim shuffles and I almost expect him to make his standard crack about the two of us growing old together in the ancient homos home for the prematurely senile, pinching all the candy stripers' butts, but he doesn't.

He sits down on the bed in the exam room. After he catches his breath he says, "Nice drapes."

There aren't any drapes. The room is sterile and white, too bright. Jim leans back in the chair and breathes out hard. The only other sound is the fluorescent light. He coughs.

"Say something, Tonto. Tell me story."

"—I . . . uh . . ."

I pick up a packet of tongue depressors. "Hey, look at all these. How many you think they go through in a week?"

He doesn't answer.

I pick up an instrument off a tray. "How 'bout this?" I turn to show him but his eyes are closed. I put it back down. When I close my mouth, the room is so quiet.

I can't tell stories the way Jim does.

A doctor comes in. She introduces herself as Dr. Allen and asks Jim the same questions he's just answered at the front desk—his fevers, his sweats, his appetite, his breath. She speaks softly, touching his arm as she listens to his answers. Then she pats his arm and says she'll be back in a minute.

In a few seconds a nurse comes in and starts poking Jim's arm to hook him up to an IV. Jim is so dehydrated she can't find the vein. She pokes him three times before one finally takes. Jim's arm is white and red. He lies there with his eyes closed, flinching.

Then Dr. Allen comes back with the other doctor who asks Jim the same questions again. The doctors ask me to wait in the private waiting room because they want to do some tests on Jim. I kiss his forehead before I leave. "I'm down the hall, Jim."

Jim waves, but doesn't say anything. They close the door.

Half an hour later, Dr. Allen comes to the waiting room. She's holding a box of Kleenex.

"Are you his sister?"

I start to answer, but she puts her hand on my arm to stop me.

"I want you to know that hospital administration does not look favorably upon our giving detailed medical information about patients out to nonfamily members. And they tend to look the other way if family members want to stay past regular visiting hours."

"So," I say, "I'm his sister."

"Good. Right. Okay, we need to do some more tests on Jim and give him another IV, so he needs to stay the night." She pauses. "He doesn't want to. I think he needs to talk to you."

She hands me the box of Kleenex.

Jim is lying on his back, his free elbow resting over his eyes. I walk up to him and put my hand on his leg.

"Hi."

He looks up at me, then up at the IV.

"I have to have another one of these tonight so I need to stay."

I nod.

"It's not the flu. It's pneumonia."

I nod again, and keep nodding as if he were still talking. I hear the whir of the electric clock, the squeak of nurses' shoes in the hall.

"I haven't asked what kind."

"No."

He looks at me. I take his sweaty hand in mine.

"I don't mind going," he says, "or being gone. But I don't want to suffer long. I don't want to take a long time going."

I try to say something to him, but I can't. I want to tell him a story, but I can't say anything.

Because I've got this picture in my head of Jim's buddy Scotty, who he grew up with in Fort Worth. And I'm seeing the three of us watching *Dynasty*, celebrating the new color box Jim bought for Scotty to watch at home, and I'm seeing us getting loaded on cheap champagne, and the way Scotty laughed and coughed from under the covers and had to ask me or Jim to refill his glass or light his Benson & Hedges because he was too weak to do it himself. Then I'm seeing Jim and me having a drink the day after Scotty went, and how Jim's hands shook when he opened the first pack of cigarettes we ever shared, and how a week later Jim clammed up, just clammed right up in the middle of telling me about cleaning out Scotty's room. And I think, from the way Jim isn't talking, from the way his hand is shaking in mine, that he is seeing Scotty too.

Scotty took a long time going.

Jim stays the night at Swedish. The next night. The next.

He asks me to let some people know—his office, a few friends. Not his parents. He doesn't want to worry them. He asks me to bring him stuff from his apartment—some clothes, a couple of books. I ask him if he wants his watercolors. He says no.

I go to see him every day. I bring him *The Times, The Blade, Newsweek*. It's easy for me. I only work as a temporary and I hate my jobs anyway, so I just don't call in for a while. Jim likes having people visit, and lots of people come. Chubby Bob with his pink, bald head. Dale in his banker's suit. Mike the bouncer in his bomber jacket. Cindy and Bill on their way back out to Vashon. A bunch of guys from the baseball team. Denise and her man Chaz. Ange and Jeannie call him from Olympia.

We play a lot of cards. Gin rummy. Hearts when there are enough of us. Spades. Poker. We use cut-up tongue depressors for chips. I offer to bring real ones, but Jim gets a kick out of coloring them red and blue and telling us he is a very, very, very wealthy Sugar Daddy. He also gets a big kick out of cheating.

We watch a lot of tube. I sit on the big green plastic chair by the bed. Or Dale sits on the big green chair, me on his lap, and Bob on the extra folding metal chair: We watch reruns, sitcoms, *Close Encounters*. Ancient, awful Abbott and Costello's. Mini-series set between the wars. But Jim's new favorites are hospital soaps. He becomes an instant expert on everything—all the characters' affairs, the tawdry turns of plots, the long-lost illegitimate kids. But also on the real stuff—the instruments, the lingo, signs and symptoms. He sits up on his pillows and rants about how stupid the dialogue is, how unrealistic the gore:

"Oh, come on. I could do a better gunshot wound with a paint-by-numbers set!"

"Is that supposed to be a bruise?! Yo mama, pass me the hammer now. Now!"

"If that's the procedure for a suture, I am Betty Grable's legs."

He narrates softly in his stage aside: "Enter tough-as-nails head nurse. Exit sensitive young intern. Enter political appointment in admin, a shady fellow not inspired by a noble urge to help his fellow human. Enter surgeon with a secret. Exit secretly addicted pharmacist."

Then during commercials he tells us gossip about the staff here at Swedish, which is far juicier than anything on TV. We howl at his trashy tales until he shushes us when the show comes back on. We never ask if what he says is true. And even if we did, Jim wouldn't tell us.

But most of the time, because I'm allowed to stay after hours as his "sister," it's Jim and me alone. We stare up at the big color box, and it stares down at us like the eye of God. Sometimes Jim's commentary drifts, and sometimes he is silent. And sometimes when I look over and his eyes are closed, I get up to switch off the set, but he blinks and says, "I'm not asleep, Don't turn it off, Don't go," because he doesn't want to be alone.

Then more and more he sleeps and I look up alone at the plots that end in nothing, at the almost true-to-life colored shapes, at the hazy ghosts that trail behind the bodies when they move.

Jim and I met through the temporary agency. I'd lost my teaching job and he'd decided to quit bartending because he and Scotty were becoming fanatics about their baseball team and consequently living really clean. This was good for me because I was trying, well, I was thinking I really ought to try, to clean it up a bit myself. Anyway, Jim and I had lots of awful jobs together—filing, answering phones, Xeroxing, taking coffee around to arrogant fat-cat lawyers, stuffing envelopes, sticking number labels on pages and pages of incredibly stupid documents, then destroying those same documents by feeding them through the shredder. The latter was the only one of these jobs I liked; I liked the idea of it. I liked being paid five bucks an hour to turn everything that someone else had done into pulp.

After a while, Jim got a real, permanent job, with benefits, at one of these places. But I couldn't quite stomach the thought of making that kind of commitment.

We stayed in touch though. Sometimes I'd work late Xeroxing and Jim would come entertain me and play on the new color copier. He came up with some wild things—erasing bits then painting over them, changing the color combos, double copying. All this from a machine that was my sworn enemy for eight hours a day. We'd have coffee or go out to a show or back to their place so Scotty could try out one of his experiments in international cuisine on us before he took it to the restaurant. Also, Jim helped me move out of my old apartment.

But Jim and I really started hanging out together a lot

after Scotty. Jim had a bunch of friends, but I think he wanted not to be around where he and Scotty had been together so much—the dinner parties and dance bars, the clubs, the baseball team. So he chose to run around with me. To go out drinking.

We met for a drink the day after Scotty. Then a week later, we did again. Over the third round Jim started to tell me about cleaning out Scotty's room. But all of a sudden he clammed up, he just clammed right up and left. He wouldn't let me walk home with him. I tried calling him a lot but he wouldn't answer.

Then a couple weeks later he called me and said, "Wanna go for a drink?" like nothing had happened.

We met at Lucky's. I didn't say anything about what he had started to talk about the last time we'd met, and he sure didn't mention it. Well, actually, maybe he did. We always split our tab, and this round was going to be mine. But when I reached for my wallet, he stopped me.

"This one's on me, Tonto."

"Tonto?"

"The Lone Ranger." He pointed to himself. "Rides again."

He clinked his glass to mine. "So saddle up, Tonto. We're going for a ride."

We had a standing date for Friday, 6 o'clock, the Lucky. With the understanding that if either of us got a better offer, we just wouldn't show up and the other would know to stop waiting about 6:30 or so. However, neither of us ever got a better offer. But we had a great time talking predator. We'd park ourselves in a corner behind our drinks and eye the merchandise. Me scouting guys for him; him looking at women for me.

"He's cute. Why don't we ask him to join us."

"Not my type . . . But mmm-mmm-mmm I think somebody likes you."

"Who?"

"That one."

"Jim, I've never seen her before in my life."

"I think she likes you."

"I think she looks like a donkey. But hey, he looks really sweet. Go on, go buy him a drink."

A few times I showed up at 6 and saw Jim already ensconced in our corner charming some innocent, unsuspecting woman he was planning to spring on me. I usually did an abrupt about-face out of Lucky's. But one time he actually dragged me to the table to meet whoever she was. Fortunately that evening was such a disaster he didn't try that tactic again.

After a while our standing joke began to wear a little thin. I cooled it on eyeballing guys for him, but he kept teasing me, making up these incredible stories about my wild times with every woman west of the Mississippi. It bugged me for a while, but I didn't say anything. For starters, Jim wasn't the kind of guy you said shut up to. And then, after a longer while, I realized he wasn't talking just to entertain us. His talk, his ploys to find someone for me, were his attempts to make the story of a good romance come true. Jim had come to the conclusion that neither he, nor many of his brotherhood, could any longer hope to live the good romance. He told me late one bleary, double-whiskey night, "Us boys are looking at the ugly end of the Great Experiment, Tonto. I sure hope you girls don't get a mess like us. Ya'll will be okay, won't you? Won't ya'll girls be okay?"

Because Jim still desired, despite what he'd been through with Scott, despite how his dear brotherhood was crumbling, that some of his sibling outlaws would find good love and live in that love openly, and for a good long time, a longer time than he and Scott had had. He wanted this for everyone who marched 3rd Avenue each June, for everyone that he considered family.

He's sitting up against his pillows. I toss him the new *Texas Monthly* and kiss him hello on the forehead. He slaps his hands down on the magazine and in his singsong voice says, "I think someone likes you!"

I roll my eyes.

He gives me his bad-cat grin. "Don't you want to know who?"

"I bet you'll tell me anyway."

"Dr. Allen."

"Oh come on, Jim, she's straight."

"And how do you know, Miss Lock-Up-Your-Daughters? Just because she doesn't wear overalls and a workshirt."

"Jim, you're worse than a Republican."

"I am, I am a wicked wicked boy. I must not disparage the Sisterhood." He flings his skinny hand up in a fist. "Right On Sister!"

I try not to laugh.

"Still, what if Dr. Allen is a breeder? I'm sure she'd be very interested in having you impart to her The Love Secrets of the Ancient Amazons."

"Jim, I'm not interested . . ."

"Honey, I been watching you. I seen you scratching, I know you be itchin' fer some bitchin'."

He makes it hard not to laugh.

"Jim, if you don't zip it up, I'll have to shove a bedpan down your throat."

"In that case I'm even more glad it's about time for Dr. Allen's rounds. She'll be able to extract it from me with her maaaar-velous hands."

And in sails Dr. Allen, a couple of interns in tow.

I get up to leave.

"Oh, you don't have to leave." She smiles at me. "This is just a little check-in with Jim."

Jim winks at me behind her back.

I sit down in the folding metal chair by the window and look at downtown, at Elliott Bay, the slate-gray water, the thick white sky. But I also keep looking back as Dr. Allen feels Jim's pulse, his forehead, listens to his chest. She asks him to open his mouth. She asks him how it's going today.

"Terrific. My lovely sister always cheers me up. She's such a terrific woman, you know."

I stare out the window as hard as I can.

Dr. Allen says how nice it is that Jim has such nice visitors then tells him she'll see him later.

"See you," she says to me as she leaves.

"Yeah, see you."

The second she's out the door, Jim says, more loudly than he usually talks, "That cute Dr. Allen is such a terrific woman!"

"Jim!!" I shush him.

"And so good with her hands," he says, grinning. "Don't you think she's cute? I think she's cute. Almost as cute as you are when you blush."

I turn away and stare out the window again. Sure, I'm blushing. And sure, I'm thinking about Dr. Allen. But what I'm thinking is why, when she was looking at him, she didn't say, "You're looking good today, Jim." Or, "You're coming right along, Jim." Or "We're gonna have to let you out of here soon, Jim, you're getting too healthy for us."

Why won't she tell him something like that?

There's a wheelchair in his room. Shiny stainless-steel frame, padded leather seat. Its arms look like an electric chair.

He's so excited he won't let me kiss him hello.

"That's Silver. Your dear friend Dr. Allen says I can go out for some fresh air today."

"Really?" I'm skeptical. He's hooked to an IV again.

"Gotta take advantage of the sun. Saddle up, Tonto."

He presses the buzzer. In a couple of minutes an aide comes in to transfer the IV from his bed to the pole sticking up from the back of the chair. The drip bag hangs like a toy. I help Jim into his jacket and cap, put a cover across his lap and slide his hospital slippers up over his woolly socks.

"Are you sure you feel up to this?"

"Sure I'm sure. And if I don't get a cup of nonhospital coffee, I am going to lynch someone."

"Okay, okay, I'll be back in a minute. I gotta go to the bathroom."

I go to the nurses' station.

"Can Jim really go out today?"

The guy at the desk looks up.

"Dr. A says it's fine. You guys can go across the street to Rex's or something. A lot of patients do. They uh . . . don't have the same rules as the hospital." He puckers his lips and puts two fingers up to mime smoking.

"Uh-huh. Got it."

Back in the room I take the black plastic handles of the chair and start to push.

Jim flings his hand in the air, "Hi-yo Silver!"

I wheel him into the hall, past doctors and aides in clean white coats, past metal trays full of plastic buckets and rubber gloves and neat white stacks of linens. Past skinny guys shuffling along in housecoats and slippers.

The elevator is huge, wide enough to carry a couple of stretchers. Jim and I are the only ones in it. I feel like we're the only people in a submarine, sinking down to some dense, cold otherworld where we won't be able to breathe. Jim watches the elevator numbers. I watch the orange reflection of the lights against his eyes.

When the elevator opens to the bustling main entrance foyer, his eyes widen. It isn't as white and quiet as he's gotten used to. In his attempt to tell himself he isn't so bad off, he's made himself forget what health looks like. I see him stare, wide-eyed and silent, as a man runs across the foyer to hug a friend, as a woman bends down to pick up a kid, as people walk on their own two feet. I push him slowly across the foyer in case he wants to change his mind.

When the electric entry doors slide open, he gasps.

"Let's blow this popcorn stand, baby." He nods across the street to Rex's. "Carry me back to the ol' saloon."

I push him out to the sidewalk. It's rougher than the slick floor of the building. Jim grips the arms of the wheelchair. We wait at the crosswalk for the light to change, Jim hunching in his wheelchair in the middle of a crowd of people standing. People glance at him then glance away. I look down at the top of his cap, the back of his neck, his shoulders.

When the light changes everyone surges across Madison. I ease the chair down where the sidewalk dips then push him into the pedestrian crossing. We're the only ones left in the street when the light turns green.

"Get a move on, Silver."

The wheels tremble, the metal rattles, the IV on the pole above him shakes. The liquid shifts. Jim's hands tighten like an armchair football fan's. His veins stand up. He sticks his head forward as if he could help us move. I push us to the other side.

We clatter into Rex's. There's the cafeteria line and a bunch of chairs and tables. I steer him to an empty table, pull a chair away and slide him in.

"Jesus," he mumbles, "I feel like a kid in a high chair."

"Coffee?"

"Yeah. And a packet of Benson & Hedges."

"Jim."

"Don't argue. If God hadn't wanted us to smoke, He wouldn't have created the tobacco lobby."

"Jim."

"For God's sake, Tonto, what the hell difference will a cigarette make?"

While I stand in line, I glance at him. He's looking out the long wall of windows to Madison, watching people walk by on their own two feet, all the things they carry in their hands—briefcases, backpacks, shopping bags, umbrellas. The people in Rex's look away from him. I'm glad we're only across the street from the hospital.

I put the tray on the table in front of him. He puts his hand out for his coffee, but can't quite reach it. I hand him his cup and take mine.

"Did you get matches?"

"Light up."

"It's good to be out . . . So tell me, Tonto, how's the Wild West been in my absence?"

"Oh, you know, same as ever . . ."

"Don't take it lightly, pardner. Same as ever is a fucking miracle."

I don't know whether to apologize or not.

When we finish our cigarettes, he points. "Another."

I light him one.

"You shouldn't smoke so much," he says as I light another for myself.

"What?! You're the one who made me haul you across the street for a butt."

"And you drink too much."

"Jim, get off my case."

He pauses. "You've got something to lose, Tonto."

I look away from him.

He sighs. "We didn't used to be so bad, did we, Tonto? When did we get so bad?"

I don't say, After Scotty.

He shakes his head as if he could shake away what he is thinking. "So clean it up, girl. As a favor to the Ranger? As a favor to the ladies? Take care of that luscious body-thang of yours. Yes? Yes?"

I roll my eyes.

"Promise?"

"Jim . . ." I never make promises; nobody ever keeps them.

"Promise me."

I shrug a shrug he could read as a no or yes. He knows it's all he'll get from me. He exhales through his nose like a very disappointed maiden aunt. Then slowly, regretfully, pushes the cigarettes toward me.

"These are not for you to smoke. They're for you to keep for me because La Dottoressa and her dancing Kildar-ettes won't let anyone keep them in the hospital. So I am entrusting them to you to bring for me when we have our little outings. And I've counted them; I'll know if you steal any."

"Okay."

"Girl Scouts' honor?"

"Okay, okay."

The cellophane crackles when I slip them into my jacket.

"Now. Back to the homestead, Tonto."

The Riding Days:

One hungover morning when Jim and I were swaying queasily on the very crowded number 10 bus to downtown, I bumped into, literally, Amy. She was wearing some incredible perfume.

"Hi," I tried to sound normal. I gripped the leather ceiling strap tighter. "What are you doing out at this hour? On the bus?"

"Well, the Nordie's sale is starting today and I want to be there early. But Brian's car is in the shop so he couldn't drop me off."

"Jeez. Too bad."

"Oh, it's not that bad. He'll be getting a company car today to tie us over."

"How nice."

She smiled her pretty smile at Jim but I didn't introduce them. She got off at the Nordstrom stop.

After she got off, Jim said, "She's cute, why don't you—"

"She's straight," I snapped. "She's a breeder. Now. She used to be the woman I used to live with. In the old apartment."

"The one you've never told me about," he said.

I stared into the back of the coat of the man squished in front of me. "Jim, shut up."

"I'm sorry, babe . . ." He tried to put his arm around me. I wriggled away from him.

"Hey, she's not that cute," he said when I jumped off the bus at the next stop. It was several blocks from work, but I wanted to walk.

That afternoon, Jim sent me a box of chocolates. The chocolates were delivered to me in the Xerox room. The chocolates were delivered with a card. "Forget the ugly bitch. Eat us instead, you luscious thang." I shared the chocolates

with the office. They made the talk, the envy of the office
for a week. I kept the contents of the card a secret.

Jim sweet-talked my apartment manager into letting him
into my tiny little studio apartment so he could leave me
six—*six*—vases of flowers around my room when I turned
27. He taught me how to iron shirts. He wore a top hat when
we went to see the Fred and Ginger festival at the U. He
knew that the solution for everything, for almost everything,
was a peanut butter and guacamole sandwich. He placed an
ad in the *Gay News* for Valentine's Day, which said, "Neu-
rotic lesbian still on rebound seeks females for short, intense,
physical encounters. No breeders." And my phone number.
Then let me stay at his place and laughed at me because I
was afraid the phone might ring. He brought me horrible
instant cinnamon and fake apple-flavored oatmeal the mornings I slept on his couch, the mornings after we'd both had
more than either of us could handle and didn't want to be
in our apartments alone, and said, "This'll zap your brain
into gear, Mrs. Frankenstein," and threw me a clean, fresh,
ironed shirt to wear to work. He fed Trudy his whole-food
hippie cookies to keep her quiet so he and I could sneak out
to Jean and Ange's porch for a cigarette and a couple of
draws on the flask.

He wore his ridiculous bright green Bermuda shorts and
wagged his ass like crazy, embarrassing the hell out of me,
at the Gay Pride March. He raised his fist and yelled, "Ride
on, sister, ride on!" to the Dykes on Bikes. He slapped high-
heeled, miniskirted queens on the back and said in a husky
he-man voice, "Keep the faith, brother." I got afraid some
guy might slap him or hit him with his purse, or some woman
might slug him. When I started to say something, Jim
stopped. The march kept streaming down 3rd Avenue beside
us. The June sun hit me on the head and Jim glared at me.
He crossed his arms across his chest like he was trying to
keep from yelling.

"Tonto, what the hell are you afraid of anyway? You may
like to think of us all as a bunch of unbalanced, volatile

perverts, but every single screaming fairy prancing down this
boulevard and every last one of you pissed-off old Amazons
is my family. My kith and my kin and my kind. My siblings.
Your siblings. And if you're so worried about their behavior
you should just turn your chicken-shit ass around and crawl
back into the nearest closet because you are on the wrong
fucking ride.''

I didn't say anything. He stared at me several seconds.
Then a couple of punky women dancing to their boom box
dragged Jim along with them. I watched their asses wag off
in front of me. I started to walk. But I was ashamed to march
with him again. Then, when he saw the Educational Service
District workers contingent in front of us, their heads covered in paper sacks because you can still be fired from your
state school teaching job for being queer, Jim turned around
and hollered, "At least you don't have to keep your sweet
gorgeous sexy face covered like that anymore, Tonto." I
stared at my pathetic, scared, courageous former colleagues.
Jim pranced back to me and yanked me into a chorus line
where everyone, all these brave, tough pansies, these heroic,
tender dykes, had their arms around each others' backs. Jim
pulled me along. I felt the firmness of his chest against my
shoulder.

"This is the way it's gonna be, Tonto. Someday it's all
gonna be this great."

This is what Jim believed.

He laughed at his own stories and he clapped at his own
jokes. And he never, never, despite how many times I asked,
told me which stories he'd made up, which ones were true.

And sometimes when he's holding court from his hospital
bed, and he's in the middle of telling us some outrageous
story, making all of us laugh, and we're all laughing, I forget.
When he's telling it like there's no tomorrow—no—like
there *is*—I just forget how he is in his body.

He gets over something, then gets something else. Then

he gets better, then he gets worse. Then he begins to look okay and says he's getting ready to go home. Then he gets worse. Then he gets something else.

On the days they think he's up to it, they let me take him out. A couple times both of us walk, but other times he rides. They call it his constitutional. We call it his faggot break.

I bring him a cup of Rex's coffee and throw the cigarettes across the table to him. He counts them, purses his lips and says, "You *are* a good Girl Scout." Then he leans toward me, gestures like a little old lady for me to put my ear up close to him.

"She's just trying to make you jealous," he whispers.

"What?"

"Doc-tor A-llen," he mouths silently.

He nods across Rex's to a table in the no-smoking section. Dr. Allen is having a cup of coffee with a woman.

"She knows we come here, she hopes you'll see her with Another Woman and be forced to take action."

"Jim . . ."

I'm sure Dr. Allen has seen us, Jim and me and the cigarettes, but I'm hoping she's taking a break from being doctor long enough to not feel obliged to come over and give Jim some healthy advice.

"She likes you *very much*, you know."

"Jim, I've probably had five minutes of conversation with the woman," I whisper. "All about you."

"Doesn't matter. It's chemistry. Animal maaag-netism."

He wants me to laugh.

"Come on, Jim. Give it a rest . . ."

He turns around to look at Dr. Allen. Then he looks back at me. He takes a long drag on his cigarette. He tries to sound buoyant. "Hey, I'm just trying to get you a buddy, Tonto. Who you gonna ride with when the Ranger's gone?"

One time Jim told me, this is what he said, he said, "A lie is what you tell when you're a chicken shit. But a story is what you tell for good."

"Even if it isn't true?"

"It's true. If you tell a story for good, it's true."

I'd had them twice and they were always great. They truly, truly may have been the best sour cream enchiladas on the planet. But that time, after two bites, Jim threw down his fork.

"These suck."

"Jim, they're fine."

"They suck."

He pushed the plate away. "I can't eat this shit."

I handed him the hot sauce and the guacamole. "Add a little of these."

"I said I cannot eat this crap." He lifted his hands like he was trying to push something away. I started to clear the table.

"Leave it. *Leave it.*"

I put the plate down. I looked away from him. Then at him. "Let's go out for Chinese."

He didn't say anything, just nodded.

I ordered everything: egg rolls, hot and sour soup, moo goo gai pan, garlic pork, Chinese veg, rice, a few beers. He asked me to tell him a story and I did. A lewd, insulting, degrading tale about a guy at the temp agency, a swishy little closet case we both despised. I told about him being caught, bare-assed, his pecker in his paw, in the thirty-fifth-floor supply room by one of the directors. Jim adored the story. He laughed really loud. He laughed until he cried. He didn't ask if it was true.

We ate everything. All the plum sauce. All the little crackers. Every speck of rice. But we didn't open our fortune cookies.

On the way home, Jim put his arm around me and said, "You're learning, Tonto."

The enchiladas were a recipe of Scotty's.

———

The door is half closed. I take one step in. There's a sweeping sound in the room, a smell. The curtain has been drawn around the bed. I see a silhouette moving.

"Jim?"

"Go away." His voice is little. "I made a mess."

An aide in a white coat peeks around the curtain. He's holding a mop. He's wearing plastic gloves, a white mask over his mouth and nose. I leave.

I go up to the Rose. Rosie sees me coming through the door. She's poured a schooner for me by the time I reach the bar.

"Jesus, woman." She leans over the bar to look at me as I'm climbing onto the bar stool.

"Shrunken body, shrunken head . . . Gonna be nothing left of you soon, girl."

I reach for the beer. She stops my hand.

"We don't serve alcohol alone. You have to order something to eat with it."

"Gimme a break, Rosie. I have one dollar and"—I fish into my jeans—"55 . . . 56 . . . 57 cents."

"Sorry, pal. It's policy."

"Since when?"

"Since now. It's a special policy for you."

"Rosie, please."

"Don't mess with the bartender."

I drop my face into my hands. "Please, Rosie."

She lifts my chin and looks at me. "If you promise to clean your plate, we'll put it on your tab."

"You don't run tabs."

She points to her chest. "I'm the boss."

As I'm finishing my beer she slaps a plate in front of me —a huge bacon-cheeseburger with all the trimmings. A mound of fries. A pint glass of milk.

She writes out the bill and pockets it. "We'll talk."

"Thanks."

I take a bite. She puts her elbows on the bar.

"How's Jim?"

"The same." My mouth is full.

She cocks her head.

I swallow. "Worse."

"Jeez . . ." She touches my arm. "Eat, honey. Eat something."

I eat. Sesame seed bun. Bacon. Mustard. Lettuce. Pickles. Tomatoes. Cheese. Meat. Grease on my fingers. I chew and swallow. It is so easy.

Jim on the drip-feed. Jim not keeping anything down. Or shitting it out in no time. His throat and asshole sore from everything that comes up, that runs through him. His oozy mouth. His bloody gums.

A hand on my back. "Hi."

I turn and almost choke.

"You're Jim's—"

I nod. "Yeah, right." I swallow. "You're Dr. Allen. Hi."

I wipe my mouth and hands on the napkin.

She's saying to the woman she's with, "This is Jim's sister," as if her friend's already heard of Jim. Or of me. Dr. Allen extends her hand to me. "Please, my name's Patricia."

I shake her hand.

"And this is my sister Amanda. It's her first time here— I mean—here in Seattle." She does this nervous little laugh. "She's visiting from Buffalo."

It's the woman she was having coffee with at Rex's.

"Oh, Buffalo," I say, "how nice."

"I've come to see if poor Pat's life is really as boring as she tells me it is. Doesn't have to be, does it?" the sister says with a grin.

I don't know what to answer. I do this little laugh.

They both look around the bar. Not wide, serious checkout sweeps of their heads, but shy, quick glances. They certainly aren't old hands at this. And I think I see two different varieties of nerves here. I try to read which is the tolerant, supportive sister, and which is the one who wanted to come to this particular bar in the first place.

"Mind if we join you?"

"Uh, no. Sure. Great."

I gesture to the empty bar stool next to me, then I stand up and gesture to my own. "But I was just going, actually . . . Here, have my stool." I down half the glass of milk. "Gotta be at work early in the morning," I lie.

They look at each other and at me. I feel like one of them's about to laugh, but I don't know which. Dr. Allen sits on my stool. Jim's right. She is pretty cute.

I gulp down the rest of the milk, slap my hands on the bar and shout into the kitchen, "I owe you, Rosie!"

I say to the sister, "Nice to meet you. Have a nice time in Seattle." And to the doctor, "Nice to bump into you. See you 'round."

Then I'm standing outside on the sidewalk, shaking.

Because maybe, if I had stayed there in the bar with them, and had them buy me a beer or two, or a coaxed a couple more out of Rose, maybe I would have asked, "So which of you is the supportive sister, and which of you is the dyke?" Or maybe I would have asked, "So how 'bout it, ladies. Into which of your lovely beds might I more easily insinuate myself?"

Or maybe I would have asked—no—no—but maybe I would have asked, "So, Dr. Allen, you are pretty cute, how 'bout it. How long till Jim goes?"

I bring him magazines and newspapers. *The Times, The Blade, The Body Politic*. They all run articles. Apparent answers, possible solutions, almost cures. Experiments and wonder drugs. A new technique. But more and more the stories are of failures. False starts. The end of hope.

Bob's been coughing the last few times he's been here. He's still at it today.

Bob coughs. I look at Dale. He looks away.

One evening in the middle of *Marcus Welby*, Jim announces, "I'm bored outta my tits, girls. I wanna have a party."

Mike, who's been drooping in front of the TV set, sits up.
"I say I am ready for a paaaaar-tay!"
Mike says, "Jimmy boy, you're on."
We okay it with Dr. Allen. Mike raids the stationery store
on Broadway for paper hats and confetti and party favors
and cards. We call everyone and it's on for the evening after
next. They limit the number of people allowed in a room at
a time, so Mike and I take turns hanging out by the elevator
to do crowd control. Jim shrieks, he calls me "Tonto the
Bouncer" and flexes his arm in a skinny little she-man biceps.
It's great to see everybody, and everyone brings Jim these
silly presents: an inflatable plastic duck, a shake-up scene of
the Space Needle, a couple of incredibly ugly fuzzy animals,
a bouquet of balloons. Somebody brings him a child's wa-
tercolor set; it's the only gift he doesn't gush about.

When I start to clean the wrapping paper, he says, "Oh,
leave it a while." He likes the shiny colors and the rustling
sound the paper makes when he shifts in bed.

When anybody leaves, he blows a kiss and says, "Bye-
bye, cowpoke. Happy trails."

He knows what he's doing.

I see it when I'm coming down the hall, a laminated sign
on the door of his room. I tiptoe the last few yards because
I don't want him to hear me stop to read it, acting as if I
believe what it says. It's a warning, like something you'd see
on a pack of cigarettes or a bottle of pesticide. It warns about
the contents. It tells you not to touch.

I push myself into his room before I can give myself a
chance to reconsider. I push myself toward his bed, toward
his forehead to give him his regular kiss hello.

"Don't touch me."

When he pushes me away, I'm relieved.

"Do you realize they're wearing plastic gloves around me
all the time now? Face masks? They've put my wallet and
clothes into plastic bags. As if me and my stuff is gonna jump
on 'em and bleed all over 'em, as if my sweat—"

"Jim, that's bullshit. This isn't the Middle Ages, it's 1984.

And they're medical people, they should know they don't need to do that. Haven't they read—"

"Why don't you go tell 'em, Tonto? Why don't you just march right over to 'em with all your little newspaper articles and you just tell 'em the truth."

"I will, Jim, I'll—"

"Oh for fuck's sake, Tonto, they *are* medical people. They know what they're doing." He covers his eyes with a hand and says wearily, "And I know what my body is doing."

He holds his skinny white hand over his eyes. I can see the bones of his forearm, the bruises on his pale, filmy skin. He looks like an old man. The sheet rises and falls unevenly with his breath.

I ought to hold him but I don't want to.

"Jim?" I say, "Jim?" I don't know if he's listening.

Inside the belt line of my jeans, down the middle of my back and on my stomach, I feel myself begin to sweat. I start to babble. A rambling, unconnected pseudo-summary of articles I haven't brought him, a doctor-ed précis of inoperative statements, edited newspeak, jargon, evasions, unmeant promises, lies.

But I'm only half thinking of what I say, and I'm not thinking of Jim at all.

I'm thinking of me. And of how my stomach clutched when he said that about the sweat. I'm thinking that I want to get out of his room immediately—and wash my hands and face and take a shower and boil my clothes and get so far away from him that I won't have to breathe the air he's breathed. Then further, to where he cannot see how I, like everyone I like to think I'm so different from, can desert him at the drop of a hat, before the drop of a Goddamn hat, because my good-girl Right-On-Sister sympathies extend only as far as my assurance of my immunity from what is killing him. But once the thought occurs to me that I might be in danger, I'll be the first bitch on the block to saddle up and leave him in the dust.

I don't know what I say to him; I know I don't touch him.

After a while he offers me a seat to watch TV, but I don't sit. I tell him I've got to go. I tell him I have a date. He knows I'm lying.

I look around for Dr. Allen. She tells me she thinks this recent hospital policy is ludicrous. "It just increases every-body's hysteria. There's no evidence of contagion through casual contact. If these people . . ." But I don't listen to the rest of what she says. My mind is still repeating *no evidence of contagion through casual contact*. I'm so relieved I'm taken out of danger. I realize I'm happier than if she'd told me Jim was going to live.

I don't listen until I hear her asking me something. I don't hear the words, just the tone in her voice.

"Huh?"

She looks at me hard. Then shakes her head and turns away. She knows what I was thinking, where the line of my loyalty runs out.

The next day before I visit him, I ask Dr. Allen, "Are you sure, if I only touch him . . ."

It's the only time she doesn't look cute. She practically spits. "You won't risk anything by hugging your brother."

Her eyes make a hole in my back as I walk to his room.

I hug him very carefully, how I believe I can stay safe. He holds me longer than he usually does. He doesn't say any-thing, when I pull away, about the fact that I don't kiss his forehead, which shines with sweat.

"Come here," he says in his lecher voice, "Daddy's got some candy for you."

He hands me a hundred dollar bill.

"What's this?"

"What I still owe you for the TV."

"What?"

"The hundred bucks I borrowed for the color TV."

Jim wanted to buy it for Scotty when all Scotty could do was watch TV. Jim wasn't going to get paid until the end of the month so I lent it to him. He wanted to pay me back immediately but he kept having all these bills.

"Dale withdrew it from the bank for me."

"I don't want it."

He glares at me. "The Ranger is a man of honor, Tonto."

"Okay, okay, but I don't want it now."

He keeps glaring. "So you want it later? You gonna ride into Wells Fargo bank and tell them part of my estate is yours?"

"Dale can—" I close my eyes.

"I owe you, Tonto. Take Dr. Allen out for the time of her life."

"Jim . . ."

"Goddammit, it's all I can do."

He grabs me by the belt loop of my jeans and tries to pull me toward him but he's too weak. I step toward the bed. He stuffs the bill into my pocket.

"Now go away please. I'm tired."

Was this a conversation? Was it story?

I wish Scotty knew how I felt about him.

He knew.

I never told him. I wish I'd said the words.

He knew.

How do you know?

He told me.

Did he? What did he say?

Scotty told me, he said, Jim loves me.

Did he really?

Yes.

Did he say anything else?

Yes. He said, I love Jim.

He said he loved me?

More than anything.

Is that true?

Yes, Jim, it's true.

This is how I learn to tell a story.

We stay outside for longer than we ought. I tell him it's time to go back, but he whines like a boy who doesn't want recess to end. He chatters. For the first time since I've known him, he starts retelling stories he has told to me before, stories that lose a lot in the retelling. But finally he runs out of things to say and lets me wheel him out of Rex's.

There's a traffic jam. Cars are backed up to Broadway and everybody's honking. A couple blocks away a moving van is trying to turn onto a narrow street. People at the crosswalk are getting impatient. They look around for cops and when they don't see any, start crossing Madison between the cars.

"I'm cold," says Jim.

He puts his free hand under his blanket. I lean down to tuck the cover more closely around his legs. His face is white.

"I'm cold," he grumbles again, "I wanna go back in."

"In a minute, Jim. We can't go yet."

"But I'm freezing." He looks up. "Where's the fucking sun anyway?"

I take off my jacket and wrap it around his shoulders.

The cellophane of the cigarette package crinkles. I take care not to hit the drip-feed tube.

People start laying on their horns. The poor stupid van ahead is moving forward then back, inch by inch, trying to squeeze around the corner.

"It's moving, Jim. The truck's going."

"About time," he says loudly. "Doesn't the driver realize what he's holding up here?"

Then the truck stalls. There's the gag of the engine, silence, the rev of the motor, the sputter when the engine floods.

"Someone go tell that goddamn driver what he's holding up here."

People in their cars look out at Jim.

"I've got to get back in," he screams. "Go! Go!" He starts shooing the cars with his hands. The drip-feed swings.

I grab his arm. "Jim, the IV."

"Fuck the IV!" he yells. "Fuck the traffic. I'm going back in. I have to get back in."

"We're going, Jim, the traffic's moving now," I lie. "We're going in. Settle down, okay?"

He pushes himself up a couple of inches to see the truck.

"The truck isn't moving, Tonto."

He kicks his blanket awry and tries to find the ground with his feet. "I'm walking."

"Jim, you can't."

"So what am I supposed to do. Fly?"

"You're supposed to wait. When the traffic clears—"

"I'm sick of waiting. You said it was clearing. You lied to me. I'm sick of everyone lying. I'm sick of waiting. I'm sick—" His voice cracks.

I put my hand on his arm. "When the traffic clears I'm going to push you and Silver across the street."

"It's not a horse," he screams, "it's a goddamn wheel-chair!"

He starts to tremble. He grips the arms of the chair. "It's a wheelchair full of goddamn croaking faggot!" He slaps his hands over his face and whispers, "Tonto, I don't wanna. Don't let me—I don't wanna—I don't wanna—"

I put my arms around him and pull him to me. His head is against my collarbone. His cap falls off his sweaty head. I try to hold him. He lets me a couple of seconds, then he tries to pull away. He isn't strong enough. But I know what he means so I pull back. He grabs my shirt, one of his.

"I don't wanna—" he cries, "I don't wanna—"

I put my hands on the back of his head and pull him to my chest.

"I don't wanna—I don't wanna—" he sobs.

His hands and face are wet. I hold his head.

"Jim," I say.

He grabs me like a child wanting something good.

When we get back to his room he's still crying. I ring for Dr. Allen. Jim asks me to leave.

I pace around in the hall. When Dr. Allen comes out of his room, she says, "He's resting. He isn't good but he's not as bad as you think. He won't want to see you for a while. Now that you've seen him like this, it's harder for him to pretend he's not afraid. You can call the nurses' station tonight if you're concerned, but don't come see him till tomorrow. And call him first."

I want to tell her to tell him a story, to make him not afraid.

But I don't. I say, "I'm going to call his parents."

She looks at me.

"*Our* parents," I mumble.

"He hasn't wanted his family to know?"

"Right."

"Call them."

I call his parents that night. They say they'll fly out in the morning and be able to be with him by noon. I tell them I'll book them a hotel a five-minute walk from the hospital. They want to take the airport bus in themselves.

I call him in the morning.

"Hey, buddy."

"Yo, Tonto."

"Listen, you want anything special today? I'm doing my Christmas shopping on the way down to see you."

"No you're not."

"Who says?"

"Santa says. I called Jean and Ange this morning and you're going down there for the week. That remodeling you were supposed to help them with way back is getting moldy. So it's the bright lights of Olympia for you, Sex-cat."

"Jim . . ."

"You have to go. They're going to pay you."

"What?!"

"They said they'd have to pay somebody, and they're afraid to have a common laborer around the priceless silver.

So they want you. And it's not like you've been earning it hand over fist since you've been playing candy striper with me."

"Jim, they don't have any money."

"They do now. Jeannie managed to lawyer-talk her way into some loot for her latest auto disaster and Ange is determined to spend the cash before Jeannie throws it away on another seedy lemon. So, Tonto, you got to go. It's your sororal duty."

It was impossible to talk Jim out of anything.

"Give my best to the girls and tell Trudy the Sentinel Bitch I said a bark is a bark is a bark."

"Doesn't Alice get a hello?"

"Alice is stupid. I will not waste my sparkling wit on her."

"Okay . . ."

Were we going to get through this entire conversation without a mention of yesterday?

"So, Tonto, the Ranger is much improved today . . . My folks called a while ago from DFW airport. They're on their way to see me. Thanks for calling them."

"Sure."

"We'll see you next week then."

"Right."

He hangs up the phone before I can tell him good-bye.

I drive to Olympia. Ange is outside chopping wood. When I pull into the yard she slings the ax into the center of the block. She gives me a huge hug, her great soft arms around my back, her breasts and belly big and solid against me. She holds me a long time, kisses my hair.

"Hi, baby."

"Ange."

She puts her arm around my back and brings me inside. The house smells sweet. They're baking. Jeannie blows me a kiss from the kitchen.

"Hello, gorgeous!"

"Jeannie my darling."

I warm my hands by the wood stove. Ange yells at Gertrude, their big ugly German shepherd, to shut up. She's a very talkative dog. Jeannie brings in a plate of whole-wheat cookies. I pick up Alice the cat from the couch and drop her on the floor. She is a stupid cat. She never protests anything. I sit on the place she's made warm on the couch. Jean hands me the plate. The cookies are still warm. I hesitate. It always amazes me they can, along with Jeannie's law school scholarship, support themselves by selling this horrible homemade hippie food to health food joints.

I take a cookie. "Thanks."

"How's Jim?"

"Okay . . ."

"Bad?"

"Yeah."

"He sounded incredibly buoyant on the phone, so we figured . . . We told him we'd come up to see him next week when we've finished some of this." She nods at the cans and boards and drywall stacked up outside the spare room.

"Let's get to work."

"Yeah. Let's do it."

Ange puts an old Janis Joplin on the stereo. We knock the hell out of the walls.

They cook a very healthy dinner. As she's about to sit down, Jeannie says, "Hey, we got some beer in case you wanted one. Want one?" Ange and Jean haven't kept booze in their house for years.

"No thanks." There's a jar of some hippie fruit juice on the table. "This is fine."

They look at each other. We eat.

I sleep on the couch in the living room. Gertrude sleeps in front of the wood stove. I listen to her snort. She turns around in circles before she settles down to sleep, her head out on her paws.

Jim and I used to flip for who got the couch and who got

the tatami mat on the floor next to the dog. I lean up on my elbow to look at Trudy The Sentinel Bitch. Only Jim could have renamed her that. In the bedroom Ange and Jean talk quietly.

All the junk has been moved from the spare room into the living room. Some of it is stacked at the end of the couch. I toss the blanket off me and sift through the pile. Rolled-up posters, curling photographs. There's a framed water-color of Jim's, a scene of Ange and Jeannie by the pond, with Gertrude, fishing. They look so calm together. They didn't know Jim was painting them. They didn't know how he saw them.

I find one of all of us, three summers ago when we climbed Mount Si. Jim is tall and bearded, his arms around the three of us, me and Jeannie squished together under his left, Ange hugged under his right. All of us are smiling at the cam-eraman, Scotty.

Two nights later the phone rings late. I'm awake, light on, blanket off, before they've answered it. When Ange comes out of the bedroom I'm already dressed.

"That was Dr. Allen. His parents are with him. You should go."

They won't let me drive. We all pile into the truck; Jeannie driving, Ange in the middle, me against the door. Jeannie doesn't stop at the signs or the red lights. She keeps an even 80 on the highway. For once, Ange doesn't razz her about her driving.

I-5 is quiet. The only things on the road are some long-haul trucks, a few cars. We see the weak beige lights of the insides of these other cars, the foggy orange lights across the valley. We drive along past sleepy Tacoma, Federal Way, the airport.

"Look, would you guys mind if I had a cigarette?"

"Go ahead, baby."

Ange reaches over me and rolls down the window. I root around in my jacket for Jim's cigarettes. I'm glad I didn't make that promise to him.

We pull into the hospital parking lot. My hand is on the door before we stop.

"You go up. We'll get Bob and Dale and meet you on the floor in ten minutes."

In the elevator is a couple a little older than me. Red-eyed and sniffling like kids. We look at each other a second then look at the orange lights going up.

When the elevator opens I run. But when I see the guys in white taking things from the room in plastic bags, I stop. The man at the nurses' station looks up.

"Your parents are in the waiting room."

"My what?"

"Your parents."

Then I remember how that first night, a million years ago, when Dr. Allen had told me she couldn't tell me about Jim unless I was in his family, I had told the story of being his sister.

"Oh Christ."

"They told me to send you in when you came."

"Oh Jesus."

They've left the waiting room door open a crack. I look in. His father is wearing an overcoat. His hands lay loose around the rim of the hat in his lap. His mother is touching her husband's arm. Neither of them is talking.

I knock on the door very lightly.

They look up.

"You must be Jim's friend. Come in."

I push the door open. They both stand up and put out their hands. I shake their hands.

"Mary Carlson."

"Jim Carlson."

I introduce myself.

"The young man at the desk told us that, before she went into surgery, Dr. Allen called our daughter and that she was on her way. But we don't have a daughter."

"I'm sorry. But I—the first night Jim was here I told Dr. Allen—"

Mr. Carlson is still shaking my hand. He squeezes it hard.

"You have nothing to apologize for. Jim told us what a good friend you'd been to him. Both after Scotty, and more recently."

"Jim was a good friend too. I'm sorry I didn't call you sooner."

"We know he asked you not to. We had a few good days with him. I think he wanted to get better before he saw us," says Mrs. Carlson. "He didn't want us to have to see him and have to wait the way he had to wait with Scotty."

"Yes."

"Did you know Scotty?"

"Yes."

"He was a lovely young man."

"He was good to Jim," says Mr. Carlson. "There were things about Jim it took us a long time to understand, but he was a good son." He says this slowly. "He was a good man."

"Yes."

"We loved him." Mr. Carlson's mouth is open like he's going to say more, but then there's this sound in his throat and he drops his face into his hands. "Dear God," he says, "oh dear God."

Mrs. Carlson pulls her husband's head to her breast. His hat falls to the floor.

I pick the hat up off the floor and put it on the table. I leave the room. When I close the door, I hear his father crying.

Ange and Jean and Bob and Dale are standing at the nurses' station. The boys are in pj's and overcoats and house slippers. They look at me. I look at them. We all look at each other. Nobody says anything.

Dale walks over to the wall and puts his forehead against the wall. His shoulders shake. Bob goes over and puts his hand on Dale's back. Nobody says anything.

We get in the truck to go back to Bob and Dale's. We all insist Bob sit up front with Jean and Ange. Dale and I sit in the open back. We haul the dog-smelling woolly blanket over our knees and huddle up next to each other. I can feel the cool ribbed metal of the bottom of the truck through my jeans. Jeannie pulls us away from the bright false lights of the hospital onto Madison.

It's dark, but there're enough breaks in the clouds that we can see a star or two. The lights are off at Rex's, the streets are empty. Jean drives so slow and cautiously, full stops at the signs and lights, and pauses at the intersections. There's not another car on the road, but I think she hopes if she does everything very carefully, things might not break apart.

Jean stops at the light on Broadway. Dale and I look into the back window of the pickup and see their three heads— Jeannie's punky hairdo sticking up, Ange's halo of wild fuzz, Bob's shiny smooth round scalp. The collar of Bob's pajama is crooked above his housecoat. He's usually so neatly groomed, but now he looks like a rumpled, sleepy child.

Dale begins to tremble. I put my hand on his knee.

"Jim was a great guy, the greatest, but now it's like he was never here. What did he ever do that's gonna last? It's like his life was nothing."

"Jim was a good man," I say.

Dale nods.

"And he loved a good man. He loved Scotty well."

"And that's enough?"

"It's good," I say, "it's true."

Dale takes my hand. He holds it hard. It's the first time I notice he wears a ring.

He takes a breath. "Bob . . . you know Bob . . . I'm afraid maybe . . . I think Bob . . ."

He can't say it. I see his eyelashes trembling, the muscles in his jaw he tries to hold to keep from crying. He swallows and closes his eyes.

"Bob is a good man," says Dale.

"Yeah, Dale, I know. Bob is a good man too."

So we all go back to Bob and Dale's. I call the Carlsons' hotel to leave Bob and Dale's phone number. We drink tea and sit around in the living room until someone says we ought to get some sleep.

"Well, there's plenty of pj's," says Bob. "We can have a pajama paaaaaar-tay."

He says it before he realizes it's a Jim word. Ange and Jeannie and I try to laugh. Dale closes his eyes.

Bob and Dale get pj's for us. They wash the teacups as Ange and Jean and I change. We all look really silly in the guys' flannel pj's. When the boys come out of the kitchen and see us, they laugh. It's a real laugh. It sounds good.

Ange and Jean are going to stay in the guest room. Ange says to me, "You wanna stay with us, babe?"

And Dale says, "Or you can sleep on the couch in our room."

"Thanks, guys." I plop down on the living room couch. "This is fine with me."

Dale goes to the linen closet to get some sheets and blankets.

If I lie next to someone I will break apart.

I wake up first. I put the water on to boil. When Jean and Ange come out of the guest room, I say, "The Katzenjammer twins."

They look at my pj's. "Triplets," Jeannie says.

"Quads," says Ange when Dale comes into the kitchen. He gives us each a scratchy, unshaven kiss on the cheek. "Good morning, lovelies."

Jeannie nods toward the guys' room. "Our fifth?"

"Bob's asleep now. He was sweaty last night. I don't think we'll go to Jim's."

He goes to phone the bank and Janet, Bob's business partner. Jean and Ange and I look at each other.

"You want me to stay with you?" asks Jean when Dale gets off the phone.

"Naaaah." He smiles like nothing's wrong. "Bob'll be all right. You guys go help the Carlsons."

We take turns in the shower while we listen for the phone. We hear Bob coughing in the bedroom.

The Carlsons call. They want to meet at Jim's about ten to clean out the apartment. We say okay, and plan to get there a half an hour early in case there's anything we need to "straighten up." Not that we expect to find anything shocking, but if we were to run across something, even a magazine or a poster, it might be nicer if the Carlsons didn't see it.

We leave Dale sitting at the kitchen table, his hands around his coffee mug. He looks lost. He looks the way he's going to look after Bob is gone.

We take the truck and stop by the grocery store to get a bunch of cartons. I've got the keys to Jim's place. When we walk up the steps I think of where Jim hasn't stood since I came by to drive him to the hospital. We climb the gray-mustard-colored carpet of the stairs. The hallways smell like food. Living people still live here.

When I open the door to the apartment everything looks different. We set the empty boxes on the living room floor and begin to look in closets and drawers, intruding in a way we never would if Jim was around. There's nothing in Jim's drawers but socks and T-shirts and underwear, nothing beneath the bed but dust, stray pennies, a couple of crusty paintbrushes.

The Carlsons get there before we can go through all the rooms.

The Carlsons don't think there'll be anything they'll want from the living room, so I start packing the books and records, wrapping the TV in towels before I put it in a box.

Jeannie and Mrs. Carlson start in the kitchen. I hear Mrs. Carlson telling Jeannie about the first time Jim made scrambled eggs, about her trying to teach "my Jims," as she calls her husband and son, to cook. She laughs as she remembers the story of the eggs. It's good to hear her laugh. In Jim's room Mr. Carlson and Ange are packing shirts into cardboard cartons. I glance in. Mr. Carlson looks so small, like a schoolboy being sent away from home. He's very slow and careful as he fastens buttons and smooths collars and folds sleeves. He creases the shirts into neat, tidy rectangles. Ange

says a couple of things but Mr. Carlson doesn't answer much.
So after a while she leaves him to sort through his son's ties
and loafers, his jackets and suits, his baseball things, alone.

"This must have been Scotty's room," says Mrs. Carlson.

I'd been in there when Scotty was around. But after Scotty,
the door was never open.

The handle of the door is colored silver. Mrs. Carlson puts
her hand on it. It clicks. She pushes it open. The curtain is
drawn, the room is dark. But we can see, around Mrs. Carlson in front of us, that the bed and dresser, the night table,
are gone. The only piece of furniture is the long desk by the
window. It's crowded with clutter. There are pale gray-white
rectangles on the walls. Ange flips on the light.

And all around is Scotty. Scotty in his red-checked lumber
jacket. Scotty smiling with a three-days' growth of beard.
Scotty sitting cross-legged on a mat. Scotty with long hair,
a tie-dyed shirt and sandals. Scotty in his ridiculous bright
orange Bermuda shorts. His firm brown stomach, his com-
pact upper arms, him holding up a Stonewall fist and grinning. His fine hands holding something blue. His profile
when he was a boy. Him resting his chin in his palms and
looking sleepy. His baseball hat on backwards. His pretty
shoulders, his tender sex, his hands.

In every one, his skin is tan, his body is whole, his eyes
are blue and bright. We recognize some poses from old photographs, and some from Scotty as we remember him. But
some are of a Scotty that we never saw; Jim's Scotty. Painted
alive again by Jim.

"Dear Scotty," Mrs. Carlson says, "my Jim's beloved."

We take the stuff they can use to a center that is starting
up. We leave most of it in both their names. The TV in
Scotty's. The hundred dollar bill in Jim's.

A few days later everything is over. The Carlsons are flying
back to Texas. They don't want a ride to the airport, but
they invite us all down for coffee at their hotel. They tell us

if we ever get to Texas to come see them. We all thank each other for everything and say if there's ever anything we can do. The Carlsons take some paintings to share with Scotty's family. When the airporter arrives we put their suitcases in the storage place beneath the bus. Mr. Carlson carries the paintings rolled up into tubes. When the bus pulls out Mrs. Carlson waves to us for both of them. Mr. Carlson won't let go of the tubes.

We go back to Bob and Dale's and drink more coffee. We all get pretty buzzy. Then Jean says they shouldn't put it off anymore, they need to get back to Olympia. I mumble something about starting up temping again.

Jean says, uncharacteristically, "Oh, fuck temping."

Bob laughs. "Listen to that potty mouth."

Ange reminds me that I have to go back to Olympia to get my car, and I ought to help them finish the remodeling. Both of which are true, but it's also true they know what I can't say: how much I need to be with them.

So we say "See you round" to Bob and Dale and get in the truck to drive back down to Oly. Ange makes me sit in the middle, between the two of them.

"Wha-chew-wont, baby I got it!!" Ange howls as she shoves Aretha into the tape deck. Aretha takes a second to catch up with Ange, but then it's the two of them singing. Ange cranks the tunes up as Jean pulls the truck out onto 15th. We turn at Pine. Jean slows the truck as we pass the Rose in case anyone cute is casually lounging around outside; no one ever is. There's a moment of stillness at the red light on Broadway, a moment of stillness between the tracks, then "Chain of Fools." Ange cranks it up even more as we turn left onto Broadway, then turn right again onto Madison and right into a traffic jam.

Ange rolls down the window as if she needs the extra room to sing. She loves the chain-chain-chaaaaaain, chain-chain-chaaaaaain parts and always does this ridiculously unsexy jerk of her shoulders and hips when she sings it. She gets especially crazy at the cha-ya-ya-ya-ya-in part near the end.

She squints and tries to look very mean, meaner with each ya-ya-ya. Jeannie is good at the hoo-hoo's, which she accompanies with some extremely precise nods of her chin, and some extremely cool finger points. I sit between them and laugh.

But as the song is nearing the end and we haven't moved more than ten yards, I growl, "What is this traffic shit?"

Ange pops the cassette out of the tape deck.

"What?"

"I said, what is this traffic shit."

"Quarter of four," says Jean, "I thought we'd miss it."

"The old 'burg ain't what it used to be, baby. New folks movin' in all the time. And they all have six cars and they all love traffic jams. Reminds them of good ol' LA."

"Where they can all go back to in a goddamn hand truck, thank you very much."

We inch along a few minutes then come to a complete stop in front of Rex's. Pedestrians on the sidewalk look around for cops then start walking in between the cars. Someone squeezing by in front of the truck does a knock-knock on the hood and grins in at us.

"Smug asshole bastard," I snarl.

Cars start honking.

"Jesus, this traffic sucks," I say louder.

Ange looks at me.

The car behind us is laying on the horn.

"Fuck the traffic," I shout.

"Hey, babe, take it easy," says Ange, "we'll get outta here soon."

I ignore her. "Fuck the traffic," I cry. I put my hands over my ears. "Fuck the traffic."

Then I hear Jim screaming, "Fuck the traffic! Don't they realize they're holding up a wheelchair full of dying faggot!" Then I hear him yelling, "So what am I supposed to do, fly?" Then he looks at me, "Tonto, I don't wanna, I don't wanna die—"

Then my head is against the back of the seat. I'm rigid. Ange's hand is on my arm.

"Baby?"

Jean grinds the truck into reverse, backs up a couple inches, whacks it back into first and climbs over the sidewalk into the Seattle First National Bank parking lot. She cuts the engine.

"Baby." Ange says it hard.

She yanks me away from the back of the seat and throws her arms, her whole huge body around me. Jeannie grabs me from behind. I'm stiff. I'm like a statue. My body can't bend and I can't see. They sandwich me in between them. Spit and snot are on my face.

"Let it go, baby, let it go."

I can't say anything. My jaws are tight.

"Let it go, babe."

Ange pulls away from me enough to kiss my forehead. I break. She squeezes herself around me tight. Then they're both around me, holding me.

And then, dear Jim, held close between the bodies of our friends, I see you.

I roll you and your wheelchair out to the sidewalk. I'm worried because in the few minutes it's taken us to get from your room to here, the sky has turned gray. I tell you we ought to get back inside, but you wave that idea away. I stand above you at the pedestrian crossing and look down at the top of your cap, the back of your neck, your shoulders.

There's a traffic jam. The cars are pressed so close not even pedestrians can squeeze through. A wind is picking up. People are opening umbrellas. Cars are honking, drivers are laying on their horns. I start to say, again, that we really ought to go back in, but you find my hand on the wheelchair grip and cover it with your own. You sigh like a tolerant, tired parent. You shake your head. You pat my hand then squeeze it.

"The traffic'll break in a minute, Jim."

But you aren't listening to me. You slip your hand from mine, and before I can stop you, you've unhooked the tooth of the drip-feed from your arm.

"Jim, the IV."

"Ssssh." You put your finger to your lips like you are finally

*going to tell the truth about a story you've been telling for so
long.*

*You slip the blanket off your knees. You stand up alone,
not needing to lean on anyone. You're tall as you used to be.
You stretch your arms out to your sides and take a deep breath.
I see your chest expand. You stretch your neck up and look
at the sky. You throw your arm around my shoulder and pull
me to you. I feel the firmness of your body and smell the good
clean smell of your healthy skin the way it was the summer
we climbed Mt. Si. You pull my face in front of you. You
hold my face between your hands and look at me. You look
inside where I can't see, where I can't look away from you.
Beneath the fear, the covered love, you see me, Jim. Then,
like a blessing that forgives me, and a healing benediction that
will seal a promise true, you kiss my forehead.*

You tell me, "Tonto, girl, I'm going for a ride."

*You fling your Right-On Sister, Stonewall fist up in the air.
You open your hand in a Hi-yo Silver wave. I watch your
hand as it stretches above you high, impossibly high. Your
feet lift off the sidewalk and you rise. Above the crowded
street, the hospital, above us all, you fly.*

*The rain begins. Cold drops hit my face when I look up at
you. But you fly high above it, Jim. Your firm taut body
catches glints of a light from the sun that no one here below
can see.*

*I raise a Right-On fist to answer you, but then my fist is
opened, just like yours, and I am waving, Jim.*

Good friend, good brother Jim, good-bye.

An Amazon Beginning

Ellen Frye

The old woman stared at the fire. I bit into an apple and waited. I knew there was more to her story, but the way she settled against the log told me that her tongue had gone to sleep. No more talk tonight, I grumbled. Cat's piss! Scraps! always scraps! I want the whole tale. I went out to tend the horses.

There were three of us on the mountain that winter—the old woman, Granny, and me. We'd all chosen a life away from the comings and goings of people: I'd run away from home, the old woman had found what she'd been searching for, and Granny? Well, the cave was Granny's home.

It wasn't really a cave; it was more like a rock house built into the side of the mountain that faced the rising sun. Inside, you could stand up straight only in the center; you had to crouch to get to the storage jars that lined the walls because the walls curved over them into a kind of dome with a smoke hole at the top. We cooked and ate and slept in that room, and almost every night after dinner, we told stories. It was mostly the old woman who talked, but Granny had stories that rode tunes. They'd start out of her mouth high, ringing against the walls; then they'd fall low and scurry along the floor like a deermouse. I wanted to sing stories, too. I reckoned that if I listened long enough and hard enough, my mouth would find their shape.

There were two rooms in the cave. Along the back of the first room, a pair of rocks leaned against each other to make a kind of doorway into the second. It was like a secret room. I wasn't allowed to go there alone. As the moon waxed and waned, we'd go back together for the bread ceremony. I got to grind the sacred flour. The old woman mixed it, and Granny shaped it into loaves and shoveled them into the fat clay oven.

There was an altar in that room, and we put the loaves on it when they came out of the oven. Next to the altar, a goddess sat on a throne. She scared me a little. She had a beak instead of a nose, and her arms naked around her broad belly, and her legs curved under wide hips. Once, when I first came to the mountain, I was kneeling at the grindstone and I got up suddenly because my feet had turned to prickles. My head started spinning, and I stumbled across the room. I thought I was going to crash right into the goddess, but she stopped me just before I fell. It was as if the air around her was strung with an invisible spider's web that caught me and held me swaying. Neither the old woman nor Granny said anything; they just kept chanting, and when I'd caught my breath I went back to the grindstone and chanted, too.

An old elm guarded our home, a tree that Granny said was older than her great-great grandmother, older than her great-great grandmother's great-great grandmother. Once the leaves had fallen, you could shinny up the trunk, step up branches like ladder rungs and see the whole world below. A river flowed through the valley; it was just a creek where it dropped down a wall of rock but it got bigger and bigger as it snake-slithered across the plain. Down in the valley I knew its loud song, but up on the mountain it was silent as the hawks that glided from one jack pine to another.

I was born in the valley where the river runs. We had winter there, too, but the wind never screamed so hard nor stung my face with such cold. Spring came sooner, too. When

I lived down there, the river-ice would groan and crack, and the anemones would poke through the snow and still the mountain'd be shrouded in gray. I know because I waited every spring for Granny to visit, and it was only after the last of the fiddleheads had unfurled that I knew it was time to search the ridge to cry her black mare. She'd stay with us until her bundles of threads were sold and her saddlebags filled with barley and millet.

Evenings she'd sit at our fire and sing. My mother would be grinding barley, my sister stitching her dowry, and me, I'd be mending my father's good pants or one of my brother's shirts. Granny would twirl her spindle and fill the room with songs about strong women who rode fast horses out into the world. Antiopi, Hippolyte and Zerinthia rode flame-red mares to places called Smyrna and Sinope. They climbed mountains and passed through piney woods filled with talking hares. They yoked the east wind to build their cities and they hung their secrets on a pair of quarreling laurels on a riverbank.

My mother didn't like the singing. Late at night I'd hear her complain to my father, but he always laughed and said the songs were harmless. "The days of the Amazons are over," he'd tell her. "Times have changed; let the children listen."

Once, when Granny and I were shelling peas in the yard, I asked her what made Amazons different from other women, that they could ride out in the world like men. She leaned close to me. "It's because we live without them," she whispered. Then she straightened her back. "Your mother doesn't understand. We don't shun men, you know. We barter with the iron-smelters for our horseshoes; we trade skins for fish from the shore-dwellers. But the Gargarensians who father our children live in another place."

"How could they be fathers if they didn't live with you?" I remember asking, but Granny only stood up and rolled the peas into the pot of steaming barley. I looked over to where my mother was pulling crusty loaves from the fat clay

oven. She'd gotten my sister and me up before dawn to start
the baking; we'd tended the cows and set the milk to clabber;
we'd carried water from the upper spring and bundled clothes
down to the flat river rocks to pound them clean. Now we
were making the midday meal. My father and brothers would
come in from the fields soon and they'd have worked hard,
too. But when their bellies were full, they'd sleep while we
hung the laundry from the quince tree and hung up the
dripping curds. In the evening they'd go down to the village
plane tree and gossip with the other men while we bedded
the animals and turned the cheese. If my father and brothers
lived in another village, I thought, no one would sleep while
someone else worked.

On the mountain that winter, it was just that way. Each
of us had our own tasks: the old woman carded, Granny
spun, I tended the horses; I carried the water, Granny
ground the barley, the old woman cooked. When we worked,
we all worked; when we slept, we all slept. And around our
evening fire, we shared stories.

The old woman's stories didn't ride tunes like Granny's;
they fell out of her mouth in plain speech. She wasn't an
Amazon, either. She came from a place way to the south of
our mountain, a place where the sun was warmer than ours
and even when it wasn't, their river never turned to ice. She
was born in a house that stood like a crane in the marsh,
she said, but she grew up in a marble-and-gold palace, slave
to a princess. The city was called Troy, and it was built like
a mountain with narrow streets at the bottom and bigger
ones along the middle and wide, wide spaces on the top
where the palace stood. Every stone in the city wall was big
as ten oxen, and the wooden gates that let you in and out
were tall as the elm that guarded our mountain home.

I tried to imagine the view from the West Gate. Only a
thin green strip, she said, kept the blue Aegean from spilling
into the harbor. Dark shadows on the horizon marked some
island's mountains. A river, the Skamander, foamed down
from a green plateau and eddied through the lowlands. On

top of the plateau—her eyes flashed when she said this—
horses ran free, the finest horses under the sun. Merchants
came from across seas to trade gold and Chinese jade for
them.

Some nights the old woman had us playing hopscotch with
her princess; other nights she carried us astride an old chestnut mare wandering the foothills of Mount Ida. Sometimes
she filled the Trojan plain with bronze-wheeled chariots and
men with shields and swords. Her stories were as grand as
Granny's songs, but like Granny's songs, they came out of
her mouth in pieces: the middle of one, the beginning of
another. I asked her once to tell me how to fit them all together, but she just said, "You're tall as a filly, but mares
know where to crop." No answer at all, but it stopped my
tongue.

On the longest night of the year, I was out in the stable
with my mare and Granny's black one and the old woman's
piebald. The stable was just a lean-to when I came, so when
the wind started biting, I'd daubed its cracks with mud and
thatched a grass roof. A clay silo close by kept the barley
mash dry. My mare was heavy with foal, and on that cold
night, she was heaving. I was singing to her—one of Granny's
stories, or at least as much as I remembered of it. I wanted
to be awake when the little head poked out to sniff the world.

"Iphito!"

The old woman's voice cut through the night air, and I
ran to the cave. Granny lay like death, her face twisted into
a mask. Not all of her face, though. One half was calm as
if she were sleeping; the other side rigid and angry.

"Quick," the old woman whispered, "fan the fire and set
water to boil. Then run out and fetch a hellebore—there's
one blooming by the downpath. Pull gently so its roots come
out whole."

I blew on the coals until they were dancing flames and set
the water jug over them. I knew exactly where the hellebore
was. Carrying water past it every day, I wondered at its

delicate winter-blooming flowers. By the time the tea was steeped, Granny's blue eyes were open, but her face was still a mask and her speech only gruntles. The old woman's arm strong around her shoulders, she sipped the steamy tea. I lit a lamp to Hekate and hung thyme over the bed to give her courage.

I left the old woman watching and ducked out of the cave. It had started to snow, the first of the year. The flakes melted when they hit my cheeks and ran with my tears. "Hang on, Granny," I muttered, shivering, "I've got so much to learn." I begged Hekate for time, and she must have heard me; Granny's breath was steady through the night. Toward dawn I heard a groan from the stable and went to tend the foaling mare.

The birthing was a breech. The mare's coat was soaked, her eyes wild. A single tiny hoof hung out of her, not moving. I'd seen lambs drop every spring and I knew the creatures came out headfirst and fast. I ran back to the cave.

"I'll tell you what to do, and you'll do it," the old woman said. Her hands were comforting Granny who, like the mare, was soaked in sweat. "One of the legs is likely twisted. Reach in your arm and turn it right." I gulped. "You can do it," she said, "better than I. Your arm won't tear her. Here, take this dittany." She pulled a handful of dry leaves out of her bundle of herbs and let me smell their mintiness. "Light it next to the mare's front feet. Stroke her nose to make her stand still. Then go round and do your job."

I did as she told me, and a colt slid into my waiting hands. I laid him on the straw, but he straightened his hind huckles immediately; the front two followed, and he stood there wobbling. I turned to tend to the afterbirth and was astonished to see a second head poking its way into the cool dawn.

Stubborn mare. I might have known. The season other mares rutted, that one's flower had been tight as a berry, and she'd frolicked away from the village stud. Then at midwinter her berry had swelled, and she'd slipped the tether. I'd left the goats half-milked to search for her and found her at nightfall in the next valley romping on a mudbank with a gray stallion. My mother smacked me for acting like a boy, but my father said, "What do you expect? She's half-Amazon. Let her be." Then he said the foal, when it came, would be mine.

So that night I had twins. The colt, the difficult one, was gray like his daddy; the filly, who arrived in this world like water falling from a cleft, was flame-red with a white snip on her nose.

Each foal found its way to a teat, and I left them nursing. Back in the cave, Granny's jaw was still frozen, half mettled, half grooly. She was sitting up, though, and when I told her about the twins, she grunted through her locked teeth. Suddenly one arm flailed, the other one still limp, and somehow I knew she wanted her stick. I let its silver horse's head catch her waving hand. She sat rigid on her rug pile, her useless legs sprawled, her eyes fixed on the fire. She sang. I stared at her. Unable to talk, she lifted her speech onto a tune and sent it soaring.

> I sing of full-breasted Zerinthia
> astride her black mare, a twin at each breast
> she rides with the dawn . . .

Her voice stopped. Sweat beaded her brow, and the stick clattered to the floor. I turned to the old woman, astonished. She smiled. "It happens that way, sometimes," she said. "A song can live even when the speech is gone." We turned Granny's body to rest. The song hung in the air, and I prayed to Hekate to let it be a horse to carry her into the spring.

The sun turned in its course, and the nights began to shorten. The northwind's rime stayed on the cave walls, though, no matter how much I stoked the fire. Granny learned to jam her distaff into her good arm's crook and twirl her spindlewhorl one-handed. I learned to understand her grunts and gurgles. Here and there speech tumbled out—upsidedown, sideways or backwards—and I'd listen hard to be able to tell her straightways what she was trying to say. When my guess was right, she'd clap her good hand against her thigh.

I told her about the filly stealing the colt's barley mash, and she told me about a horse she'd had when she was my age that stole eggs from under a nesting hen. I said that I'd seen lynx tracks in the snow, and she told me about a bobcat she'd killed as it stalked her mare and then how she'd fed its orphaned litter until they were big enough to forage on their own. She cackled and whinnied; she growled and mewed. Still, while the wind howled, she grew bonier, and white wisps came out when I braided her hair. Some days she'd sleep all day; other days she sat up but knocked her distaff aside, furious, and shook her good fist in the air. Sometimes her mutters turned into weeping, and the old woman would rock her until she slept again.

I'd hunted out the near woods, so I began to spend my mornings running the trapline on up the ridge as far as the divide. The snow was deep up there, and I strapped on rawhide webbing to keep my feet from plunging me waist-deep into a drift. I liked the silence in the woods—and then the sudden *dr-dr-dr-dr-dr* of a woodpecker grubbing its dinner. The tracks that crisscrossed each fresh fall of snow made me imagine a sleek shrew urging her family back to the burrow at dawn, a flying squirrel gliding out of a hollow tree to dance in the moonlight.

Sometimes in the still woods, I'd think about my family in the village and wonder if they missed me. I missed them. Even if the work wasn't fair, I missed the way my father swung me round when he came in from the fields and how my sister's baby lurched across the courtyard when they came to visit. I even missed my mother's rough hands sweeping my hair from my face to braid it.

It was the betrothal that made me leave. The oaks had just begun to tip red when my mother told me to get ready to become a wife. I knew what marriage meant: go to a strange house and get scolded because you stir the soup the wrong way. My sister's husband's little brother had hit her once because she told him to wipe up his own spilt milk, and then her husband didn't speak to her for days because she'd shamed him.

Kotys was the boy they'd chosen for me, and he didn't like the idea any better than I did. He lived in the house where the path turns off to the upper spring. I used to set down my water jug and walk with him halfway to the goat meadow. We weren't family yet, so we weren't supposed to talk, but I wanted to know about the world beyond our village, and he liked to speak his dreams. The men under the plane tree had told him about a sea where the water is the sweetest in the world. There were storms there, they said, that drove cattle over cliffs to join splintered ships below; there were rocks that moved through the waves and caught galleys between them. Kotys said he'd welcome the storms and the clashing rocks. He was going to take his father's piebald, he said, and find his way to the sea. He'd bend an oar on a merchant ship and sail to the uttermost bourn and back. I didn't tell him about my dream, about living in a world without men so that everybody would work the same and no little boy could hit a grown woman.

After I heard about the betrothal, I decided to wake up my dream. I waited for the late summer vintage. That was the best day of the year because we girls got to go out to pick grapes with the boys. Old Crimpfoot wailed his reedy aulos over the whole valley, and as the sun rolled westward, we'd smell the lamb roasting all the way from the village square. After the hills had swallowed the sun, the boys wound vines all around themselves and tried to make us think the vineyards were dancing. I knew everyone would stay at the bonfire until the moon went to bed, so I slipped away and untied the full-bellied mare. My father had promised me her nestling, after all, so I thought I'd borrow her until she foaled and return her the following spring. I rode downstream, walked her across the ford and started up the mountain.

Married Ladies Have Sex in the Bathroom

Sally Bellerose

We did it everywhere. We were middle-aged women with middle-aged husbands and school-aged boy children. Mostly in daylight. Mostly in twenty minutes or less. Mostly in places so common that they'd never suspect.

Every room of both houses, and the cellar, and the garage, and the neighbors' children's four-foot wading pool. And then there were the bathrooms, the women-only rooms, the bathrooms of Fitzwillies, the Girls Club, Caldor's, Shop Rite, and the bushes in back of the bar at the end of the street.

We did it on her picnic table and under my picnic table. We did it in every extreme, prepared for inclement weather. Coming fully clothed, hats, scarves, boots, and mittens. Coming buck screaming naked, in the hot dirt of some god-forsaken road, with the bugs of August crawling, in the woods that never gave back her pink lace panties.

We did it lying flat on the kitchen floor, our heads pressed up against the kitchen door. Our bodies barring our boys entrance.

We did it seated, in my car, moving. On our knees, in her car, at the body shop. Standing, outside my brother's car, at the airport. Flying, on a plane to Baltimore, while she calmly discussed Women, War, and Peace with the woman in the next seat. Floating, in the hot tubs, even though I hate the hot tubs. Against the damp wall, on the stairs outside the hot tubs, not waiting for the women inside to come out.

We did it with phones ringing, kids screaming, dogs barking, tubs overflowing, and dinner burning in the pot. We did it with fingers so hot that we thought we'd be branded forever. We did it with bodies so tired, hearts so heavy, that doing it was the last thing on our minds. But still, something greedy whispered—get it while you can girls because you never know if or when you're going to get it again.

We did it with a roar and called it power, dared man or nature to deny that it was anything but sacred. We did it with a whimper and named it adultery.

We flaunted. We hid. Our lives were tense and tangled. Sometimes we forgot when to run, when to taunt.

We did it till we stopped, caught our breaths, confronted. Like dogs in heat, we fought. Held each other, uprooted. Recovered, to fight and blame some more. In the end, cared for ourselves, enough to stay in this world. Alive. Together.

And a year, and a year, and the years go by. Less and less we press each other. Still we love. But oh the sex. It's never been the same. Life on the edge is an addiction. Honest life is pleasant. Better, definitely better, but so damned tame.

Author Biographies

Madelyn Arnold was born in the Bible Belt during the beginning of the postwar baby boom. She fell in love with microscopes at age 4, published her first poem at 12. She has a B.A. in Microbiology from Indiana University, an M.A. in Writing from the University of Washington, and has also attended Ball State University and Seattle Central Community College. She joined the first Gay Liberation Chapter at Indiana University (1969), the very first week of its existence. While she worked at jobs ranging from microbiologist to cabdriver, she wrote articles for the Zodiac News Service, women's liberation journals, and weekly newspapers. Her first published novel was *Bird-Eyes*; her latest book is a collection of short stories, *On Ships at Sea*. Principally she writes fiction because she likes to tell stories.

Sally Bellerose is a fiction and poetry writer. Her work has been published in several journals and anthologies and appears in Joan Nestle's *The Persistent Desire: A Femme-Butch Reader*, Tee Corrine's *The Poetry of Sex: Lesbians Write the Erotic*, and Roz Warren's *Women's Glibber*.

Lucy Jane Bledsoe teaches creative writing to new adult learners (literacy students) and to homeless and formerly homeless women in San Francisco's Tenderloin district. Her writing has been awarded an NEH Youthgrant, the PEN Syndicated Fiction Award, and a Barbara Deming Memorial Money for Women Fund grant. Bledsoe's fiction has been published in magazines including *Newsday, Conditions, Evergreen Chronicles, Girljock, Focus, Caprice*, and in anthologies including *Dykescapes* and *Word of Mouth*.

Rebecca Brown is the author of three works of fiction: *The Haunted House; The Children's Crusade*, a finalist for Britain's prestigious Guardian Fiction Prize; and *The Terrible Girls*. Her work has been translated into Dutch and German and enjoys great critical acclaim in England. Her stories have been adapted for theater in the United States, Scotland, and England. She lives in Seattle where she writes, teaches writing part-time at the University of Washington, Extension, and is active in the AIDS community.

Michelle Cliff's latest book is *Bodies of Water*, a collection of short fiction.

Nona Caspers grew up in rural Minnesota and currently attends the MFA program at San Francisco State University. Her short fiction and poetry have been published in journals such as *Hurricane Alice, Plainswoman, Evergreen Chronicles*, and *Negative Capability*. Her stories also have been anthologized in *Word of Mouth, Stiller's Pond*, and *Voyages Out 2*. Her first novel *The Blessed*, experiments with humor and horror, salvation, and personal ghosts.

Nisa Donnelly is the author of *The Bar Stories: A Novel After All*, her first book, which won the second annual Lambda Literary Award for Lesbian Fiction in 1990. Now in its fourth printing, *The Bar Stories* has repeatedly been on nationwide best-seller lists in the gay and lesbian press, and in women's and gay bookstores. Stories from that book also have appeared in various magazines, including *Common Lives/Lesbian Lives*, and anthologies, including *Erotic Interludes*, an anthology of women's erotica, edited by Lonnie Barbach.

Donnelly is currently completing work on a novel, *The Love Songs of Phoenix Bay*. She has reviewed books for *Lambda Book Report*, and was on the organizing committee for Out/ Write '90 & '91, the national lesbian/gay writers conference. She has worked and studied for several years with Judy Grahn. Nisa Donnelly lives and writes in San Francisco.

E. J. Graff's first short story appeared in *The Iowa Review*. This is her second short story. Her poetry and essays have appeared in such journals as *The Threepenny Review, The American Voice, Sojourner*, and *The Women's Review of Books*. She is a marketing writer who lives in the Boston area.

Annie Dawid's "Invented Sisters" is part of her first novel, *York Ferry*. Her fiction, essays, and poetry have appeared in *River Styx, AIDS: The Literary Response*, and *SIFRUT: The Northern California Jewish Literary Bulletin*.

Ellen Frye is the author of *The Other Sappho* and *Look Under the Hawthorne*. She recently completed a collection of linked tales entitled *Remember the Mother: Amazon Tales*; "Beginnings" is one of the tales.

Naomi Holoch lives in New York City and has been teaching French at the State University of New York at Purchase for the past seventeen years. She is the author of several short stories and a novel, *Offseason*.

Helen Hull was born in 1888 in Albion, Michigan. She was a Wellesley College English writing instructor, a professor of creative writing at Columbia University, an active worker for women's suffrage, and a member of the vital Greenwich Village women's organization, Heterodoxy. Helen Hull, a lesbian who enjoyed a fifty-year relationship with children's book author Mabel Louise Robinson, was also a professor at Columbia University. Hull wrote more than sixty short stories and twenty-five novels, including "The Fire," first published in Century Magazine in 1919, *Quest* (1922), and *The Labyrinth* (1923). Historian Patricia McClelland Miller wrote important biographical introductory essays on Helen Hull when both *Quest* and *The Labyrinth* were recently republished. Helen Hull died on July 15, 1971. [bio prepared by Judith Schwarz]

Edith Konecky is the author of *Allegra Maud Goldman* and *A Place at the Table*. She has published a number of short stories and is currently at work on a new novel.

Jennette Lee (Barbour Perry), according to the third edition of *Who Was Who in America*, was born in Bristol, Connecticut, in 1860. She received her A.B. from Smith College in 1886, married in 1896, and bore a daughter. She taught English at Vassar from 1890 to 1893 and at Smith College from 1901 to 1904. After settling in Northampton, Massachusetts, in 1933, she authored more than twenty novels and numerous short stories, including this one which appeared in the 1919 *Ladies' Home Journal*. She died in 1951 in Northampton.

Cathy Lewis has previously published in *Woodwriter, Texas Journal of Women and the Law*, and *Pleiades*. Presently, she is a police officer for the city of Tallahassee and is working on her Ph.D. in English at Florida State University.

Jesse Mavro received her masters degree in Creative Writing from Brown University and her masters degree in Fine Arts in Dramatic Writing from Brandeis. Her poetry has been published in newspapers and in small magazines in the United States. In 1983, she won first place in The Brush Hill Poetry Competition. Her plays have been produced in the Boston area. In 1990, her coming-out play, *Cowpalace*, was produced by the New Ehrlich Theatre as part of their Newworks Festival. Her enduring inspirations include her mentor, Martha Collins, her writing partner, Marty Kingsbury, and her life partner, Annie O'Connell. "Eating Wisdom" is dedicated to Donna, because she is wise, loving, and true. It is also dedicated to the author's father, the short-story writer Max Flannery, for his unconditional love and support of her, as a writer and a person.

Cherríe Moraga is a Chicana poet, playwright and essayist. She is the author of *Loving in the War Years* and the co-editor of *This Bridge Called My Back: Writings by Radical Women of Color* which won the Before Columbus Foundation's American Book Award in 1986. In 1990, she received The Fund for New American Plays Award for her play, *Shadow of a Man.* Her most recent play, *Heroes and Saints*, premiered in San Francisco in 1992, produced by Brava! For Women in Arts. Currently an Artist in Residence at Brava!, Moraga teaches Writing for Performance to gay youth and women of color groups. Her most recent collection is *The Last Generation*.

Cherry Muhanji in 1985, after seventeen years at the Detroit Phone Company, came to Iowa City for downtime and to begin college at age 46. Once there, she started writing what she wanted to read. Her first love, poetry, comes out through her prose at odd moments. She's a mother of four and grandmother of five. At present, after receiving her B.A., she's attending graduate school. She is coauthor of *Tight Spaces* (Aunt Lute Books, 1987) and author of *Her*. She was the winner of the 1991 Ferro-Grumley Award.

Eileen Myles is a poet and performer whose recent book of poems *Not Me* [Semiotext(e)] was nominated for a Lammy. Her collections of stories are *Bread and Water* and *1969* from Hanuman. In 1992, she ran as a write-in candidate for President of the United States.

Merril Mushroom is a 50-year-old committed lesbian. She is a frequent contributer to lesbian anthologies and periodicals. Her fantasy novel, *Daughters of Kharton*, is about a world of women and flowers.

Cass Nevada is an artist and writer living in Seattle, Washington. She owns a TV but rarely watches it. Really.

Joan Nestle is co-founder of the Lesbian Herstory Archives of New York City and author of *A Restricted Country* as well as editor of *The Persistent Desire: A Femme-Butch Reader*. She is delighted at the abundance of lesbian writing in the bleak Bush-Quayle years.

Gerry Pearlberg's poetry and fiction have appeared in *On Our Backs, The Portable Lower East Side's* now-infamous Queer City issue, and the *Apalachee Quarterly*. Her non-fiction book, *Women, AIDS, and Communities: A Guide for Action*, was published in 1991. She lives in Brooklyn.

Brigitte Maria Oluwa Roberts is an African-American lesbian writer who was born, raised, and currently lives in Brooklyn, New York. She is a social worker, publisher, producer, and activist. Her work has appeared in *The Brooklyn Trend* and the chapbook titled, *In the Spirit of Affirmation*.

Lexa Roséan was conceived in Cuba, born in Florida, and raised in the Rocky Mountains. Living in New York City since 1976 as a poet and mystic, she received her B.A. in English Literature from Yeshiva University (and also officially came out of the closet within the walls of that same institution). Lexa has written three plays and was a founding member of the Women's Ensemble Theatre. In 1991, she published *Elements*, an art/poetry book. In the 1980s Lexa performed as "The Snake Poet" outside the Delacorte Theatre with her 11½-foot python, Lily. Lexa is also a High Priestess of the Goddess, and teaches classes on Tarot, Astrology, Kaballah (Jewish Mysticism), and the Minoan Sisterhood (a lesbian study group focusing on healing and finding the goddess within).

Gail Shepherd is a poet, fiction writer, and videographer living in Pittsburgh, where she teaches creative writing and coordinates the Frick Summer Writer's Conference. Her poems have appeared in many journals, including *Poetry, Prairie Schooner, The Iowa Review*, and *Chelsea*. She is currently working on a collection of short stories with a lesbian focus. Her awards include a creative writing fellowship from the Florida Arts Council and an Emerging Artist's Video Grant from Pittsburgh Filmakers. "Snake in the House" is excerpted from a novella in progress.

Carolyn Weathers left her native state of Texas to move to Los Angeles in 1968, where she lives with her partner, artist Jenny Wrenn, and their three dogs. She and Wrenn run Clothespin Fever Press. She has published three books: *Leaving Texas: A Memoir* (1986), *Shitkickers and Other Texas Stories* (1987), and *Crazy* (1989), all published by Clothespin Fever Press. Her most recent work appears in the anthologies *Common Bonds: Stories By and About Modern Texas Women, The Poetry of Lesbian Sex, Banned Books*, and *Loss of the Ground-Note: Women Writing About the Loss of Their Mothers*.

Jacqueline Woodson is the author of a number of books for young adults, including *Maizon at Blue Hill* and *The Dear One*. She has been a fellow at The MacDowell Colony and The Fine Arts Work Center in Provincetown and is currently working on a novel, *Writing My Name on Water*.

Mary Wings was born in Chicago, Illinois, where she worked as a school bus driver and a drug delivery router before becoming a graphic designer. She lived in Amsterdam for seven years and speaks fluent Dutch. She is the author of two novels—*She Came Too Late* and *She Came in a Flash* as well as numerous short stories. She now lives and plays in San Francisco.